THE STIRRING

ROBERT MOELLER

THOMAS NELSON PUBLISHERS
Nashville • Atlanta • London • Vancouver

Published in Nashville, Tennessee, by Thomas Nelson, Inc., Publishers, and distributed in Canada by Word Communications, Ltd., Richmond, British Columbia.

Scripture quotations are from the NEW KING JAMES VERSION of the Bible, Copyright © 1979, 1980, 1982, Thomas Nelson, Inc., Publishers.

This book is a work of fiction. Any similarity to real life in the scenes, characters, timing, and events is merely coincidence.

Library of Congress Cataloging-in-Publication Data

Moeller, Robert
  The stirring/ by Robert Moeller.
    p. cm.

  ISBN 0-7852-8136-3
  1. Revivals—Middle West—Fiction. I. Title.
813'.54—dc20   94-11476
                                                              CIP

Printed in the United States of America

1 2 3 4 5 6 7 — 99 98 97 96

ACKNOWLEDGMENTS

I wish to thank the numerous individuals who played a role in the publication of this story.

First and foremost, I would like to thank my wife, Cheryl. It is because of her untiring efforts and long hours of investment in this project that it moved from the idea stage to reality. Thank you so much, my wife, my colleague, and my best friend.

I wish also to thank Jan Dennis, Jennifer Horne, and the people of Thomas Nelson for believing in us when we approached them with this story in mind. Their encouragement, wisdom, and expertise has made this undertaking a joy to complete. We shall always owe them a debt of gratitude.

Finally, I must acknowledge our friends and family who took the time to read the manuscript, offer helpful insights, and urge us to press on. My thanks in particular go to Marilyn Hiebler for her thorough and helpful critique of the early manuscript. Thanks also to our parents, Homer and Inez Moeller, and Roy and Gladys Webster, for their love and helpfulness. To all those who prayed for us and this project, thank you so much.

DEDICATION

To my wife Cheryl, and to our four children.
May our hearts always be turned toward
one another.

Advance Praise for *The Stirring*

"Sensational, convincing, convicting, and relevant . . . the realities of a spiritual battle that exist in all communities today place this book in the must read category. The convincing part for me is that the truth of the gospel and its power to reconcile when all else is lost is vividly and actively portrayed."

Dr. Raleigh Washington,
Pastor, Rock of Our Salvation Church

"Through fiction, Robert Moeller powerfully identifies the spiritual battle being waged today for control of our culture. *The Stirring* not only reminds us that prayer can pierce the voice of our times, but that it can transform our families and our nation as well."

Beverly LaHaye,
President, Concerned
Women for America

"I just finished reading Robert Moeller's *The Stirring*, and I couldn't put it down. It's a great story—a page-turner—but more than that, it stirred my heart. If we had an awakening in America, I suspect it would be something like this. I found myself praying that God would turn the fiction into reality. Read this book. You'll be glad you did."

Steve Brown,
President of Key Life Network and
Professor of Practical Theology,
Reformed Theological Seminary,
Orlando, Florida

"A thrilling story! Robert Moeller makes us face crucial moral and social issues in our generation while weaving a gripping account of what God can do in true spiritual revival."

Dr. Robert E. Coleman and Marietta Coleman,
Director, School of World Missions and
Evangelism,
Trinity Evangelical Divinity School;
Director, Institute of Evangelism, Billy Graham
Center

"Heart-pounding action with a faith-strengthening message. Don't miss this one."

> Kevin A. Miller,
> Editor, *Leadership Journal*,
> Christianity Today, Inc.

"I pray that the kind of 'stirring' which Robert Moeller shares so powerfully in this exciting volume will become a reality in our day."

> Paul Cedar,
> President,
> Evangelical Free Church in America

"I do not usually read novels, but found that I could not put this one down. The story threads woven with powerful suspense throughout [*The Stirring*] are spellbinding. I consider this book a must read for all evangelical pastors, leaders, and parents."

> Don Argue,
> Former President,
> National Association of Evangelicals

"One of the problems people have in praying for revival is they don't know what it [revival] looks like. A century ago, the bestseller, *In His Steps*, provided that picture for people. Robert Moeller's *The Stirring* could well do that for the people of this generation. I hope so."

> David Mains,
> The Chapel of the Air

PART ONE

PART ONE

ONE

Three Years From Now

Two women met in the back room of a bookstore in Covington Park, an affluent suburb in the greater Chicago area.

"Ingrid, I'm looking to you for guidance," Rachel Brewster said. A somber forty-five-year-old woman, Rachel's eyes were as fiery as her red hair. To look deep into them was to find only emptiness, or something like emptiness. She had sought out Ingrid Gustav, a woman in her forties known for her power.

"I'm telling you, Rachel," she said with a glazed expression, "Warner must go. He's dangerous. We feel something is ready to happen, but we don't know what it is. And we can't take any chances. He must be neutralized. Once he's gone, you'll have much more freedom—and more power."

"Thank you, Ingrid. I want to have what you have."

"Power comes only through obedience," she said in dead earnestness. "If you want admission to the higher levels you must destroy a pastor first. Those are the requirements."

"I want what you have," Rachel repeated. "And I intend to get it."

"What about your husband? Will he cooperate?"

"He's fine. He knows nothing."

"Good. This shouldn't be difficult at all."

Brenda Warner, a small, blonde woman in her early forties, trudged back into the kitchen and picked up a bowl to stir it one more time.

Where's Steven? He said he'd be home by now.

During eighteen years of marriage to a busy minister, Brenda often ate alone. She also was used to leaving supper in the microwave for him to heat when he finally did get home.

She walked to the bottom of the stairwell and shouted into the hallway darkness, "Eric, turn off the music and come down. It's time for supper."

In less than a minute, Eric, their fifteen-year-old son, a sophomore in high school, thundered down the stairs. Though deaf to a hundred other requests, he always managed to hear the call to supper.

"I'm starved. Let's eat," he said.

"Your dad isn't here yet," she said.

"Oh great," he mumbled. He knew what that meant.

Brenda loved her tall, handsome boy who now struggled to become a man. Even when he irritated her, she found it difficult not to like the kid. Just when she was certain his adolescent antics would drive her nuts, he would lean over and kiss her on the cheek and say, "I love you, Mom." He meant it, too.

Eric walked past her into the kitchen. "So where's Dad tonight?" Eric said. He really didn't need to ask. He stuck his finger in the dessert.

"He'll be a few minutes late."

"Maybe I'll get something to eat by ten tonight."

"Eric, watch what you say. He had a counseling appointment." Eric put his arm around his mother and grinned, "Pretty please, Mom? Just a little something to tide me over?" Brenda could feel herself weaken. His big grin and soft eyes were too much.

"Okay. Let's start supper. Dad should be home any minute."

As Eric piled spaghetti on his plate, Brenda glanced at the two empty chairs at the table. One was Steven's, the other belonged to Karin, their daughter, who was now away at college. She missed her very much these days.

"Aren't you hungry, Mom?" Eric asked.

■

"So tell me, Tiffany," Steven Warner said, leaning back in his black leather executive chair, "what's troubling you?"

Across the desk from him sat a beautiful woman who looked forty or so. Her immaculate hair, flawless complexion, and professional wardrobe seemed at odds with her quivering voice.

"I needed to talk to someone about my life . . . it's all been so confusing lately," she said. She reached in her purse and fidgeted with something that appeared to be a cigarette case. She had only recently started to attend his church and had called to ask for an appointment to discuss her marriage problems.

Steven opened a file on his desk and scribbled a few lines. At forty-three, his jet black hair and ocean blue eyes added to his natural charisma and commanding presence. "Please go ahead, Tiffany, I'm making notes only for my own records."

As the pastor of First Community Church of Covington Park, an upscale church of nearly twelve hundred members, Steven Warner was the envy of his colleagues. Oddly, he was still a very insecure person. Once a much more spiritual man, life had simply become too complicated to spend much time praying or in solitude. He considered himself the CEO of the Covington Park church, and that demanded administrative savvy, well-chosen moves, and above all, a painstakingly maintained executive image.

"When my husband and I were dating, he enjoyed spending time with me," Tiffany said. "We would spend hours together at a restaurant, sipping wine, finding reasons not to leave. When I'd get home, he'd call me and we'd talk another two hours. Then . . ."

She stopped for a moment and looked away. Steven assumed she was deciding just how much she wished to share. As of yet, her husband had never attended church with her.

"And has that changed?" Steven said.

Tiffany looked down, then away. It was obvious she didn't want to cry in front of him. She drew a deep breath.

"Yes, it has changed," she said. "Now, he spends his whole life at the office. If he calls, it's to remind me to pick up dry cleaning. He usually doesn't get home until eight o'clock. When he walks in, he heads to the refrigerator for a beer and then switches on ESPN. It's as if I don't exist." Perhaps out of nervousness, she again reached into her purse. "Tom says he needs time to unwind. But by the time he's relaxed and the game's over, I'm asleep. The next morning we get up and start it all over again. I feel more like a roommate than a wife."

She paused and looked up. "What am I doing wrong?"

Steven looked at her. *Why would your husband ignore you?* he wondered. Steven happened to glance down at his watch. *Oh, no. It's already six o'clock.* An ache went through his soul. He had promised to be home by 5:30. Then a second realization smacked him like a forearm across the chin. *I promised Brenda I'd pick up our airline tickets.* He fidgeted with his pen and bit his lower lip. *How am I going to explain this to Brenda?*

He glanced around the room, needing a graceful way to bring the session to a quick conclusion.

"We're never intimate anymore. I think Tom has a girl-friend," she said.

The statement shook Steven out of his thoughts. "Tiffany, do you know for certain Tom is having an affair?"

"I've never caught them together if that's what you mean. But if it's not an affair, what's going on?"

"Who is 'them'?"

"The new woman at work. She's twenty-five, a size six, and has an MBA from the university. Drives a red Porsche. She works right next to Tom in his division."

"You might be jumping to conclusions, Tiffany. There are other reasons why men sometimes retreat in a marriage. Stress. Exhaustion. A sense of failure. Is Tom under a lot of pressure at work?"

"Yes. He was promoted to regional manager last fall."

Steven smiled. "That could be it, Tiffany. Your husband may just be trying to keep his head above water at work." He realized he was defending a man he had never met.

He glanced at his watch again. It was now 6:15. "Tiffany, I really have to apologize—"

"I can't live with Tom much longer. I'm thinking of leaving him . . ." She had decided to surrender her professional image and sobbed.

Steven's frustration escalated. If he didn't leave in the next few minutes all the travel agencies would all be closed.

"I'm so sorry for acting like this," she said.

"No apologies necessary; in fact, I must apologize. Tiffany, I'm embarrassed to admit this, but I have an appointment I just realized I had completely forgotten." Steven knew it was quite unprofessional of him to break off the counseling session at such a delicate moment, but he felt he had no choice.

"Oh, I'm so sorry I've kept you." She tried to hide her disappointment.

"Please, talk to Elizabeth and reschedule. I promise I'll not have to rush off the next time." She bravely nodded and put away her Kleenex. Steven got up and so did Tiffany. She reached out to shake his hand. He returned the courtesy.

"Again, I'm sorry to end this prematurely," he said.

"I understand, Pastor. This has really helped. Just to talk to you. You're such a good listener."

Karin Warner, a nineteen-year-old college sophomore, looked so much like her mother—blonde, petite, with brown eyes that seemed to dance.

As she sat in the front seat of the car, wrapped in the arms of Jeff Mortenson, her newfound love at college, their lips met in a slow, passionate kiss. Then another, then another. The afternoon seemed to slip away. Neither one seemed to notice, or care.

They said very little, interrupting their kissing only to give each other a hug.

"I love you so much, Karin," Jeff whispered as his lips brushed her ear.

"Don't say it unless you really mean it," she whispered back.

"I do."

"Are you sure?"

"Yes, I'm sure." Jeff moved closer to her. He became more passionate. Karin drew back, a mixture of fear and longing in her eyes.

"What's wrong, Karin?" Jeff said, upset by her strange expression.

"Jeff, I don't think you'd understand."

"Try me. Am I doing something wrong?"

"No, sweetheart. That's not it."

"Then what is it, Karin? Tell me. Please."

"It's just that . . . that . . ." Karin played with the collar on his shirt. She struggled for the right words.

"Jeff, I'm scared of how much I've come to love you. I'm afraid of what I feel. How strong it's become."

"Is that all?" he said in a low and soothing voice. He took Karin's chin and made her look directly into his eyes.

"Karin, you've changed my life. I . . . I can't concentrate. I can't sleep. I miss meals. All because of you."

Jeff kissed her again. He moved his hands up and down her back. Without warning, Karin drew away.

"What's wrong, why are you acting this way?" Jeff said.

"Because you said you love me."

Jeff let go of her. He was frustrated. "All right, Karin, I won't say it anymore."

"Oh no, please, Jeff, I need to hear it." She leaned toward him and put her arms around him. "Don't try and understand," Karin whispered. "Just hold me."

An hour later, as Jeff walked Karin back to her dormitory, they found a stairwell hidden from view. He took her into his arms and kissed her again. Karin was slow to let go of him. As she opened the door to her dormitory, both refused to break their gaze.

Karin walked down the hallway; the smile on her face betrayed her emotions.

"Hi, Karin. Can I borrow your notes from English today?" It was Jane Phelps, a freshman who lived on her floor.

"Sure, sure, they're in my closet."

"Your closet? Karin, for heaven's sake, why would you put your lecture notes in your closet?"

Karin never heard the question. She just kept walking.

It was nearly eight o'clock when Steven pulled his metallic green Honda Accord into the driveway of his home. He was ready for the inevitable confrontation.

It would be the Same Old Fight. *Where were you?* I had business. *Did you forget about us?* Yes, I did. I'm sorry. *Never mind, it doesn't matter.* That's not fair, Brenda. *It's not me, it's Eric and Karin I feel badly for.* And so it always went.

One night, two years earlier, after Steven had missed his daughter's final senior high band concert to emcee a sports banquet at church, he came home to find the whole family laughing at the table. When he tried to break into the conversation, no one seemed to pay any attention to him. Later, he confronted Brenda about it.

"Do you think I deserve to be treated that way?" he said. "Ignored, like a delivery man or something?"

"I'm sorry, Steven. I guess we've just learned to get along without you."

The incident had frightened him, but not enough to convince him to change. Ironically, Steven's father had been a pastor, and he was always gone. He had grown up resenting the church. He had sworn he would be different from his dad. But each day he seemed to become a little more like his father.

Steven opened the door from the garage to the back hallway. The kitchen was dark. An empty plate and glass were the lone sentries on duty in the deserted outpost.

Steven glanced inside the refrigerator, then opened the microwave to see what might be left over from supper. He took the lid off a container. The spaghetti looked cold and dried out. He decided he wasn't hungry. He loosened his tie, then made the decision to go upstairs. This wouldn't be easy.

"I'm home, darling," he hollered up the stairwell.

"Up here," came the reply.

As Steven walked through the bedroom door, he tried hard to appear casual. It was an elegant room, complete with a four-poster bed, white canopy, and large down quilts. Brenda sat propped up by pillows, reading a book.

"Any phone calls for me?" Steven said as he took off his coat.

"Just Ed Brewster. Wants you to call him back. Did you eat?" Brenda kept her eyes on her book.

"Yeah. I picked up a gyro sandwich at Junk Food Heaven." That was their name for the fifteen fast-food counters at the mall. Ten different stands offered everything from hot dogs to Cajun chicken.

"Did you pick up our tickets?" Brenda said.

"Uh, no. All the agencies were closed by the time I got there. I'll get them in the morning."

There was a long silence. Steven felt a sense of shame sweep over him as he hung up his sport coat. *Here we go again.*

"What time did you leave church?" Brenda said. She put down her book.

Steven swallowed hard. "Oh, about quarter to seven. I just had an appointment run late, that's all. You know how that goes."

Another long silence.

"Yes. I guess I do."

"I can take care of it tomorrow."

"Steven, if you don't want to take this trip, why don't you just say so? Let's just forget about it."

"I said I was going to the mall tomorrow. Isn't that good enough for you?"

"It's the second time you've forgotten. If your heart's not in it, I don't want to force you—" Brenda's voice betrayed her hurt.

"Why don't you let me be the judge of where my heart is?" Steven pulled his tie off with a jerk and walked into the closet.

Brenda bit her lip to fight back the tears. "I'm sorry, Steven. I just sometimes feel—"

"Feel what?"

"Sometimes I just feel like I'm second, maybe third place in your life."

He whirled around toward her. "Okay, that's it. If you want to take a cheap shot at me, here I am." He held up his arms pretending to be an easy target.

"Steven, calm down."

"Why should I? What are you saying? That I'm a poor husband? A lousy lover?" His voice had gotten louder. "That I'm cheating on you?"

"No, Steven, I'm not saying that. I just want you to talk to me. I want the man I married back. The man who took Cs on his semester finals in seminary to go home to announce our engagement. The man who took a week off work when Karin and Eric were born. I want the husband back who would call me at work and say things over the phone that made me blush."

It had been some time since Brenda had unloaded this much. Steven didn't even try to argue. He knew this was coming from her soul.

"Why do I, why do Karin and Eric always have to share you with others?" said Brenda. "Do you really believe the kingdom won't come unless you work seventy hours a week?" She took a deep breath and delivered her final blow. "Are you on some type of special mission from God, Steven?"

Steven turned and walked over to the window. He tried to control his anger, but it was difficult. He wanted to say something to hurt her.

"Don't you see it, Steven?" Brenda said. "Karin is grown and gone. But Eric is only fifteen. There's still time. He needs you, Steven. He worships you. But he isn't sure if you even know he's alive."

Brenda turned and buried her head in a pillow. Steven continued to say nothing. After a minute or two, Brenda got up and walked into the bathroom. She closed the door behind her.

Steven just stood and gazed out the window at the winter landscape. In the darkness the trees stood naked, stripped of all their foliage, shadowy, barren, dead.

TWO

The church was cold, lonely, and quiet on Thursday mornings. Steven Warner always arrived at work by seven o'clock; it gave him time for paperwork before the interruptions of the day started. He walked down the empty corridor toward his study when he noticed something on the bulletin board. It was a photocopied announcement crossed out in red pen and marked "Canceled." He took the notice off the wall and studied it closely. It was the Women's Roundtable Luncheon. *I'm scheduled to speak at this next week. That's strange,* he thought. *No one told me it was canceled.* A bit miffed, he made a mental note to call the chairwoman of the committee later that morning.

He flipped on the light in his spacious, book-lined study and was confronted by the pile of unopened mail he hadn't gotten to the day before. He thumbed through it quickly, looking for first-class mail. He stopped when he came to a letter marked "Personal and Confidential." The handwriting looked like a man's. Steven used a knife with a carved handle to slit open the envelope. He unfolded the letter and scanned its contents.

Dear Reverend Warner,
  I'm wise to you. I know things about you no one else does. This might be a good time to leave, while you still can. If you don't, you may end up wishing you had.

There was no signature at the bottom. Steven picked up the enveloped and studied it. The postmark indicated it had been sent from West Oaks, a nearby suburb, but there was no return address.

Steven had received hate mail in his career—every pastor does. But this letter had a different feel to it. It seemed almost a threat. His usual policy was to immediately toss unsigned letters. *What if there is something to this? It could be from someone in the church,* he thought. *But maybe not.* He decided for now he would show it to no one. He locked the letter in his personal filing cabinet and went back to his mail.

Later that morning he walked out into the reception area where several of the office personnel worked. By now all the lights were on in the building, and the lobby buzzed with activity. Two women sat at the front desk.

He walked up to the older woman who answered phones and leaned across the desk. "Barbara, have I told you that you do the work of three people?" The woman, who wore a loud floral dress, just grinned. Before she could answer him, the switchboard signaled an incoming call. He schmoozed for a minute or two with the others out front and then walked into the office of Elizabeth, his executive secretary. She was fifty-five years old, her hair pulled back in a bun. She wore huge glasses and no makeup. She had come to First Community through a temporary employment agency, but her efficient, no-nonsense manner had caught Steven's attention. She was soon offered a permanent job as his personal secretary.

"Elizabeth, do you know anything about the Women's Roundtable Luncheon that's been canceled for next week? I saw the notice this morning."

The woman shook her head in bewilderment. "No one called me about it." She never forgot details.

"Would you run this down and see what happened? I don't particularly care for schedule changes that no one tells me about."

"Yes, Dr. Warner. Where can I reach you this afternoon?"

"I have a conference at my son's school. I'll be back by 3:30 at the latest."

"Don't forget you have a finance committee meeting to-night."

Steven reached up and rubbed his forehead, "Oh, no. The finance committee." The chairman had called Steven late Tuesday evening and suggested a special meeting to deal with the church's financial crisis. "I was supposed to take Eric to a Bulls game tonight. Todd Branstrom gave me tickets from his law firm."

Elizabeth smiled sympathetically.

"Oh well, Eric will just have to understand. I can't afford to miss this one."

"Is the giving even worse?" she asked.

"I'm afraid so. The last two weeks have been disasters. Howard says we're going to have to put a freeze in place if things don't turn around soon."

"Maybe it's just a short-term thing, Pastor."

"I wish." Steven was twice-discouraged. He not only had to cancel with Eric, but he knew he'd face hard questions in the meeting as to why giving was on the slide. That's why he couldn't miss this one. If he wanted to control the outcome, he'd have to be there. Steven rarely missed meetings.

Just after lunch Steven Warner stood in the hallway of Roosevelt High School. He enjoyed the smell of freshly waxed hardwood floors. All around him lockers opened and slammed shut while students pushed by each other on their way to class. Pep rally banners hung from the ceiling.

Steven worked his way toward a pay phone near the main office. He opened his date book and thumbed through it. He found the number he wanted, dialed it, and plugged his ear to listen for the ring.

"Huntington and Associates, may I help you?"

"Good afternoon, this is Dr. Steven Warner. May I please speak with Mr. Ed Brewster?"

"Just a moment Dr. Warner, I'll see if he's available."

Steven was put on hold. He noticed a young couple leaning against a locker. The boy, obviously attracted to the young girl, stood over her with one arm against the wall. She was trapped, but she didn't seem to mind.

Stupid kids. When I was in high school, a wrong decision could get you a disease. Today it could cost you your life. Don't they know that? Their unrestrained display of affection irritated him, so he turned away. His thoughts were interrupted by a voice on the other end of the phone.

"Hello, Pastor. I suppose you're calling to see if we're broke," said the voice in a half-teasing manner.

"No, Ed, I already know that much. I was just calling to ask, 'Can you spare a Mastercard?'"

The two of them laughed. Steven genuinely liked Ed Brewster, the newest member of the finance committee. Articulate, detail oriented, yet easy to work with, Ed was the ideal committee chairman.

"Listen, Ed, I need a favor. Can you fax me the budget report before tonight's meeting? I need to look at it before the piranhas get to it."

"Sure thing, Pastor. I won't fool you, the numbers don't look good. We fell behind another two thousand dollars last month, and we haven't paid the missionaries for January yet."

"Okay, Ed. Let's put the best face we can on it this evening. Can I count on you?"

"Certainly."

"Thanks, I'll talk to you later."

Steven Warner hung up the phone and walked around the corner into the Roosevelt High guidance counselor's office. The receptionist offered to page the guidance counselor for him.

Within two minutes the door opened and a middle-aged man walked in wearing a dark blue sweater and khaki pants. He had the look of a coach, short black hair and a strong, muscular build.

"Hi, I'm José Martinez."

The two shook hands.

"I'm Steven Warner."

"Let's go back to my office."

The two men walked behind the main desk and down a short hallway and then into the counselor's office. When they were both seated and comfortable, Martinez leaned across his desk and looked Steven in the eye.

"I'll get right to the point, Reverend. I called you because we're looking for parents to serve on our Drug Awareness Week committee. With your high profile in the community, you'd make an excellent member."

Steven was flattered by the counselor's remark. "What would be my responsibilities?" he said. He was, after all, a busy man.

"Our theme for this year is 'Kids: Do You Know Where Your Parents Are?'" said Martinez. "The idea is to encourage teenagers and parents to spend more time together. I'm sure you know the statistics. Studies show teenagers who spend significant time with both parents each day rarely abuse alcohol and drugs. They are also less likely to get involved with gangs. I don't know if you're aware of this, Reverend, but we've had some gang-related incidents at Roosevelt."

"I've heard rumors," said Steven. "Are they true?"

"Yup," said Martinez. "All it takes is some lonely kids, AWOL parents, and a need to belong. Like I heard a comedian say the other night, it's either cocoa-wheats with the parents or cocaine with the gang."

"There's some truth to that," Steven said.

"Two-income families, business travel, latchkey kids. We're looking at a lonely bunch of young people out there. Parents just don't seem to have time for them."

Steven sat up and crossed his legs the other way. "You're right, Mr. Martinez. Today's kids are a high-risk generation."

"That's where you could help us. We'd like to raise the awareness in the community about the relationship between neglect, substance abuse, and gang activity."

"Sounds good to me."

"Can I count on you?"

"Of course."

The two men stood up, shook hands again, and Steven left the office. He was almost out of the building when he remembered the finance committee meeting. He had to find Eric and break the bad news. The Bulls game would have to go on without him. But he had no idea where to begin looking.

Just above him a bell rang and students poured into the hallway. Steven lost ground as a wave of teenagers pushed past him. He stood up on his toes and scanned the horizon for any sight of his son. No luck. Then, just thirty seconds before the next bell was to ring, a familiar brown head with blue eyes and a New York Knicks basketball jersey appeared around the corner.

"Eric!" Steven shouted. Eric stopped to see who had called his name. Their eyes met.

"Dad?" the boy gasped. A look of delight crossed his son's face. Steven walked up to Eric, and they gave each other a high five. A tall, lanky kid, Eric wore a close crew cut. The dark circles under his eyes also conveyed a certain sadness to his features, but for the moment he was all grin, from ear to ear.

"Dad, what are you doing here?"

"I had business in the counselor's office. I've been invited to serve on the parents' committee for Drug Awareness Week."

By now Dustin and Rob, two of Eric's friends, had joined them. Steven had seen the boys once or twice but had forgotten their names. "Good afternoon, fellas, good to see you again."

The two boys wore nylon jackets emblazoned with sports emblems. They seemed a little embarrassed. Dads were a rare sight at school. No one was quite sure how to act.

"Hey, I was just telling Dustin and Rob about tonight's game," Eric said. "The Atlanta Hawks are in town. We've got front row seats."

"Cool," said Dustin Jacobs. Rob agreed.

Eric stood there, showing off the one trophy every boy in the school coveted—a dad.

The bell came alive just above them. "We gotta get to class," said Rob. Eric's two friends took off at a sprint down the hallway.

Eric glanced down the hallway, "Sorry, Dad, I gotta run. I'm late."

"Hang on just a minute, son," Steven said.

"What is it, Dad?" Eric said, anticipation gleamed in his eyes. "You wanna leave early so we can beat the traffic downtown?"

"Uh, no Eric, that isn't it," Steven said. "Uh, I'm not going to be able to go with you to tonight's game."

Eric lost his smile but said nothing.

"Sorry, big guy, but I forgot an important finance meeting tonight. But hey, Todd Branstrom, the guy who gave me the tickets is going. I called him. He'll give you a ride. Look, here's twenty bucks." Steven held out his hand with a crisp bill. "Take one of your friends, Dustin, Rob, or whoever, and have a good time. I'd really like to come with you, but I've got problems at church. Giving is way down . . ."

Eric didn't stay to listen. He picked up his backpack, slung it over his shoulder, and walked down the hall toward his class.

"Eric, wait."

The boy ignored him and disappeared through a classroom door. Steven was upset. "Have it your way, Eric," he muttered. He turned around and walked away. He never looked back.

"And please, Lord, bless our study this afternoon." The heads of all the women in Rachel Brewster's living room remained bowed as she prayed. "We only want what's best for your church. Just restore the love that seems to have left our congregation. Let it begin here. Amen."

Rachel Brewster looked up. The group of women smiled at her. It was Thursday afternoon and her small group had now grown to ten women. She felt good about the variety of women she had recruited. Some were single, some divorced, and several were just tired young mothers appreciative of the free baby-sitting. Rachel had a keen sense of who was vulnerable. This was a hand-picked group.

"Thanks for coming, ladies," she said. "It's really important that we all get fed from God's Word at least *once* a week." The little barb went unnoticed by most of the women, but two of the older ladies smiled knowingly at one another.

Rachel leaned forward in her overstuffed chair and opened a large, leather-bound Bible she held in her lap.

"In light of the problems at church," she said, "I thought the Lord would have us study this portion of Scripture." Clearing her throat, she read from 1 John, chapter 4, out loud, "'Beloved, do not believe every spirit, but test the spirits, whether they are of God; because many false prophets have gone out into the world. . . . We are of God. He who knows God hears us; he who is not of God does not hear us. By this we know the spirit of truth and the spirit of error.'"

With a somber expression, she closed the Bible and looked straight at the women from First Community Church.

"During my quiet time this morning, this passage kept coming back to me. I don't know why. Perhaps God is trying to warn me. I mean, who knows what will happen to our church if we stop trying to discern truth from error and true preaching from false preaching? Like I read in a book the other day, 'When truth departs, love soon follows.'"

One of the younger women in the group, Melissa, a new mother and homemaker, spoke up. "Rachel, I'm new to the church, but I've experienced nothing but love and acceptance at First Community. Why do you feel our church is an unloving place?"

Rachel smiled at Melissa. "I'll be glad to answer that. Then maybe some of you will have things you'd like to add." Several in the group nodded in anticipation.

"For starters, I know two families that just left the church because of the pastor," Rachel said. "This week I talked with a woman who told me Warner, er . . . I mean Pastor Warner, never even visited her husband when he was in the hospital."

Scowls appeared on several faces. "And," Rachel said, "my husband, Ed, tells me giving has been way down lately. That all adds up to a pretty sorry situation, don't you agree?"

"I don't know," Melissa said. "The church has over fourteen hundred people on Sundays. It's got to be hard to keep track of that many people. Maybe no one told Pastor Warner about her husband in the hospital."

"He knew," someone said.

Melissa ignored the interruption. "Rachel, isn't it normal for a church our size to lose people? I don't know if it's fair to blame the pastor every time someone leaves."

Rachel tried hard not to lose her smile and remain sweet. "Melissa, you're a new Christian. I'm much more, what shall we say? Experienced in these things? My father was a pastor. Personally, I have nothing against Pastor Warner. But he's not doing his job as a shepherd. That's all I'm saying."

The group sat silent.

"I don't know if I can go along with this," Melissa said. "I came to this group to study God's Word, not to criticize Pastor Warner. How do the rest of you feel?" She glanced around the room, looking for support.

The other women said nothing. Then, an older woman spoke up.

"Melissa, dear," she said, "no one's suggesting Pastor Warner should leave. We're just sharing prayer concerns. You do believe in praying for your pastor, don't you?" She raised her cup of hot tea to her lips and took a delicate sip.

The young woman looked anguished. "I don't know," Melissa said. "Doesn't it say somewhere in the Bible we should respect our leaders and try and make their work a joy?"

"Of course, dear," the woman said. "What better way to lift someone else's burdens than to pray for them? But we can't pray intelligently for someone if we don't discuss their real needs, can we?"

"Well, I, uh, suppose not. So how should we pray for the pastor?" Melissa said.

"Let's pray he'll see his need to be more loving," another woman said.

"Yes," several others responded.

It was obvious the group was in agreement.

"Are there any other prayer requests?" Rachel said. She was pleased with how things had gone so far, and she didn't want to jeopardize her gains.

"I'd like you to pray for Anita's husband, Sam. He's back on cocaine again," a woman volunteered.

"I'm so sorry. We'll stand with her," Rachel said. "Anyone else?"

"Please pray for Ralph; he just got demoted this last week," another said. "His boss says he has terrible people skills."

Rachel carefully wrote down each of the requests.

"Isn't it wonderful we can have this kind of honesty with one another?" Rachel's older counterpart said in an elegant voice. She waved her hand across the entire room. "This is just what the church is supposed to be."

THREE

Eric trudged up the icy sidewalk of his home, his baseball cap turned backward and a duffle bag slung over his shoulder.

How could Dad do this to me? he thought. *I told all my friends I was going to the Hawks game. I don't believe it. I just don't believe it. His promises aren't worth a thing.*

He pushed the door open.

"Mom?" His voice was loud enough to be heard in the kitchen. There was no reply. Eric was relieved. *Good, I won't have to talk to anyone.*

After poking around in the refrigerator for a minute, he pulled together a sandwich and grabbed a Coke and headed for his bedroom. He nudged the door open with his foot. The floor was covered with debris everywhere—socks, books, compact discs, and everything else he didn't feel like picking up.

Angry and exhausted, he flopped down onto his mattress. The bed creaked under his weight, then the room grew quiet. Eric stared at the poster tacked to the ceiling directly above him. He reached over and grabbed his portable CD player. He popped in a compact disc and closed his eyes. He punched the controls until he found the track he wanted.

A clear and melancholy male voice came softly through the earphones. Eric spent almost an hour lying on his bed listening to music. Even when the phone rang several times, he just ignored it. He was starting to relax, and he didn't want anything to interrupt his mood.

"Can I get you another cup of coffee?" It was the voice of the waitress at the fashionable Espresso Elegant, a coffee bar located in the downtown area of Covington Park.

"No, no thank you, this is enough," said Brenda Warner. "I'll keep this one and finish it." The waitress nodded and left to tend to other customers. Seated across from her was Maggie Dunlop, a seventy-five-year-old widow from their church. A stately African-American woman, Maggie was a surrogate mother to several women in the church. Her gentle eyes and calm expression belied all the years of difficulty she had experienced in her life. Her husband had died of a sudden heart attack in his forties. Maggie went back to college, earned a master's degree, then raised all three of the children on her own. She'd had a bout with breast cancer eight years ago, but so far it had not returned.

Despite all these trials, as far as anyone could remember no one had ever heard Maggie complain.

"It's good to see you again, child," said Maggie, her face aglow with a soft smile. "But you do seem worried about something today. Tell Maggie about it."

Brenda looked up into the patient brown eyes of her good friend. If it had been anyone but Maggie, Brenda might have passed on the request to share her thoughts. But with Maggie she felt safe. Heaven and earth could pass away before Maggie would ever gossip.

"It's Steven," said Brenda.

"Ah, yes, you married a wonderful man, Brenda," she replied. "He's a powerful preacher. He's a ten-talent pastor. In fact, you're a ten-talent person yourself." She reached out and patted Brenda's hand. Brenda responded by squeezing her friend's hand. All at once tears came.

"I know he's a wonderful man," Brenda said. "But the last few years, as the church has grown, someone is always wanting something from him. He's on the phone till late at night, he's gone before breakfast to an appointment, and he spends Saturdays at the office to finish business he couldn't get to during the week."

"You love him, don't you?"

"Of course."

"And you know he still loves you?"

"Yes, I . . ."

"Then things aren't as bad as they could be, are they?"

Brenda felt embarrassed for complaining in front of her friend. After all, Maggie had spent the last thirty years without her husband. The older woman squeezed her hand and then let go. They each took a sip of coffee.

"I'm overdosing on self-pity today, Maggie. I'm sorry."

"Shh, child, don't apologize to me for anything," she smiled. Brenda acknowledged Maggie's smile with a slight grin of her own.

"Why, Maggie?"

"Why what, Brenda?"

"Why would God call Steven to a church that leaves him no time for his family?"

Maggie just stared into the eyes of her friend. It was almost thirty seconds before Maggie responded. "Success can be as dangerous as failure, child—even more so. You and I need to pray more for Steven."

Brenda used her finger to wipe her eyes; it left mascara smudges. "Oh, Maggie, of course I pray for him. But it doesn't seem to do any good."

"I'm not talking about that kind of prayer, sweetheart. I'm talking about *PRAYER*."

"I'm not sure I entirely understand, Maggie."

"Brenda, your husband knows more good theology than any other preacher I've ever listened to in my whole seventy-five years. But he may still need to learn something."

"What's that?"

"That God loves him."

"Ed, why don't you open in prayer?" said Steven.

It was 7:02 P.M. The last member of the finance committee had straggled into the conference room at the church. It was a tastefully decorated boardroom with a polished mahogany table that ran almost the length of the narrow room. Oil paintings of the medieval French countryside adorned the walls.

Steven Warner and Ed Brewster sat side by side at the head of the table. Nearly everyone had had to forego supper to make it to the meeting on time.

"Shall we pray?" said Ed. The faces at the table bowed their heads as if on cue. "Lord, once again we need Your help. Help people understand that churches run on money. We can't do Your work on good intentions alone. Get us through this present crisis. Amen."

Earlier in his career, Steven might have squirmed a little at Ed's theology of money. But now he saw things pretty much the way Ed did. No money, no ministry. Simple as that. A church these days had to be bottom-line oriented. And it was his job as pastor to make sure that the bottom line was always in the black.

"I've passed out the monthly balance sheet," said Ed. "You can see for yourselves we're taking on water." The glum committee members scanned the document. "It's more of the same," Ed continued. "The general operating budget is behind again. This time it's twenty-three hundred dollars. I've transferred money from our contingency funds to cover the shortfall. But if this keeps up much longer, we'll be in serious trouble by Easter."

"I move we cut the heat and light to the pastor's study," said a committee member. The sullen room now erupted in laughter. Steven was quick to respond.

"And I move we let the junior high youth group choose the music for Sunday morning worship," he said. Again the room responded with laughter.

"Pastor, do you have any idea what's causing the drop-off in giving?" asked Bruce Craig, a black executive with a major brokerage firm in Chicago. The room quieted down all at once. Steven felt his stomach tighten.

"Yes, I've given that some thought." The truth was Steven had thought about little else for the last eight weeks. Here it was early winter, when giving was supposed to be gangbusters. Instead, giving was limping along at summer levels, traditionally the pits for church finances.

But like a good card player, Steven wasn't about to reveal his hand first. He wanted to get a sense of what the group was thinking. "But before I share my ideas, let's hear your thoughts," he said.

"People are just more selfish than they used to be," blurted out one member. "They spend everything on themselves. They don't have anything left for the church."

"It's debt. Our young couples can't afford to do anything but pay their bills," said another.

"It's the economy," guessed another. "Consumer confidence is down everywhere." The speculation went on for several minutes.

"You all may be right," said one of the older members in conclusion, "but it doesn't put a dime in the bank. What we need is a pledge campaign like the kind we had back in Missouri." He pointed his finger at Ed and Steven. "In that church they published what people gave in the church bulletin. Yes sirree, people thought twice before they passed the plate by."

Steven gulped. He knew it was time to speak up before this discussion got away from him. "Thanks, Frank, you've given us something to think about," he said.

He took his Waterford pen out of his pocket and turned it over with his fingers, then looked out at the group, "The trend in business is toward downsizing and eliminating middle management. It's time we took a fresh look at our organizational structure. I believe we may be bloated in the middle. It could be we could get by if we eliminate some mid-level staff positions."

The room grew tense.

"Who are you thinking of letting go, Pastor?" asked Ed.

"I think it would be premature to mention specific names," Steven said calmly. "But it's obvious it's time to reduce our cash outflow. Personnel right-sizing might cause some problems in the congregation, but we can ride it out. And if we handle this right, we could give staff members a few months to find jobs. It would save us paying severance."

"But what if people get upset?" asked a member. "Won't that just hurt giving more?"

"Leaders lead," Steven said. "We might get some flak, but we'll get through it."

One of the finance committee members had been strangely quiet throughout the discussion. It was Phil Crawford, a retired missionary from Indonesia who lived in a house the church owned nearby. He laid his glasses on the table and looked toward the pastor.

"Steven, do you suppose God is trying to say something to us as a body through this financial crisis?"

"Like what?" said Steven.

"That we need to be praying more."

Oh terrific, thought Steven, *another sermonette on prayer by Phil Crawford.* Prayer seemed to be Phil's answer for everything, from water in the basement to problems in the choir. "I'm all for prayer," Steven answered. "In fact, a great deal of prayer goes on in this church each week, Phil."

"I agree, Pastor. But I'm still challenged by the example of the Indonesian church. Those folks got up early to pray every day of their lives."

Someone groaned. "My nerve endings don't fire until I have my first cup of coffee at 6:30." The group burst out in laughter again. That is, everyone but Phil.

"Phil," Steven replied in his most spiritual voice, "we could all use more prayer. Why don't you organize something like that? But quite frankly, I don't think prayer alone can solve our problems. We need to use common sense and business sense. In this case, I think it means reducing cash flow and reevaluating staff. Don't you all agree?"

Everyone around the table nodded. Phil rested his chin on his hands and looked down.

By 11:15 P.M., the business meeting was over. The commit-tee members headed into the dark parking lot to find their cars. Steven Warner walked down the hallway and clicked off lights. He walked around a corner to check one more room when he bumped into someone.

"Oh, Phil, are you still here?" he said. *Thanks for the little lecture on prayer*, thought Steven. But Steven knew better than to say what he was thinking, and chose instead to be diplo-matic. "Thanks for your input tonight, Phil," Steven said. "You were right on."

"Can I count on you to be part of a new prayer group, Pastor?" he replied. "Your leadership might make this thing work."

"Give me a time, and I'll check my schedule," said Steven. "If not, I'll send Ron." Ron Simmons was Steven's senior associate pastor.

Phil stood quietly for a moment, then smiled at Steven. "Okay. I'll check with Elizabeth. Good night, Pastor," he said.

"Good night, Phil." Steven reached for a switch, and with the turn of a coded key the entire church went dark.

"The history of early eighteenth-century England is remem-bered as a time of unprecedented social decay," the professor said as she wrote on the blackboard. "For example, prior to what historians call the Great Revival, which began in the early eighteenth century, there were over two hundred fifty capital offenses on the books. Public hangings were a routine weekly event. Large crowds would gather for the spectacle in London and refreshments would be sold. Sadly, even children were hung for what we consider today relatively minor crimes. Ironically, as the laws grew more severe, the crime rate sky-rocketed . . ."

Karin Warner doodled on her notes and didn't pay much attention to her European History professor. It was Friday morning, and her mind was elsewhere. Her thoughts kept going back to the night before with Jeff.

"Large gangs of youth roamed the cities and the countryside robbing and terrorizing the population, much like urban gangs do today," the professor said. "Substance abuse was everywhere. Alcoholism became rampant after the British government deregulated the gin industry. Six thousand new pubs opened in London in one year alone. Signs read, 'Drunk, six pence. Dead drunk, ten pence.'"

Karin reached in her purse and pulled out a picture of her and Jeff taken during homecoming.

"At that time in English history, the king, the prime minister, and the Prince of Wales were all living in open adultery," the professor continued. "Literary pornography was the order of the day. The authors of the age turned out little but prurient and obscene novels. The standards of public morality pointed toward the eventual collapse of the society . . ."

I wonder where Jeff is right now? Maybe I could catch him before his next class, thought Karin.

Karin's daydreaming was interrupted when she noticed that the other students were writing something down. She popped her head back up to try to catch the assignment for Monday.

"I want all of you to read the next three chapters of the text. Monday we'll talk about the uplifting impact of the Great Revival on England's poor and destitute. Class dismissed." The room immediately became a blur of activity as students pushed past each other to get on to their next class.

A young woman stopped by Karin's desk. "Hey, Karin, how about joining us on Saturday?" It was Lisa Fredrickson, the resident assistant on Karin's floor. "We're hitting the outlet malls. Jane's got her dad's Visa card, and she says by the time he finds out, it will be too late." The two girls laughed.

"I'd like to, Lisa, but Jeff and I talked about going downtown together that day."

"Oh, come on, Karin. Since you've met Jeff we never see you anymore. Can't lover boy go a day without you?"

"I don't know. I'll let you know. I may just crash on Saturday."

"Okay, but if you change your mind, you're welcome to come with us."

"Thanks, Lisa, I really appreciate it."

Karin walked out into the hallway of the administration building and noticed two of Jeff's friends, Brent and Andrew, leaning across the locker. They seemed nervous. One waved at her; the other smiled.

They reminded her of Jeff. She smiled back at them and walked away. She was warm with the feeling of love. Life didn't get any better than this.

FOUR

"Good morning, sweetheart," said Brenda.

Steven opened his eyes and looked over at Brenda, who smiled at him. It was seven o'clock on Saturday morning. Eric had spent the night at a friend's home and the house was quiet and empty. The soft morning light was just beginning to bring shades of yellow to their bedroom.

Steven put his arm around his wife and pulled her closer to him. "How's my Belinda?" he whispered. Belinda was the nickname Steven had given Brenda when they were engaged. The clerk at the courthouse had misspelled her name on the marriage license application. They both thought it was funny, and somehow the name had stuck through the years.

"Steven, have I told you lately how much I love you?" said Brenda softly.

"And I love you too. You know that."

"It doesn't hurt to hear you say it now and then."

Steven pulled away and adjusted his pillow. "What's on the agenda for today?" he asked. "When do we pick up Eric from Dustin's house?"

"Not till nine," Brenda said.

"Good." It looked as if this was going to be an ideal Saturday morning.

Brenda sat up. "Steven, do you realize it's been almost a week since Karin's called? Do you think she's okay? She's really crazy about Jeff."

Steven pulled a pillow over his face. He hated it when Brenda brought up difficult issues this early in the morning. With a muffled voice he said, "Oh, her mind is probably on macho man. She'll probably call sometime this weekend. Can we forget it?"

Brenda knew Steven didn't care for Karin's latest boyfriend. "Okay," she said, "but I'm still a little worried about her."

"You worry about too many things. Will you please relax? It's Saturday morning."

"All right," she said. She tried to relax, and Steven put his arm around her and pulled her close again. Suddenly, the quiet was shattered by the sound of a phone ringing in the next room.

"Let it go," Steven said.

"Fine with me," Brenda said. *Why can't life be like this every day? Just the two of us, alone, sharing our feelings with each other.* The sound of a man's anxious voice could be heard on the answering machine.

"Pastor Warner, this is Bill Cedar. I'm sorry to bother you at such an early hour, but there's been a break-in at the church. I just got here about ten minutes ago. The sanctuary is a real mess. Someone's really done a number with spray paint. The carpet has been ripped up. I think you need to come over here right away."

Steven bolted out of bed, grabbed a robe hanging by the door, and dashed into the office. Brenda put on her own robe and followed him into the office. Steven jerked the phone up to his ear. The answering machine went silent.

"Bill, this is Steven. What's going on?"

"Oh, Pastor, I'm glad you heard my message. We've got real problems here. It looks like a burglary."

"Are you sure?"

"Yup. Some sound equipment has been stolen. Ripped right out of the console. The lid was broken off and the mixer is gone. At least two speakers are missing too."

"Have you called the police?"

"They're on their way. I called you just after hanging up with them."

"Is there any chance someone is still in the building?"

"No, I don't think so. The spray paint on the pulpit is dry. So is the mud on the carpet. I'd say this happened at least three or four hours ago."

Brenda could see the mixture of anger and disbelief in her husband's face.

"Have you checked the offices, Bill? Anything missing there?"

"No, that's where I'm calling from. I used a key to get in here, and everything looks normal."

"How about the safe?"

"No one's touched it that I can see."

"Okay, Bill, wait there. I'll be over in ten minutes." Steven put the phone down and looked up at Brenda. "Someone's trashed the sanctuary and stolen sound equipment. It doesn't make any sense."

"Did they catch them?" asked Brenda.

Steven shook his head. "I don't think so."

"Was the alarm system on?"

"I forgot to ask. I would assume it was."

"Then why didn't the police show up?"

"Maybe it malfunctioned. Maybe it . . . I don't know. I need to get there and see for myself."

"I'll get you something to eat on the way, sweetheart."

"I'm not hungry." Steven got up and hurried back into the bedroom and got dressed. He grabbed a cup of instant coffee Brenda offered him, kissed her good-bye, and then disappeared into the garage. Steven's green Accord squealed out of the driveway, then roared off down the block.

Blue and red lights flashed in the parking lot of First Community Church as Steven pulled up to his parking place. A policeman sat in the front of his squad car and filled out a report. He didn't bother to look up as Steven ran into the rear entrance of the church.

Bill Cedar, a man in his late sixties wearing a plaid work shirt and coveralls, stood in the hallway talking to another police officer. The patrolman was about forty years old with bright red hair and a 250-pound frame. A large service revolver hung at his side. The officer's tired eyes and the deep lines in his face conveyed that he was a veteran of the night shift.

"Are you the reverend?" he asked.

"Yes, I'm the pastor," Steven said.

"Can I have your name and address?" Steven obliged him with the information.

"Officer, can you tell me who did this?"

The officer put down his small spiral notebook. "I don't know, Reverend."

"Was there any sign of forced entry?" Steven said.

"Nope. At least not any we've found so far."

"Have you been through the entire building yet?"

"We did an initial sweep around the perimeter when we first arrived. We were hoping that we could catch them still inside."

"You say 'them.' Does that mean there was more than one person involved in this?"

"Look, Reverend, your speakers are about six feet tall. I doubt very much one person could carry two of them off by himself. There had to be at least two people involved."

"Would you mind if I look around?" Steven asked.

"Go right ahead. I'm about to search the rest of the building more thoroughly to look for evidence. Do you have a key I could use?"

"I have one," Bill offered.

"All right. We'll start in the attic. They may have come in through the roof. Let you know if we find anything, Reverend." The two men started down the hallway.

Just before they disappeared, Steven had a thought. "Officer, excuse me," he said. The policeman turned around.

"Yeah, what is it?"

"Why didn't the alarm go off at the station house? We're wired into the system."

The bulky officer thought for a moment. "I checked with the dispatcher a few minutes ago. No alarm went off at the precinct station. It looks as if it failed on your end. Who knows? Maybe a power outage."

"Does that ever happen?" Steven said.

"Reverend, everything happens," smirked the officer. He started up the stairs toward the upper levels and the attic.

Steven wanted to see the sanctuary for himself, but his anxiety grew with each step. He was curious and frightened at the same time, like the time he was twelve years old and went to see his grandmother's body at the funeral home. *I don't need this right now, God,* he thought. *Not with the financial problems we're having.*

Steven knew insurance would cover most of what had happened, but it would mean forms, delays, deductibles. It would only draw more attention to the financial problems the church was having. *And tomorrow is Sunday,* he thought. The thought of his sanctuary in shambles with no sound system made him ill.

Steven decided to use the side door to enter the sanctuary. He pushed the door open, then stopped dead in his tracks.

The telephone rang in the kitchen of the Warner home. Brenda Warner was getting ready to go out and buy some groceries before she picked up Eric. She stopped halfway to the phone and debated whether or not to answer it. *It might be Steven,* she thought.

"Good morning," she said.

"Brenda, is that you? This is Rachel Brewster. Ed just got a call from Bill Cedar at church. I just can't believe it—" Rachel sounded as if she was going to cry.

"Oh, Rachel, it's you. Isn't it unbelievable? Who in the world would do something like that?"

"I just think it's another one of Satan's fiery darts," answered Rachel. "It's because your husband is preaching the true Gospel that we're going through these kind of trials."

"It's one more problem, Rachel."

"Brenda, the enemy is attacking our church. We've got to stand together. Is there anything we can do to encourage you? This must be a terribly hard time for both of you."

"Thanks, Rachel. For now there's nothing to do but pray. I suppose the police will take fingerprints and see if they can find any other clues."

There was a long pause.

"Good," Rachel said. "Whoever did this needs to be punished. Imagine, someone doing something like that to the house of the Lord. Well, as the Bible says, 'Justice is mine. I will avenge.'"

Brenda glanced up at the clock on the wall. "Rachel, I really appreciate you calling, but I've got to go pick up Eric. Let's talk later today."

"You two are.in my prayers, Brenda."

"Thanks, it means a lot."

Steven felt as if he had just been punched in the stomach.

The pulpit lay on its side like a toppled statue. Its rich wood was covered with spray-painted fluorescent obscenities. The carpet on stage was torn up in several places; padding bulged through like rising styrofoam dough.

Down in front, the altar's table legs had been broken off on one end, and the table now drooped to a thirty-degree angle. Microphone wires dangled aimlessly from the ceiling, the 2000-dollar microphones missing.

Oh Lord, who would do such a thing? thought Steven. He stumbled out onto the stage and just stared at the wreckage. *We'll never be able to get this cleaned up before tomorrow.*

Discouraged by the sight of his once immaculate sanctuary in ruins, Steven slumped down on a chair on stage. The familiar sense of shame once again descended on his soul.

What have I done to deserve this, God? Why have You done this to me? His perfect church was no longer perfect. Irrational as it was, he felt afraid. Things seemed out of control.

It took several minutes for the waves of emotion that assaulted his soul to pass. Finally he stood up and walked down onto the main floor area of the large sanctuary. The first few rows of pews had been hit the hardest. Hymnals and pew Bibles were spewed everywhere, torn up and tossed aside.

Steven kicked his feet among the debris until he spotted something familiar on the floor. It was the altar Bible—the one his father had given him the day he graduated from seminary. Steven picked it up as if it were a fragile vase. The leather cover with his name had been ripped off. Whole sections were missing.

Tears came into his eyes. This was one of the few personal gifts he had ever received from his father. It symbolized a bond, an act of approval on Steven's life work.

Steven remembered the beautiful June day almost twenty years ago when his dad had presented him with this gift. Two hundred students in black robes and colorful hoods had mingled with professors and family in the seminary commons area.

"Steven, don't trust anything or anyone but this book," his dad had said as he thrust the Bible into his hands. "I'm giving you the most worthwhile possession in all the world. Take good care of it."

Steven looked down at the torn book in his hands.

For the next few minutes Steven simply wandered through the debris. He behaved much like the victims of a tornado do when they enter the ruins of what were once their homes. They'll often set up a table or lamp right in the middle of a room with no roof over it or no walls on either side.

"Are you okay, Pastor?"

Bill Cedar's voice shook Steven out of his melancholy. He appeared through the same door Steven had used.

"What did you find out?" Steven said. "Did they come in through the roof or one of the windows?"

The older man shook his head. "Nope. Whoever did this didn't force their way in. The police say it's an inside job."

■

"So there you are. I thought I'd never find you," whispered Karin. She had to keep her voice down in the library. Jeff Mortenson looked up from his molecular chemistry textbook and smiled.

"Hey, am I ever glad to see you," he said. He pushed away from his study carrel and took Karin's hand. "Let's get out of here. I'm sick of chemistry tables. Besides, when it comes to radioactive elements, you're more my style."

Karin blushed a little, "Don't overdo it, Jeff."

The two walked hand in hand down the hallway to the college coffee shop. It was Saturday mid-morning, and students stumbled in for a late breakfast. A few looked bedraggled, perhaps from too much partying the night before.

"Had breakfast yet?" Jeff asked.

"No, I don't feel hungry," Karin said. "Besides, Sally and I are on a diet where we only eat one meal a day. And that's lunch." Sally Jensetter was Karin's roommate.

"Okay, Karin, but I'm buying if you're interested." Jeff walked over to the bright stainless steel counter and ordered a waffle. The smell of hot breakfast foods wafted across the room.

Jeff was soon back and sat down next to her. He took her hand under the table. "Hey, I'm sorry about missing you the other day after history class. I got invited to a pickup game of basketball in the athletic center. I looked at the clock and realized how late it was."

"Why didn't you call?"

"I figured you might be angry, and I didn't have a good excuse. Are you angry?" He bent over so he could look directly into her eyes. He smiled.

Karin wanted to look upset, but she couldn't keep a straight face. A smile started to appear at the creases of her lips.

"I can see you weakening," Jeff said.

Karin burst out laughing. "I hate it when you do that to me."

"Mortenson, your order is ready," boomed the intercom.

"Save that thought, sweetheart," Jeff said. He leaned over and kissed her. In a moment he returned with a waffle smothered with strawberries, maple syrup, and whipped cream.

"Want a bite?" he said.

"I'd better not. Sally will kill me if she finds out I broke the diet." Karin watched as Jeff devoured the waffle, then downed two glasses of orange juice.

"Jeff?"

"What is it, sweetheart?" Jeff mumbled with his mouth full.

"Would you go with me to my dad's church tomorrow? It would mean a lot to him. I'll drive."

Jeff put down his glass of orange juice and his face tightened. "I'd like to, Karin, but your dad makes me nervous. He doesn't like me."

"That's ridiculous, Jeff," Karin said, trying to sound cheerful. "Daddy just isn't an expressive person. He likes you. I know he does."

"Has he ever said so?"

"Well, no. But I can tell."

"See, I told you so."

"That's just the way he is, Jeff. He's got things on his mind. He was that way with me when I was growing up."

Jeff stabbed at the last piece of his waffle and then put it back down on his plate. "Karin, you want me to tell you the truth?"

The question made her just a little nervous. "Sure," she said tentatively.

"He's jealous. He resents me stealing his little girl."

"Jeff Mortenson, that's about the most ridiculous thing you've ever said. I can love my father and you at the same time."

"Yeah, but can he love both of us at the same time?"

Karin paused for a moment. "Jeff, come to church with me tomorrow. For me. Please."

Jeff studied the table for a moment. "For you . . . all right. But on one condition."

"What's that?"

"We sit at the back. I want out of there when it's over. Okay?"

"Fair enough." The two shook hands, but Jeff didn't let go. He pulled Karin toward him and kissed her.

"Jeff Mortenson, people are watching!"

"What people?"

Karin pulled away. "I've got an idea," she said. "Let's take the train downtown and catch a movie this afternoon."

"Sounds good to me, sweetheart." They grabbed their backpacks and headed out the door. An hour later they caught a commuter train into the city and spent the afternoon in the heart of Chicago. After catching a matinee, they ate pizza at Gino's East, one of the city's renowned Italian restaurants. The walls of the booths were covered with initials people had carved into the wood. It was part of the charm of the place.

After Jeff had finished his spumoni, he took out his Swiss army knife and scratched a heart on the wooden back of the booth. "JM + KW."

Satisfied, he put his knife away. Then, on second thought, he pulled it out and snapped out the blade again. He smiled at Karin, then scratched an arrow that went right through the center of the heart.

FIVE

"Senate Fight Breaks Out Over Children's Right to Suicide: Confirmation of New Supreme Court Justice Now in Doubt." Steven Warner scanned the headlines as he walked in from his front porch. It had always been his habit to get up on Sunday mornings at five o'clock and rehearse his sermon. He was proud of the fact that he preached his messages without notes and entirely from memory, but that meant getting up early to rehearse it.

He walked into the living room, where he spotted Eric lying on the couch. "Hey guy, what are you doing up so early?"

"I was feeling kind of sick to my stomach, Dad," said Eric. "I came down to get something to drink. I thought it might help." He took a long slurp from a can of Coke.

Eric's body filled the entire length of the couch. *The kid is almost as tall as me,* thought Steven. He both loved the boy and was frustrated by him. *If only you would try harder in school.* Steven had been an honor student, and here was Eric pulling Cs consistently. *He has the talent, why can't he do better?* Steven wondered.

Steven could see the boy was obviously nauseated. He put aside his disappointments with Eric's academic performance. "Let's see if Dr. Warner can get you the right prescription," he joked.

"Thanks, Dad, I don't want to hurl on the carpet."

"Let's see what Mom has stashed in the medicine cabinet." Eric moaned and got to his feet. Steven put his arm around the boy as they walked into the bathroom. He poked around in the medicine cabinet and found some Pepto-Bismol.

"Dad, that tastes like chalk," objected Eric.

"I'll give you an eraser to swallow, too, if you think it would help," said Steven.

"Dad, you've got a sick sense of humor. Careful or I might decide to hurl in your direction."

"Tell me about it. When you were two years old you came into our bedroom one night feeling sick. You thought our closet was the bathroom. I had to throw away two pairs of shoes."

"Yeah, bring it up now, Dad."

"Just drink it, will you?"

Eric downed the pink fluid and made a sour face. The two Warner men walked back toward the kitchen. Steven turned the coffeemaker on and sat down to read over his notes.

"What are you preaching on this morning, Dad?" said Eric. The question caught Steven off guard. Eric wasn't usually interested in his dad's sermons.

"Well, let's see. This morning I'm talking about fear."

"Can I read what you're going to say?"

"Not now, Eric." Steven didn't like discussing his sermons with anyone in advance. But he could see his son was trying to reach out to him. "All right, you can look at my notes when I'm done going over them."

Steven continued to scan his notes. "Are you ever afraid, Dad?" said Eric.

"Sure, all of us are sometimes," he said without looking up.

"What are you afraid of?"

"Eric, I'd like to talk with you but I'm under a deadline."

"Okay. I guess I'll go back to bed." Eric started to get up when Steven realized he'd made a mistake.

"Please, Eric, sit down. I'm sorry. Now what was your question?" The boy turned around and came back to the table.

"Are you ever afraid to die?" Eric said.

"That's sure a morbid subject for 5:30 in the morning. But to answer your question, of course there are times when I'm afraid to die. Why do you ask?"

"Oh, no reason. I just didn't think you were ever afraid of anything." He played with his thumbs on the table. "Dad?"

"Yeah?"

"What happens to you when you die? A teacher of mine says you go through a long, white tunnel with a light at the end."

"No one knows for sure, Eric. Those stories may be true, they may not be."

"Oh," grunted Eric. He popped open a second Coke and took a long gulp.

"Eric, I'd really like to discuss this with you, but now isn't the right time."

The tall boy got up. "Hey Dad, if I feel better, how about some one-on-one basketball after church? You know, just you and me. I'd like to show you my monster dunk."

"Like to Eric, but Mom and I are invited out to lunch after church. You can have the house to yourself this afternoon. Maybe tomorrow."

Eric had learned to act as if he didn't care when his parents went places without him. He picked up a basketball near the door and dribbled it as he left.

"Eric, please, I've asked you not to bounce that thing in the house. I'm trying to concentrate."

"Sorry, Dad." He picked up the ball and went upstairs. He closed his door and sat down in front of his computer in the pitch black. He shoved in a diskette and switched on the PC. Soon the dark room lit up with the brilliant colors of his favorite video game, "Basketball's Hottest Moves." The energy and excitement of the game made him forget about his sour stomach.

It was 8:15. The hallways of First Community Church were filled with people. All the talk was about the break-in. Curious, the people had gotten there early to get a look at the damage, though the janitors had worked all night to get the sanctuary back in order. Speculation on the identity of the vandals ranged from gangs to occult groups to paroled criminals.

The smell of hot coffee and pastry filled the gymnasium as families and children crowded in. When the bell sounded at 8:25, the crowd broke up and went to their classes. The room was left empty except for two women standing in the corner, deep in conversation.

"Things like this never happened with the last pastor," said one.

"Oh, Rachel, it's not the pastor's or anyone else's fault. Crime happens everywhere today."

"Don't you believe God judges people, Diane?"

"Of course I do. But why would God judge our church?"

Rachel Brewster looked around to be certain no one was listening. "Do you promise you won't tell anyone else what I'm about to tell you?"

The eyes of the other young woman widened. "Sure . . . sure, I guess so. What is it?"

"There are members of the board who are beginning to question Pastor Warner's leadership."

"But why?" Diane looked stunned. She leaned closer as Rachel whispered more information. As far as Rachel knew, the room was empty. She was right, except for an older woman pouring herself a cup of coffee in the kitchen who could see them through the large serving window. She had stopped to pick up a cup before going to the class on prayer she taught.

The woman watched from the kitchen as Rachel gestured forcefully with her hands. The conversation went on for nearly ten minutes.

Maggie Dunlop put down her cup and saucer and stared at the two women as they walked off together.

"Lord, have mercy on us," she prayed quietly.

SIX

"Karin, come here and give your dad a hug," Steven reached out and pulled his daughter into a huge embrace. The receiving line at church was forced to wait while the pastor and his daughter shared a moment together.

"Daddy, I heard about the break-in at church yesterday. I'm really sorry." Karin had always tried hard to encourage her dad.

Steven had Karin walk over to a corner where they could talk with more privacy.

"Thanks for your concern, sweetheart. Some idiots did about twenty thousand dollars worth of damage, when you count the missing sound system." Steven glanced back at the line of waiting parishioners. "Look, I've got to go back and finish greeting these people. Can you come home tonight? Your mom's really been worried about you."

"Uh, no, Dad. Jeff and I are going to study for a chemistry test." At the mention of Jeff's name Steven quit smiling.

"Oh, I see," he said in a flat tone. "Is he here with you? I thought I saw you sitting next to some boy in the balcony."

"Yes, Daddy. And his name is Jeff, not 'some boy.'"

"So where is he?"

"He had to leave and get back to campus right after the benediction. You'd like him if you just got to know him, Daddy. I know you would. Maybe the three of us could get together sometime. You know, just to—"

"Ahem . . ." A woman with a large hat tapped her foot and cast a scowl in the direction of Steven and his daughter. A few people had already given up and left the line. The chairman of the deacon board, Howard Svendsen, also stood waiting to talk to him.

"Uh, sorry, honey, I've got to go back and press the flesh."

"Go ahead, Daddy, we can talk later." Karin pulled her long blonde hair back and smiled. Steven gave her a quick kiss on the cheek, then went back to the receiving line. He apologized to several people for making them wait.

Karin was used to sharing her dad. *I'd better hurry or I'll make Jeff wait,* she thought. She turned and started through the crowd. She scanned the sanctuary for her mother but couldn't find her. *I'll have to find Mom another time,* Karin decided.

Once in the parking lot, she looked back at the beautiful spire of the church. It glistened in the early winter light. *Why doesn't Daddy like Jeff? He hasn't even given him a chance.* Karin felt pulled in two directions at once. *I wish Dad and Jeff could get along. I need them to get along.*

Back in the church, most of the people had left the building. "Listen, Steven, we may have trouble on our hands," said Howard Svendsen, the chairman of the deacon board. A man in his late sixties, he was dressed in a 600-dollar business suit and expensive Italian-made shoes. He had pulled Steven aside just as soon as the pastor had shaken hands with the last person. "Word has somehow leaked out about the finance committee meeting. Two of your staff approached me this morning and asked me if they still have jobs."

"Who was it?"

"Stu and Ron." Stu was the youth pastor, and Ron was the senior associate.

"What did you tell them?" Steven said.

"I told them not to worry about it."

"Who did it?" Steven bristled. "Who leaked the information from the meeting?"

"I don't know."

"That discussion was strictly confidential. I'm going to call every person who was there. Elizabeth took minutes. She could give me a list of committee members and phone numbers this afternoon."

"Now just hold on, Steven."

"Somebody's talking and we need to find out who," insisted Steven. "Let's call a committee meeting this afternoon and get to the bottom of this."

"I don't think that's necessary," the chairman said. "Let's not overreact."

Steven's face flushed with anger. "Howard, this is critical. I'm facing a staff rebellion because someone on the committee couldn't keep his—or her—mouth shut."

Howard was a mild-mannered banker who seldom raised his voice. "I can understand why you're upset, Steven, but please, let me handle this. Someone probably said something privately and someone else overheard. You know how much trouble we have around here keeping secrets. Remember the tenth anniversary surprise party we planned for you? Somehow you were even mailed an invitation." Howard laughed and nudged Steven's shoulder.

Steven reluctantly smiled. "Yeah, I remember. I even got an envelope in the mail asking me to contribute to my own gift."

"Steven, it's no big deal."

Steven stared at the floor for a minute, then in a slow and measured way looked up at the chairman. "Howard, do you think someone is working against us on this committee? Why else would they leak this?"

"Let's not assume anything just yet, Steven. It could have been an innocent remark."

"Howard, can I trust you?"

"Of course you can, Steven, you know that."

Steven stopped and looked around to be certain no one was listening. A few children ran down the hallway; otherwise there was no one in sight. "A little over a week ago I received an anonymous letter."

"So what's new?" the chairman said. "Remember the last time you preached on a hot topic? You needed asbestos gloves and a bomb-sniffing dog to open your mail for two months."

"This letter included veiled threats against me."

Howard furrowed his brow, "Why didn't you tell us sooner?"

"I didn't think there was anything to it. Now this break-in, I'm beginning to wonder . . ."

"Steven, don't be an alarmist. They may not be related at all."

"I know it sounds farfetched Howard . . ."

"Steven, I've never known you to buckle under pressure," said the banker. He put his hand on the pastor's shoulder, "This all is likely a coincidence. The board is 100 percent behind you. So are the people. I'll just call Stuart and Ron this afternoon and assure them again the board is not about to take any action with regard to staffing."

"Thanks, I appreciate you handling this for me," said Steven. "Would you like to see a copy of that letter? I've got it locked up in my office."

"That may be a good idea."

The two men walked back toward Steven's office. They greeted the few families left who were cleaning up Sunday school rooms. "It's right here," said Steven as he unlocked his filing cabinet. He pulled out the file without opening it and handed it to Howard. The chairman sat down in an overstuffed chair.

"Steven, is this the right file?" he asked.

"Of course."

"Then I'm afraid we do have a problem. The letter is gone."

St. James on the Park, an upscale restaurant, was jammed with people. Todd and Ashley Branstrom smiled over the table at Steven and Brenda. Todd was a young attorney and Ashley was a teacher. They had started attending First Community six months before. Steven had accepted their invitation to lunch because it seemed a good move. He knew Todd was a junior partner in a prestigious law firm and might be future leadership material for the church. It had always been Steven's philosophy to groom leaders several years in advance before putting them on the board. He wanted to make certain they would be loyal if elected.

"Pastor, where did you get your doctorate?" Todd asked.

Steven didn't answer. He was lost in thought about affairs at church.

"Steven," his wife nudged him under the table. "Todd asked where you earned your doctoral degree."

"Oh, I'm sorry," Steven said. "Princeton. I earned my doctor of ministry degree from Princeton."

Brenda realized she was going to have to cover for her husband. Ever since the church break-in his mind had been elsewhere. She steered the conversation away from Steven and got Todd and Ashley to talk about their vacation to Switzerland last summer.

Who had access to my files? Steven asked himself. *I know I put that letter away. Didn't I? Where did it go? Howard must think I'm a nut.*

The waitress stopped by their table with the coffee pot and a tray of four glasses of ice water. She held the steaming pot in one hand and balanced the ice water with her other hand.

"I'll take a warm-up," said Brenda.

The waitress leaned across Steven to pour Brenda's coffee. Suddenly the glasses on the tray shifted. In a split second the entire tray became imbalanced and all four glasses of water plunged off the platter and onto Steven.

"Oh no!" cried the waitress. She let go of the pot of coffee and the container hit the ground right next to Steven's feet.

"Ow!" he cried. He stood up, soaked with water from his waist to his cuffs. The hot coffee had splashed on his right ankle and had left it slightly scalded.

"Steven!" shrieked Brenda. "Are you all right?"

"Look what you've done!" he shouted at the waitress.

"I'm so sorry, I'll get a rag . . . If you'll just—"

"Can't you do something simple like pour coffee? Is that too much for you?" Like a scene from his boyhood kitchen, he poured on the shame over a mistake. "Terrific. Just terrific. I want to see the manager and fast."

"Steven, please . . ." She tried to get him to sit down. Todd got up and offered Steven his napkin. Tables everywhere grew quiet to watch the spectacle.

"Well just don't stand there, do something!" he shouted.

Steven's tirade had reduced the young waitress to tears. She stooped down to wipe off his shoes. "Please, let me help you," she said.

"I said call your supervisor," demanded Steven.

"Yes, yes, of course—I'm so sorry . . ."

Brenda sat with her head down. The waitress finally left and disappeared through a door into the kitchen. In a matter of moments a short, heavy-set man in a long-sleeved shirt and tie appeared.

"Sir, I'm terribly sorry. I'll be glad to have your suit and tie dry-cleaned at our expense."

"You might be facing a lawsuit, mister."

Brenda couldn't look up.

"I apologized to you, sir," came the short reply.

Brenda had seen Steven this angry at home before, but never in public, and never in front of two parishioners.

Brenda reached for her purse and slid back from the table. "Todd, Ashley, you'll have to excuse us," she said. "We'd better get home and take a look at Steven's foot."

"We understand," said the couple sweetly. They stood up and shook hands with the Warners. Steven left first. Brenda stayed a moment to offer a parting apology to the waitress. She caught up with him as he stormed out of the door of the restaurant.

"Who was that guy?" whispered a couple who sat at a nearby table.

"Some jerk," said the manager under his breath.

■

Steven sat alone in the living room that afternoon and just stared. His outburst at the restaurant had left him feeling ashamed and embarrassed. He was also worried, particularly about his image in the church. If Todd and Ashley spread word of this . . .

Steven decided to call the young couple to apologize for his temper. Todd assured him that they understood and would say nothing of the incident to anyone. Relieved, he hung up and laid down on the couch.

What's happening to me, God? Steven prayed. *I can't believe the way I'm acting.* Steven reached for the remote control and flicked on the television. He surfed through the channels until he found an NBA game. *Basketball. Eric,* thought Steven. *I missed taking Eric to a game for a crummy finance committee meeting that got me into hot water with my staff.* The game on television featured two teams he had no interest in, so he flicked it off.

He picked up the Sunday paper. He sometimes could relax by reading the opinion page. He leafed through the heavy Sunday edition, then stopped. On the front page of the travel section was a picture of a couple lying in lounge chairs on the deck of a luxury cruise liner.

A vacation, our vacation, he thought. *Brenda. Our anniversary.* She had said nothing more about the trip since their blowup two weeks ago. After their fight, Steven had put off ordering tickets. The paper listed toll-free numbers to call about cruise vacations. Intrigued, Steven walked into the kitchen and picked up the phone. He punched in the 800 number and listened.

"Welcome to the Royal Pacific Dream Line. Imagine yourself for fourteen days sailing into the pristine blue waters of Hawaii . . ."

Steven took down the information for booking and reservations. Next he called a 24-hour travel service in San Diego. In less than ten minutes, the arrangements were made. He hung up the phone. "Yes!" he said out loud. "I'm out of here. And no one can stop me."

Hands above his head, he snapped his fingers and pretended to do the Mexican hat dance. Steven's momentary exhilaration at the thought of surprising Brenda with a quick vacation was checked by another thought. *I have no one to cover for me. I haven't even checked with Howard or the board. I can't just walk away without arranging for substitutes.* He suddenly had second thoughts about his impulsive decision to book a vacation.

Steven trudged upstairs into his study. He dropped down into his swivel chair, put his feet up on his desk, and leaned back. *Who in the world could I get to cover for me on such short notice?* he wondered. *That is, anyone who's any good.* Steven sat up and made a list of names. He didn't like any of them. He could feel the exhaustion of the day. No, the exhaustion of the last few years. He put his head down on his desk. *Please, God,* he prayed. *I need to get away from all this.*

He heard a small, accusing voice inside. *Who are you to think you can just up and get away? Did your dad ever walk away just because things were tough? What kind of pastor are you anyway?*

Guilt pangs shot through him. *The church needs me,* he thought. *It won't work if I'm gone. We're in trouble as it is. I've got to call and cancel this whole thing. I can't leave now.*

Steven eased back again in his chair when his eyes caught his seminary diploma on the wall. He stared at it for just a moment. Then a smile broke out on his face.

"That's it," he said. He whirled around on his chair and pulled out a filing cabinet drawer next to his desk. He thumbed through several files under "H" in the alphabet, then pulled out the one he wanted.

The adrenaline started to flow. He studied the phone number on the letterhead in the file and then picked up his cordless phone. He read the number off the stationery and dialed the number.

The phone rang once, twice, three times. He let it ring a fifth time and decided to hang up. Then, at the last second, he heard a familiar voice with a southern lilt on the line.

"Good afternoon, this is the Intercession Hotline, Ray Havens speaking. How may I serve you?"

"Dr. Ray, is that you?"

"Why, yes it is," came the courtly reply. "And whom, may I ask, am I speaking to?"

"It's Steven Warner. Your former student." There was a long pause as the elderly gentleman tried to remember who Steven was. "You remember me," Steven said. "I graduated twenty years ago. I was in that class you took down to the bus station to witness with a bullhorn. You were arrested for not having a permit. Remember? I bailed you out of jail."

"Well, my stars, it's you, Steven," laughed the professor. "How can I ever forget that class? We saw some remarkable answers to prayer. It's so good to hear from you, son."

"It's good to hear your voice too," replied Steven.

For the next several minutes the old professor and Steven reminisced about seminary days. Steven had loved Dr. Ray. In many ways he had been a father to Steven. He seemed to treat everyone with warmth, affirmation, but most of all, love.

Dr. Ray had a special room with an entire wall covered with a picture of a serene mountain lake. Troubled students were welcome to come in anytime to pray. If Dr. Ray happened to be in the office, he'd offer a small glass of chilled grape juice from his small refrigerator.

But the professor was by no means popular with everyone. Some viewed him as too lax or unorthodox in his teaching methods. It wasn't unusual for Dr. Ray in those days to start class by telling all his students to get down on their knees right next to their desks. He might have the class pray for the entire hour—for each other or for the special needs that had been phoned in on the Intercession Hotline. His phone rang day and night with calls coming in from all over the world.

"If students are going to learn about prayer, they need to begin by praying," he would answer his critics.

Dr. Ray was retired now, living in southern Mississippi, his native home. But he still maintained his Intercession Hotline.

"Well, to what do I owe the honor of this particular call?" asked the old professor.

"I have a favor to ask you, Dr. Ray," said Steven.

"Certainly. How can I pray for you? Let me get my prayer diary out here—"

"I need you to do something more than pray, Dr. Ray. I need you to come to First Community and preach for me for three weeks."

Ray hesitated for a moment, "Gracious me, what a privilege."

"We have over fourteen hundred people on Sunday mornings."

"Land sakes, son, you've nearly got yourself a denomination. But I'm very busy at the moment. I have very few dates available until next summer."

"Of course," said Steven. He took a deep breath and decided to go ahead with his request anyway, "I apologize, Dr. Ray, but I need you to come in two weeks and stay for three."

"Two weeks from now? Have mercy, are you up against it, Steven?"

"I'm afraid I am, Dr. Ray. I'm also afraid I'm losing my ministry." For the next several minutes Steven poured out his heart to his old friend and mentor. He told him all about the drop in finances, the problems in his marriage, the hate mail, and now the vandalism in the sanctuary.

"And to top it all off, Dr. Ray, this afternoon at lunch, I lost my temper and humiliated a waitress in front of two new members of my congregation. I was loud, obnoxious, and mean. Just plain mean. I didn't care who heard me or how loud I got." Steven's voice started to quiver. "Dr. Ray, I'm worried.

I don't know what's happening to me. I need to spend some time with you."

"My, my, my," said the professor gently. "We're going to have to get on the main line and get you out of this mess."

"Dr. Ray, can you come?" He hated to pressure his old friend, but Steven felt he had no choice.

"Well, my dear wife, Beulah, and I were scheduled to conduct a prayer summit near Paducah, Kentucky, on the twenty-ninth. Let me see . . . ." His voice trailed off as he turned the pages of his calendar.

"I'll see the church pays all your expenses," Steven offered. "We'll put you up at the Ambassador Suites and have a rental car available."

"Let's see here, on the second of next month I was going to attend meetings in Marietta, Georgia . . . ." As long as Steven had known the old gentleman, he was never in a hurry.

"On the eighth I was going to Atlanta for a meeting with the editor of *Our Daily Provisions* . . . ." Steven bit his lip. There was a long pause again.

"Well, heaven have mercy," came the voice finally. "It will mean putting some hogs in a different pen. And they're likely to squeal a bit, but I think we could manage it." He chuckled in that distinctive down-home style that made him so lovable.

"Thank you, Dr. Ray. You don't know how much this means."

"But you remember, Beulah and I don't fly. We'll have to take the bus." Steven had forgotten the old gentleman's aversion to airplanes. His brother had died in an airplane years ago, and Dr. Ray had never boarded one since then.

"That's fine," said Steven. "I'll make all the arrangements. I can't thank you enough."

"Son, you write me a letter and tell me the times of your services and how often I have to preach. I'm going to call several of my prayer associates and have them add you and your church to their list. In fact, we're due to have a meeting start here in about half an hour. You wouldn't know Virginia Stubbles, but my, how that lady can pray."

"I need all the prayer I can get, Dr. Ray. So does my family." Steven had forgotten that you never mention a prayer request in Dr. Ray's presence unless you were ready to pray right then and there.

"Lord, we bring this servant of Yours before You this afternoon," said Dr. Ray. "You have said our adversary roams about as a roaring lion seeking whom he may devour. Yet Your name shuts the mouths of lions. Lord, bless this devoted man, our brother Steven. Set him on a high place. Don't let discouragement get the best of him. We ask You to give him hope and let him see light. In the name of Jesus, we pray. Amen."

For the first time in months—maybe even years—Steven felt at peace as he hung up the phone. Maybe, just maybe, things were going to get easier for him.

SEVEN

Karin, Karin, where are you?"

It was 8:30 on a Tuesday morning and Sally Jensetter was in a hurry. She paced up and down the dormitory hallway, poking her head in various rooms where the door was open, trying to find her roommate. A tall, attractive sophomore, Sally was also an honor student. She and Karin had roomed together for two years.

Frustrated in her search, Sally pushed open the door to the lavatory at the end of the hallway. There was Karin, standing motionless in front of the mirror.

"There you are. Come on. We have class in five minutes."

Karin didn't answer her. She stood with her back toward her roommate.

"Karin, did you hear me? We're going to be late. Today's the midterm, remember?"

Finally Karin turned around. Sally couldn't believe her eyes. Karin's eyes were red and swollen, and her face was pale as a sheet.

"Karin, what's . . . what's wrong?" she said. Karin didn't say a word. Instead, she held up a small vial containing blue liquid and handed it to her roommate.

"What's that?" Sally said.

"I'm pregnant," Karin whispered.

"You're what?"

"I'm pregnant."

It took a moment for Sally to absorb what she had just heard.

"Karin, you're joking, right?"

Karin shook her head.

"You must be—you couldn't be—oh my word, Karin." Karin took the vial back from her stunned roommate. In a colorless voice she said, "I bought this pregnancy test at a Phar-Mor drugstore last night. The pharmacist said it's 98 percent accurate. No change in color, you're safe. But if it's blue . . ." There was no doubt about the color. It was definitely blue.

"Oh, Sally!" Karin collapsed into Sally's arms. Still off balance herself, Sally held onto her roommate, unable to say anything. She feared Karin would drop to the floor if she let go.

"My father, my mother . . . Oh, Sally—"

Sally felt Karin's body convulse with each sob.

"Why did God let this happen to me?"

Sally was at a loss for words.

Not knowing what else to say, Sally asked, "Did you have any idea?"

"Yes. I was late this last month. But I thought it might be just stress or something. That's happened to me before. But finally I went to the drugstore. I knew it was possible."

"What are you going to do, Karin?"

"I don't know. I . . . don't know."

Sally stood and cradled her roommate on her shoulder. When Karin had regained some composure, Sally let go of her. She walked over and poked her head out the door. Everyone else on the floor had either left for class or decided to sleep in. Carefully, she led Karin down the hallway to their room.

"Karin, listen to me," she said as she closed the door to their room behind her. "You're going to see a doctor before the day is over. What if you are one of the two percent that gets a false positive? Before you go and tell Jeff or anyone else you're pregnant, you need to know for sure."

"But where can I go?" said Karin.

"I've got an idea," answered Sally. "There's a 24-hour medical clinic in Kensington Heights. You don't need an appointment. You can just walk in. We'll go there. Let me hurry and go take the midterm. I'll tell the professor you're not feeling well. When I come back, you be ready to leave, okay?"

"I just need you to promise me one thing," said Karin. Her dark, sad eyes cut right through her roommate.

"Sure, Karin, what is it?"

"Sally, promise me you will never, under any circumstances, tell my parents. Do you promise?"

"Sure."

"Under no circumstances."

"Okay, Karin. Whatever you say."

Sally grabbed her coat and books and ran off to class. For the next hour Karin just lay on her bed, sometimes crying, sometimes feeling nothing at all.

An hour later she got up and smeared on some makeup to try to hide her swollen and red eyes. At last Karin heard a car honk and looked outside the window. Sally had pulled in front of the dorm. Karin walked down the hallway and out the door without saying a word to anyone.

As Karin rode through busy traffic, nothing seemed real. She had no sense of time. It was all a bad dream. *Oh, please God,* she prayed, *please, don't let me be pregnant.*

The phone rang in the Warners' kitchen.

"Good morning," said Brenda in a cheerful voice.

"Just calling to see how you're doing this morning."

"Oh, Maggie, it's good to hear from you. I'm doing terrific. Steven surprised me yesterday with two tickets for a fifteen-day cruise to Hawaii, then a week more on Oahu."

"Hawaii?" shrieked Maggie. "That's fabulous, absolutely fabulous."

"I know, I can't believe it," said Brenda. "Last month was our twentieth anniversary. Steven had promised we would do something special. So he called the board chairman last night. Then he called the other deacons. They said yes! Maggie, can you believe it?"

The two women squealed with sheer delight.

"Well, the Lord does move in mysterious ways, doesn't He?" said Maggie. "I asked Him to bless you two, but I didn't think it would be this soon."

"We're leaving a week from Monday. Steven arranged for one of his former seminary professors to fill in for him while we're gone."

"Child, who's going to take care of Eric?"

"We're still looking, Maggie. I called my parents, but they can't come. So I have a call in to my sister."

"Well, quit calling, dear."

"What do you mean?"

"What I mean is that you have found your house sitter. I'll come over and take care of your boy while you're gone. We'll get along just fine."

"Oh, Maggie, do you mean it? Would you?"

"Of course. It wouldn't do any good to pray for people if you're not willing to be part of the answer, would it?"

"Maggie, what can I ever do to repay you? I'm going to call Steven at the office and tell him the moment we hang up. Maggie, I love you."

"And I love you, too, daughter. You just start making up a menu for that boy. It's been a few years since I cooked for a teenager, but I think I still remember."

"Eric will love you, Maggie. I can't believe this. Guess where I'm going this afternoon?"

"Where, dear?"

"I'm going to Michigan Avenue to buy my cruise wardrobe. I have to plan to be in the sun for three weeks."

The two women laughed. Their celebration was interrupted by the doorbell.

"You'll have to excuse me, Maggie. Someone's at the door." Brenda raised the curtain on the kitchen window and saw a delivery truck parked in their driveway. "I think it's UPS or someone, Maggie. I'll call you tonight when Steven and I have the plans worked out better. Gotta run. 'Bye."

When Brenda opened the door, she was greeted by a florist's delivery man. "Sign here," he said politely. Brenda scribbled her signature, then walked back into the house. She held in her hands a dozen long-stemmed yellow roses.

When she had closed the door behind her, she opened the card. "My dearest Belinda, Two decades is too long to wait for another honeymoon. I love you, Steven."

The bright yellow sun of the early winter sky poured through the windows of their home. Brenda sat down on her couch and read the card over and over again.

"Steven, may I come in and see you?"

"Of course, Elizabeth. I'm not busy at the moment." The light on Steven's interoffice phone went off as he set the receiver down. In less than thirty seconds there was a knock at his office door.

"Come on in." Steven's secretary came and sat down in the chair directly in front of his desk.

"You asked me to check on that canceled luncheon with the women's group."

"Yes." Steven continued writing something in his calendar. It was common for him to be doing two things at once. Elizabeth had gotten used to it.

"I called Doris Shumway, who's on the committee. She said the new president made the decision to postpone it."

"Who's that?" Steven said as he looked up.

"Rachel Brewster."

"Ed's wife?"

"Yes."

"Did she say why?"

"Rachel just said she felt the women needed something different. They're planning at this point to get an outside speaker."

"Huh." Steven tapped his pen on the desk and looked out his window.

Just then Steven's phone rang. It was the receptionist. "There's a Tiffany Evans waiting in the reception area. That's your ten A.M. appointment, Dr. Warner."

"Thanks, send her in in just a moment, will you?" Steven leaned forward and in a lower voice said, "Elizabeth, I've never asked you to do something like this before. But I need a favor from you."

"Certainly, what is it?"

"Get me a copy of the latest Women's Ministry minutes. And remember, I never asked you to do this." Elizabeth nodded an approving smile and walked out.

As Elizabeth walked out, she met Tiffany in the hallway. The woman was wearing a white mink and long gold earrings.

A middle-aged bureaucrat at the IRS had just about opened all the morning mail in Kansas City, the regional center for the Treasury Department. He thumbed through the remaining letters on his desk when he spotted one labeled "Confidential."

Slitting it open, he took out the letter, which was typed on stylish stationery.

To whom it may concern:
    I wish to remain anonymous, but as a member of First Community Church in Covington Park, Illinois, my conscience will not allow me further silence. The pastor of my church, along with a select few from the official board, are involved in practices that could at best be considered fraud.
    Money is being laundered through church accounts to qualify individuals for charitable tax deductions. Yet, the money doesn't go to the church or to missionaries, but back to the donor's account. I suggest you take this note seriously.

The bureaucrat put the letter down and turned to his boss. "Jack, will you look at this?"

His older supervisor got up from his desk and walked over to the man's desk. He took the letter and scanned it quickly.

"What do you think? Is it worth sending on upstairs?"

"I don't know. It could just be a crank."

"What's policy on these matters?"

The older supervisor rubbed his chin. "We're very careful about unsigned letters. We can end up wasting a good deal of time chasing rabbit trails." The supervisor looked at the letter once more. "I suppose we'd better be safe than sorry. Send it upstairs and mark it to Joe McDonald's attention. He handles investigations for the Chicago area."

The bureaucrat scribbled a memo to McDonald and stapled it to the letter. He then put it in his out basket.

Eric sat alone in the cafeteria with his Walkman headphones on. The noise inside the lunchroom was almost deafening, but all he could hear was the beat of one of his favorite rap groups.

Someone pulled one of his earphones away from his ear. "Hey man, anyone home?" Eric whirled around to see who it was.

"Dustin, you fool. Don't do that to me."

Dustin Jacobs was one of Eric's best friends at school. His parents ran a successful real estate agency in Covington Park and worked long hours. Dustin had come home to an empty house since he was seven. Now he sat down next to Eric, his baseball cap turned backward.

"Eric, stop by my locker after school."

"Why, man?"

"I brought something today I want to show you."

"What are you, some type of druggie now?" Eric sounded annoyed.

"Shut your face, Eric. This is something it took me a long time to get."

"Okay, if you say so. But remember, I've got to catch the bus."

When the last bell rang at 3:20, Eric made his way through the maze of teenage humanity toward Dustin's locker. Students pushed from every direction, but Eric was finally able to break through the crowd.

"I didn't think you were coming, Warner," said Dustin.

"This had better be good," said Eric. Dustin looked around to make certain no teachers were in sight. He spun the numbers on the combination lock, then opened his locker. A long trench coat hung inside.

"Reach in the pocket, but don't take it out," Dustin said calmly.

Eric looked at him as if he were crazy. He reached into the locker and put his hand inside the coat. His fingers felt cold steel and a short barrel.

"Are you out of your mind?" said Eric.

"Shut up, you'll attract attention," Dustin warned.

"You could be arrested, you idiot."

"Look, I'll tell you who's the idiot. It's anyone who comes to school without one. Just last week I had to turn over my new jacket to one of those Squires." Dustin cursed. "I won't do it again. I won't get shaken down again."

Eric felt fear move down his spine. The look on Dustin's face was pure hatred.

"You really mean this, don't you, man?"

"Watch and see."

That night Eric went home shaken. He was quiet while his mom and dad discussed their trip to Hawaii.

"Oops, it's almost 6:30," Steven said. "I've got a deacon's meeting at seven. Did you bring homework home, son?"

"Yeah, it's upstairs," said Eric.

"Good, I'll stick my head in your door if I get home before 10:30. You've got a good mind, Eric—use it."

Steven stood up and gave Brenda a quick kiss good-bye and was out the door.

"You want dessert, Eric?" asked Brenda.

"Naw, I'm not too hungry tonight."

"I'll leave it on the table if you change your mind. I'm going over to Maggie's for a few minutes tonight. We've got some last minute details to settle before the trip. You'll enjoy her company. She's raised two boys herself."

"Sure," mumbled Eric.

"Can I get you anything while I'm out?"

"No, I'm fine."

But that night, Eric had trouble falling asleep. One thought kept going through his mind: *If Dustin has a gun, who else does?*

It was past midnight. Karin emerged from her room with a look of steel resolve in her eyes. She walked down the stairs into the basement of the dormitory. The hallway was dimly lit. The only sound she could hear was the steady humming of a dryer still running in the laundry room.

Just outside the laundry room was a pay phone. She dropped a quarter in it and dialed the number from memory.

A male voice answered. "Hello?" He sounded groggy and irritated.

"Greg, is that you? This is Karin. I need to talk to Jeff. Right away."

"He's not here, Karin."

"Where is he?"

Greg hesitated. "He's . . . uh, he's—"

"Greg, this is really important," Karin interrupted. "Just tell him it's me."

"Karin, I'm really zoned. It's past midnight. I'll leave him a message that you called."

"Greg, don't hang up. I need to talk to Jeff. Where is he?"

"How am I supposed to know?" Greg started to sound angry. "Look, I don't want to get involved in your relationship, okay? Good night." Karin heard a click.

"Greg, Greg, are you still there?" No response. Karin slammed the receiver down in frustration.

"I'll tell you where Jeff is," came a voice out of the shadows. Karin looked over, startled. A woman stepped out of the darkness into the light. It was Lisa Fredrickson, Karin's resident assistant. She stood with a laundry basket in her hands.

"Oh, Lisa, I'm glad it's you. You nearly scared me to death."

"No, I need to apologize. I didn't mean to eavesdrop on your conversation. But about Jeff."

"Yes?" said Karin, her voice tense.

"Why don't we go in the laundry room where we can talk?"

The two girls pushed open the door to the laundry room. They were immediately bathed in bright fluorescent light. The entire room glistened with white porcelain washers and dryers. Lisa motioned for Karin to sit down by the folding table. "Karin, I wish I wasn't the one telling you this."

"Telling me what?"

"About Jeff."

"What about Jeff?"

"I went to the mall earlier tonight to get a passport photo taken for my overseas trip next semester. I ran into Jeff as he was coming out of a movie."

"So? He likes to go to movies. It helps him unwind." Karin was defensive.

"So he was with . . ." Lisa paused. She looked truly pained to say what she was about to say.

"Yes?"

The resident assistant looked down. "He was with another girl. A freshman from Florida, Janelle Baker."

"What?" Karin felt weak.

"I asked around on the floor when I got back. It seems Jeff has been seeing her for some time. I thought I should tell you. I don't want to see you hurt."

The next morning Jeff and Karin sat across from each other in a booth in the far corner of the campus coffee shop. Except for a few students who had wandered over to play video games, the place was empty.

"I think I hate you," said Karin. Her tone was quiet yet almost menacing.

Jeff refused to look into her eyes. "Why is this my fault?" he shot back. "Why didn't you take more precautions?"

"Because it wasn't my idea to begin ending dates that way. You said you loved me, remember? You said you had never wanted another woman as much as me. I believed you." She glared at him. Neither said a word for over a minute.

Karin took a deep breath and appeared to gain control over her anger for a moment. "Jeff, I think for the baby's sake we ought to get married." She began to blink back tears.

"Married? Karin, you must be joking," Jeff said. Flustered and red in the face, he continued, "We're both still in college. We have the rest of our lives ahead of us. I'm not ready to get married. I don't even know if I . . ." He stopped.

"Go ahead, Jeff, say it. You don't even know if you love me. Is that it?"

"Karin, calm down—"

"I get it, I was just a good time. Now that it's over, you're ready to go back to your buddies, your car, and more easy women. Right?"

"Look, Karin, I like you. Don't get me wrong. It's just that—"

Before Jeff could finish his thought, Brent and Andrew, two of Jeff's friends, walked up. They had walked away from Karin the day she spotted them outside her history class. Now it was her turn to ignore them.

"Hey, Jeff," Brent smirked. "Someone's looking for you. Something about wanting to study biology together."

He bent over with laughter. Andrew glanced at Karin. He punched Brent and said, "Shut up, you fool. Can't you see Jeff's busy?"

A glare from Jeff sent the two of them on their way. But the incident had given him time to think. "I need space, Karin, that's all. I'm not ready to just date one girl."

Karin glared at him. "I gave you part of myself I've never given anyone else, Jeff. I did it because you said you loved me."

"Well, I do . . . in a way."

She pointed straight in his face. "You used me, Jeff. You used me! And what we did was wrong."

"Shh, shh, Karin. There are people around." Jeff glanced over his shoulder. "Look, we can take care of this little problem. We don't have to have a baby, and we don't have to get married."

"What do you mean?"

"You know what I'm talking about. I hear it only costs about 350 dollars." He leaned forward. "I'll pay for half of it."

"An abortion?" she said out loud.

"Will you quiet down, Karin?"

"I don't believe you! I just don't believe you!" Karin stood up. "I never realized just how slimy one human being could get." Her eyes burned with rage. "Get out of my life, Jeff. Get out!"

Without saying a word, Jeff picked up his books and walked out of the coffee shop. Two students by the video games looked down as he went past them. They pretended they hadn't heard the conversation.

EIGHT

It was the middle of the night when Maggie Dunlop woke up. She sat up in bed and yawned. She glanced over at the digital clock on the dresser. The red numbers glowed 3:45.

"Heaven have mercy," she said out loud. She fell back on her pillow. *Lord, tomorrow is going to be such a busy day,* she prayed. *Please, help me to get some rest.* She pulled the oversized comforter over her head and tried to get back to sleep.

Instead she tossed and turned for several minutes. That's when she heard the inner voice. *Get up and pray. Pray for your pastor and his family.*

"I'm too tired, Lord," she said. "I'll pray in the morning." She was bone tired, in fact. She had spent nearly twelve hours the day before helping a stroke victim in the church move to a residential care facility. Every muscle in her body ached from lifting boxes, scrubbing cupboards, and packing clothes.

The subtle voice spoke again. *Pray for them, Maggie.*

"Oh, all right," Maggie sighed. She swung her feet to the side of the bed and stood up. She flicked the night stand light on. She suffered from mild arthritis, so she hobbled stiffly over to her dresser, where she reached for her tattered and worn red leather Bible.

She trudged back to her bed and sat down on the edge of the mattress. She adjusted the earpieces of her reading glasses and then flipped through the pages. At last she found the passage she was looking for, Psalm 28:8–9, "The LORD is their strength, and He is the saving refuge of His anointed. Save Your people, and bless your inheritance; Shepherd them also, And bear them up forever."

"Lord," Maggie prayed, "I know You don't wake people up unless You have a good reason. So whatever it is, it must be important. Please protect my pastor and his family. I love them, Lord. I love them all like they were my very own. Protect our church too, Lord. You said not even the gates of hell would prevail against Your church. Slam those gates shut, God. In the strong name of Jesus. Amen."

Maggie closed her Bible and lay down again. As she did, a deep, serene peace settled over her soul. The feeling reminded her of when she was a little girl in Texas. She and her sister, Gloria, would climb up the haystacks and lie on top, soaking in the warm summer sun. Remembering that sensation, she was soon sound asleep.

That same night, a group had met in secret across town.

"Let's have the list of names," a woman said in a shallow voice.

A young man got up from the table and handed the list to Ingrid. She studied the list for a few moments, then set it down.

"Let's join hands," Ingrid said. The group immediately obeyed. "As you know, communal energy flows between us," she said. "It is the same cosmic life force that immerses all living beings in an endless ocean of power. It is the life force of Gaia, the goddess of the earth. It is what makes us one with all living creatures. That power is ours to harmonize life and to disrupt it."

The group of men and women in the New Consciousness movement sat mesmerized at her every word.

"As I read this list of names, if you are willing to serve as a channel through which power can flow to punish our enemies, please stand," she said.

One by one the group stood as the leader read the names on the list. At last there were just three names left on the list. Ingrid looked at them and smiled. "Steven Warner, Karin Warner, and Eric Warner," she said. She looked across the table at Rachel.

Rachel look frightened but managed to rise to her feet. "Is . . . is it necessary to punish his children as well?" she asked.

"Can you think of a better way to neutralize him?" Ingrid replied.

"No . . . no, I see the wisdom of your words," Rachel said. She put her head down. The group stood together, joined in a trancelike state for nearly an hour.

When they finally left, it was still dark outside. Rachel glanced at her watch. It was a quarter to four in the morning.

There was the strong smell of diesel fumes mixed with icy cold air outside the downtown bus station. A large, sleek Greyhound bus pulled into the unloading area. Its air brakes hissed as it swung into its designated spot.

Once the bus came to a stop, the large door swung open and the bus disgorged its passengers. Teenagers, mothers with small children, and a number of soldiers climbed off.

"Where is Dr. Havens, Steven? I don't see him," said Brenda.

"Don't worry, honey, he's here somewhere." Steven smiled. He pulled his wife close to him as they shivered in the cold winter air.

Just as the last of the passengers climbed off, a man in a broad black felt hat cocked slightly to one side stepped off. He turned and helped a woman wearing a nylon scarf and bright red wool coat down the bus steps.

"Dr. Ray, over here!" yelled Steven as he pushed his way through the crowd.

The older gentleman heard his name and searched the crowd for the voice. Steven broke through the line and headed straight for the older couple, his hand outstretched.

"Well glory, it's you, Steven," smiled the tall professor as the two men embraced. "Son, where's that lovely bride of yours I remember from seminary?"

Brenda caught up with him. The two couples all hugged and shook hands.

Dr. Ray's arrival made Steven feel like he was twenty-five years old again. The courtly old gentleman had hardly changed. His large round face, the oversized glasses, and the bald spot on the top of his head were just as Steven had remembered.

"Mrs. Havens, I'm so delighted you could come as well," said Brenda. "It's so good to see you again."

"Yes, dear, I remember both you and your husband," said Beulah in a long, sweet southern way. Her bright red lipstick, wavy brown hair, and dark eyes made her an attractive woman, though she was now in her mid-seventies.

"Let's get your bags and get you two out of the cold," Steven said. He and Dr. Ray walked over to the line of suitcases the driver had produced from underneath the bus. Dr. Ray pointed out four olive green Samsonite pieces that were theirs. Each looked like they had seen better days.

Meanwhile, the two women sought shelter inside the terminal. "It was sixty-eight degrees when we left Jackson last night," said Beulah as she wrapped her arms around herself to keep warm.

"It's so kind of you two to come on such short notice," said Brenda. "Steven has been an entirely different person since Dr. Ray said he'd come and preach."

Beulah just smiled and nodded. "Listen, dearie. I discovered long ago that I married a traveling man. I thought Ray might slow down a little when he retired, but I was wrong. He's as busy now as he ever was. Just last month we conducted a prayer workshop for navy and marine chaplains in San Diego. Mercy sakes, Ray insisted we go on a tour of a battleship."

"You dear woman, how do you make it?" said Brenda. "Well, I promise you, this is going to be a relaxing time for both of you. We've rented a furnished suite for you stocked with groceries. Steven's arranged every detail. You won't have to worry about a thing. You can just enjoy your time together here."

"That's so kind of you, dear," said Beulah. "But I imagine Ray will want to get out and visit some people."

"Oh no, we've got staff members who do visitation," said Brenda. "All Dr. Ray will have to do is preach."

Beulah stopped, took Brenda's hand, and looked right into her eyes. "Dearie, you'd better get a list of people together right now who need a visit. Dr. Ray can't sit still. Chances are he's already made a call or two while we've been standing here chattering."

Both women laughed and headed out the automatic doors onto the sidewalk. Steven and Dr. Ray pulled up in Steven's car.

Once Steven was on the expressway, he hit the accelerator and weaved around several cars. Aggressive driving was the name of the game in Chicago. Dr. Ray spoke up. "Why don't we have a word of prayer here for our trip?" he said. He put his hand on the dashboard, "Dear Lord, give Your angels protection over this vehicle. We want to go to heaven, but not before our time. Amen."

Steven got the message. He slowed down to sixty-five miles per hour.

NINE

Eric glanced at the clock on the wall. It was 11:20.

Good, he thought. *It's only ten more minutes until lunch.*
He hated his English literature class, and the last few minutes
before lunch were always the worst. He turned around and
made a face at Dustin, who sat in the back row. The boy
grinned back and flashed a signal.

"Mr. Warner, do we have a problem the entire class should
know about?" It was Mrs. Bratten, or "Mrs. Bratt-Worst" as
the students called her behind her back. She wore tent dresses
and still styled her red hair in a "Paris Beehive."

"No, ma'am. No problem here," Eric said.

"Then please direct your attention this way. If there's
another distraction, I'll let you and the vice principal discuss
it," she said. With that, the fifty-five-year-old English teacher
returned to diagramming Shakespearean sonnets on the blackboard.

The bell finally rang, and Eric jumped out of his seat. He
was the second person out the door.

"Hey, Warner, you nearly got busted," Dustin said once
they were out of earshot of Mrs. Bratten.

"And it was all your fault, Dustin, you loser," said Eric. "I'm
hungry. How about a little food action?"

"Fine by me," said Dustin. "You paying?"

"No way."

The two boys worked their way into the line that was
forming outside the cafeteria doors. The aroma of tacos, pizza,
and hot dogs wafted through the air. The two teenagers
salivated as they walked down the serving counters filled with
à la carte items suited to adolescent taste.

"It's pizza day for me, man," said Eric. He piled two huge slices of pepperoni on his plate.

"Cool," said Dustin as he grabbed three pieces.

The boys found the last two spots at a lunch table and tore into their lunch. The long, stringy white cheese hung down from Eric's mouth as he chomped into his first piece.

"Did you see the Bulls last night?" said Dustin. "A three-pointer with two seconds left to win the game. Awesome."

Eric nodded; his mouth was too full to respond at the moment.

"Yup, they shut down Phoenix for the third time in a row. Too sweet, man. Too sweet."

Just across from the two boys sat two seniors. Without warning, one suddenly jumped to his feet, took his milk carton, and threw it straight up to the ceiling. "Let's go, Archer!" he yelled out.

Five tables over, another boy stood up and threw his milk carton halfway across the cafeteria. That ignited a chain reaction. Like a wave that suddenly swells and thunders onto the beach, a roar erupted as lunch plates, silverware, and tacos flew through the air.

"It's a food fight!" yelled Dustin.

"Head for cover!" laughed Eric. Dustin dove under the table just as a tray of food sailed over his head.

"Hey, what do you think you're doing?" said Eric. He picked up a piece of pizza and whipped it like a Frisbee at a group of guys three tables over. He dodged a milk carton and smirked, "Too bad, dude. Maybe next time." Suddenly something went splat against his face. He reached up. It was fruit salad.

"Warner, get down here," said Dustin, crouched beneath the legs of the folding lunch table.

"Not until I even the score," said Eric. His face was covered with whipped cream. Half a maraschino cherry stuck to his cheek.

He reached over and picked up a hot dog from an otherwise empty plate. He stuck it onto his fork, cocked his hand, and let it fly. It hit the back of a senior student lunchroom monitor who had tried to hide behind a pillar for protection.

"Oops," said Eric. He dove down before the monitor could see who threw it.

In less than sixty seconds it was over. The lunchroom was a disaster area. Apparently the food fight had been preplanned. Several students had smuggled chicken eggs that were supposed to be incubating from the biology lab. The yolk dripped from the ceiling and the glass walls of the cafeteria.

"Did you get anyone, Warner?" asked Dustin as the two boys hid underneath the table.

"Yeah. I took out one of the student monitors with an Oscar Mayer cruise missile." The boys rocked with laughter.

"Total impact, man?"

"Total."

Dustin gave Eric a high five. Eric's hand was covered with pizza sauce.

"Ooh, ugly, man."

The principal announced over the intercom during the next class period that over one thousand dollars of damage had been done to trays, silverware, and the cafeteria. "Another food fight in this school will not be tolerated," he warned.

Unfortunately, the second lunch period had gotten word of the free-for-all during the first period. They were not to be outdone. All it took was one surface-to-air taco launch, and Roosevelt's second food fight of the year was under way.

"Karin, your mom and dad are down in the lobby. They want to see you." Karin looked up from her desk and saw Sally standing in the door to their room.

"Mom and Dad? What are they doing here?" Karin asked. She had found excuses not to go home since the day Sally took her to the doctor.

"Looks like they've got some packages for you," said Sally. "I ran into them on my way to class. They asked me to come get you. Shall I tell them you're here?"

Karin felt a little sick on the inside. She hadn't been to church either since she had learned she was pregnant. It had been a week since the doctor had confirmed her worst fears. According to his estimates, she was now seven weeks along. She had struggled for many days—and nights—with just how to tell her parents.

"Karin, you need to go talk to them," said Sally. "They're your parents. Sooner or later you're going to have to tell them."

"Let me be the judge of that," said Karin as she slammed her book shut.

"I'm sorry, Karin, I didn't mean to . . ."

"How would you like to tell your dad and mom you were pregnant, Sally? Did you ever think of that?"

"Karin, I'm sorry. I didn't mean to—"

"What should I say? Oh, by the way, Dad and Mom, you're going to be grandparents."

"Karin, I'm sorry, I was only trying to help."

"Well, help someone else."

Sally turned around and walked away.

Karin knew Sally didn't deserve her anger. "Sally, wait. I'm sorry. If it hadn't been for you these last two weeks . . ." Karin covered her face and fought back her tears. Sally quietly walked over and put her hands on her roommate's shoulders.

"Karin, your parents are downstairs. Go see them."

"Okay. Tell them I'll be down in five minutes."

Sally reached out and hugged her roommate. "Good, Karin. I think you're making the right decision."

Karin got up and combed her hair, dried her tears, and put on fresh makeup. Satisfied she didn't look too miserable, she headed out the door to the elevator.

The doors closed in front of her. Karin quietly prayed out loud, "Dear God, this is the hardest thing I've ever done. Please help them to understand. Please don't let them reject me. Please, God, I'm so scared."

The doors opened to the lobby, and several women got on the elevator as Karin got off. Her legs felt wobbly underneath her. Her heart seemed to burn in her chest. She felt a tingling sensation in both hands. Every fiber in her body told her to turn around and go back to her room.

Make up some excuse, a voice inside said. *Any excuse to get you out of here.* But Karin knew her hour had come.

Steven Warner sat on a sofa calmly reading the newspaper while his wife glanced through a magazine. At the sight of their daughter, Brenda jumped up.

"Oh, sweetheart, how are you?" She hugged Karin so tightly she thought she might break. Karin found comfort in the familiar smell of her mother's perfume.

"How's my little girl?" said Steven, joining the two in a hug. He hadn't even bothered to take his coat off.

"Mom, Dad, I'm so glad to see both of you," Karin said in her bravest voice.

"Why haven't you come home, darling?" asked Brenda. "I've missed you so much."

"Oh, you know. Schoolwork. Papers. Midterms."

Brenda hugged her daughter again. "I keep your room clean just in case," she smiled.

"Thanks, Mom."

Steven had already sat down again on the couch. "Can you believe this?"

"Believe what, dear?" said Brenda.

"The Bulls traded their best point guard for two undisclosed draft picks. I could run a team better than they do."

"Steven, we're here to see Karin, remember?"

He put his paper down and smiled. "So how's my scholar?"

"Fine," said Karin quietly. She started to feel weak again. She prayed her parents wouldn't notice her jitters.

"Glad to hear it," he said. He reached into a Marshall Field's shopping bag and produced several packages. "We wanted you to have these before we left on our trip." Steven handed his daughter several boxes, all neatly gift wrapped.

"What are these for?" Karin asked. The beautifully wrapped presents seemed out of place at a moment like this.

"Because we love you, that's why," said Brenda.

Karin kept up a brave front as she tore the paper off the first box and opened it. It was a lovely cashmere sweater. "Oh, Mom, it's beautiful."

"I thought so, too, when I saw it. It was just our way of telling you how proud we are of you. I always knew our little girl would go to college and become an honor student."

"That's right, Karin," said Steven. "You've made me one proud father. Imagine, you go to school in the city where I'm serving a church. What more can a dad ask?"

Karin opened the next box. It was a white silk blouse. The third box had a pair of black dress slacks. She could feel the emotion welling up inside her. "Thanks, guys. But you really shouldn't have . . ."

"Well, we're going to miss your birthday while we are away in Hawaii, so just consider this your party in advance," said Brenda.

"Oh, thank you." Karin went over and hugged her father. She did the same to her mother. Her eyes were filled with tears.

"Hey, there's nothing to cry about," said Steven. "You deserve these things. You've earned them."

How can I tell them? thought Karin. *But I've got to. I can't go on like this any longer.*

"Look Dad, Mom, I'm wondering if we could talk for a few minutes?"

"Why certainly, darling," said Brenda.

"Sure, Karin," said Steven. "But I am due back in the office in a few minutes."

Karin felt a determination well up inside. The lobby was empty. She was not going to miss this opportunity to face the truth. In a calm but firm voice she said, "I need to tell you both something."

"Yes?" Steven looked puzzled.

"I've got this problem . . ." She could feel her pulse quicken and her hands began tingling again. The expression on her mother's face became one of concern. Karin took a deep breath and prayed for courage. This was unquestionably the hardest moment of her life. Both her parents stared at her, waiting for her to finish her sentence.

"Could we go somewhere where we can talk?" she said in a nervous voice.

"What is it, Karin?" said Brenda.

Before she could answer her mother's question, Steven reached inside his coat pocket and pulled a small black object off his belt. It was his silent beeper. A vibration on his belt had just indicated he was being paged. He squinted as he tried to read the numbers on the liquid display panel.

"This looks important, Karin. Do you have a phone somewhere close? It should only take a minute."

Karin couldn't believe this was happening, not now. "Sure," she mumbled, "there's one right next to the door going downstairs."

"I'll be right back, I promise." Steven got up, walked over to the phone, and dialed the number from his pager. Karin could see him furl his brow, an expression she had seen a million times growing up. That meant trouble. He talked only a minute or two, but she knew he was as good as gone.

Steven walked back to the two women with an anxious look on his face. "Karin, you're going to have to forgive me, but Jack Freeman's wife had surgery this morning. She's gone into a coma. I'd send someone else to the hospital, but . . . well, Jack is an elder. I always handle elder family problems myself." Karin felt a wave of disappointment sweep over her.

Brenda could see that she was troubled.

"Karin, I know what you're going to tell me," said Brenda.

"You do?" Karin felt as if she might faint. *Who told her? How did she know? Did Sally say something?*

"Sure I do. It's about you and Jeff, isn't it?" she said.

Karin felt dizzy. So her mom did know.

"Oh, Mom," she cried. She rushed into her arms.

"Karin," said Brenda. "I know. You and Jeff had some big fight. You're wondering what to do next. Don't worry, sweetheart. These things work themselves out. The same thing happened to your dad and me when we were dating."

"I've always thought you can do a lot better than Jeff," said Steven, who had put his coat on to leave. "Why not date around? You may find someone who deserves you more than he does."

Brenda shot a scowl at Steven.

"Then again, maybe you should try and work it out," he said halfheartedly.

Karin just stood there, unable to respond. *Then they don't know,* she thought.

"Don't worry about it, honey," Steven said. "When we get back, I'll have Elizabeth call and set up a lunch date for the three of us. You may have worked it out by then."

Brenda wiped her daughter's eyes with her handkerchief and hugged her again. "Are you going to be all right?" she asked.

Karin nodded.

Steven buttoned his coat and grabbed his appointment book. "Take it from me, Karin, your whole life is in front of you. This Jeff character isn't the only guy out there. Remember that."

"Good-bye, sweetheart," said Brenda. She took Karin's hands and looked into her daughter's eyes. "Always remember, Dad and I love you. Okay?"

"Okay," smiled Karin.

Steven pulled on his gloves, then reached in his pocket, "Here, I want you to have this." He held out a fifty-dollar bill. "Buy something nice for yourself. Mom and I will call you from Hawaii. Sorry we have to run."

Karin slowly reached out and took the money. Steven leaned over and kissed her on the forehead, then took Brenda's hand.

"Come on, honey. We need to get to County General right away. Jack's wife is in serious condition."

Reluctantly, Brenda said good-bye to Karin and followed him out the door.

Karin just stood there, hands by her side, feeling numb. "Good-bye, Mom. Good-bye, Daddy," she whispered.

Two days later, Dr. Ray Havens and his wife stood pressed against the window of the departure gate and waved good-bye as a giant 757 pulled away from the O'Hare terminal.

"Look, there's Brenda, dear," said Beulah. She had spotted Brenda by a window seat and waved to her. Brenda smiled and waved back. The plane backed away and taxied down the tarmac to the takeoff point. Five minutes later, the huge plane roared down the runway, its monstrous jet engines shaking the terminal windows as the nose of the aircraft pointed up into the air. In less than ten seconds it was out of sight.

"I hope they have a lovely time," said Beulah. "They both looked so tired. Poor souls. Brenda told me this was their first vacation alone in nine years."

Dr. Ray was silent as the elderly couple walked down the busy concourse toward the parking lot. Once in the car, Dr. Ray seemed lost in his thoughts.

"It's not like you to be so quiet, dear. Are you worried about how you'll get along with this giant congregation of Yankees?" She meant it as a joke, but Dr. Ray didn't laugh.

"No, my dear. That's not it."

"What is it?" she said.

"I don't reckon as if I can put my finger on it, my dearest. But my heart has been heavy since the day we arrived at this church."

"What are you saying, Ray?" Beulah asked.

"Beulah, do you remember that church in Murfreesboro I preached in back in the late seventies?"

"Why, of course I do," she said. "Bobby Lee Vinson had been the pastor there for years. That poor man. Didn't someone in his church get angry and pour sugar into his transmission? Ruined his brand new Chevrolet if I remember right."

Dr. Ray nodded as he signaled to change lanes on the busy expressway. "Indeed. That poor preacher boy lost his health and quit the ministry after that church."

A loud honk from behind suggested that Dr. Ray needed to speed up. "Land sakes, what a hurry these people are in," he said. He pushed hard on the accelerator. Still, the car behind him pulled alongside, then shot by him. The driver shook his fist at Dr. Ray as he went by.

"Bless you, my brother," Dr. Ray said. He meant it.

"In Murfreesboro," Dr. Ray continued, "I just remember such a heaviness about that place. The building particularly. It was the gloomiest place I had ever been in. It wasn't until folks got praying that the sun seemed to shine on that property again."

"There was a remarkable change in that congregation wasn't there?" said Beulah. "They ended up going to two services."

Dr. Ray adjusted his black felt hat so it tipped to the other side of his head. He always did that whenever he had reached a decision. "Beulah, may I ask you a favor?"

"Why of course you can, dear. What is it?"

"Would you spend the next day in prayer and fasting with me? I feel the Lord would have us begin our time here this way. I'm concerned I'm up against something I don't understand."

"Let's start tonight after supper," she answered in a pleasant voice.

Dr. Ray looked over at her and smiled. "Aren't you still the prettiest woman in Mississippi? Why in the world did you ever consent to marry such a homely old preacher in the first place? You should have lived in the governor's mansion. Instead, you ended up in some broken-down parsonage in the hill country."

"And I've never regretted a day of it, Raymond Havens. And I'll have you know I think I married the handsomest man in Hot Coffee, Mississippi. Even Mama agreed. She told me I'd better set the hook and reel you in or I'd lose the trophy of my life."

The two elderly people reached out and squeezed each other's hands. They had had this same discussion for nearly fifty-two years. Each knew the other's lines by heart.

"One other thing we need to do," Dr. Ray said.

"What's that?"

"We need to find out who the people are who pray in this church. You do suppose they have some souls who believe in prayer, don't you?"

"I believe they do," said Beulah. "The Lord never leaves an outpost unguarded, does He?"

"No, dear, He doesn't."

Beulah slid over next to her tall husband and leaned on his shoulder. "I'm a fortunate man, Beulah, a fortunate man."

Just then another driver honked at them.

The next morning Karin walked out to her car behind the women's dormitory. The frigid weather made the vinyl seats brittle as she eased into the car and slammed the door next to her.

She could see her breath as she turned the ignition key. Jeff had refused to speak to her, or even look at her, since their confrontation in the coffee shop. On Friday, Karin had seen him walking across campus hand in hand with his new girl-friend, Janelle.

Karin had wanted so much to tell her parents everything. But they were gone now, at least for the next three weeks. *Besides,* she told herself, *it would have been selfish of me to ruin their first vacation in years.*

By the time they'd get back she would be almost eleven weeks pregnant. She would probably be showing by then. The morning sickness wasn't getting any better. It had forced her to drop her eight A.M. class. Time was against her. She felt more desperate by the day. While she had many friends on campus, including caring professors, she was determined to guard her secret.

Today Karin was just exploring her options. At least, that's how she had convinced herself to make this appointment.

It took nearly an hour to reach her destination in Glenwood Bluffs, a far western suburb. Glenwood Bluffs was known for its elegant Victorian homes. She searched the streets until she found the address she had been given over the phone. She finally found the sign she had been looking for—Women's Health Clinic. She swung her car into the back lot of the gray, two-story brick building. She took one last look at her sad, tired eyes in the rearview mirror. She got out and walked across the black, cracked pavement toward a large black metal door with a green security glass window. Across the street a silent prayer vigil was in progress. One woman held a sign that read, *The Women of St. Kolbe Love You and Your Child.*

She pushed the buzzer and waited.

Nothing happened. So she pushed it again. This time a voice crackled over the intercom speaker.

"May I help you?"

"Yes, my name is Jill Davis," she stammered. She had decided to use a false name to protect her identity. She didn't want word of this getting back to anyone. "I have a 10:45 appointment." There was a long pause as the receptionist checked the schedule for the morning. Karin started to get chilled in the winter wind.

"Yes, Ms. Davis, we do have you down." A loud buzzer sounded next to her and the lock on the door clicked. She reached over and pulled the cold metal handle and the door swung open.

Karin still felt chilled as she walked into the reception area. An odd assortment of people were seated in front of her.

There was a mother with long, unkempt hair, wearing a blue nylon bowling jacket and smoking a cigarette. Several children played on the floor beside her. Next to her sat a smartly dressed woman who appeared to be in her early forties.

Across the tile floor sat a young teenager with short, black hair. *She can't be more than fifteen years old,* thought Karin. *What's she doing here?*

Karin walked over to the receptionist. The woman was busy highlighting patients' names with a yellow marker.

"Excuse me," Karin said. "I'm Jill Davis."

"I'll be with you in a moment," the woman said. She never looked up but continued to sort through files. Behind her stood stacks of file folders. In fact, the entire wall was a sea of folders. *There must be thousands,* thought Karin. Finally, the receptionist looked up. "What's your name?"

"Davis, Jill Davis."

The woman frowned as she rummaged through her file. "Here you are," she said. She picked up a clipboard and handed it to Karin. "Please be seated and fill this out," she said. "Make sure you indicate who's responsible for payment."

At first Karin hesitated to take the clipboard from her.

"I'm in a hurry," said the receptionist. "Will you please take this?"

As Karin reached for the clipboard, her hand trembled. When she finally took hold of it, it was as if something shut down inside. She no longer felt anxious or scared. In fact, she felt nothing at all. Instead, she turned and walked back to a cloth-covered chair and sat down.

Karin read the questions and scribbled her answers. She was halfway down the form when she stopped. It was question number eleven that made her put her pen down.

"Have you ever undergone an elective abortion before? If yes, please indicate date and complications, if any."

TEN

Karin stared at the large circular clock on the wall. She had been in the waiting room for over an hour. *I'm only here to get information,* she told herself. *I haven't made a decision. There's nothing wrong with just talking to these people. I'm just talking to them. That's all.*

But try as she might to convince herself there was nothing wrong with what she was doing, it didn't work. A cacophony of inner voices started to shout for her attention.

How's my little girl?

Look, Karin, we can take care of this little problem. We don't have to get married.

Karin, you have to tell your parents . . .

Sure I like you, but I'm not ready to settle down yet.

I'm so proud of you, darling.

Karin put her head down in her hands, trying to quiet her inner confusion. *Oh, God, I'm so scared,* Karin prayed. *What am I doing here? Where have You gone?*

"Jill Davis."

Karin thought she heard yet another voice.

"Is there a Jill Davis here?"

She suddenly remembered her assumed name and looked up. A short woman in her late fifties with closely cropped hair, stylish glasses, and a professional gray suit stood in front of her.

"Are you Ms. Davis?" she asked matter-of-factly.

"Yes, I'm Jill Davis."

The woman extended her hand, "Hi, I'm Ellen Belstrom-Donahue. I'm one of the clinic's client advocates. Would you like to come with me back to my office?"

Karin got up and followed the woman through a door and down a busy corridor. Ellen walked several steps ahead of her. Karin happened to catch a glimpse through a door left slightly ajar. Inside sat a young girl, probably junior high age, who waited alone. Karin looked away.

"In here, if you will, Ms. Davis," the counselor said. She pointed to a small office with two chairs that faced each other in front of a desk. "We can talk undisturbed in here."

Karin sat down as the woman closed the door and took her place in the other chair. Ellen looked down through the top half of her glasses as she reviewed Karin's case.

"Now, Jill, let's see, you're nineteen years old. You're a college student. And you're single. Is that correct?"

"That's right."

The woman continued to study the chart. "Hmm, and you think you are eight weeks along. Is that right?"

"Yes."

"Have you seen a doctor? Did she confirm you're pregnant?"

"Yes," Karin whispered.

The woman looked up. "I'm sorry, I couldn't hear you."

"I said, yes." This time Karin's voice was unnaturally loud.

The woman put down the chart and smiled, "Jill, I know this is a difficult time for you. I imagine you're scared and confused. Maybe feeling guilty for even being here. Am I right?"

Karin couldn't respond. She knew that if she said anything she'd start to cry. The woman reached out and tapped Karin's knee with a pen. "Listen Jill, I know what you're going through. The same thing happened to me when I was your age. Only in those days, women had no rights over their own bodies. I had to go to Mexico to find the help I needed. It was a nightmare. Thank heavens those days are gone forever."

"He was the first man I had ever been involved with," said Karin.

"Dear, you need to quit blaming yourself. All of us have the right to express our sexuality. You're an adult, and adults are sexual beings."

"But what I did was wrong," Karin said.

"You loved him, didn't you?"

"Yes."

"Then how can you say it was wrong?"

"Well, it's what I was taught to believe. You see, my dad is a . . ." Karin stopped short. "What I mean to say is, I come from a very religious family."

"So do I, Jill," replied Ellen. "But what's right or wrong is for us to decide, not some male figure in a black robe shouting at us from behind a pulpit. Jill, I'm a person of faith. But my faith includes the right to make responsible choices."

"But I was brought up to believe abortion is wrong. That it's . . ." She hesitated to use the word. Sin. "It's killing a baby. And I've never harmed any living thing in my entire life." Her stomach began to hurt again.

Ellen's face lost its warmth. "Abortion is not 'killing,' Jill. It's the termination of a potential life. Let's get that straight from the beginning. What's growing in you at this moment is a nonviable fetus. You might be interested to know that at this stage in your pregnancy . . ." she stopped to glance at the chart, "it's no larger than a fingernail. To call a cell mass the size of a fingernail a *person* is simply ridiculous."

Karin looked out the window and took a deep breath. "I know it's small, but still, it's a human being isn't it?"

The counselor put down her chart and folded her hands. She leaned forward and spoke in a soft voice. "Jill, are you ready to raise a child?"

Karen shook her head. "No. I've still got two more years of college. And then I hope to go on to graduate school after that."

"Have you told your family you're pregnant?"

"No. I tried to, but they wouldn't listen. Besides, I'm not sure my mom and dad could handle it right now. And the school I go to—"

"Would expel you, right?"

"Yes."

Ellen sighed and rolled her eyes.

"It's my fault that I'm here, not theirs. Sex before marriage is wrong," Karin said.

"I apologize. I didn't mean to offend your choice in education," the counselor said. "Jill, I won't ask you which college you attend. But I think I know. Let me assure you, you aren't the first client we've had from there."

Karin looked down. The idea that she was part of a group from Randolph University that had secretly sought out abortions upset her. Sure, she had heard the rumors from time to time in the dormitory, but she didn't think anyone from Randolph would do something like that.

Now, here she was, living proof that a few rumors were more than just idle gossip.

"Jill, only you should make the choice whether to continue this pregnancy or not. But let me remind you, you have the rest of your life to start a family. Right now, if I'm hearing what you're saying, you don't have the support of a husband, your family, or your college. Am I right?"

Karin nodded.

"If you choose to continue this pregnancy, you'll have to drop out of school and live on your own. Won't you?"

Karin meekly nodded yes.

"You'll end up either putting your child in day care to go to work or going on public assistance so you can stay home. Are you ready to make that choice?" Karin noticed how tight the skin on the woman's face had become.

"I guess I hadn't thought that far ahead," Karin replied. She looked down and fiddled with a nail on her right hand. "Why can't I put my baby up for adoption? Then I could go on with school."

"That's one possibility," said Ellen. "But are you aware of the emotional and psychological side effects of adoption?"

"No, not really. I always thought adoption was a good thing. You know, people who can't keep a baby give it to people who can't have one. It seems everybody wins that way."

The woman sat up and straightened her suit jacket, then put her folded hands on her knee. "Jill, I must tell you adoption is an unnatural process. It's a violation of nature. You're forced to surrender your child to strangers. The trauma of handing your baby to someone you'll never see again is soul wrenching."

"But isn't it better than . . ."

"Let me finish, Jill. Then, if you decide you want your baby back someday, you're forced to go through a legal chamber of horrors. Even if you don't try and locate your child, studies predict you'll grieve for years, possibly decades, over your missing child. Are you ready for that?" Ellen demanded.

Karin didn't know what to say.

"Here, let me give you an article to read," said Ellen. The counselor turned in her chair and opened a file drawer. She pulled out a three-page photocopied article from a leading women's magazine and handed it to Karin. Karin read the title: "What They Never Told Me About Adoption: Ten Years of Death in Limbo."

The woman stared at Karin with a somber expression. "Jill, I'm here only as your advocate, not as your parent. But let me assure you, the procedure is safe and relatively painless. You'll be back in class in three or four days. No one will ever have to know. As part of our client services, we offer one month of free after-care."

Karin had come here only to explore her options. Now she was starting to weaken. Ellen seemed so logical, so persuasive. The woman leaned forward and looked straight into Karin's eyes. "Jill, the longer you wait to make your decision, the higher the risks involved. You need to make your decision soon. Don't wait until your second trimester."

Karin bit her lip and said nothing. *Maybe she's right. This would solve everything. No one would ever know except Jeff and Sally. This whole nightmare could be over.*

"If money is an issue, Jill, don't worry. We receive generous federal and state grant money to cover cases like yours. We believe all women should have equal access to the health care they need. All you have to do is fill out a simple form I'll give you, and we can set a date for the procedure."

"I don't know. I'm just not ready."

"Jill, God, whoever you understand her to be, wants you to go on with your life. Surely you believe that, don't you?"

"I don't know what God thinks anymore," said Karin. For the first time in the conversation real tears began to show. "I used to think I knew. Not any more."

The counselor leaned over and took Karin's hands and held them in her own. "If God is a God of love, which I believe she is, then God will understand why you have to do this. After all, the Supreme Being doesn't want any child brought into the world who won't be loved. It wouldn't be fair to you, to the baby, or to anyone else, would it?"

Karin didn't know what to say.

"Would it?" the counselor said.

"No, I guess not. Not when you put it that way."

"Jill, here's my card. Take it home and call me when you've made your decision. If you do decide to terminate this pregnancy, you should do so as quickly as possible. I'd recommend you have it done on a Friday. Perhaps a week or two from now. That way you would have the weekend to recuperate. Could you arrange for someone to bring you in and drive you home afterward?"

"Sure," said Karin. Truth was she had no idea who she could get to help her. Sally certainly wouldn't go for this. Lisa wouldn't. Then it hit her. Ellen had her talking as if she had already decided to go through with the abortion.

"I really need to be going," said Karin.

"Believe me, Jill, once it's over with, you'll be feeling back to normal in just a few days," replied Ellen. She took one final glance over her chart.

"Jill, this doesn't say what your father's occupation is. I'm just curious, what does he do?"

"Uh, he's . . . he's an executive of a large corporation. He's a busy man. Very busy. He has a job that's always taken him away from home."

"Of course," Ellen said. "But you don't need someone else to make this decision for you, do you?"

"Uh, no." It was the worst lie Karin had told all day.

Karin stood up to leave.

"Jill, one more thing. It's purely voluntary for our clients, but we recommend they be tested for HIV."

HIV? thought Karin. *I never thought of that. What if Jeff has been with other women?* Karin started to turn pale. The counselor noticed her change in color.

"Why don't you sit down for just a moment?" Ellen said. "You look a little unsettled."

Dr. Raymond Havens walked up the steep brick steps to the Randolph University campus chapel. A cold winter wind swept through the open spots on campus. An inch of snow had fallen the night before. He wrapped his scarf a second time around his neck, then pushed on.

A loud bell bonged mournfully in the steeple above the chapel. It was ten in the morning, time for chapel. A small group of students rushed past him up the stairs. Dr. Ray smiled. *My, my, I wish I was their age again,* he thought. *So much of life still to be lived.*

The Greek Revivalist architecture of the chapel, with tall white pillars and high elegant doors, made the building the most beautiful structure on campus. As Dr. Ray stepped through the door onto the slate tile in the lobby, his eye caught the inscription chiseled in marble above the entrance: "Not by might, nor by power, but by My Spirit."

Once inside, he took off his black felt hat, unwrapped his wool scarf, and hung his coat up in a cloakroom. He found a mirror on the wall and took a comb out to straighten what little hair he had left. He could hear the powerful strains of the pipe organ through the wall as it played Bach's *Fantasia. One of my favorites,* he thought.

He followed some students headed through the doors of the lobby into the main auditorium. It was a magnificent room. There were high arching windows, an elevated choir loft, and rich wood benches. Yet only a third of the pews were filled. The balcony was entirely empty. He scanned the room for faculty members. He counted twenty at most.

A young female student stepped up to the microphone. "Good morning, everyone. Can I have your attention?" The noise in the room continued. "Excuse me," she said in a louder voice. In a moment the room grew quiet. "Thank you. I've been asked to make the announcements on behalf of the student activities office. Grandhurst Dormitory will be showing *Bonfire of the Vanities* tonight. Tickets are one dollar. This weekend Sigma Chi will sponsor their 'Day at the Beach Party.' Feel free to wear whatever you wear to the beach."

"Yes!" a young man shouted from near the back. The other students laughed.

The woman blushed momentarily, then pressed on, "Music will be provided by Junta, a new rhythm and blues group from Chicago. Tickets are seven dollars at the door."

The young woman paged through her notes. "Oh, yes. There's one more announcement. This is from the Student Missions Coalition. 'If you would like to attend the Unreached People Group Prayer Fellowship, we meet in Chaplain Vincent's office at seven each Tuesday morning.' That's all the announcements for now."

The young woman left the stage and was followed by the campus chaplain, Dr. Dexter Vincent, a young man in his thirties who wore a beard and wire-rimmed glasses. "Good morning, and welcome. In just a moment I'll be introducing this morning's guest, Dr. Thurmond Albred. Dr. Albred is an expert on indigenous and tribal medicine. He'll be sharing the results of his latest trip to the Amazon region of Brazil. But first, let's join together in singing one of my favorite hymns, 'Joyful, Joyful, We Adore Thee.'"

As the rich pipe organ filled the room with the first measures of the Beethoven melody, the entire group rose to their feet. Afterward, Dr. Albred's lecture proved to be fascinating, and the hour soon ended.

As Dr. Ray put his coat and hat back on, he happened to overhear a conversation going on around the corner.

"You're telling me the truth. They don't check your I.D. at Hopper's?"

"I'm serious, man."

"Okay, I'll meet you there at nine tonight. Will you give Cindy and Megan a ride?"

"For you, yes. You know me. I'm always ready for some action. I'm the official party animal chauffeur on campus."

"Thanks."

Back at the church office, Dr. Ray closed the door behind him. He opened his Bible and took out tattered notes he always carried with him. He had decided to use one of his tried and true messages for Sunday.

The buzzer on his phone went off. He picked up the receiver and pushed several buttons until he found the right one.

"Dr. Havens here. How may I serve you?"

"I apologize for the interruption, Dr. Havens, but the chairwoman of our women's ministries was wondering if she could have a minute with you."

"Why, of course. Please send her in."

Dr. Ray soon heard a knock on his door. Always the gentleman, he got up to open it. But before he could reach it, Elizabeth opened it and ushered in the guest. The woman, dressed in a white sweater and pants, smiled at the older pastor.

"Dr. Havens, I'm so pleased to meet you. I'm Rachel Brewster."

The pastor reached out his hand. "Pleased to meet you, Mrs. Brewster." As the two individuals shook hands, Dr. Ray's expression changed just slightly.

"Can I bring you two coffee?" Elizabeth asked in a cheerful voice.

"Not for me," said Rachel.

"No, I don't believe I will have any either. Thanks just the same, Mrs. Swift," said Dr. Ray.

"Call me if you change your mind." Elizabeth walked out and closed the door behind her.

"Won't you please sit down, Mrs. Brewster?" Dr. Ray said.

Rachel obliged. Once she was comfortable, she looked at the pastor and said, "I don't want to take more than a minute of your time. I just wanted to drop in and let you know how excited we all are to have you here."

"You are too kind."

"I enjoyed your first sermon so much. So did everyone else I talked to," Rachel said.

"Thank you."

"Really, you are so . . . *believable*. That's the word."

"I'm just a country preacher filling in until the real preacher gets back, Mrs. Brewster," said Dr. Ray. The two talked for several minutes about children, how Rachel and her husband met, and the high cost of living in the Chicago area. Rachel displayed her usual charm and poise.

"I wish you and your wife could stay longer with us," she said.

Dr. Ray smiled. "But that wouldn't be fair to you folks. After all, you have one of the most gifted preachers ever to come through our school."

"Uh . . . yes, I suppose you're right, Dr. Havens," Rachel said. "Would you mind if I ask you a question?"

"Go right ahead," said Dr. Ray.

"It's a question of biblical interpretation."

"I'll do my best."

"Don't the Scriptures say even if we speak in the tongues of men and angels, but have not love, we are only a clanging cymbal or a noisy gong? Isn't that in the Bible?" Rachel began to pick apart a piece of paper she held in her hands.

"Why, yes, it is. You are to be commended for your knowledge of the Scriptures, Mrs. Brewster."

Rachel blushed slightly. "Thank you, Dr. Havens. You're so easy to talk to. What I'm getting at is . . . what several of the women in my group are wondering is . . . what do you do if you don't feel love from one of the leaders in the church?"

"If it were me, I would look at my own heart first. I would ask myself, 'am I a loving person?' If I'm not loving others, I'm not open to receiving love from others."

"Okay, but what if you had done everything you could to show love, and you still felt shut out by someone on the staff. What would you do then?"

"Well, Mrs. Brewster, I would do what the Scriptures say you ought to do in that type of situation."

"What's that?"

"You're to go to that person and tell them your concern. What grieves the heart of our Lord is when folks in the church talk behind each other's backs. That's how many a church has split through the years."

"A church split?" said Rachel. "Oh, heaven forbid." Rachel looked down and realized the floor beneath her was covered with tiny pieces of paper she had torn up. "Oh, look what I've done. Forgive me, Dr. Havens, it's a terrible nervous habit of mine." She leaned over to pick them up.

"No need to do that, Mrs. Brewster. Our fine custodian, Mr. Styles, will be sweeping the room this evening," said Dr. Ray.

Rachel stood up, somewhat embarrassed, "I guess I should be going."

They stood up and shook hands. "Good day, ma'am," he said.

Once she had left the room, Dr. Ray went over to the window and bowed his head.

Meanwhile, Rachel walked down the hallway in a huff. She ignored several of the staff members who greeted her and headed straight to Elizabeth's office.

Once Rachel was in the room, Elizabeth closed the door. "How did it go?" she asked.

"It didn't," Rachel said. "I couldn't get him to say anything I could use against Warner."

"Don't worry, Rachel, this day might not be a total loss," Elizabeth smiled. She reached in her drawer and pulled out a large plain envelope. "You might find this interesting reading tonight." She handed Rachel the envelope. The two women smiled a wicked grin at each other.

"Elizabeth, you are so good at what you do."

"I know," she replied.

Although the food fight damage at Roosevelt High made the local papers, what went under reported was the growing number of gang-related activities in the high school. Two groups in particular were developing dangerous reputations—the Excalibur and the Squires.

Because the school district included both Covington Park and a more economically deprived community next to it, the two gangs were made up of different groups. The Excalibur were drawn from the lonely and neglected children of upper-class families, while the Squires came almost exclusively from working middle-class homes.

Eric and Dustin knew enough to try to keep out of the path of the rival gangs at school, but that wasn't always possible. A few days after Eric's parents left for Hawaii, the two boys decided to stay late and finish their projects in the metal shop.

While Eric hammered away on an anvil, Dustin worked intently to bend square corners on his galvanized metal tool-box. He hoped to give the project to his dad as a birthday gift.

"I'll be back in a minute boys," shouted Mr. Rostowlski, the shop teacher, over the din of hammers and exhaust fans. He left to take his lesson plans down to the office. Moments after he walked out, three members of the Squires stepped through the doorway.

"Eric, don't look now, but I think we're in trouble," said Dustin. Eric continued to hammer away on his project.

"I can't hear you. What did you say?" said Eric. He was completely unaware of the three figures in starter jackets who approached him from behind. Eric gave the anvil another loud hammer blow, and the clang echoed through the room.

"What do we have here?" said one of the three teenagers. He picked up the toolbox Dustin had been working on.

"Hey, that's mine," said Dustin.

"Oh, is it?" said the teenager. "I once took a shop class myself. It looks to me like this needs a little straightening." He turned to one of his companions and tossed it to him. "Here Mike, help this twerp get his corners straight."

The other boy broke out in a menacing grin. He walked over to the anvil where Eric stood. "Give me the hammer," he snarled.

Eric hesitated, and before Eric could react, the boy grabbed it from him. He pushed Eric out of the way and dropped Dustin's box onto the anvil. He smirked at Dustin and then raised the hammer.

"Don't!" yelled Dustin. "Please. I've worked four weeks on that. It's half my grade."

"Stop," barked the leader. The teenager put the hammer down and laughed. The leader turned to Dustin and got right up into his face. "It seems my friend is in a destructive mood today. I'm not always able to stop him once he gets in these bad moods. Understand?"

"What is it you want?" said Eric. The leader turned and walked over to Eric.

"Now there's a good question," said the leader. "Let's call it a little insurance payment. You pay us thirty dollars a week.

In return, we insure nothing happens to you or your homework." The leader kicked the metal braces Eric had been working on off the anvil.

"I don't have that kind of money," said Dustin.

"Oh, you don't?" said the leader. "That's too bad." He turned toward the teenager holding the hammer and nodded. The boy slammed the hammer into the center of the tool box and collapsed it into a sheet of twisted metal.

"No!" yelled Dustin.

"Shut up!" said the leader. He pushed Dustin against the cement wall. "Look, you loser, I want thirty bucks from each of you, each and every Monday. That's every Monday. Delivered to my locker. Or next time my friend might use the hammer on something else—like your face." Dustin looked terrified.

Eric came alongside his friend. "You had no right to do that," said Eric.

"Oh, so we have a hero, do we?" said the leader. He shoved Dustin away and grabbed Eric. "Now what did I hear you say?"

"I said you had no right to do that. Dustin's never done anything to you."

"Eric, please, it's okay," said Dustin. His voice trembled.

The leader turned to the third member of the gang, "Go and keep look out." The student ran over to the door, looked out, then nodded to the leader.

"It seems you have a big mouth, my friend," said the leader. He leaned into Eric's face. "Do you know the cure for a big mouth?"

Eric refused to answer.

"You seal the mouth shut," the leader said. He motioned to the other gang member who set the hammer down on the anvil. The teenager walked over to a long green metal cylinder of acetylene gas connected to an acetylene torch. The torch was used for heating metal to make it more pliable. He picked up the nozzle of the device, twisted the valve on it, and using a flash-pot, ignited it. A clear blue flame shot out.

"No—no—you wouldn't . . ." said Dustin.

"You stand back, or you'll be next," said the leader. He motioned to his companion. "Give it to me." The other boy handed him the torch. He held it in one hand and pulled Eric closer to him with the other. "As I was saying, the way to deal with a big mouth is to seal it. Permanently." He started to turn the torch toward Eric.

"Please, don't! I'll do whatever you want," Eric cried.

"Well, I see we aren't such a tough guy anymore, are we?" said the leader. With a quick thrust he threw Eric backward. "I was being generous at thirty dollars, but since you've got such a big mouth, it's going to cost you fifty dollars a week, geek."

Eric just stood there, afraid to say anything.

"That's five, zero, each Monday. Can you remember that? Or do I need to warm up your brain a little?" said the leader. He waved the torch over the top of Eric's head and singed part of his hair.

"Ow!" cried Eric.

"The teacher's coming back!" shouted the sentry at the door. The leader turned the torch off and dropped it on the floor, and the three gang members ran through a storage room and out another door.

Dustin ran over to see how badly Eric was hurt. Eric shook from both fear and pain. "Let me see it, man, are you hurt bad?" Dustin ran his finger over the small burned patch on the top of Eric's head. The smell of acetylene and burnt flesh lingered in the air.

"Ouch, let go!" said Eric. He pushed Dustin away and staggered over to a seat. He sat down and held his forehead. "Were they Squires?"

"Yeah," said Dustin. "I think it's the same thugs that threatened to break Bill Farris's kneecap with a baseball bat. He refused to pay them protection money. He said he was going to the police. They could have hurt him bad if a teacher hadn't come along. See why I've got the gun, man?"

Eric looked up with rage in his eyes, "Yeah, I do now."

Mr. Rostowlski stepped into the room, took a whiff of the scent, and walked over to the boys. "What's going on in here? Did one of you boys use the torch? I told you never to do that while I was out of the room."

Dustin and Eric gulped. Eric quickly reached up and covered the burn on his head. "I'm sorry, Mr. Rowstowlski, I . . . I needed it to fix a solder joint that had broken," said Eric.

The teacher was a large man who wore his gray hair in a crew cut. His green work apron barely reached around his large waist. He had only two years left before retirement, and his patience with students was nearly exhausted.

"Listen, Warner, you do something like that again when I'm gone and you're out of this class for good," he snarled. He pointed his finger at Eric. "Do you understand me?"

"Yes, sir," mumbled Eric.

"And that goes for you too, Jacobs." He shook his head. "I thought I knew you boys better than that. Now get this area cleaned up. It's time to close down for today."

He walked back to his desk mumbling to himself about students.

"Eric, I think we should tell him what happened," whispered Dustin.

"No."

"Why not?"

"For two reasons, idiot. First, no one saw the Squires come in here except us. It would be our word against theirs. Second reason. If we do squeal on them, they'll take us out for good."

"What about your dad, Eric. He'd believe you."

"He's gone, remember? He's with Mom on some vacation I wasn't welcome to go on. So right now I'm living with some old lady from church. She's nice and all that, but she doesn't have a clue what's going on at school." Eric put his head down.

The pain from his burn had given him a headache. "Let's get out of here," he said.

The two boys quickly threw their projects into a locker. Dustin swept the floor while Eric put the tools back on the wall. Dustin could see that Eric was in pain.

"Good night, Mr. Rowstowlski," said Dustin as he walked out the door behind Eric.

"Yeah, yeah," he replied. The teacher continued working on his grade book.

Dr. Ray tried to study his notes, but he couldn't concentrate. The visit with Rachel had left him deeply troubled. She seemed so sweet, so concerned, so spiritual. Yet something didn't seem right.

It's no use, he said to himself. *I'm not going to get anything more done today.* He closed his Bible and pushed away from the desk. He reached over for the phone. *Now which button is it I'm supposed to push?* he thought. He took a stab at the top one.

"Yes, Dr. Havens?" came a voice.

"Elizabeth, I think I'm going to call it a day. I shall talk with you in the morning."

"Certainly, Dr. Havens. Good night."

"Good night." He hung up and got up from the desk. He walked slowly over to the coat tree in the corner and picked off his black felt hat and camel hair coat. He turned the lights off, closed the door behind him, and started for the parking lot. Then he thought better of it. He turned toward the sanctuary.

He followed the arrows that pointed the way to the auditorium. He soon came up to the doors that led into the sanctuary. He pushed on one. It didn't move. He pushed the other. It was locked too. *Lord, have mercy, I need a place to pray,* he thought.

He turned around to go home when he heard the doors unlock behind him. Someone else was already in the sanctuary.

For a moment he was startled—he remembered Steven's story about the break-in.

In the dim late afternoon light a figure stepped out of the door. It was a woman. The two stood face-to-face about ten feet apart.

"Dr. Havens? Is that you?"

"Yes."

"Excuse me, sir. It's me, Maggie Dunlop."

"Mrs. Dunlop, my gracious, you're the lady taking care of the Warners' son?"

She walked toward the pastor and extended her hand, "Yes, sir, that's me. And you're taking care of their church while they're gone."

"I believe I might trade you this afternoon," chuckled Dr. Ray.

He remembered that Maggie was the woman Brenda Warner had called the "prayer pillar" of the church.

"Why, may I ask, are you here so late in the day?" said Dr. Ray.

"I often come here by myself late in the afternoon to pray. The deacons gave me a key."

She held up a brass-plated key. "And what brings you here?"

"Much the same thing," said Dr. Ray.

"Have mercy, Dr. Ray. Who else do you think the Lord is going to send here this afternoon?"

Her words were no sooner out of her mouth when a tone sounded over the intercom system, followed by a female voice. "Dr. Havens, if you're still in the building, could you please call the office?"

"Now how in the world did they know I was here?" Dr. Ray chuckled.

"There's a courtesy phone on the back wall," said Maggie. She pointed him toward a white receiver by the door.

"Thank you, Mrs. Dunlop. Imagine, telephones in the sanctuary of the Lord. Is there no place to get away? I do believe I prefer First Church of Hot Coffee to this." He excused himself and walked over to the phone. It was a maze of blinking lights.

"The top button, sir," said Maggie.

Dr. Ray nodded appreciatively and picked up the phone.

"Dr. Havens here," he said. He listened for a moment and then nodded. "Please do me the courtesy of sending him down to the sanctuary. Thank you so much. Good-bye."

He hung up the phone and clapped his hands. "Heaven be praised!"

"What's that, Pastor?" said Maggie.

"Why, that was the secretary informing me a Mr. Phil Crawford is in the building trying to find me. Pastor Warner told me he's the one who wants to start an early morning prayer meeting."

"Glory!" said Maggie. "It looks like we have our two or three gathered in His name, doesn't it, Dr. Havens?"

In less than two minutes Phil Crawford appeared through the door into the sanctuary.

"Why, Maggie, what a delight to see you," said Phil.

"Welcome to our first glory get-down prayer meeting with Dr. Ray," said Maggie. Phil and Dr. Ray exchanged courtesies.

"Pastor Havens, let me explain why I came down here to see you. It's my opinion that this church is in the middle of a tremendous spiritual battle," said Phil. "Our pastor is discouraged, the giving is down, there is dissent on the board, and the sanctuary was ransacked only a few weeks ago. My wife hears talk that there are some in the congregation who want the pastor to leave."

"Heaven forbid," said Maggie. "Pastor Warner's not the problem. The problem is that this church has quit praying. We don't pray for the pastor, we don't pray for the unchurched, we don't pray about giving. All we do is complain."

"I'd have to agree, Maggie," said Phil. The sun was fading and the stained-glass colors fell across the three as they stood in a circle. "Do you see our point, Dr. Havens?"

"I do indeed, sir." The three of them walked into the sanctuary and knelt at the altar. For the next hour they prayed with great intensity. Only those who have done the hard work of prayer can understand how difficult and strenuous it can be. But that afternoon, when the three of them got up from their knees, they knew something had been accomplished.

"Could you join us here on Friday mornings?" said Phil. "Say six o'clock. And would you bring Beulah?"

"I'd be delighted to," said Dr. Ray.

"Count on me," said Maggie.

ELEVEN

The ship's white signal flags flapped easily in the cool ocean breeze. From Steven's vantage point on deck of the luxury cruiser, the *Pacific Crowned Prince*, the banners looked like pristine white birds, flying in perfect diagonal formation. Sea and sky captured Steven's attention as he jogged around the deck.

"Watch out!" a voice yelled. Suddenly, Steven was hammered by the impact of another person slamming into his shoulder. The blow spun him into the guardrail, then down to the deck. The other body recoiled backward but managed to remain upright. A bit dazed, Steven looked up like a hapless prize fighter who had just been knocked out.

Above him stood a man in a nylon running suit. He looked about forty-five. He was tanned, with his blond hair combed straight back. He leaned over Steven and extended his hand. "I guess we should exchange driver's license numbers," he said. He pulled Steven back on his feet.

Steven brushed himself off and returned the quip, "Are you insured?"

"It depends—are you a lawyer?"

"No, but if this had happened in Chicago they would have already scheduled a court date." The two men laughed and shook hands.

"Hi, I'm Ted Carlson."

"I'm Steven Warner."

"Would you like to run with me?" said Ted. "It might be safer for both of us if we were going in the same direction."

"Why not? Who knows who else we might run into."

The two joggers turned and headed off to lap the ship's perimeter twice more. Later, exhausted from their run, they slumped down in lounge chairs that faced the jasmine blue ocean. Sea gulls echoed their plaintive cry about fifty yards off starboard. A waiter in a starched white jacket and black bow tie walked up to take their order. "May I get you two something to drink?" he asked.

"I'll take sparkling soda on ice," said Ted.

"Make mine a fruit juice," said Steven.

"Very good," the waiter said. He turned and headed toward the bar to fill their order.

"You're not half bad as a runner," said Ted. "I don't know many people who can keep up with me."

"Or with your modesty," grinned Steven. "I'm from Illinois, how about you?" They were interrupted by the waiter who delivered the cool drinks. Steven signed for the bill.

"I'm from the Midwest too. Ohio," said Ted. "I'm a V.P. for Human Resources at Rorvik International. How about you?"

"I'm a pastor, but don't let that scare you," said Steven. Ted gestured with his hands not to worry. "Looks like we both came here to get away from people, huh?" said Steven.

Ted leaned back in his chaise lounge chair and closed his eyes. "Yeah, I needed a rest. I usually handle seven to ten crises a day. The problems never seem to end. You name it, I'm in charge of it."

"Life is grim, isn't it?" said Steven. He took a slow sip of his fruit juice. "Ah, now if only we could do *this* for a living."

"A little burned out?" said Ted.

"This is the first vacation I've taken alone with my wife in almost nine years," said Steven. "I came unglued at a restaurant two weeks ago when a waitress dumped five glasses of water on my lap. That's when I knew it was time to get away."

"At least it wasn't coffee."

"She dropped that too."

"Ouch," said Ted.

"Do you have kids?" asked Steven.

"Two. How about you?"

"I've got two myself. My girl is in college and my son is still in high school."

The two men finished their drinks and agreed to meet the same time the next day for another run.

Hot orange flames leapt high into the night sky. The sounds of sirens filled the air with penetrating screams. Outside the church building, police formed a perimeter to keep curiosity seekers back.

A section of the main roof collapsed, sending a million sparks into the cold, dark sky. It was an inferno of destruction, a galaxy of consumption spinning out of control. Firemen aimed hoses at the top of the church to try and control the raging fire.

"It's no use," said the captain on the scene. "We can't save it. Redeploy our main unit. Let's try and keep it from spreading to the neighbors."

"You can't let the church burn down, you've got to do something!" a woman pleaded. An explosion inside the church sent a new pillar of fire racing into the nighttime sky. Several cries could be heard from the crowd.

"There's nothing we can do," said the captain. "There's nothing we can do."

Brenda sat up with a start. She struggled to get her breath. Her whole body was covered with a cold sweat.

"Are you okay, honey?" mumbled Steven, still half asleep.

Brenda looked around the cabin and realized where she was. "Oh, Steven. I had the worst nightmare. I dreamed the church was . . . oh, never mind. It was crazy."

"You can tell me in the morning," he said. He buried his head in his pillow and went back to sleep. Brenda's heart was still racing. She got out of bed, put on her robe, and sat down by the small table in their cabin. She looked for a while out the porthole and could see the white light of the moon glisten on the gentle waves of the Pacific.

"Lord," Brenda prayed, "help me to calm down." She glanced over at her sleeping husband. "And take care of Eric and Karin. And our church. Please, God." She walked back to their bed and crawled under the covers.

Agent Joe McDonald had been with the IRS for seventeen years. It was nine o'clock in the morning when he stepped off the plane in Chicago and checked his watch. He walked over to a bank of phones on the wall and punched in a telephone number.

"Give me Eckstrand," he said. "Tell him Joe McDonald is on the line."

McDonald was put on hold. Streams of humanity passed before him in O'Hare, the world's busiest airport. Flight attendants pulled suitcases behind them, mothers struggled to hang on to their toddlers, and businesspeople in well-tailored suits walked by with newspapers under their arms.

McDonald heard a voice break in on the other end. "Yeah, this is Eckstrand."

"Bob, Joe McDonald here. I've just landed at O'Hare. Kansas City sent me here to look into a possible fraud case. It's a church in the suburbs, let's see . . ." He fumbled with the piece of paper he had in his coat pocket. "Yeah, it's First Community Church of Covington Park. You ever heard of them?"

"Nope. What's the deal?"

"We've got information they might be involved in a laundering scam. We checked their records in K.C. and everything appears clean."

"So what can I do for you?"

"I'm going to need some help reviewing bank deposits and other data. Can you spare somebody for a few days?"

"I'd like to Joe, but we're understaffed as it is. There's eight million people in this city, remember?"

"I know, Bob. All I need is one other person to do some footwork for me. Or do I need to call Kansas City?"

"Okay, Joe. But just for two weeks, got it?"

"Got ya. And Bob, I owe you one."

"I won't let you forget it either," Eckstrand countered.

"I'll be staying at the Westin O'Hare if you need to get hold of me," said McDonald.

"Stay in touch."

Joe McDonald hung up the phone. He set his briefcase up on the metal edge of the phone booth and flipped open the latches. He dug around in his papers until he found what he was looking for. It was a copy of First Community's 501 (c)(3) tax exempt status form. He also pulled out a copy of the anonymous letter sent to Kansas City. Satisfied he had what he needed, he put them back in and slammed his briefcase shut.

He and another agent spent the next two days reviewing bank records and monthly statements from First Church. They combed through microfilm records at the two banks the church had accounts with. There had been a marked decrease in deposits as of late, but there was no evidence of any wrongdoing.

By the third day McDonald was ready to label the tip a hoax and close the file. He sat in his hotel room and prepared his final report on a small laptop computer. He looked up and noticed the red message light on his telephone was blinking.

He walked over and picked up the phone and pushed zero.

"Front desk, may I help you?"

"Yeah, this is McDonald in Room 712. Do I have a message?"

"Oh yes, Mr. McDonald. We just received a fax for you. We'll have it waiting at the front desk."

"Thanks, I'll be right down." The agent saved the information on his screen and flicked his computer off. Downstairs the front desk clerk handed him four sheets of smooth fax paper.

"Any charge for this?" asked McDonald.

"A dollar per page, sir. We've already added it to your account," answered the clerk.

"Figures," mumbled McDonald. He walked over and sat down in an overstuffed lobby chair. The fax was from the Kansas City office. It was marked, "Personal and Confidential."

The first page was a short note from his supervisor:

Dear Joe,
   I received these faxes this morning. Since you're handling the investigation, I thought I'd send them your way. Call me when you've had a chance to review them.

McDonald set aside the first page and studied the next one. It was a photocopy of correspondence. The church's letterhead was at the top of the page. It was addressed to a Mr. James Stillwell in Costa Mesa, California.

It read:

Dear Jim,
   Greetings. We received your last check for $3000 and put it through our accounts. I appreciated your little 'gift,' but I think this is too risky to continue. I won't do this again for you. I expect my 'honorarium' soon.

                                             Sincerely,
                                             Steven

McDonald put that page down and studied the final one. It was a photocopy of a handwritten note on a check request form from the church. It read: "Ed, put this through. It doesn't need to appear in the budget. Trust me. S.W." The check request was for three thousand dollars to be made out to Stillwell Enterprises, San Juan Capistrano, California.

McDonald folded the papers up and rubbed his chin for a moment. He got up and hurried over to the elevator. Back inside his room, he sifted through his briefcase until he found the document he wanted. It was a copy of Steven Warner's last income tax return. He held the fax letter up next to the income tax form. The two signatures matched identically.

"Bingo," he said.

■

"Are you ready, dearest?" asked Dr. Ray.

"Just a moment, honey," replied Beulah. She leaned toward the mirror and applied a last bit of red lipstick. Satisfied with what she saw, she tied a scarf around her shoulders and then turned toward her husband. "All ready, Ray."

"My, don't you look lovely," he said.

"You know, Ray, it's colder than a dead dog's nose out there. I'm not sure if my winter coat is warm enough to take this frigid air."

"These northern winters are a fright, aren't they?" he replied. "We'd better get going, Beulah. Our first appointment is in just twenty minutes. I need some time to get lost in this huge city."

"You are a brave one, Ray, to drive in this crazy traffic," said Beulah. "I can't wait until we get back home where folks drive like they want to live another year."

Twenty minutes later the couple stood on the doorstep of a fashionable home in a new subdivision in Covington Park. The house's high, vaulted cathedral ceilings, polished oak floors, and three-car garage said it all. This family had earned themselves a piece of the pie.

Dr. Ray rang the doorbell, and a multitone carillon announced their arrival.

The door swung open, and a good-looking man in his late thirties stood in the foyer. "Dr. Havens, won't you come in?" he said. "Cindy," he yelled down the hallway, "the Havens are here." A pleasant but somewhat tired-looking woman appeared through one of the hallways leading to the foyer.

"Good evening," she said politely. "I was so pleased when Richard told me you were going to stop by this evening."

"Well, I'm just an old-fashioned Mississippi preacher who still believes in making home visits," said Dr. Ray. "We won't stay but a minute. Beulah and I just wish to get a little better acquainted with the leaders of this fine church."

"Come right in," the young man said. "I don't believe we've ever received a house call from a pastor, have we, Cindy?"

"You're right, dear. I think this is a first. Why don't we go and sit down in the living room?"

They walked down a glistening hallway with expensive vases and oil paintings on either side. In the next room stood a giant television with two teenagers plopped in front of it. The screen had to be five feet tall.

"Boys, I'd like you to meet our guests, Dr. and Mrs. Havens," said the father. The two boys turned around and offered a quick "hi" and "hello," then went back to playing their video game. On the screen a hooded player grabbed the other and slammed him to the floor. Blood spurted out and an unearthly cry shook the room in stereo. The conquering player then chopped off his opponent's head, which produced more blood. "Yes!" shouted one of the boys. Finally, the hooded hero reached down and pulled the entire spinal cord from the lifeless body.

Beulah gasped.

"Boys, what in the world are you two playing?" said their mother.

"Martial Retaliation," answered the younger of the two teenagers. "You bought it for my birthday, remember?"

The mother and father both turned flush red. "Well, I certainly didn't know it contained scenes like this," said the mother. "Give me the cartridge this very minute."

"Why, Mom?" they moaned.

"Right now, boys." She marched over and held out her hand.

"But Mom . . ." the older boy complained, "you've let us play worse games than this."

"Do as your mother says this minute," said the father. He turned toward the Havens, who both tried hard to appear unshaken by the gore they had just witnessed in living color. "You'll have to forgive us," said the father. "Both Cindy and

I work long hours. We don't always have time to stay up on the latest in video crazes."

"No apology needed, good sir," said Dr. Ray. "It looks as if you have two handsome boys there."

The Havens stayed less than twenty minutes then headed on to make other calls. Over a three-night period, they began to see a pattern at work. What they consistently discovered was one worn-out and stressed-out family after another.

The last night of their visits brought them to the home of Bill Cedar, the trustee who discovered the break-in at church. He welcomed them in.

They chitchatted for a few minutes, then Beulah innocently inquired, "And where is Mrs. Cedar?"

Bill smiled nervously, "She is away at her sister's. They haven't seen each other in years. She lives in New York."

"How marvelous she could spend time with her family," said Beulah. "Families are so spread apart these days, aren't they?"

"Yes, yes they are," replied the man.

"I hope we can meet her before we leave Chicago," said Beulah. "This must be a lonely week. I know I find it so difficult to be away from Ray, even for a week's time." Ray and Beulah smiled at each other.

"Why don't we have a word of prayer for you and your dear wife and pray for her safe return?" said Dr. Ray.

"I would . . . would appreciate that, Pastor."

Dr. Havens took Bill's hand, then his wife's hand and the three bowed their heads. "Our gracious Lord and Savior, we thank You for allowing us the privilege of meeting this fine brother tonight. What a choice servant of God he is. We ask that You bless his dear wife in New York this evening—"

Dr. Ray's prayer was interrupted by the sound of a man weeping. He let go and looked up and saw Bill's face buried in his hands, sobbing. Dr. Ray's instincts told him what was happening. He looked over at Beulah and motioned for her to join him. He stood up walked over and put his hands on the man's shoulder, as did his wife. He continued to pray, "Lord, only You know the burdens and problems this man carries tonight."

"She's gone, and she's not coming back," sobbed the man.

The Havens looked at one another in sorrow.

"Oh, you poor soul," said Beulah.

"She left last week—she didn't even say good-bye. She warned me, but I didn't believe her." The man broke down and wept harder than before.

Dr. Ray and Beulah each took a hand of the brokenhearted man.

"I was so afraid of letting anyone know. We've been married nearly forty-three years. I was too ashamed to tell anyone at church," he said as he wiped the tears from his eyes. "Thank you both. Thank you both for coming by this evening."

"Certainly, my dear friend," said Dr. Ray in a soothing voice. "You're not alone in this. You're not alone."

An hour later Dr. Ray and Beulah walked out into the winter night and got into their car.

"You would never guess there's so much pain behind the walls of these beautiful homes would you, dear?" said Beulah.

"No, dear, you would not. I remember hearing something the old preacher Joseph Parker used to say: 'Always remember there's a broken heart in every pew.'"

"I'm so glad I'm married to you, Ray," said Beulah. "Seeing that poor man all alone made me realize how lucky I am to have you."

"And for me to have you, my dear," said Ray. "By the way, why did you ever marry a homely old preacher like me, Beulah?"

"I've told you a million times, Raymond Havens, because you were the handsomest man to ever come out of Hot Coffee, Mississippi."

And so they started again.

TWELVE

Lord, You know we only want what is best for this church,"
prayed Rachel. "If we should need to stand up to a false
and ungodly shepherd, give us the courage to do so. We pray
that the eyes of the people in the church would be opened so
they will see how they have been deceived by Pastor Warner.
Lord, may he please resign before he splits the church. Restore
your church here in Covington Park before it's too late.
Amen."

The circle of women who held hands let go of each other
and looked up. The air was charged with an electricity, the
scintillating sensation that comes from being part of something
a little dangerous, even forbidden. The group of six women
had met, by invitation only, in the basement of Rachel Brewster's home. It was one o'clock in the afternoon.

Rachel had spent the last several months carefully gathering
grievances against Steven Warner. Like Absalom, the rebellious son of King David, who fomented an uprising in the
king's own courtyard, Rachel had recruited her disgruntled
cohorts in the very lobby of the church.

Things were coming together quite nicely.

"Alice, do you have the latest list?" said Rachel.

"I sure do, and believe me, it continues to grow every day,"
said the young woman.

"Good, why don't you read it to the group?" said Rachel.

The young woman cleared her throat, "Example number
one: Jim and Denise Fontano. Pastor Warner replaced Jim and
Denise as youth sponsors when a new youth pastor was hired.
Little or no explanation was ever given despite their seven years
of service."

"I remember Denise cried for an entire week when that happened," commented one of the women.

"Example number two," continued the young housewife, "Dorothy Shayer. She left First Community after Pastor Warner failed to make mention of veterans in his Memorial Day sermon. Her brother had been killed at Anzio during World War II. The pastor never called or inquired as to why she left."

"Can you imagine that?" said one of the women. "But remember, pastors are exempt from fighting in wars." She rolled her eyes. "They leave that to the rest of us."

"That's right," said another.

"Please, go on reading," said Rachel.

"Let's see here. Example number three: Randy and Kathleen Byers. When Randy's father died, Pastor Warner refused to do the funeral because he had a speaking engagement in Milwaukee. An associate pastor did the service and delivered a horrible sermon. Randy and Kathleen have never gotten over it."

"That man has such an incredible ego," someone sighed.

"He doesn't have time for little people like us," said another.

"Example number four: Gary Rodriguez. Gary is a seminary graduate who now works as a computer analyst. He has detected numerous doctrinal errors in Pastor Warner's sermons. He tried to talk with the pastor and correct his errors. Pastor Warner will no longer take his calls."

"Is Gary willing to stand up and help us when it's time?" said Rachel.

"I think so. He told me he has a detailed record of Pastor Warner's doctrinal problems on his computer. Gary will bring a complete printout with appropriate proof texts when it's time to expose Warner's false teaching."

The young woman looked at Rachel, "Should I keep reading?"

"No, you can stop there. I think we have what we need," Rachel said. She turned toward Florence, the oldest woman in the group. "Florence, do you have the petitions ready?"

"Right here, my dear," said the older woman. She held up a file folder filled with photocopied petitions.

"Florence and I spent nearly four hours yesterday drafting this," said Rachel. "Would you ladies tell me if we need to add anything?" The women nodded in agreement.

Florence got up and handed each woman a copy. She did so with the grace and poise of a woman serving a formal tea. "One for you, and one for you . . ."

The women were quiet as they studied the document.
It read:

Whereas we the people of First Community Church of Covington Park are committed to preserving the "unity of the Spirit in the bond of peace" (Ephesians 4:3), and our church today suffers from discord and disunity due to the ungodly leadership we are receiving; and whereas we are warned by Jesus that "many false prophets will rise up and deceive many" (Matthew 24:11), and we have consistently received false teachings and distorted truths from the pulpit; and whereas we are commanded in the Bible to "Cast out the scoffer, and contention will leave; Yes, strife and reproach will cease" (Proverbs 22:10), and yet today our body is rent with strife, quarrels, and insults due to the insensitive and unloving behavior of our pastor; therefore we, the undersigned, petition the elder board to remove Pastor Steven Warner from his position as senior pastor, effective immediately. We request an interim pastor be named at once who will restore love, unity, and sound doctrine to our congregation.

"An elegant statement, don't you think?" said Florence. She turned to the other women. "This was mainly Rachel's work. She deserves most of the credit." Florence bit down on one of the gourmet cookies she had baked for the group and smiled sweetly as she chewed on it.

"Rachel, when do you think we should pass them out?" asked one of the women.

"Wait for my call," said Rachel. "I think we'll go for it after the service this Sunday. Dr. Havens doesn't have a clue what's going on at church."

The group snickered. "The timing of him coming here was perfect," beamed Rachel. "We can hold the no-confidence vote before Warner has an opportunity to rally his lackeys on the board."

"Will the church constitution allow it?" asked one woman.

"I've checked with a lawyer who's willing to help us. A business meeting can be called on just three days notice if 20 percent of the membership request it. We easily have that many on our side."

"I believe the Lord is in this," said one of the women. "Look how He's orchestrated everything so the people won't have to fear Warner. They can speak their hearts. I know I plan to."

Karin sat in the cafeteria at Randolph University and poked at her food. Her salad made her feel sick. She had avoided the table of laughing women seated next to her. From what she could overhear the subject was boys, homework, and more boys. Lately, the topic of romance had lost all its appeal.

She got up and carried her tray to the gray conveyor belt. She watched it disappear through a window to the dish room.

On her way out of the cafeteria she noticed a new poster on the glass door in front of her. It read: "Is someone you know pregnant? Frightened? In need of someone to talk to? Call the Crisis Pregnancy Center at 1-800-NEW-LIFE." Karin studied the number for a moment, then realized people might be watching. She shoved down on the metal arm of the door and walked out into the cold wind.

Back in her dorm room she sat down on her bed and stared at the phone. She knew Crisis Pregnancy Centers didn't believe in abortion. Calling them would only add to her confusion.

"Oh, God, what should I do?" whispered Karin. An odd image passed through Karin's mind. It was a picture her dad had kept in his office. It was of Eric when he was only ten months old. He sat on a small gold chair surrounded by stuffed animals, smiling.

She opened her eyes and picked up the receiver. Then she set it down again. Then she picked it up again. *I can always hang up whenever I want to,* she told herself. *These people can't make me have this baby.* She punched the toll-free number. 1-800-NEW-LIFE was easy to remember.

The phone rang once, then twice.

"Good evening, New Hope Crisis Pregnancy Center of Chicago. Julie Ann speaking."

Karin hesitated.

Again the voice spoke, "Hello, hello . . . is anyone there?"

"Yes. My name is Jill."

"Hello, Jill, I'm Julie Ann. Is there something I could do to help you this evening?"

"I don't know. I'm not even sure why I called."

"I see. Jill, are you having some problems?"

"You could say that."

"May I ask a question, Jill?"

"Yes."

"Are you pregnant? Are you trying to decide what to do with the baby?"

"I've already made up my mind."

"To do what?" asked the counselor.

"I'm going to have an abortion. I don't like the idea, but it seems my only way out."

"Fair enough. No sermons. But tell me, Jill, it sounds like you're a little scared right now. Like the world is closing in on you. Am I right?"

"I don't want you to try and talk me out of this, okay? My mind is made up. My boyfriend broke up with me, I can't tell my parents, and I'll get kicked out of school if they find out. So don't try and tell me God loves me and this baby is a person because I can't deal with that right now." Karin surprised herself with her hostility. She usually never talked to people that way.

The counselor remained calm and polite. "Jill, I'm not here to try and tell you what to do with your life. That's your decision. I'm just here to tell you that you might have more options than you think."

"Like what? Hiding out for the next seven months in a women's shelter in another city? Tell my parents I'm in South America doing missions work?"

"Jill, are you from a Christian family?"

"Maybe."

"You mentioned missions. You must have some church background," said the counselor.

"Okay, so my dad's a pastor, how's that? I'm a pastor's daughter and I'm pregnant. Are you satisfied?"

The counselor continued to refuse to respond to Karin's anger. "Jill, if I were sitting next to you right now, do you know what I'd do?"

"No. What?" said Karin in an abrupt voice.

"I would hug you. Regardless of the choice you make, I would want you to know that I care about you, Jill. I really do."

"I'm so tired of this. I just want it to end," said Karin.

"Listen, Jill. Even though it seems like the end of the world, it's not. Your life is still ahead of you. I suspect that if your parents knew the truth tonight, they would love you as much as they always have."

"That's easy for you to say. You don't know my dad. He loves me because he thinks I'm this sweet little girl he used to push on a swing. Well, I'm not that little girl anymore." Karin started to cry.

"Jill, I think you're wrong. Your dad loves you just the way you are. Yes, he'd probably be hurt by what's happened, but God gave parents an incredible capacity to love their kids, even when they make mistakes."

"So what am I supposed to do? I don't have a job. I have no husband. And I'm about to have no place to live."

"Jill, there are people who would be glad to take care of you if your parents won't. There's more to this decision than where you'll live. We're talking about a new life. A precious baby that's growing in you at this very moment."

"I happen to believe it's just a fetus." Karin hardly sounded convincing.

"How far along are you, Jill?"

"A little over two months."

"Did you know you can hear your baby's heartbeat now? Your child even has fingerprints. Everything is in place for the development of a beautiful boy or girl."

"But it couldn't live outside my womb. How can it be a person if it can't live outside my body?"

"Jill, without a lot of love and nurture from our parents, none of us could survive, even after we're born. But we're still people, aren't we?"

"I guess so."

"Let me ask you another question. Do you believe you have a soul?"

"Yes. Why?"

"When did that soul enter your body? When you were conceived or when you were born?" asked the counselor.

"I've never given it much thought," said Karin. "I don't know. My dad's the expert in theology, not me."

"Let me read you something from the Psalms, Jill. It's found in Psalm 139. Listen to this: 'My frame was not hidden from You, When I was made in secret . . . And in Your book they all were written, The days fashioned for me, When as yet there were none of them.'"

"So, if God loves me so much, why did He let this happen to me?" said Karin.

"God gave you the ability to make choices, Jill. He won't stop you from making a bad choice just because it's bad. Unfortunately, our right to make wrong choices can bring painful consequences. That's the reality of sin. But that doesn't mean God has stopped loving us. If His love was based on our performance, none of us would ever be able to earn His love."

"I sure don't feel loved right now, by anyone."

"Of course you don't, you're in too much pain. But believe me, Jill, Jesus loves you as much tonight as the day you were born."

There was a long pause on the phone. "I only wish I could believe that. But I can't. Not anymore." Karin didn't want to cry, but she couldn't help it. "I appreciate your time, Julie Ann," she said. "I appreciate you talking to me, I really do. But it's just too late. My life is too messed up."

"It's never too late, Jill. Never. God says He loves us with an everlasting love. There's no sin you've committed that God won't forgive. Believe me."

"I want to believe that, I really do. But I can't. I just can't."

"Jill, please don't hang up—"

Julie Ann's heart sank as her phone went dead.

"Good night, Mrs. Madigan. And do call me if I can be of further help to you," said Maggie. Maggie waved good-bye to a frail-looking woman in her late eighties. She lived alone in a two-room flat on the west side of Chicago.

Maggie put on her gloves, dropped her purse over her arm, and headed down the sidewalk. Her car was parked halfway down the block. The sidewalks hadn't been shoveled so Maggie chose to walk in the street.

The orange glow of the mercury-vapor lamp above her cast a shadow in front of her. Maggie hurried toward her car. She had just put her key in the car door on the driver's side when someone jerked her arm. She turned around and saw a tall man in a dark jacket. He grabbed her purse and shoved her back against her car. Her head hit the car window.

"Oh," she cried, then slumped to the pavement. The silhouetted figure disappeared into the night. Maggie lay facedown perpendicular to her car. Her body extended halfway into the street.

—125—

Two blocks away, a car with two teenagers raced down the side street at forty-five miles per hour. The music was on full blast in the car. The two laughed and rocked to the radio. The driver sped up as he started down the second block. After sundown it was hard to see well on side streets.

"Look out!" cried the teenager on the passenger side.

"What is it?"

"Someone's in the road!"

"What—" The driver hit his brakes. The car skidded wildly out of control. And then it hit something.

THIRTEEN

Brenda and Steven walked hand in hand down the length of the luxury ship. It was another perfect tropical day. In just a few hours they would celebrate the halfway mark on their journey to Hawaii. It would mean another special outdoor brunch.

"How do you think the kids are doing?" asked Brenda. She leaned her head on her husband's shoulder.

"Just fine," said Steven. "They're big kids now, Brenda."

"I know. Still, I just wish I could talk to them. Should I call Maggie?"

"You worry way too much," said Steven. He stopped and rubbed his hands up and down her arms. "Besides, who ever heard of a couple calling their kids on their honeymoon cruise?"

Brenda laughed, "Okay, okay. But I'm still calling Maggie tomorrow."

"Do you know how much a ship-to-shore call costs?"

"As much as one of your golf games at the Banetree Country Club back home," said Brenda.

"Touché," said Steven.

Steven glanced down at his watch, "Oops, I promised Ted I'd meet him in the fitness center at eleven o'clock this morning. Do you mind?"

"As a matter of fact, I do."

Steven was about to argue, then he looked down into his wife's lovely brown eyes. "Okay. I can always work out some time later. Let's go for a swim."

They stopped and looked at each other for a moment. Brenda smiled. Steven leaned toward her and their lips met. She closed her eyes.

"Steven, we're out in public," she whispered.

"I don't see anyone," he whispered back.

"That's because you're not looking." Her protest was faint, and Steven kissed her again. The two lovers decided to cut their walk short.

The next day Ted and Steven climbed onto treadmills right next to each other. They were in the workout room, just below the main deck. After ten minutes of vigorous exercise, Ted wiped the sweat off his face. "I don't know about you, Steven, but the tips and gratuities I'm going to owe when we reach port is going to leave me a galley slave."

"Isn't that the truth?" puffed Steven. "I've heard settling up runs as high as four hundred dollars per person. The food may be free, but the service certainly isn't." He pushed an incline button on his treadmill and the machine nosed up another ten degrees. "I'm thinking of staying on board for another reason."

"What's that?" said Ted.

"This trip has done something for Brenda and me. I know it sounds weird, but I'm discovering how much I love my wife."

"Not weird at all, my friend," said Ted. He wiped his face with his towel, then hung it again around his neck. "Most marriages today lack one essential element."

"What's that?"

"Time together," said Ted. "In my master's degree work I took a course on family systems. The professor claimed couples having an affair spend on average fifteen hours alone with each other each week. Can you imagine that? Fifteen hours. I can't seem to find five hours a week to spend with my wife."

"I guess we find time for what we want," said Steven.

"You got it."

"Time is what I don't have," said Steven. "I mean, I feel guilty when I'm not with my family. But when I'm not at the office, I feel like a slouch." Steven looked into the mirror in front of him. His face was red, his shirt was soaked with sweat, and his eyes were drawn. It was a perfect picture of how he felt inside.

"Do you ever take your anger out on your wife or the kids?" said Ted. "I'm afraid I do it to Denise all the time."

The question cut Steven like a knife between the ribs. Steven remembered his last conversation with Eric, just before they left for the trip. He had asked Eric to pick up his room. On the way out the door he glanced in Eric's room and saw clothes lying everywhere on the floor. Eric was on the bed listening to music. Steven had exploded at his son. He stood in the doorway and shouted while Eric scurried to pick things up. Later, once he and Brenda were in the air, he felt bad about what he had done. But it was too late to apologize—it would have to wait until he got home.

The treadmill started to beep. "I guess my five miles are up," said Steven. "I think I'll do some weights."

"Join you in a minute or two," said Ted. As Steven walked over to the bench press, his thoughts turned to Karin. As he pushed the bar above him, he remembered how often he would push Karin away when she was a little girl with dirty hands. "Look what you've done to Daddy's clean suit," he would scold her.

Steven laid the heavy weight down on the bar above him. Then there was the day years ago when Brenda had come down with pneumonia. She had called and asked him to come home, but he told her to wait because he had a lunch engagement he couldn't miss.

As Steven took a deep breath and pushed up the 150 pounds above him, it all became so clear. His life had been nothing but constantly lifting weights, at home, at church, in his relationships. *The sad part is,* he thought, *each year I'm expected to lift more. Oh, God, help me. I can't keep this up forever.*

■

"Maggie, can you hear me?"

It was the voice of Phil Crawford. A heart monitor and an intravenous feeding machine stood next to her bed. Maggie opened her eyes, but nothing was in focus. She tried to reach up and touch her head, but an excruciating pain shot through her arm. She set it down again once she realized it was in a cast.

"Where am I?" she moaned.

"You're in County General Hospital, Maggie," said Phil. "I have Eric here to see you. You're going to be all right. You were hit by a car yesterday and your arm is broken. You also have a concussion." Eric approached the bed cautiously.

"Hello, Mrs. Dunlop," he said.

"How . . . how—I don't remember anything," said Maggie.

"Shh, don't try just now, Maggie," said Phil. "Dr. Ray and his wife are right here with us, too. We'd like to pray for you."

"Please do, please do," said Maggie. "My head hurts so bad."

Dr. Ray walked over to her bed, and Beulah went around to the other side. Phil and Eric stood at the end.

"Oh, you dear woman," said Beulah.

Maggie drifted off into unconsciousness.

"We'd better call a nurse," said Phil.

A young man in his mid-twenties stepped in and took her pulse. "She's slipped in and out like this all afternoon," he said quietly. "She probably needs to rest."

"Of course," said Dr. Havens. "We were just set to pray for her. Could we do that before we go?"

"Of course," said the young man.

Dr. Ray bowed his head. "Lord Jesus, bind up the wounds of this dear woman. Raise her up again, in Jesus' name, Amen."

The male nurse smiled. "Amen." He picked up his stethoscope and charts and left the room.

■

The next morning Karin decided to check her mailbox between classes. She reached in and pulled out a letter. The corner of the envelope said *Office of the Dean.* Karin swallowed hard. *What's this about?*

She tore the envelope open and scanned the contents. "Dear Miss Warner," it read. "Dean Prestwick requests you call her office for an appointment immediately. Please call extension #347. Thank you."

Karin dropped her arms to her sides. "She knows," she said aloud.

An awful sense of fear and anxiety swept over Karin. *Who told her?* she wondered. *How did she find out? It must be Sally. It had to be Sally. How could she do this to me?*

There was no use putting this off. Karin walked over to a campus phone. Her hand trembled as she dialed the number.

"Dean's office," came the voice.

"Uh, yes. This is Karin Warner. I received a note from you today that I'm, um, supposed to meet with the dean."

"Oh yes, Karin. The dean wants to see you right away. Could you come in, say, at 11:30 this morning?"

"Sure. May I ask what this is about?"

"The dean didn't say. She just wants to see you as soon as possible."

Karin gulped again. "Okay, I'll be there. Good-bye." She slowly hung up the phone and leaned against the wall. Her whole body seemed to shake. For a moment, Karin considered the possibility of running out to her car and leaving campus forever. She'd go somewhere that no one would ever find her.

Who am I fooling? she thought. *If the dean already knows, there's no point in running. Besides, I can always deny it.*

Karin glanced at her watch. It was just eleven o'clock. She had time to put better clothes on. It would help her appear as calm and confident as possible.

Karin hurried out the door and back to her room. Twenty minutes later she stood outside the door to the dean's office. She caught a reflection of herself in the glass wall. *Jeff used to like this suit,* she thought. She pushed open the door. She introduced herself to the secretary and took a seat to wait. She was ten minutes early. It was the longest ten minutes of her life.

"The dean will see you now," the secretary finally said. "Please follow me."

Karin got up and followed her into a beautiful office, replete with ornate wallpaper and draperies, a solid walnut coffee table, an expensive couch, and a rather large, crescent-shaped desk. The dean was seated behind the desk reviewing correspondence. She looked up as Karin walked in.

"Won't you please come in?" said the dean. Dean Prestwick was a distinguished-looking woman in her early sixties. She wore a black dress with a string of white pearls. Her soft, gray hair and the frames of her tortoise-shell glasses added to her scholarly appearance.

Karin found a seat on the floral-covered couch and tried as hard as she could to look relaxed. Once the secretary closed the door, the dean got up and sat down in a Queen Anne chair across from Karin.

"I believe you are Dr. Warner's daughter, are you not?" she said.

Karin nodded. "Yes."

"A superb preacher, simply superb," she said. "May I pour you some hot tea?"

"No, thank you," said Karin. She wondered if the dean had noticed her perspiring.

"Very well," said the dean, "please allow me to get to the point of this meeting. I have a question to ask you."

Karin could feel her face burn. Yet, her hands felt icy cold.

"Do you recall earlier this semester when Professor Dobbs submitted a short story you had written to the Faulkner Society?"

"Yes, I remember," said Karin.

"Well, I am pleased to announce to you the results of that competition," said the dean. She reached behind her and took a letter off her desk. She put her half-glasses on to read it.

Dear Dean Prestwick,

On behalf of the distinguished review committee of scholars and journalists that comprise the Faulkner Society, I am pleased to announce that Ms. Karin Warner, a student from Randolph University, is this year's scholarship award recipient. This $7500 scholarship may be applied toward current tuition or graduate school, whichever Ms. Warner should determine. On behalf of the committee, let me offer our congratulations.

Cordially,
Dr. Emily Warsaw-Chapman, Chairperson,
Faulkner Society Review Committee

Karin let out a large gasp of air that caught the dean off guard. "Are you all right?" she said.

"Oh, yes. Fine. Just fine."

"I don't blame you for being excited," she said. "I would be, too, if I were in your place, Karin."

"Oh, yes, ma'am. I mean Dean Prestwick. This isn't at all what I was expecting," said Karin. "What I mean is, this is really a surprise." She reached up and felt her face; her cheeks were burning hot. The dean tried to hide her amusement.

"I don't believe in the history of Randolph we have ever had a Faulkner Scholarship recipient from our ranks," said Dean Prestwick. "I plan to make this award known in chapel next month. I understand your father and mother are out of the country at the moment. I think we should postpone making the presentation until they return, don't you, Karin?" The dean picked up a cup of tea and sipped it.

"Yes, definitely," said Karin. Her momentary exuberance was cut short by a return to a sad reality. *If I wait until next month, I'll be showing,* Karin thought to herself. "On second thought, Dean, perhaps there's no need for such an assembly.

Why don't we forego the ceremonies? It's enough for me that I was selected."

"Nonsense, my dear. You have achieved a significant academic milestone. All of Randolph needs to share your accomplishment. The matter is settled. There will be a public award ceremony. I'll check with Chaplain Vincent and set a date for the presentation."

"Thank you. Thank you so much," Karin said in a weak voice.

A few minutes later, as Karin closed the door to the dean's office, she was struck by how unfair it all seemed. *I'm going to receive a scholarship I won't be able to use, unless I . . .*

Karin walked over to the campus coffee shop. *That's it,* she decided. *This settles it. I can't give up my future for a baby Jeff doesn't even want. I have a right to be happy, to finish my education. I'm not going to give up the biggest honor of my life for a man who won't even speak to me.*

Karin had made up her mind. She suddenly experienced a surge of new energy. She spotted a group of her girlfriends talking in the corner. She walked over and joined in the conversation. No one had seen Karin this happy in weeks.

"Will you look at this?" said Barbara, one of the church secretaries. She pointed to her computer screen nestled in a cloth-walled cubicle in the offices of First Community Church.

The screen in front of her seemed to have a mind of its own. It flashed numbers, scrolled indecipherable words up and down the page, and made weird noises. Two lines appeared at the top of the screen. "Divide overflow. System halted."

"I've never seen anything like this happen before," said Barbara. Ron Simmons, the senior associate pastor, stood nearby. He fancied himself an above average computer hacker. "Let me take a look at it," he said. He punched several keys and waited. Nothing happened. "That's strange," he mumbled.

He sat down in front of the computer and rolled up his sleeves.

Barbara stood behind him. "All I tried to do was call up the numbers for giving last month. Mr. Branstrom had called to verify the amount of his last gift. Then, the screen went crazy."

Ron switched the computer off, then turned it on to reboot it. It hummed and beeped as it booted up. He typed in the correct password and a menu appeared before him. "What information were you looking for?" he said.

"Branstrom. Todd Branstrom. The file name would be BranTodd.bal." Ron typed in the appropriate command to retrieve the data. They both waited. Then the screen flashed bright blue. Then numbers began to scroll wildly across the screen, just as before. Then the two lines appeared again at the top of the screen. "Divide overflow. System Halted."

Ron shook his head. "This doesn't make sense. We couldn't."

"Couldn't what?" said Barbara.

"Couldn't have a virus."

"A virus? What are you talking about?" asked Barbara.

"I'm talking about big trouble," said Ron. "Depending on how extensive it is, our entire data base may have been corrupted."

"Which means?"

"Which means all of our financial records on the mainframe have just been destroyed," said Ron.

He turned around in his swivel chair and looked up at Barbara. "Let me try something else," said Ron. He walked into his office and came out with a floppy disk.

"What's that?" said Barbara.

"A virus scanning program." He inserted the diskette, then rebooted the computer again. Several minutes later he slammed his fist on the desk.

"Rats, it isn't working. Barbara, we may have been sabotaged," said Ron.

"Oh, my word."

The associate continued to stare at the blank screen. He tried to think of some way to counter the virus. "Where are the backup tapes?" he said.

"We keep them in the safe," Barbara answered.

"I've got the keys." She walked over to her desk, reached inside, and produced two keys. Both had to be inserted to open the vault. "I know right where they keep the backup tapes."

They walked into the room where the safe was stored. She inserted the keys into the huge metal door and turned them both. The six-foot door swung open and Barbara reached in and turned on the light. The safe was a narrow room the size of a large coat closet. On either side were shelves of various boxes.

"They should be right here," she said confidently. "We've kept the last seven years all on tape. IRS rules require keeping receipts that long."

She reached for a long plastic box, took it down, and opened it. "Oh, no," she whispered.

"What's wrong?" asked Ron.

"These are all 3M tape. We've used Memorex tapes for as long as I've been here." Her face turned pale. "Ron."

"Yes?"

"These are different tapes. Look, the labels are missing too."

He grabbed the box and walked out into the daylight. He studied several of them, then walked into the youth pastor's office. The secretary followed him. He sat down at the desk with the laptop computer in front of him.

It was used by the youth pastor and wasn't connected to the other computers. Yet it used the same program as the others did. He loaded the tape software. He shoved one of the tapes into the computer and typed in the command to restore the data.

The computer flashed a short phrase at the top of the screen; "No files found. Tape media not formatted."

"It's empty," he muttered. "The tape is empty." He took another tape out of the box from the safe and shoved it into the tape drive. Same story. He tried another, and another.

He looked up at the bewildered secretary. "Barbara, we've been robbed," he said quietly.

FOURTEEN

"I regret that our scheduled speaker for this morning has had to cancel her appearance," announced Randolph University Chaplain Dexter Vincent. "Pam Grunway of the National Nutrition Coalition was to address us this morning on the topic of 'The Beta Carotene Revolution.' However, she was forced to cancel due to illness."

"Maybe she's got a vitamin deficiency," someone shouted in the back. The students roared with laughter.

"Has she tried Flintstone Vitamins yet? They're chewable," shouted another.

"Excuse me," said the chaplain. He scowled at a group of young men seated near the back. The group quieted down.

"Fortunately, I was able to secure a guest speaker from First Community Church, the Reverend Doctor Raymond Havens." Chaplain Vincent picked up the resumé in front of him. "Dr. Havens is serving as interim pastor while Dr. Warner is on an extended vacation. Dr. Havens is the former professor of intercession and spiritual formation at Commonwealth Theological Seminary. He is now the current director of the International Intercessory Prayer Institute. He is an ordained pastor, and he and his wife, Beulah, make their home in Greenville, Mississippi.

"Will you please welcome with me Dr. Raymond Havens to our chapel service this morning?"

There was polite applause.

Dr. Havens got up slowly to walk to the podium. Over six feet, four inches tall, he was an imposing figure behind a pulpit.

Chapel was voluntary and it suffered from sporadic attendance. This day, the auditorium happened to be less than half full. As Dr. Ray looked out, he could see students yawn, scratch their heads, or lean forward on pews as if already asleep.

"I once attended a banquet where the speaker went on way too long," he began in his distinctive southern drawl. "The emcee was seated right behind the man. By and by, the emcee decided it was time to get the speaker to sit down, but the man loved the sound of his own voice. So he went on way past his allotted time.

"The emcee decided to get the man's attention in a polite manner. So first, he tried tapping his spoon on a glass of water. But someone in the audience coughed, so the speaker never heard the spoon. He just kept on talking."

Several students chatted quietly among themselves, and ignored Dr. Ray.

"Next, the emcee tried tugging on the speaker's coattail. But wouldn't you know it? The man leaned forward and the emcee couldn't reach him.

"Finally, the emcee was as anxious as a long-tailed cat in a room full of rocking chairs. So he picked up the wooden gavel he had used to call the meeting to order. He swung as hard as he could at the man. But the speaker stepped aside to make a gesture, and sure enough, the gavel missed him. Instead it caught another man on the back of the head.

"The man was momentarily dazed from the blow, but once he had recovered, he said in a loud voice, 'Hit me again, I can still hear him.'"

The chapel erupted in laughter, first one wave, then another. Dr. Ray gestured his appreciation.

"Well, I don't know much about the value of carrots or beta carotene," he said. "But I was raised in the hills of Mississippi, and I can tell you this much. I've never seen a rabbit die of a heart attack. So whatever these beta carrots are, they must be good for you." The students laughed again. A few even sat up.

"Since I'm not a nutrition expert, I'll have to speak to you on a topic I know more about. May I read to you from one of my favorite passages in the Bible? Did any of you bring your Bibles with you this morning? I'd like you to follow with me."

Here and there, students reached into their backpacks, dufflebags, or under a pile of books and produced a Bible.

"Turn to Isaiah, chapter six, verses one through eight," said Havens. "'In the year that King Uzziah died, I saw the Lord sitting on a throne, high and lifted up, and the train of His robe filled the temple. Above it stood seraphim; each one had six wings: . . . And one cried to another and said: "Holy, holy, holy is the LORD of hosts; the whole earth is full of His glory!"'"

Dr. Havens paused for a moment. "Are you staying with me, friends? Hang on, I'm almost done." He continued to read. "'And the posts of the door were shaken by the voice of him who cried out, and the house was filled with smoke. So I said: "Woe is me, for I am undone! Because I am a man of unclean lips, and I dwell in the midst of a people of unclean lips; For my eyes have seen the King, the LORD of hosts."

"'Then one of the seraphim flew to me, having in his hand a live coal which he had taken with the tongs from the altar. And he touched my mouth with it, and said, "Behold, this has touched your lips; Your iniquity is taken away, and your sin purged."

"'Also I heard the voice of the Lord, saying: "Whom shall I send, And who will go for Us?" Then I said, "Here am I! Send me."'"

Dr. Havens closed his Bible and looked out at the students. "People have strange ideas about how to please God. I read recently where there's a religious cult that believes letting the air out of other people's tires earns points with God. I'm serious. Imagine the hallelujah time they must have in the parking lot of a football game."

The students laughed. "Truth is, my young friends, we can't please God. That is, not on our terms. Nor does it do any good to try and hide our sin. Like Isaiah, we can only be used by

God when we're willing to admit, 'I am a person of unclean lips.'

"It reminds me of the story of King Frederick II, an eighteenth-century king in Prussia, what is today Germany. He was on a visit to a prison in Berlin when the inmates crowded around him to proclaim their innocence. All except one man. He sat quietly in the corner, head bowed.

"Frederick walked over to him and said, 'What are you here for?'

"'Armed robbery, your majesty,' the man replied.

"'Are you guilty?' the king asked.

"'Yes, sir. I deserve this punishment.'

"The king turned to the guard and ordered, 'Set this guilty man free. I don't want him corrupting all these other innocent people.'"

The crowd laughed again, but the point had hit home.

"Young people, finding God's pardon in our lives begins by admitting our guilt. To insist we are innocent when we are not leaves us in a prison of our own making. Yet when we admit our need, God offers us grace and forgiveness. Imagine, if you could start your life all over today. You can do that by placing your faith in the sacrifice of God's one and only Son." Most of the audience was now listening.

"Some of you are feeling like Isaiah this morning, filled with remorse over what you've done wrong, but uncertain of what to do about it." Nervous coughs sounded from the back row. "But the way to God isn't by trying harder, or cleaning up your act, as I believe you say. It's by faith. Faith in the finished work of Christ on the cross.

"Listen here to Ephesians, chapter two, verses eight and nine: 'For by grace you have been saved through faith, and that not of yourselves; it is the gift of God, not of works, lest anyone should boast.'"

Dr. Ray happened to glance up at the clock. He had only two minutes left. "Let me put it another way. I want to finish before Chaplain Vincent here reaches for the gavel."

The chaplain smiled.

"Let me leave you with this challenge, dear young men and women. Give up trying to please God on your own terms. Instead, let God touch your lips with His tongs of forgiveness through Jesus. Put your faith in His death on your behalf. And then when God asks, 'Who shall I send? And who will go for us?' you can say, 'Here am I! Send me.'

"If you would like to take that step of faith this morning, to put your trust in what Christ has done for you, I urge you to do so this morning. God bless you as you make your decision," said Dr. Ray. With that he turned around and sat down.

Chaplain Vincent appeared moved by the message. He stood up to the podium and struggled for words. His eyes glistened with tears. "I know it is our custom to dismiss on time and not infringe on the class schedule for the day. But perhaps . . . perhaps we could make a small exception this morning. Let us take a few moments to pray."

The organ began to play a quiet Bach piece, and many students remained in their pews to pray. Several professors were seen kneeling by a pew.

Jeff Mortenson, seated near the back, felt miserable.

"Come on, Jeff, let's get out of here," said one of his friends. "There's too much religion here for me."

"Just give me a minute to think, will you?" said Jeff.

"What? You can't be serious," Andrew whispered.

"Leave me alone," said Jeff.

"Okay, man. Okay. I'll catch you later." Andrew got up, yanked his backpack over his shoulder, and headed out the door. He looked back one more time at Jeff. Jeff got up and followed him out the door.

Across the chapel Karin Warner sat with red eyes. *It's not too late, Karin,* a voice inside seemed to say. *This is your opportunity.*

No, no, it's too late, another voice seemed to argue inside Karin. *God doesn't love you anymore. He might love the other*

people here, but not you. You've done too many bad things.
You're hopeless.

Karin got up from her pew and walked out the door.

Dr. Ray was praying when the chaplain tapped him on the shoulder. "Dr. Havens, there's a young man down here who says he needs to talk to you. Could you give him a few minutes of your time?"

"Certainly, certainly," Dr. Ray replied.

"When do we start handling snakes in chapel?" said the irate faculty member. He paced back and forth in front of Dean Prestwick's office. "Is this what it's come to? Altar calls and the sawdust trail of tears? I was under the assumption that Randolph University was an institution of higher education, not an Elmer Gantry evangelism circus," he continued.

"Dr. Porter," said Dean Prestwick, "I fully appreciate your concerns about religious excess and manipulative emotionalism. I'll not tolerate that for a moment either. But I saw none of what you are characterizing as a 'circus' in this morning's chapel service. Quite the contrary, I found the entire service both decent and well ordered. I'm afraid I don't fully comprehend the nature of your anger."

The faculty member whirled around and pointed his finger at the dean. "I'll explain my anger to you. Students weeping in their seats. Several fellow faculty members kneeling like penitent rescue mission derelicts. An old-time religious huckster telling students their problems would soon be over. The man's a charlatan."

"Really, professor," said Dean Prestwick.

"What's worse, we gave him an opportunity to peddle his backwoods ignorance and corn-pone theology to our students. Simply inexcusable!"

"Please, professor," the dean said calmly. "The only inappropriate display of emotion I've witnessed this morning has just occurred in this office."

The professor raised his arm and was about to launch into a second tirade when he thought better of it. He dropped his arm, smiled at the dean, and sat down in a chair. "Why, of course," he said. "I must apologize to you, Dean Prestwick. How foolish of me to carry on this way."

"I accept your apology," said the dean. "Now, may I pour you some tea?"

"Please, if you would."

The dean walked over to a steaming pot of water on a coffee maker and poured two cups of hot water. She picked up a mahogany box filled with assorted teas and offered him his choice. He selected an herbal orange. She served him hot water, and the two resumed their discussion.

"I don't object to sincere explanations of one's religious experiences," said the professor in a deliberate and calm voice. "Freedom of inquiry on a college campus must allow for a variety of religious experiences to be explored."

"Granted," said the dean. She took a sip from her cup and nodded for him to continue.

"But the idea that God would punish us for not adhering to the right theology is as errant as it is bigoted," said the professor. "This 'Doctor' Havens, or whatever his title, would have students believe that unless they share his understanding of God, they will be punished in the afterlife."

"Go on," said the dean.

The professor leaned back. "Though New Testament study is outside my discipline, on my last sabbatical I focused on a redaction-critical examination of the Gospels about heaven and hell. I can safely say that most scholars agree that Jesus' alleged sayings on the subject can be disregarded as later additions to the New Testament."

"I would take exception, but your point, professor?" said the dean.

"My point is this. I find the idea of a literal heaven a strenuous, if not whimsical, notion to believe in. But the idea of a loving God sending anyone to hell is simply preposterous.

It's the product of a dangerously narrow, perhaps even bizarre, notion of justice and punishment. I simply cannot believe such a God exists," said the professor.

"I see," said the dean. She put down her teacup and leaned forward. "Would your point be that all of us, whether or not we wish to, will enter heaven upon our death?"

"I suppose if you were to characterize my theology at this point, I could be described as a latent universalist. But yes, if there is such a place, all of humanity will assemble there in one form or another," he answered.

"I find it odd, professor," said the dean, "that you would assign all people to such a place, even against their will. Why would the agnostic or atheist, who desires no relationship with the Almighty, be forced to spend eternity with God? Your heaven sounds rather like Dr. Havens's hell." She raised her eyebrows at him and stirred her tea.

Porter was quiet for a moment. Tension once again entered his eyes. "Dean Prestwick," he said in a controlled voice, "I have great respect for your work as a scholar and your leadership as an administrator. If it were not so, I would have left this institution years ago. But I must warn you, if you insist on bringing this so-called 'doctor' back to chapel again, I shall be forced to raise the issue before the faculty."

"Professor, that sounds to me rather like a restriction of freedom of expression," replied the dean. The firmness in her voice was unmistakable. "I would carefully consider the ramifications of such an action first."

The professor stood up, his faced flushed, "What's next, Dean Prestwick? Be reasonable. You and I both know Havens and others like him have no place on this campus. Good day." He picked up his leather satchel and stormed out the door.

Once he was gone, the dean sat back down in her high leather chair and smiled. She pushed the button on her intercom.

"Yes, Dean Prestwick?" the secretary answered.

"Lois, call Dr. Havens and ask him if he and his wife would be my guests tomorrow in the Rutgers Room. Please invite Chaplain Vincent and his staff. And Lois, ask him to select a few students to attend as well. Perhaps from among those who responded this morning in chapel."

"What will be the agenda? Should I come prepared to take minutes?"

"No need for minutes. We're going to have a different sort of convocation tomorrow. We're going to pray."

"Did you say pray, Dean Prestwick?"

"That's right, Lois. All we're going to do is pray."

Even though Joe McDonald now had copies of apparently incriminating letters from Steven Warner and First Community Church, he knew he needed more evidence if he was to go before a grand jury. He had only one other solid lead. It was a letter a bank officer had given him from a member of First Community. The man had requested to see the church's financial statements from the last twelve months. Because he was not a signatory on the account, the bank had refused his request.

McDonald decided to pay the man a visit after supper. Later that night, he stood in the shivering cold in front of a townhouse in a posh subdivision east of Covington Park. He rang the doorbell and waited.

A young man looked out from behind the white lace curtains on his Victorian oak door and then opened it.

"Yes, may I help you?" he said.

"My name is Joseph McDonald. I'm a criminal investigator with the Internal Revenue Service and Treasury Department." He produced his badge and held it up for the man to read. "Are you—" and the investigator read the name from the letter.

"Yes, that's me. I've been expecting you."

"I'd like to ask you some questions."

"Please come in, Mr. McDonald," he said. "I believe we have much to talk about."

The two men spent the next sixty minutes in intense discussion. Joe McDonald set a miniature tape recorder on the table to record the man's deposition. When it was over, Joe McDonald stood up and shook hands with the young man.

"Do you realize you might be called before a grand jury to testify?" said McDonald.

"I'd be glad to."

"And you still maintain that the pastor and other leaders deliberately destroyed the computer data dealing with the church's finances?" said McDonald.

"Absolutely," said the young man. "Just a few days ago I was told a 'virus' conveniently destroyed the data base. And if my information is accurate, Warner also had arranged to have backup tapes stolen from the safe and destroyed."

"You're willing to say this under oath?"

"You bet I am. It's time someone exposed this scam. I won't pay more taxes because religious frauds like Warner keep others from paying their fair share."

"I appreciate your sense of integrity," said McDonald. "I wish there were more people in the world like you."

"Mr. McDonald, my wife and I are Christians. Our faith won't allow us to look the other way."

"I appreciate your cooperation," said McDonald. McDonald clicked the tape recorder off and put it back in his briefcase. "You'll be hearing from me soon," said the agent. "And please, don't say a word about this meeting to anyone."

"You can count on it," agreed the young man.

The bell rang at Roosevelt High and students jumped from their seats.

"Don't forget, tomorrow's test will cover bisecting triangles," said the middle-aged math teacher. "Review chapter six for the test." The noise in the classroom drowned out the teacher's plea for the students to study hard.

Out in the hallway, a girl accidently knocked Eric's notebook from his hand. He stooped down to pick it up, then noticed a pair of male legs standing straight in front of him. He looked up. It was one of the Squires. Eric gulped.

Eric stood up and tried to walk past him. The teenager grabbed his shirt. "Not so fast, loser boy."

Eric clinched his teeth. "Let go of me."

"Not until you make a little down payment on our agreement," said the teenager. "Say, ten dollars?"

Eric again tried to push past him, but the boy held his grip. "You said fifty dollars on Mondays," said Eric. "This happens to be a Thursday, remember?"

"Don't get smart with me, Warner," growled the teenager. "I want money now, or you may get another little suntan. You wouldn't want that, would you?"

The rage and fear Eric had carried for days suddenly boiled over. He stamped on the teenager's foot, bringing all 150 pounds to bear on the boy's toes. The gang member crumpled in agony. Eric didn't wait to see what would happen next. He took off down the hallway at a full sprint. He left the teenager hopping on one leg.

He raced down two flights of stairs to his physical education class. The bell rang just as he burst into the locker room. Most boys were already dressed for class and ready to head upstairs to the gymnasium.

"So, Warner, did you need some extra time from the ladies?" Eric looked up. It was Mr. Grissup, his gym teacher. Grissup was a former Marine drill sergeant who took great delight in humiliating young boys. He stood with his hands on his hips, waiting for an answer.

"Uh, no sir, I had to run to my locker for something," said Eric.

"Get down and give me fifteen right now," said the teacher. Eric paused to put on his other sock. "I said fifteen right now! Or I'll make it fifty, Warner!" shouted Grissup. Eric lunged to the floor and immediately began his push-ups.

The former drill sergeant put his right foot on Eric's back to make it more difficult for him to push up from the floor.

When he had paid his dues, Grissup let Eric get up. He quickly got dressed and ran up the stairs to the gymnasium. As he stood in line for inspection, he noticed they had combined classes with another section that day.

Straight across from him stood a member of the Squires. Eric glanced away, hoping the boy hadn't noticed him. But when he looked his way again, he could see the boy staring straight at him.

Does he know what happened in the hallway? wondered Eric. Eric's heart pounded so hard he was certain other people could hear it. The instructors divided the boys into two groups for a basketball scrimmage. Eric's squad was to sit out first. That was a relief to Eric; at least he was surrounded by his classmates. He hunched down, staring at the floor.

After five minutes of scrimmage, Mr. Grissup whistled play dead. "Blue team, my class. Red team, Mr. Danson's class. On the floor. Hustle!" Eric jumped to his feet with four other boys and ran out onto the court.

Across the circle from him stood the gang member. He pointed at Eric and said, "Warner's mine." Eric pretended not to notice. The teacher threw the ball in the air and play began.

The tip went to the other team. Eric raced down the floor to play defense. The ball was passed several times. One of the opposing team players tried a cross-court pass. Eric saw it coming and circled underneath to intercept it. The boys on his bench yelled their approval. "Go for it, Warner!" He drove down the court and headed for what looked like an easy lay-up.

Just as he left the floor to lay the basketball up against the backboard, he felt a tremendous blow to his spine. The force of the impact drove Eric forward into the blue padding hanging against the cement wall in front of him. He crashed full force into the wall and dropped to the ground.

A loud whistle blew immediately. "That's a flagrant foul, Snyder!" said Grissup. "You're outta here." The teenager gave Eric a small kick in the ribs and walked off with a smirk.

Eric was slow in getting up. Mr. Grissup came over and bent down by him, "Hey, Warner, you all right?" Eric tried to sit up, but the room seemed to spin all around him.

"Warner, you woman, can't you take a hit?" someone from the other team shouted.

"Get up, son. Be a man," said Grissup. He made Eric get up, and Eric wobbled back toward the bench. The other teacher came over and inspected the knee that had hit the wall.

"Where does it hurt, son?" he asked.

"Ouch! Right there, Mr. Danson," said Eric.

"You better go downstairs and put some ice on it," the teacher said. "It's probably just a bruise. But you're tough, right?"

"Yes, sir."

"Thatta boy." He turned toward the others, "All right you wimps, let's get back to the game." He blew his whistle and the game resumed.

Eric walked past the other bench and saw his assailant smirking at him. The gang member mouthed the words, *You're a dead man.* Eric pretended not to notice.

Later, as Eric lay on the cot in the first-aid room, he thought, *They're going to kill me. I know it. I just know it. And I can't tell anybody.*

"Now how in the world does this new-fangled machine work?" said Dr. Ray out loud. He had stayed late to photocopy a prayer action list, but the machine was jammed.

Never entirely comfortable around modern technology, Dr. Ray opened up the machine and searched for the piece of paper caught inside. He poked here and there and finally found another wrinkled piece of white paper. He yanked it once, then twice, and at last it came out.

"Glory," said Dr. Ray. But he had smudged his white shirt with black toner dust. He tried to wipe it off, but it only made matters worse. "Beulah won't be pleased with this. No sirree, she won't be happy at all."

He pushed the machine's parts back down into place. He reached over and flipped the green switch to turn it on again. The buzz of the machine was sweet music to his ears. He sat down to wait for the machine to warm up.

Out of curiosity, he glanced at the wrinkled paper he had retrieved from the copier. His facial expression changed from curiosity to dismay. The paper read:

A Petition of the Congregation to the Elder Board of First Community Church of Covington Park Requesting a Congregational Meeting for the Purpose of Conducting a Vote of No-Confidence in the Ministry of Reverend Dr. Steven Warner, Pastor

Whereas we the people of First Community Church of Covington Park are committed to preserving the "unity of the Spirit in the bond of peace" (Ephesians 4:3), and our church today suffers from discord and disunity due to the ungodly leadership we are receiving;

and whereas we are warned by Jesus that "many false prophets will rise up and deceive many" (Matthew 24:11), and we have consistently received false teachings and distorted truths from the pulpit;

and whereas we are commanded in the Bible to "Cast out the scoffer, and contention will leave; Yes, strife and reproach will cease" (Proverbs 22:10), and yet today our body is rent with strife, quarrels, and insults due to the insensitive and unloving behavior of our pastor;

therefore, we, the undersigned, petition the elder board to remove Pastor Steven Warner from his position as senior pastor, effective immediately. We request an interim pastor be named at once who will restore love, unity, and sound doctrine to our congregation.

"What in the world?" he whispered. He looked down at the paper once more. *Somebody must have been copying several of these and left one jammed in the machine,* he thought. *Or maybe they had to leave in a hurry.*

The elderly man reread the document then shook his head in disbelief. He stood up and walked back to his office in a slow, even gait. He did what came naturally to him in such situations; he closed the door and got down on his knees. He laid the sheet of paper out on the chair in front of him, as if to let God read it, and prayed.

That night he made several calls to members of his prayer group. He didn't explain, but he asked each of them to come even earlier than usual the next morning.

The next morning at 5:30, seven people made their way through the back door of First Community Church. Dr. Ray led them into a small conference room, where they took their coats off and found their places at an oblong table.

Dr. Ray's face was particularly drawn and serious, yet he still somehow retained a look of peace in his eyes. He scanned the group of people seated at the table. There was his wife, Beulah, Phil and Mildred Crawford, Howard and Virginia Svendsen, and finally, Melissa, a young mother who had recently left Rachel's women's group. She had approached Dr. Ray on Sunday morning and asked if she could be a member of a different small group. He had invited her to join him and the others.

"Dear friends," Dr. Ray began, "it has not been our custom to divulge confidential matters in this group. Our purpose has always been to pray for the needs of our church and the nearby college. We have prayed for spiritual awakening. And we have prayed for Pastor Warner and his family. Beyond that, we have only mentioned the needs of the sick and the grieving."

Everyone in the group nodded in agreement.

"But this morning I must make an exception. A matter of grave urgency has arisen, which I believe the Lord Almighty has allowed me to discover."

The group smiled their support. He continued, "While trying to photocopy something last night, I discovered a piece of paper jammed in the machine. Allow me to read it to you."

Dr. Ray produced the crumpled petition and read it word for word.

"Oh, no," whispered Melissa.

"Heaven have mercy," said Beulah.

"I can't believe this, who would start such a thing?" demanded Phil Crawford.

The rest of the group sat in stunned silence.

"I have no idea, and there is no proof of who might be behind this awful plan," he said. "But God knows."

"I think I know who it is," said Melissa. All faces turned toward the young woman. Her voice trembled, "I was part of a group—oh, dear Lord, forgive me—a group that spent most of their time criticizing Dr. Warner. At first I didn't understand their agenda. Everyone sounded so spiritual. They even quoted the Bible—often. At first it was only prayer requests regarding the pastor. Then it turned into long discussions about his preaching. Then his family, even the furniture he owned."

"My, my, my," said Beulah in a quiet voice.

"Finally," said Melissa, "to be accepted by the group, you had to bring some sort of dirt about him or his family to the next meeting. That's when I decided to quit." The tears rolled down her cheek.

Beulah got up and put her arm around Melissa. "There, there, you sweet girl. It's not your fault."

Melissa wiped her eyes with her sleeve.

"I can't believe anyone would go to that extreme to get rid of Dr. Warner," said Phil Crawford.

"It's true, Mr. Crawford," said Melissa. "What they called 'convictions' I believe the Lord would call something else."

"What's that?" asked Beulah in her deep southern voice.

"Hate," she answered.

Brenda had just returned from the ship's pool when there was a loud knock at the door.

"Who is it?" asked Brenda before she opened the door.

"Room service, ma'am. I have a telegram for a Dr. Steven Warner," answered the male voice. Brenda opened the door. There stood a ship's steward dressed in a starched white tuxedo jacket and pressed blue trousers with a gold stripe that ran down each leg. He held out a sealed yellow envelope on a silver tray. "Will you sign for this?" he asked in a courteous voice.

"Of course," said Brenda. She scribbled her initials on a sheet of paper. "Thank you."

"Very good, madam," he said. He bowed slightly, then turned and headed down the plush hallway. Brenda closed the door and studied the telegram. She used a nail file to slit open the envelope. Steven was still up on deck finishing his mid-morning swim.

She unfolded the telegram and scanned its contents. It was from Dr. Havens.

Dear Brother Steven,

I apologize for this interruption. A matter of grave urgency has arisen. The deacons asked I contact you immediately. I considered calling you but was uncertain how confidential the line might be.

I have reason to believe a faction in the church is preparing to demand your resignation. Petitions may have already been circulated. I am told by a reliable source that this group may be able to force a recall ballot. I have no more information for now. We are in constant prayer for you and your family. Contact me as soon as possible by whatever means you think best.

Your brother in Christ,
Ray Havens

Brenda folded the telegram back up and stumbled over to a chair. *How could they do this to us?* she asked. *To Steven? To our children? Dr. Ray must be mistaken. It must be a rumor of some sort. No one would do anything like that.*

During the next few minutes, as she reread the letter, Brenda's emotions went from shock to rage. She got up and looked out the porthole at the blue Pacific waters. *This can't be for real*, she thought. *Not during the only vacation Steven and I have had alone in nearly a decade. No, it can't be.*

But as she stared at the ocean, the pieces of the puzzle started to come together. The canceled appearance at the women's luncheon. The drop in giving. The women who had started to walk to the far side of the hallway at church when she approached.

What about the break-in? Could that have something to do with all this too? Brenda knew it would be a few more days before they reached Hawaii. This trip had been the first time she had seen her husband relax in years. He had started to show her real attention again. Romance had returned to their relationship.

If I show him this now, it will destroy the rest of the trip. It will drive Steven crazy. He won't think of anything else. It will be the Same Old Fight. I can't believe it. Once again his mistress, the church, will have invaded our privacy.

Brenda slammed her fist on the desk top. "No!" she shouted to the empty room. "No! You can't have him. Not this time."

She stuffed the telegram into her purse, reached for her sunglasses, and walked out of the room. Like a woman on a mission, she marched up the steps to the main deck. She jostled her way past several vacationers until she reached the railing of the ship.

"Forgive me for what I'm about to do," she whispered. She reached in her purse and took out the telegram. Slowly, methodically, she tore the telegram in half, then in half again. And again. She reached over the railing and opened her hand. The pieces of paper floated down toward the sea like a gentle snowfall in December.

"He's mine," she whispered. "For once in my life he's mine, and I won't let you have him."

The ship blew a long and mournful whistle to greet a passing ship. The other ship returned the courtesy.

PART TWO

PART TWO

FIFTEEN

"W ill you look at this, Ray?" said Beulah.

She pointed out the window of their furnished suite at the five inches of fresh snow that had fallen overnight. A northwest wind had caused the snow to drift over cars and trees so they resembled clouds come to earth. "Do you think we should cancel church this morning, dear?" she asked.

Dr. Ray still had shaving cream over half his face as he stepped over to see for himself. "Land sakes, it's a howling mess out there, isn't it?"

"It may be too dangerous to ask people to come out, particularly for the elderly folk," said his wife.

"If this was Mississippi, folks with any sense at all wouldn't come out until the dogwoods blossomed," said Dr. Ray.

"You've got that right, honey," said Beulah. She left the window and went back to the kitchen to pour herself her first cup of morning coffee.

"I'm going to call the deacon chairman, Beulah. With the hornet's nest stirring at church, it might be the Lord's will we not have church this morning," said Dr. Ray. "Land sakes, I wonder why I haven't heard from Steven yet? I sent him that telegram two days ago."

"It's good he's taking time to think it over," said Beulah. "I respect him for that."

"Dear, where is my appointment book?" asked Dr. Ray.

"Sorry, honey, I don't have any idea."

Dr. Ray went over to his briefcase and searched through it. "Here it is," he said. He opened it and looked for the list of important phone numbers Steven Warner had left him. "Let's see, yes, here's Howard's number. He picked up the phone and dialed the number.

"Good morning, Howard Svendsen speaking," said the voice on the other end.

"Good morning to you, Mr. Svendsen, Ray Havens calling."

"Ah, it's you, Pastor. I bet you're calling to ask if we arranged this little northern welcome just for you this morning."

"Well, sir," said Dr. Ray, "if you prayed for snow, it's obvious you get real answers, my friend." The two men shared a brief laugh then got down to business.

"Have you heard from Pastor Warner yet?" asked Howard.

"No, but I suspect he's taken some time to pray over the matter before he gets back to us," said Dr. Ray. "He was always a praying boy when he was in school."

"What about the weather, Dr. Ray? It's up to you. Should we cancel? The weatherman says there's another storm right behind this one."

"Down where I come from, if folks got up and saw this much snow, they'd put another piece of wood on the fire and pull the covers over their head," said Dr. Ray.

"Not a bad idea, Pastor. But the road crews have been out plowing and salting all night. I would guess the main roads are clear for travel. As my Swedish dad used to say, 'Howard, if it ain't up to your elbows, it's just flurries.'"

"I never like to cancel worship," said Dr. Ray. "Will some folks show up in this blizzard?"

"Oh, sure," said Howard. "I think you could expect as many as two hundred people. We have some old Norwegians out there who would show up every week even if we entered another Ice Age. If the doors are open, they're there."

"Then let's do it," said Dr. Ray.

"Fine with me."

The elderly pastor paused for a moment. "Howard, do you think I could impose on you?"

"Certainly, Pastor, you're our guest. What can I do for you?"

"Would you mind sending someone to pick up Beulah and me? I can drive a lame mule across a flooded river pulling a load of bricks on three wheels, but this here snow is a different matter."

The chairman laughed, "Why, of course, Dr. Havens. My son has a four-wheel drive Jeep Cherokee that he just loves to show off in weather like this. Why don't you and Mrs. Havens be ready about 8:15? Give me the suite number again where you two are staying."

Dr. Ray gave him the information and thanked him for the chauffeur. The pastor hung up the phone, and his wife handed him a cup of coffee.

"Sakes alive, they're going to have church this morning," he said. "We need to get ready."

"Heaven have mercy," sighed Beulah. "Why do people want to live in this part of the world?"

Forty-five minutes later a bright red Jeep Cherokee appeared in the hotel's parking lot. Dr. Ray and his wife pulled up their collars, held onto their hats, and plunged out into the storm. Howard's son helped them both up into his vehicle, then slammed the doors behind them. Back in the driver's seat, he reached down and jerked the shift into four-wheel drive. With a groan, the vehicle slowly moved forward and out into the street.

The two elderly passengers held hands as the vehicle bounced and bumped over snow and ice. Several times they had to duck to keep from hitting their heads on the roof.

"Well, sweetheart," said Dr. Ray, "the Lord parted the Red Sea for the children of Israel. I do believe He is going to part the white drifts for us this morning."

Not far away, on the campus of Randolph University, four young men bent over the altar rail at the front of the college chapel. They had been there all night.

"Lord," one prayed out loud, "I confess to You that I've carried resentment toward my father. You know how much he drank when I was growing up. But it's never right to hate someone. And I've hated Dad. I've hated him ever since I can remember. He beat Mom, my sister, and me. But I can't go on this way, God, I just can't. Forgive me. And give me a heart to forgive my father."

Three young men knelt close by. One got up and put his arm around his friend. "Lord, You've heard the prayer of this brother of mine. Give him freedom from the hate he's carried. I ask this in Jesus' name, amen."

The young man seemed to relax. Soon his body shook with soft, muffled sobs.

Another member of the group spoke up. "Heavenly Father, it's time I settle up with You. It's about something I did last fall that wasn't right. I started a rumor about Dennis that wasn't true. I did it to get even with him. I need to go and apologize. Give me the courage to do that."

Prior to Dr. Havens's message in chapel on Friday, the four men had planned to go out for their usual partying on the weekend. But Dr. Ray's message had made an impact. By Saturday night, all four were feeling such inner turmoil about their lack of a relationship with God, they decided to skip the parties and spend some time in the chapel. They ended up staying the entire night.

Now, even as the wind howled and the snow flew outside, they each sensed God was somehow in that auditorium with them.

"What time is it?" asked one of them.

"My watch says 7:15," answered another. "The cafeteria's open."

"Should we get some breakfast?"

They all looked at each other.

"I'd rather stay here, what about you guys?" said one.

"Same here."

"Me too."

"Then it's settled. We stay. What would you think if I called Brent and Andrew to come join us?"

"Go for it, man," came the reply.

Dr. Havens sat at his desk in Steven's office going over his sermon notes for the last time. He thought he saw something move outside his door, which he had left half open. Curious, he got up and walked to the entrance. He was startled to find a young couple hiding right around the corner. Both looked extremely nervous.

"Pardon us, Dr. Havens," said the young man. "We didn't mean to interrupt you. It's just that my wife and I, we've been standing here . . . I mean we've been wondering if we could ask you—is it true?" Both the young man and his wife stood there wide-eyed, their faces a mixture of worry and anticipation.

"Is what true?" said Dr. Ray.

"You know, about Pastor Warner. His condition and all," said the woman.

"I must apologize, but I don't believe I understand what you're talking about," said Dr. Ray.

"You haven't heard?" said the woman. "Pastor Warner has had a nervous breakdown. He's been hospitalized in a psychiatric unit on the West Coast. We were just crushed when we heard." It was clear from their expressions that the couple was utterly sincere.

"May I ask where you heard this news?" said Dr. Ray.

"From friends of ours. It's all the talk down in the coffee room this morning," said the husband.

"I see," said Dr. Ray in a low voice. "Well, I can give you my personal assurance that no such thing is true. Your dear pastor and his wife are still on their long-overdue vacation. I expect to hear from him in a few days."

"Really?" the two said together.

"But we had heard there was going to be a congregational meeting to discuss naming an interim pastor," said the wife.

"Who did you hear that from, if I may ask?" said Dr. Ray.

The wife hesitated and looked at her husband. He knew what she was thinking.

"Go ahead, honey, you need to tell him," he said.

The woman glanced each way down the hall, then took a deep breath. "I don't want to be divulging personal confidences, Dr. Havens, but it was from Rachel Brewster. She . . . she called me yesterday and told me to be in prayer. When I asked her what about, she said she couldn't tell me details, but that there was a crisis in the church. But she did say Dr. Warner was going to resign. Then when we got to church this morning, she told us about the pastor's nervous breakdown."

"I see, I see," said Dr. Ray with a gentle voice. "I thank the two of you for having the courage this morning to come to my office and verify this information. Unfortunately, it's just a false rumor. I will speak to the issue from the pulpit later this morning."

"Then Pastor Warner isn't resigning?" said the husband. A look of hope entered his eyes.

"No siree, he's not leaving. He's just getting his batteries charged to come back and lead you folks another dozen years," said Dr. Ray.

"But I heard he's in clinical depression and may have even attempted suicide," said the wife. "We were told he's in a hospital in Southern California under lock and key."

Dr. Ray just shook his head. "Heaven, have mercy. There isn't a shred of truth in what you have heard."

"Thank goodness," said the wife. "We love the pastor. And his wife. I just can't understand how someone would start a story like that."

Dr. Ray reached out and put his arms around the couple. "My granddaddy used to say, 'Just because a mouse lives in the cupboard, doesn't make him a can of soup.'"

The two thanked him again and left his office. Dr. Ray walked back into his office and stared out the window. *Why hasn't Steven gotten back to me?* he wondered. *He must have received my telegram.*

Through the drifting snow he could see the headlights of cars pulling into the parking lot. He bowed his head, "In all my fifty years of ministry, Lord, I don't ever remember being in a predicament like this one. If You don't help me out, Steven may not have a church to come back to." A verse Ray had memorized years ago came back to him: *I will build My church, and the gates of Hades shall not prevail against it.*

Dr. Ray opened his eyes for a moment and watched the wind whip the branches back and forth. The storm seemed a perfect metaphor for what was going on inside the church. "Now defend your church against those gates this morning," he prayed.

The battle was about to begin.

Dr. Ray walked out onto the stage with Ron Simmons, the associate pastor, at precisely five minutes before eleven o'clock. There was a palpable sense of tension in the air. Only occasional conversation broke the silence, punctuated by nervous laughs. Several in the audience deliberately avoided eye contact with Dr. Ray. The auditorium was about half empty, mainly because of the blizzard.

The orchestra played the introduction to Handel's *Messiah.* Dr. Ray sat down, tall and dignified in his immaculate dark blue suit. Beulah had picked out a red and blue striped tie and stuffed a red handkerchief in his coat pocket. "Always look your best on Sundays," he used to tell his seminary students. "Even if no one else shows up, you know you are preaching to the angels that morning."

His dark-rimmed glasses rested peacefully on his nose, a look of serene gentleness on his face. If he was worried, it certainly didn't show.

The congregation rose to sing the first hymn, "All Hail the Power of Jesus' Name." After the final strain, Ron offered the opening prayer and then shared several announcements. Following a short dramatic skit and then several choruses, it was time to take the offering. Perhaps it was just his imagination, but Dr. Ray seemed to notice more people than usual pass the plate without putting in a cent.

A young soloist got up and sang a beautiful rendition of "Amazing Grace." As she did, a warm sense of the presence of God began to wash across Dr. Ray's soul. His concerns about the morning began to subside.

"Through many dangers, toils, and snares, we have already come," the woman sang. "'Tis grace that brought me safe thus far, and grace will lead me home." Dr. Ray continued to experience a growing sense of the nearness of God. The feeling got stronger, more intense by the moment. Dr. Ray put his head down, hot tears of joy running down his cheeks. He wondered if he could bear much more of it.

"When we've been there ten thousand years, bright shining as the sun," the woman sang as her voice reached a crescendo. "We've no less days to sing God's praise, than when we first begun." As the last note ended, the woman bowed her head and walked off the stage. There was a moment of holy silence. Dr. Ray seriously doubted if he could get up to speak, he was so overcome by divine love.

Ron walked up to the large pulpit. "We want to thank Marta Williams for filling in at the last moment. Marta worships at another church in the area and agreed to sing for us when Nancy Burns canceled because of the weather." The associate turned in the direction of the soloist, "Marta, which church do you attend?"

But the woman had disappeared. "I guess we won't know that till heaven, will we?" joked the associate. A mild ripple of laughter went through the congregation.

Ron turned away from the microphone and cleared his throat. "Please excuse me," he said. "It's my honor this morning to introduce to you again our guest speaker while Pastor Warner and his wife are away on vacation." Several people nudged each other. "Dr. Raymond Havens comes to us from Greenville, Mississippi, and has enjoyed a long and distinguished career as a pastor, seminary professor, and leader in a national prayer movement. Perhaps you have enjoyed, as I have, the warm and sweet spirit of Dr. Ray and his wife, Beulah. Won't you please welcome with me, Doctor Havens."

The two shook hands on stage. Dr. Ray then walked toward the pulpit, opened his large red leather Bible, and set it down in front of him. His large moist eyes seemed at odds with his warm, disarming smile.

"It's wonderful to see so many of you in church on such a wintry morning," he said. "It reminds me of the couple I knew in Tennessee who never missed a single morning of church their entire married life. Problem was, every time their preacher got up to speak, the husband would fall asleep.

"As you can imagine, this was a great embarrassment to both her and her dear husband. After numerous unsuccessful attempts to keep him awake, she decided to take matters into her own hands. She purchased four ounces of ripe, Limburger cheese, and carefully wrapped it in plastic."

A few people chuckled in the main section of the sanctuary.

"The next weekend the couple found their place in their usual pew. The preacher stood up as usual and said, 'Good morning.' Sure enough, the husband almost immediately went to sleep. But this time, she was armed and ready. She reached in his pocket, unwrapped the Limburger cheese, and wafted it under her husband's nose.

"The man woke up with a start. In a voice loud enough for everyone to hear, he said, 'Dear, get your feet off my pillow.'"

The sleepy morning congregation came to life with loud and uproarious laughter. It took almost a minute before order could be restored. Rachel Brewster tried to maintain her scowl at the speaker. Eventually she had to look away to hide her smile. It was important she remain in control.

Dr. Havens blushed a bit, hardly expecting such tumultuous laughter. "Unfortunately, it's not only pungent cheese that can spoil the atmosphere of a worship service, but so can rumors and misinformation," he said. The room immediately quieted down. Rachel Brewster stiffened.

"Without making reference to any one person, and assuming only their best intentions, I must respond to an erroneous story currently circulating in the church. The story has it that your pastor, Dr. Warner, is in ill health and unable to return to his duties."

Dr. Ray looked down at his Bible and smiled, "It reminds me of the time Mark Twain's obituary appeared by accident in a newspaper. When asked about the incident, Twain responded to the incident by saying, 'The stories concerning my death have been greatly exaggerated.'" The congregation laughed nervously.

"What I'm trying to say, dear friends, is that Dr. Warner and his wife are in excellent health—mentally, physically, and no doubt spiritually. They should be arriving at their destination in just a few days. They will, by the Lord's mercy, return to this church refreshed and prepared to serve you all for another decade."

A small group of people broke out in applause. Dr. Ray acknowledged their gesture, then turned to the Scripture passage he had chosen for the morning.

"Allow me, dear friends, to read to you what I believe is the most beautiful description of love ever penned by a mortal. Turn with me to the thirteenth chapter of the first epistle to the Corinthians." Dr. Ray pushed his glasses back up his nose. They had a habit of slipping down whenever he lowered his head to read.

"'Though I speak with the tongues of men and of angels, but have not love, I have become sounding brass or a clanging cymbal. And though I have the gift of prophecy, and understand all mysteries and all knowledge, and though I have all faith, so that I could remove mountains, but have not love, I am nothing. And though I bestow all my goods to feed the poor, and though I give my body to be burned, but have not love, it profits me nothing.' Now pay careful attention to what it says next," said Dr. Ray.

"'Love suffers long and is kind; love does not envy; love does not parade itself, is not puffed up; does not behave rudely, does not seek its own, is not provoked, thinks no evil; does not rejoice in iniquity, but rejoices in the truth; bears all things, believes all things, hopes all things, endures all things. Love never fails.'"

Several individuals readjusted themselves in their pews.

"What is love?" said Dr. Ray. "It is the practical expression of the character of God in everyday life. It is not so much what we say, as what we do." Havens's trademark smile appeared again, a sure tip-off he was about to tell another story.

"As a young pastor, I was assigned to a church in a very poor area of Birmingham, Alabama. It was during the war, and a lot of folks were struggling. I discovered talking about love and salvation didn't go very far when families had empty stomachs at night. So our small congregation prayed for some way to demonstrate the love of Christ to these poor folks in our neighborhood.

"So after a week or two of praying over the matter, lo and behold, I got a call from a wealthy farm owner in another county. He said, 'Pastor Havens, I hear tell your church wants to do something to feed the hungry. Well, I've got an overstock of potatoes sitting here on the loading dock. The company that was set to buy them went out of business last week and never told me. If you want 'em, I'll deliver 'em.'

"'You bring 'em right over,' I said. Now I must confess to you all, I had not taken the course in seminary on potato evangelism. So I plumb forgot to ask him how many potatoes he intended to bring. In my youthful exuberance, I had also forgotten to ask where he planned to put them. The next thing I knew, a dump truck arrived at the parsonage. Before I could get out to the driver, he had dumped the entire load in my garage. Friends, that left me with over two tons of potatoes."

"Now look here, this was late summer in the deep South. I mean to tell you, the humidity in those parts was so bad it made us stick together, in good times and bad." Several men laughed out loud. Rachel leaned over and shook her head to a friend who sat close to her.

"Land sakes, I had never seen so many potatoes in my life. I had no idea what to do. They sat in my garage for nearly four days while I tried to devise a plan to get rid of them. By and by, a foul-smelling liquid started to ooze down my driveway from the bottom of the pile." A few older people in the audience groaned.

"I take it a few of you know what ripe potatoes smell like," said Dr. Ray. "Now remember, these here were the days of Prohibition. I tell you the truth when I say I was the only minister in Birmingham making vodka in his garage." The congregation howled with laughter. Several people clapped. Rachel looked around to see who was laughing and who was not.

"By and by I called an emergency meeting of the deacons," said Dr. Ray. "'Gentlemen, if we don't get rid of these potatoes, they'll all go to ruin,' I said. We decided to cart them in wheelbarrows down to the alley from the parsonage, to the church, then dump them on the lawn in front. And that's just what we did.

"You should have seen that sight, heaven have mercy. There were seven grown individuals down on their hands and knees, crawling through the pile of potatoes like little children playing at the beach.

"Well, by and by we attracted a good bit of attention. I remember one mother and her two poorly dressed sons just stood and watched us. 'Just what kind of church is this?' she asked. I reckon she feared some new religious sect had moved into town that worshiped potatoes."

The crowd was now into this story.

"By noon that day, we had retrieved over twenty-four sacks of fresh potatoes and handed them to grateful and tearful neighbors."

Dr. Havens paused. He had come to the point of his story. "That hot day, slogging through rotten potatoes in order to try and feed hungry people, was the start of a new spiritual awakening in our congregation. We went beyond telling folks, 'God loves you,' to actually showing them He did.

"Friends, God has gotten down among the rotten potatoes of our lives to show us what true love looks like. He went beyond saying He loved us to showing us He really did. The death of Christ on the cross, the ultimate expression of the love of God, is the best answer I can give when someone asks, 'How can I know that God loves me?'

"Let me ask you a personal question this morning. Have you experienced the love of God firsthand? Have you ever allowed His love to control your life? The apostle Paul said it was possible to spend your entire life in church, fill your mind to the brim with doctrinal knowledge, even go so far as to offer yourself up as a martyr, but still not have love.

"He put it this way: 'Though I bestow all my goods to feed the poor, and though I give my body to be burned, but have not love, it profits me nothing.'"

Dr. Ray studied the congregation with a softness in his face that was a sermon in itself. "Only as we trust in Christ's finished work on the cross can we experience the true extent of the love of God in our lives. But once we've experienced that transforming love, it is not ours to keep. We must give it away—to a hurting, broken, bleeding world—and to each other."

By now Rachel held her head in her hands as if she had a headache.

"And the place to first experience that love is right here, among God's people."

Rachel got up without looking at anyone and went out the back door. A young couple also quietly excused themselves and left the sanctuary.

"Jesus didn't say it would be our big offerings, or our large building programs, or even our eloquent sermons that would convince people that God's love is for real," said Dr. Ray. "He said this: 'By this all will know that you are My disciples, if you have love for one another.'"

Dr. Ray walked out from behind the pulpit. He stood with hands folded in front of him. "I'm set to dismiss you all. I'm sure you'll want to get an early start home in this bad weather. But if there is anyone who would like to stay behind and pray, either to receive Christ or to get something straightened out in your relationship with God or someone else, I'll be right here."

He then raised his hand to offer the benediction: "And now may the love of God the Father, and the grace of our Lord Jesus Christ, and the fellowship of the Holy Spirit, rest and abide on your life, now and forever. Amen."

The instrumentalists reprised the strains of "Amazing Grace." Dr. Ray went back to his chair and sat down. He closed his eyes and prayed for a minute or two by himself. When he looked up, he couldn't believe his eyes.

Not a person in the entire congregation had left.

He looked over at Ron, who seemed as puzzled by the lack of movement as Dr. Ray was. Ron gestured toward Dr. Ray as if to say, *What do we do next?*

Somewhat flustered, Ron got up from his seat and went to the microphone. "Perhaps it wasn't clear to you that Dr. Havens has dismissed you," he said. "You are free to go. Only those desiring special prayer should stay."

Again no one moved.

Instead, one by one, individuals began to get up from their seats and move toward the front of the sanctuary. At first, it was only a trickle. Then more followed. Then still more after them. Soon the entire altar rail was lined with people from one end to the other.

The next wave of people to come forward had to kneel behind those already at the altar. Only when the line of kneeling members was three deep did people stop coming forward. Then, they knelt by their pews or in the aisles, wherever they could find space to pray.

As the music continued, Dr. Ray was overcome by the magnitude of what he was witnessing. It was beyond anything he had ever experienced. A sense of awe, conviction, and mystery filled the room. It seemed to be a continuation of what he had experienced at the beginning of the service, only stronger.

For ten, maybe fifteen minutes, the sound of whispered prayers and the soft music were the only sounds heard in the auditorium.

As the service ran overtime, volunteers from children's church began to wander into the sanctuary to see where the parents were. Their reaction was uniformly the same. Without anyone explaining what was going on, they sank to their knees as well. The reality of God was so strong in the room that no one could resist it.

All over the sanctuary husbands and wives wept and bowed in prayer with each another. In some cases, entire families formed circles in the aisle.

Single adults and teenagers also knelt side by side at the altar or prayed with each other in small groups.

In all of his fifty years of ministry, Dr. Ray Havens had simply never seen anything like it.

By noon the prayer group in the college chapel had grown to a dozen students. Several young men and women had joined the gathering, as had one professor.

Though no one particular person was in charge, there was a sense of order and tranquility. Sometimes the group sang. At other times someone would read a portion of the Bible. For long periods of time the entire group would just sit in silence.

Some wrote in their journals. Others knelt by the communion rail, praying for relatives or friends.

"I'll go get sandwiches," offered one of the students. The group took up a small collection and sent the individual on his way to the cafeteria.

As the young man stood in line with twenty sandwiches piled on his tray, the cashier asked, "Who's all this food for?"

"For people over in the chapel. It's hard to describe, but it's like we're meeting with God. It's incredible."

"Meeting with God? You're jiving me."

"Honest. I'm not. Come see for yourself."

"Really?"

"Sure, bring anyone you like."

By the time the student returned to the chapel with the food, he had collected seven more people on the way.

At two o'clock that afternoon, the phone in Dean Prestwick's apartment rang. She had stayed in that day because of the snow. Chaplain Vincent was on the line.

"My apologies for bothering you on Sunday, Dean Prestwick," he said. "But I'm over here at the chapel. Something quite extraordinary has happened."

The dean became tense. "What is it, Dexter? Is there some trouble?"

"I wouldn't say that, Dean. It is a meeting, but it's unlike anything I've ever attended. Would you be willing to come over if I picked you up?"

Dean Prestwick glanced out her window. The blowing snow obscured her view of the campus. "Dexter, you can't be serious. There's an arctic blizzard in progress out there."

"Dean, I wouldn't ask you to come out if I didn't think you were needed here."

"All right, Dexter. I trust your judgment implicitly. Give me a few minutes to find my wool scarf. This is a day for neither man nor beast . . ."

"Thank you, Dean. I'll be over in fifteen minutes."

"By the way, Dexter, what's this meeting about?"

"As far as I can tell, Dean, it's about God."

"Did you say, *God?*"

"Yes, Dean."

"I have to see this for myself."

"Friends, I must confess I have carried a grudge against another member of this congregation for over four years," said the middle-aged man who stood at the microphone. It was now three P.M., and the sanctuary at First Community Church was still crowded. The service was scheduled to end by noon, but as of yet, virtually no one had left.

Families with small children had taken them out for a quick lunch or arranged for baby-sitters, then returned to the sanctuary. Despite the blowing snow outside, the size of the congregation had actually increased through the afternoon. The sanctuary was now three-quarters full.

After the initial time of individual prayer following the morning service, several members had requested an opportunity to address the congregation.

The man who now stood at the microphone struggled to get his words out. Deep remorse was evident in his voice. "I was bypassed for a position on the elder board four years ago. I developed a bitter spirit toward the chairman of the nominating committee. I've carefully nursed that anger for the last four years. I now see the damage that did to my relationship with God, my family, and the rest of you."

The man turned toward his adversary and pointed at him, "Henry, I'm publicly asking your forgiveness. I was wrong. My ego was out of control. My wounded pride got the best of me. I want to be your brother again."

Henry stood up in the pew where he was seated and in a calm voice said, "Rick, I forgive you. And I ask your forgiveness for the insensitive way I dealt with you. I knew you were hurt when you didn't get nominated, but I didn't have the courage to come and talk to you about it. I accept the responsibility for the breakdown of our friendship."

In full view of the congregation, the two men met halfway down the center aisle and embraced. Those seated closest to them could see tears flowing down each man's face. The congregation responded by giving the two men a standing ovation.

Dr. Havens sat on stage and shook his head in wonderment. "This must be a little of what heaven is like," he said to himself. Beulah had joined him up front to watch and pray with her husband.

Next, an elderly woman came to the microphone. "As you know," she said in a frail voice, "I played the organ in this church for nearly thirty-five years. That is, until September two years ago. It was then one of the pastors suggested to me it was time for me to retire. I said yes and quietly resigned, but it crushed me. I felt like an old sweater tossed in a box and carried up to the attic."

The woman looked down and took a handkerchief from her large purse. "I must confess to our minister of music, Pastor Reynolds, that I have . . . hated you for that." Several in the audience gasped at Emma's confession. She had always seemed so sweet to everyone.

"Emma, you could never hate anybody," said the music minister seated near the front of the church.

"No, Pastor, I have hated you for taking my job away from me. I am grieved that I could allow such a vicious attitude to make its home in my heart, but I did. And I spoke against you behind your back." The woman gestured toward the congregation. "There are people seated out there this afternoon who could tell you the petty and awful things I said. I even tried to get friends to quit the choir. Pastor Reynolds, I must ask you to forgive me."

Both the minister of music and his wife got up from their pew and walked over to where Emma stood. The three of them embraced and stood wrapped together for nearly five minutes. Again the audience responded with applause. Several of the people on Rachel's list of disgruntled individuals went on to repent of their bad attitudes toward the church and Pastor Warner.

The scenes of reconciliation continued throughout the afternoon. Not every confession had to do with others in the church. Many had to do with hidden compromises or hypocrisies in their private lives.

A young man in his early thirties was next to speak. He stood almost six feet five inches tall, wore a red bandanna and faded blue jeans. His high-pitched voice belied his nervousness.

"Some of you probably noticed I left here in a hurry this afternoon," he began. "I had to. I couldn't take it. The reason was—" His voiced cracked, and he struggled to regain his composure. "The reason was I knew if I stayed, I would have to give up someone I didn't want to. A relationship that isn't honoring God. It's not important for me to go into details. But for the first time in a long time, I feel whole again."

"That took tremendous courage, my friend," said Dr. Ray. "Thank you all for the discretion you have shown today in sharing your problems. I've always believed that confession should only be as public as the sin. So, friends, if there are private matters that need to be addressed between you and the Lord, ask one of the deacons to pray with you. I can assure you, it will be kept in strictest confidence."

Indeed, very little inappropriate information was shared that afternoon. And in each and every case the congregation responded with forgiveness, love, and empathy.

By the supper hour the church was completely filled. A network of telephone calls had alerted most everyone in the congregation that something unexpected, but wonderful, was happening. Several men with four-wheel drive vehicles had volunteered to go and pick up those who had learned of the unusual service and wanted to attend.

At six o'clock, Dr. Havens had an announcement to make. "Mr. O'Donelley, who I am told owns a Kentucky Fried Chicken franchise here in town, has volunteered to bring everyone present a hot meal—courtesy of him and his wife.

The ushers will pass out cards and you may order food for you and your family."

Forty-five minutes later two service vans pulled up to the back of the church. O'Donelley had closed his stores for the rest of the day and brought his work crews over to the church to serve supper. He had offered to pay double-time if they'd go with him and help.

It turned out to be the most delightful meal the church had eaten together in a decade. Numerous people offered O'Donelley money for their meals, but he wouldn't hear of it.

By seven P.M., the usual time for the evening service, there wasn't a parking place left in the lot.

Howard Svendsen motioned to Dr. Ray to come off the stage for a moment. "Dr. Havens, I've been a member of this church since it opened its doors. But I have never seen an evening crowd this large. It's unbelievable." The main floor was full, the balcony was jammed, and chairs had been set up in the back and down the aisles.

"I certainly hope the fire marshal doesn't hear about this," chuckled Howard. "Then again, I hope he does."

Something similar had taken place at the Randolph University campus chapel that afternoon, but at a somewhat slower pace. The two dozen or so students gathered at lunchtime had grown to seventy-five by supper time.

Sally Jensetter burst through the door into her dorm room. "Karin, have you heard what's happening over at the chapel?"

"No, what?" said Karin, who lay on her bed watching a portable television.

"I don't know how to explain it," said Sally, breathless with excitement. "There's a huge group of students there who have spent all day praying. They came on their own, and they won't leave."

"So?"

"So I went over myself. Just to see. Karin, it was like . . . like God was there or something."

Karin continued to stare at the television set.

"Karin, are you listening to me?"

Obviously she was not. Karin sat with a pillow propped up under her chin watching the Channel 7 Movie of the Week, *Rampage on Flight 712*.

"Please, Karin, listen to me. There are kids over there who I know do drugs and party every weekend. Karin, they were bent over the altar rail, crying. Brad Sampton went back to his room, got his stash of cocaine, and handed it to Chaplain Vincent. You should have seen his face."

Karin turned toward her roommate, "Sally, can I be honest with you? I've got a lot on my mind right now. If you want to go to some hyped-up prayer meeting, fine. But please, give me a little peace and quiet."

Sally's face fell. "Sure, Karin. I'm sorry. I just thought you might be interested, that's all."

"Well I'm not, okay?"

Sally turned to leave, then hesitated before going out the door, "I'm going back, Karin. If you're interested, I'll save you a place."

"Fine, Sally."

She closed the door and left Karin to herself.

There was a furious knocking on the front door of the Brewster home. Ed opened the door and found a woman wrapped in a white mink coat.

"I must see your wife, immediately," the woman said in a sharp voice.

Ed hesitated for a moment. He had met this person somewhere before, but where? Always the gentleman, he said, "Won't you come in? Who may I tell her is calling?"

"Ingrid. She knows me. I'm her . . . counselor. Your wife is a member of my group. It's vital that I speak to her at once."

Rachel had never told Ed the truth about her involvement with Ingrid. She had told him instead that she was part of a self-esteem and weight-loss group. When the group met late at night, Rachel had let Ed believe that she was baby-sitting for her sister, who worked the night shift at a hospital.

"Of course, I'll get her. Won't you please sit down?" said Ed. *This is strange,* Ed thought to himself. *Since when do counselors make house calls?*

"Honey, you have a visitor," he said as he stood outside their bedroom door.

"Tell whoever it is to go away."

"Rachel, I said you have a guest," Ed persisted.

"Leave me alone."

Ed pushed open the door to their bedroom and found Rachel curled up in a fetal position on the bed. Her streaked mascara betrayed the fact that she had been crying.

"Darling, what's wrong?" said Ed. He walked over and put his hands on her shoulders.

"Go away," she said.

"Are you all right, Rachel? You look awful."

"I said go away, Ed. Tell whoever is downstairs I'm not available. I've got a terrible migraine. It hurts to talk." She rubbed the temples of her head and moaned.

"Rachel, the woman says her name is Ingrid. Do you know her?"

At the mention of the name, Rachel suddenly sat up. "Ingrid? She's downstairs? Ed, why didn't you tell me?" She pushed her husband out of the way and got up. She stopped in front of the mirror only long enough to adjust her hair. She turned to her husband. "Ed, this is a private conversation. Private, do you understand? I want you to go in your office and close the door."

"Okay," said Ed. Ed knew Rachel could act strange at times, so he usually just went along with whatever she wanted when she had a headache.

Rachel hurried down the steps, "Oh, Ingrid, I apologize for keeping you waiting. My foolish husband—he never gets things right."

Ingrid stared at Rachel with a cold anger in her eyes. "I want to know if it's true," she said.

"If what's true?" said Rachel, trying hard to sound innocent.

"Let's not play games, my dear," said Ingrid. "I'm told by my sources at First Community that some sort of spiritual awakening is going on there. Even now, the auditorium is full of people praying, and more are arriving by the minute. You waited too long to act, didn't you?"

Rachel swallowed hard. "Ingrid, I had it all planned. You must believe me. I had everything organized. There was going to be a meeting this afternoon. I had the support to force a vote."

"Shut up!" said Ingrid. "I'm not interested in your excuses. You've let the situation get completely out of hand. I was a fool to trust you with something this important."

Rachel buried her face in her hands. Her penitence did nothing to lessen Ingrid's anger. The woman paced back and forth in front of the fireplace.

"Do you know what this 'awakening' is doing!" shouted Ingrid. "I was channeling this afternoon when suddenly everything went wrong. No one could focus. No one could connect. The disruption in my aura actually caused me pain." She whirled around and pointed her finger right at Rachel's face. "And it's all your fault. You miserable excuse for a sorceress!"

Rachel walked over to Ingrid, trembling. "Please Ingrid, please give me another chance. I won't fail this time. You'll see. It's not too late."

"From now on, you stay out of this! Do you understand me?" Ingrid spoke through clinched teeth.

"Surely you can't be serious, Ingrid. I've worked so hard. I've risked so much. I've given so much to destroy Warner. I'm so close. I need just a little more time. You'll see. Just a little more time. This, whatever it is, at church will be over by tomorrow morning. I know it will."

Ingrid walked over to Rachel and stood just six inches from her face. "I know how to punish people who get in my way, Rachel. Never forget that."

"Oh, please, Ingrid. Don't do that."

"I haven't decided what I'm going to do in your case. But if you so much as step foot in First Community Church again, you will pay. From now on, he's mine." The woman spit out the last words with such venom that a shiver went through the soul of Rachel Brewster.

"I understand," said Rachel meekly.

"Perhaps you two could tell me what's going on here?" The two women whirled around and discovered Ed standing on the stairway, his hands on his hips.

"Ed! What are you doing here?" shrieked Rachel. "I told you this was a private conversation!"

Ed had decided to come down and get a cup of coffee, and he had overheard just the last few moments of their conversation. "I'm not going anywhere until I find out why this woman is threatening you," Ed demanded.

"It's none of your business," said Rachel.

"What she means, Mr. Brewster," interrupted Ingrid, "is that Rachel failed to complete an assignment I had given her. Surely you're aware of your wife's interest in becoming a self-actualized person?"

"What does all this have to do with our church?" said Ed.

"Very little, actually," said the woman. "She was merely to investigate the spiritual self-awareness of leaders in the church to gain an understanding of the spiritual matrix of your church."

"Rachel, what's this group about?" said Ed.

"I must leave now," said Ingrid as she picked up her white mink coat. She walked over to the stairs and looked up at Ed. "Let me assure you, Mr. Brewster, you'll hear no more from me. Your wife has decided to drop out of our group." She turned toward Rachel, who stood shaking by the fireplace. "Haven't you dear?"

"Yes, yes, of course."

"We shall miss you, Rachel."

Rachel nodded in fright.

"I'll let myself out," said Ingrid. She cast one more disdainful glance at Rachel, then opened the door. A cold winter wind blew into the foyer.

The moment she was gone, Ed ran down the steps and over to his trembling wife. He took her in his arms. "Rachel, for heaven's sake, what have you gotten yourself into?"

For several minutes she just stood there and shook.

That night, Rachel took Valium to help her get to sleep. Ed tucked her into bed, then slipped out of the room. He walked into his study and turned on the light.

I know it's here somewhere, he thought. He searched through a succession of bookshelves and drawers until he found what he wanted. He held up the *Pictorial Directory of the First Community Church of Covington Park.*

He turned on his desk lamp and pulled up a chair. He rubbed his finger against his chin as he turned the pages one by one, scanning rows of pictures with his finger. Three or four pages into the directory, his finger stopped at the bottom of a page.

"There she is," he said out loud. "I knew I had seen her before." Underneath the picture of Ingrid, the woman who brought such chaos into his home only a few hours earlier, was the name, *Tiffany Evans.*

SIXTEEN

My friends, it is now ten o'clock. I believe the Lord would have us all go home to get a good night's rest," said Ray Havens from the pulpit. He looked out at a church auditorium overflowing with people.

"I know several of you who have asked if you can stay on through the night and pray for relatives and friends. Certainly. Two deacons have graciously consented to stay here until morning. For those who are interested, we have scheduled a six o'clock prayer meeting here tomorrow morning and a noon prayer meeting as well. If you can't get away until tomorrow evening, we have a seven o'clock service planned."

He looked down at the altar which remained filled with people kneeling in prayer. "As we leave tonight, let's go out singing softly."

A gentle, soothing chorus filled the auditorium. It was like an echo of heaven, words and melody combining to bathe the group in an ocean of love and unity.

Dr. Ray closed his Bible and ambled down the stairs off the stage.

"This has been some day," said Ron Simmons who had followed him off the stage.

"Indeed it has," said Dr. Ray.

"Do you think this revival, or whatever it is, is over?" asked the associate. "I mean, will it continue tomorrow?"

"Maybe, maybe not," smiled Dr. Ray. "That's all up to God. If He wants it to continue, there isn't a man alive who can stop it. If He wants it to end, no amount of pump-priming can get it started again. All we can do is pray for God's will to be done." Dr. Ray reached out and patted his associate on the back, "Good night, son."

Dr. Havens turned, took the arm of Beulah, and walked back to get his coat.

That same evening, Dean Prestwick sat alone at her desk in the empty administrative building. After spending the afternoon at the chapel service, she had decided to stop and record the day's remarkable events in her journal.

This day, I have seen things I never believed I would experience in my lifetime. Certainly not in my career as a dean. It all began when I was summoned by Chaplain Vincent to the campus in the middle of a howling Midwestern snowstorm. When we arrived at the chapel, we found an intense prayer meeting underway. It had no leader, at least no visible leader.

The students, about thirty in all when I arrived, seemed drawn by a force greater than themselves to the chapel. Several faculty members joined them.

I heard student after student confess wrongs they had committed against each other. They admitted to shortcuts and cheating in their studies. Some publicly turned in drug paraphernalia and other contraband. Others confessed their faith in Christ for the first time in their lives. All this was done without the least bit of coercion, or manipulation, on the part of anyone in the group.

By supper time the size of the group had doubled. By nine P.M. the group's size had doubled again. Even now the meeting continues. I have heard that a similar spiritual occurrence has happened at First Community Church. I've yet to talk to anyone from the church to confirm that story. Based on what I've seen today, it would not surprise me.

The look of sincerity in the students' voices, the deep and thoughtful nature of their public statements, and the sheer number of the young men and women who claim to have found a new relationship with Jesus Christ today all lead me to believe something unusual is happening to our campus.

I suspect beginning tomorrow morning, I will encounter opposition from some of the more skeptical, outspoken members of the faculty. Undoubtedly, the majority of professors on this campus are pleased to see this new desire on the part of students to find an authentic relationship with Christ. Unfortunately, some will see it as religious excess or fanaticism and will try to dissuade students from participating in it.

I bear part of the responsibility for this. A few of these skeptics were my appointments, while some I inherited. Yet if I have a sin to confess in this, it's that I at times cared too much for their academic credentials alone and too little for their spiritual vitality. God, forgive me if this is the case.

The dean put down her pen, closed her journal, and looked out her window across the snowy campus. Through the bare trees she could clearly see the lights on inside the chapel. It was now eleven P.M.

Early Monday morning, a young college student stood in line at the local Wal-Mart. "Excuse me, are you the manager?" he asked.

"Yes, I am," replied a balding man in his mid-forties. "What can I do for you?" He wore a blue vest, off-white shirt, and dark trousers. His tie was already loosened at the neck. He stood next to a new employee he was trying to train on the cash register.

"I'd like to return this," said the student. He laid on the counter a compact disc.

"Do you have your receipt?" asked the manager without looking up. He turned to his trainee, a young woman in her early twenties. "Jennifer, please help the man with his return item."

"No, sir, I don't think you understand," said the student. "I don't want any money back."

He looked up, "Then why are you returning it?"

"Because I took it," replied the young man.

The manager stopped what he was doing and looked up. "Did you say you stole this CD?"

"Yes, sir, I did. I stole it from your store last month. I'm here to pay full price for it, plus interest."

The manager stared at him, then picked up the CD and turned it over. "Why?"

"Because, what I did was wrong and I want to make it right. I ask your forgiveness."

A line of people had formed behind the young man. The manager seemed at a loss for words. "In five years here, I don't believe I've ever had anyone ask my forgiveness," he said, laughing.

He took the CD and scanned the bar code on the label. The price appeared on the computer, $15.75 with tax. "Just pay me the $15.75 and you can keep it, kid. I'll give you a break this time," said the manager.

"Here's twenty dollars," said the college student. "And please, keep the change. It would make me feel better." The trainee looked at the manager, who nodded at her to take the twenty dollars. She finished the sale and handed him a receipt.

"Thank you, sir."

"Thanks," said the student. He put the receipt in his wallet and took the CD with him. Before the student left, the manager had one final question. "Why today?"

"Someone special I met last night," he replied. He left the counter and disappeared through the automatic doors.

"Must be some new girlfriend," said the manager to the trainee. "All right, who's next?"

"Professor Porter, may I have a word with you?" Sally Jensetter stood dressed in her parka, her hair tied in a ponytail. There was snow on her boots from the trip across campus.

Professor Porter was busy grading papers with a red pen. "Yes, Sally, what is it? As you can see, I'm in a hurry at the moment."

"This won't take long," she replied.

The professor swung his chair in the direction of the door. "I suppose you are here to ask about your grade on your paper.

Well, if I remember correctly, you should have spent more time on your bibliography—"

"No, sir," said Sally, "This isn't about my paper. It's about something else."

The professor nervously rubbed his forehead, "Sally, can't you see how busy I am? I don't mean to be short with you. But if you want an appointment, please contact the faculty secretary."

"Professor, I came here to ask you to pray with me."

"Pray? Whatever for?" said Porter. He took off his half glasses and stared at the young woman. "Don't tell me you're part of this so-called 'awakening' going on at Randolph. Please, Sally, I thought you had more common sense than to get caught up in this hysteria."

"Professor Porter, I'm facing a major decision. I thought maybe you would pray with me about it."

"What do you want to pray about?" His Eastern accent accentuated the sarcasm in his voice.

"I'm thinking of changing my major—to linguistics."

"Linguistics? Sally, whatever for? You are one of the most promising advisees I have. Why would you throw that away to start over in another discipline? It doesn't make any sense. None at all."

Sally hesitated. It was difficult for her to hear the criticism of a man she admired so much. "I'm thinking of joining a Bible translation missions organization when I graduate. I would like to help a tribal people put the New Testament in their own language."

The professor turned away in dismay. He took a deep breath and laid his pen down on his table. "I see. Bible translation. You wish to spend the rest of your life in the hills of Papua, New Guinea, or some such other forsaken place." He pursed his lips and stared at the ceiling for a moment. "Sally, please come in and sit down."

The young woman took off her parka and sat down across from the professor.

"Did it ever occur to you, Sally, that God gave you the talent to write?"

"Yes, I believe He did," she said.

"Then doesn't it stand to reason that you should develop your gift to the highest possible level of competence?"

"Yes."

"Then why in the world would you waste such a fine mind and promising future to follow such a ridiculous romantic notion as translating obscure jungle languages? Such an enterprise is nothing more than religious colonialism and outdated paternalism. Listen to the anthropologists, such activity destroys the indigenous culture of a people."

"I don't consider giving people the Scriptures in their own language a waste of time, sir," Sally replied. "Nor do I see it as paternalism. True paternalism is having the knowledge of how to find God and deciding some people don't deserve to know." Sally was surprised at the courage she was showing. "My decision may mean the difference between heaven and hell for them. As for the scholarly challenge, some languages in South America contain as many as twenty-five different tense forms. I consider that a worthy intellectual challenge."

"My, my, we are on our soapbox today, aren't we, Miss Jensetter? Surely you don't subscribe to the theory that the Almighty is in the business of casting obscure tribal peoples into perdition?" Porter's disapproval was hard on Sally, but she stood her ground.

"Yesterday at chapel, I was reminded of a verse I had learned as a little girl. Jesus said, 'Go therefore and make disciples of all the nations.' That's why I'm here, I think that's what God wants me to do."

The professor leaned forward, and in a rational, calm voice said, "Sally, there's a religious fervor sweeping this campus that frankly, I consider dangerous. It is bypassing all reason and inflaming sensate instincts in the adolescent population here. It will pass but not before it does a great deal of damage, I fear." The professor held out his hands as if to appeal to her.

"Please, don't make lifelong decisions based on emotions and the passions of the moment. Think about it. Let's talk about 'your call' again next fall when things have calmed down. Hopefully, people will once again be rational."

"Professor, couldn't you at least pray with me?"

"I shall remember you during my time of meditation, Miss Jensetter, will that do?"

"Thank you, sir," said Sally. "I'll be going now." Sally got up and put her coat back on.

"Remember, young lady, you have a gift. Don't squander it."

"I don't believe God will allow me to do that, Professor," she said. "Thank you for your time."

"I have you scheduled for the procedure on Wednesday, Jill," said Ellen, the clinic counselor. She handed Karin a preprinted list of instructions. "Please read these and be very careful to follow them."

"Does it take long?" said Karin.

"You'll be here at the clinic for less than five hours if all goes well," said Ellen. "And of course, there's no reason why it shouldn't," she quickly added. Karin looked anxious. "Jill, four thousand women undergo the same procedure every day in America. The risks involved are inconsequential."

"Could . . . could anything go wrong?"

"Highly unlikely, my dear," she said. "It's far more dangerous for you to continue this pregnancy given your present level of emotional distress."

"I just hope—I hope I'm doing the right thing," said Karin.

"Jill, the right thing is whatever you decide the right thing to do is. You do what you have to do. Remember?"

A faint smile appeared on Karin's face.

"Now be here by 8:00 A.M. for some blood work. The doctor will see you at 9:30. We'll watch you for a few hours and you should be out by two o'clock. Have you arranged for someone to drive you home?"

"Yes, of course," Karin lied, but she knew she still had two days to find someone.

Ellen stood up. "Jill, let me congratulate you on your academic scholarship. That's magnificent. I expect to hear great things from you in the world of English literature."

"Thank you, Ellen," said Karin. "You've really been a help."

Ellen reached out to hug Karin, "We're sisters, right?"

"Right." Karin smiled, took the list of pre-procedural instructions, and put them in her purse. She knew the way out of the clinic by now. But somehow, in the maze of hallways, she happened to take a wrong turn. Before she knew it, she had stumbled into the area just outside the room where post-procedure patients were kept.

She glanced through the windows and spotted the young teenage girl she had seen during her first visit. The girl was dressed in a hospital robe and was being led around by two nurses. She looked pale and unsure of her steps.

That's me in just a few days, thought Karin. The young girl turned away from the nurses and vomited all over the floor. The nurses held her as she bent over.

When she leaned back up, the young girl's eyes met Karin's for just a moment. Her eyes seemed to plead with Karin to take her out of this place. Karin broke off the stare and walked away. Now it was Karin's turn to feel sick.

With Maggie in the hospital, Dustin Jacob's parents had offered to take Eric in until his parents returned. After the incident in gym class, the gang members had let Eric go home without bothering him. In a way, that frightened Eric even more. He knew that the gangs never forget.

The next day, Friday, Eric had pretended to be sick and talked Dustin's parents into letting him stay home from school. On Saturday, Eric and Dustin went to the mall and bought trading cards. Sunday, the day of the blizzard, Dustin's parents had slept in, and the boys spent most of the day trying to keep the driveway clear of snowdrifts. So, Eric had no idea of the dramatic events that had occurred that day at First Community.

It was now Monday morning, and the two boys were eating breakfast in the kitchen.

"I'm not going to school today, Dustin," said Eric in a low voice.

"Look, man, you can't keep running. Besides, they didn't bother you on Thursday, did they? Just pay them their money when you get to school, and it will be no big deal," said Dustin.

"I'm not paying them anything," said Eric.

Dustin looked around to make sure his mom wasn't listening. "Are you out of your mind, man?"

"I don't owe them anything, and if I don't go to school, I don't have to pay," said Eric.

"What? You gonna stay away from school the rest of your life?" Dustin looked disgusted. "Warner, think, man. They know where you live. Sooner or later they'll find you. At least this way you've bought yourself some protection."

"I might borrow some protection," said Eric.

"From who?"

"From you, that's who."

Dustin realized what Eric was thinking. "I've thought it over, Warner. It's no use. What's one gun? You think they have just one? How many of them could you take out before they blew your head off?"

"That's why I'm staying away from school, meathead," said Eric. "My best chance of staying alive is if I don't go to school. Period. Who's to say they won't blow me away even if I do pay them off?"

"Eric, man, this is getting pretty serious. Maybe it's time to tell our parents what's going down at school."

The mention of the word *parents* made Eric's face turned hard. "Oh sure, Dustin. What should I do? Take a plane to Hawaii this afternoon? Drop in on the Love Boat? I'm not sure my dad would do something even if he knew."

"You don't know for sure, Eric."

The two boys finished breakfast and headed for the door.

"See ya, Mom," yelled Dustin.

"Be good, boys," came a voice from upstairs.

Eric and Dustin walked together to the corner of the block. Eric started down the street away from the bus stop.

"Where you going, Eric? It's cold out here."

"I've got my plans," he said.

"Please, Eric. The school is gonna find out you skipped. Just pay the money and forget about it."

"Who are you? My mom or something? I'm not going back to school. Get it?"

"Yeah, I get it."

The two boys walked off in separate directions.

The phone in the Warner's stateroom rang with a jarring sound. Steven sat up in bed and rubbed his eyes. The clock on the desk read four A.M.

"Who in the world would call us at this time of the night?" he mumbled. He stumbled over to the wall and picked it up. "Yes?"

"Is this Mr. Warner?"

"You got him."

"Mr. Warner, we have a shore-to-ship call. Will you please stand by?"

"For heaven's sake," sighed Steven, "can't a man be left alone in the middle of the Pacific? Yeah, I'll wait."

By now Brenda was awake. "Steven, what is it?"

Steven heard a faint and garbled voice say, "Steven? Steven? Can you hear me?"

"Dr. Ray?" said Steven. His voice suddenly changed to a much more pleasant tone.

"Is it something with the kids?" Brenda asked. She got up and stood by the phone. Then she remembered the telegram she had torn up a few days ago. *Oh, no,* she thought, *this is where the vacation ends.*

"Steven, praise the Lord, I got hold of you at last," said Dr. Ray. His voice sounded distant. "By my calculations, it must be seven A.M. where you are."

"Uh, no, Dr. Ray, actually it's four A.M. I think we're probably a couple of time zones farther west than you guessed. But that doesn't matter. How are things? I heard on the news you had quite a snowstorm in Chicago."

"My heavens, Steven, we certainly did. But I didn't mean to go and wake you up in the middle of the night. Shall I call you back?"

"No, no, Dr. Ray. It's good to hear from you. How are things at the church?"

Brenda bit her fingernail.

"Didn't you get my telegram a few days ago, Steven?"

"What telegram?"

"Oh my," said Dr. Ray, "I should have called sooner. Son, let me just assure you that everything is in God's hands. I really believe that."

"What are you talking about, Dr. Ray?"

"I reckon I'd better start from the beginning," he said. Dr. Ray proceeded to tell Steven the whole story: how he discovered the petition, Melissa's admission that there was an organized effort to remove him as pastor, the rumors about his nervous breakdown, and all the other sorry details.

Steven listened impassively, but by the look on his face Brenda knew his anger was building inside. Steven always spoke in a lower voice when he was angry or upset, at least at first.

"Dr. Ray, who's involved in this?" he said quietly.

"I can't say with certainty, son, but I have reason to believe Mrs. Brewster may be at the center of it."

"I see. Dr. Ray, would you please arrange a special conference call with the deacons in two hours? I don't care what it costs. The church can pay for it. It's time to deal with these people."

"Now just hold on a moment, my friend," said Dr. Ray. "That's not all the news."

"What? It gets worse?"

"No, Steven. Hallelujah, it gets better."

"How? What?"

"Steven, I'm delighted to tell you that this morning we had seven hundred people show up for a six A.M. prayer meeting."

"Dr. Ray, there must be a problem in the transmission. I thought I heard you say there were seven hundred people at a six A.M. prayer meeting. You mean seven people, right?"

"No, son, you heard me correctly. Glory to God, the auditorium was half full before the sun was up. Men and women on their way to work, children and teenagers headed to school—I've never seen anything like it in my life."

Steven sat down. "I don't . . . I don't understand. Why? Why were all those people there so early?"

Brenda moved closer to try to overhear Dr. Ray. The change in Steven's tone made her feel safer to get closer to him.

"Best as I can reckon," said Dr. Ray, "they were eager to meet with God."

Steven leaned back against the wall of the cabin.

"Steven? Steven, are you still there?"

"Yes, Dr. Ray, I'm still here."

"That's not all of it, Steven. Yesterday, the morning service ended at ten P.M."

"Dr. Ray, the line is giving us trouble again. I thought I heard you say ten P.M. You mean ten A.M., don't you?" Steven could hear the gentle laughter of his friend, even over the garbled phone line.

"No, Steven, you heard me correctly." He went on to describe the details of the unusual response of the congregation. The more he heard, the more Steven couldn't believe it.

From what little of the conversation Brenda could catch, she knew something out of the ordinary had happened at church.

Steven motioned for her to give him a pen. On ship's stationery he scratched a simple sentence. He pushed it toward Brenda. "A revival has broken out at church."

Brenda looked at Steven with astonishment. He raised his eyebrows and nodded. She leaned closer to the receiver to try again to pick up the rest of what Dr. Ray had to say.

"Is Maggie going to be okay?" Steven asked.

Brenda's face tensed up. "Steven, what's happened to Maggie and Eric?" she asked. Steven motioned for her to sit down.

"Steven, I want to know about Maggie and Eric," she demanded.

"Can you hold on a moment, Dr. Ray? I need to relay the news to Brenda about Maggie Dunlop." He covered the receiver with his hand, and said, "Maggie's been hurt and is in the hospital, but Eric's fine."

"What?" she asked. "What happened?"

"She was hit by a car and broke her arm. Eric is staying with Dustin's parents. He wasn't with her when it happened."

"Oh, no," said Brenda, "not Maggie."

"I'll tell you the rest when I hang up," said Steven. He turned back to the phone.

"Okay, Dr. Ray, go ahead," said Steven. Brenda bowed her head as she listened. The two men talked for another ten minutes. As the conversation came to a close, Brenda heard Steven say, "I'll need to talk this over with my wife, Dr. Ray. But look for us in two days. We'll catch a flight back just as soon as we reach Hawaii."

Steven glanced toward Brenda. With tears in her eyes she nodded her approval.

"Good," continued Steven. "We'll book the first plane back to Chicago. I'll call you from the islands when we have a flight number."

Steven and Dr. Ray talked another thirty seconds or so and then Steven hung up.

Both were quiet.

"Steven, I have something to tell you," said Brenda. "I have something to confess."

Remarkably, Steven said little in response to Brenda's admission that she tore up the telegram. His emotions were now beyond that. His mind was already back in Chicago.

"Steven, what did Dr. Ray say was going on at church?" she said, hoping to change the subject.

"Near as I can tell, Brenda, all hell has broken loose." Then a smile appeared on his face, which surprised her. "But according to Dr. Ray, so has all heaven."

SEVENTEEN

Ingrid drew her white mink coat around her and pushed through the door of a small office. It was located on a dingy back street near the Chicago loop. The sign on the window read, "CheckMate Investigative Services." A bell rattled as she opened the door.

"What can I do for you, ma'am?" said a man in a leather waistcoat with a short crew cut.

"I'd like to talk with a private detective," said Ingrid. "A good one."

"You've come to the right place."

Ingrid cast a disdainful glance at the bare office furniture. The office was poorly lit. A variety of yellowed certificates hung in frames on the wall. A briefcase used to conceal video equipment lay open on the next desk. "I'm in a hurry. I don't want to explain anything to anyone. I just want results. And I'm willing to pay for them."

The man casually sat up and took his feet off his desk. "I suppose you could start with me," he said. He held out his hand. "Jason Fulton is the name."

Ingrid ignored the handshake and sat down in a wooden chair near his desk. "Let's get down to business, Mr. Fulton. Your 'agency' came highly recommended to me." She looked around again at the poorly furnished room. "Although I'm starting to doubt my source. You're supposed to be highly efficient in providing incriminating evidence. Am I correct?" said Ingrid.

"We do our job, if that's what you mean," said Fulton.

"I have a little assignment for you. But I want absolutely no one on earth to know about it. Do you understand?"

"So, the old man is running around on you, huh?" smiled the detective.

"Shut up, Mr. Fulton, and just listen to what I have to say."

"Look, lady, no dame walks in here and tells me to shut up. You can kindly take—"

"Before you say something you regret, Mr. Fulton, perhaps this may interest you," she said. Ingrid spread out five crisp one-thousand-dollar bills on his desk.

Fulton reached over and picked one of the bills up. He held it up to the light.

"It's real, don't worry about that," said Ingrid. "And if you do your job right, there's more where that came from." She smiled at him, and Fulton's dour face slowly began to melt.

"Okay, lady, maybe I should hear what you have in mind," he said.

"It's really rather simple," she said. Ingrid reached in her purse and pulled out a small padded envelope. She opened it and dumped out several microcassette tapes on his desk.

"What are those?" said Fulton.

"They're tapes I made of discussions I had with a certain 'counselor' of mine. It took me several weeks to get what I needed. I want you to take them and edit them so that they clearly suggest we were more than just friends. Do you understand my point, Mr. Fulton?"

The two smiled at each other. The private detective reached over and picked up one of the microcassette tapes. "Have you two been fooling around?" he said. "Or is this some sort of blackmail scheme?"

"It's none of your business. What is your business is redoing these tapes so that not even the best lab in the country can discover they've been edited. They may be eventually used in court."

"You're talking a lot of money for a job like this, lady." He turned the tape over and over with his hands. "This type of work doesn't come cheap."

"I told you before, I don't care how much it costs. I just want it done right, understand? Or do I need to take my money somewhere else?" She reached over and picked up her bills. Fulton started to protect them, but then he let go. They weren't his, not yet.

"You realize what you're asking me to do is—"

"Illegal?" said Ingrid. "Why don't you let me worry about that?" She reached in her purse and produced another bill. She laid it down on the desk.

"Maybe we can do business," he said. He reached for the bill and Ingrid grabbed it back. "Not so fast. Do we have an agreement or don't we?"

The detective glared at Ingrid for about fifteen seconds. "You know, I don't like you," he said. "I really don't. But for ten thousand down, and another five when I deliver the tapes, I could change my mind."

"I need the new tapes right away," said Ingrid.

"What's right away? Things like this can take time," said the detective.

"I don't have time!" shouted Ingrid. She stood up and pointed her finger in the detective's face. "I'll be back in two days. They had better be ready or else."

"Or else what?" sneered Fulton.

"Or else the little conversation we've just had may find its way to the state attorney's office." She reached into her purse and pulled out a gold cigarette case. She snapped it open for him to inspect. Hidden inside was a microcassette recorder with a tape in it.

"So that's how you caught him," said Fulton.

"I'm no expert in these matters, of course," she said. "But it would seem to me that if this tape got mailed to the right person . . . well, you could very easily lose your license. Maybe even get a trip downstate."

"Why you—"

"No, no, no, Mr. Fulton," said Ingrid, waving her finger at him. "Remember? We're business partners."

"Get out of here," snarled Fulton.

Ingrid got up, snapped the gold cigarette case shut, and put it back in her purse. She smiled at the detective. "I assume that means my tapes will be ready two days from now?"

The man turned away in disgust. He refused to look at her.

"Be back here by one P.M. on Wednesday," he growled.

"Very good, Mr. Fulton. My sources were correct. You are a professional."

Fulton turned toward her and pointed his finger, "Look, lady, just don't push me too far, got it? You bring all the money on Wednesday, or you don't get the tapes. Got it?"

"Agreed, Mr. Fulton," said Ingrid. "Oh, one more thing I'd like you to do for me." She reached inside her coat and produced a business-sized envelope and handed it to the private detective.

He opened it. It contained five sheets of standard-sized stationery. He glanced through them and said, "So what are these for? They look like personal letters signed by some 'Reverend Warner.'"

"He's not a priest, he's a pastor. And if you notice, they are each written in longhand. His handwriting. And his signature appears at the bottom," said Ingrid.

"So?" said Fulton.

"So, I want you or one of your friends to study his handwriting and then compose some letters. The kind of letters one lover writes to another. The kind your clients pay you to discover."

"Lady, first you're talking blackmail, now it's forgery."

"As if that bothers you," said Ingrid.

The private detective got up and paced back and forth. He stood and looked outside, rubbing his neck. "So is lover boy supposedly sending these letters to you?"

"Yes."

"Then I need a name. What's your name?"

"Just use 'Tiffany.' That will do." She closed her purse and wrapped the mink around her once again. "Any questions?"

"None," he grunted.

She smiled and walked out the door.

As soon as she was gone he kicked over a wastebasket. He looked back at the table and saw that she had left the money. He went over and counted the bills a second time. Little by little, his angry expression turned to one of satisfaction. He put the money in his wallet, got up, grabbed his overcoat, and headed out the door to the alley.

"I'm telling you, Chief, I have a credible witness willing to testify against Warner and several others here," said Joe McDonald into the telephone.

McDonald held a hand against his ear to drown out the noise of cars on the street nearby. He had stopped to use a pay phone outside a convenience store in Covington Park.

"That's right, boss. He claims he was at meetings where the money-laundering was discussed. He's an expert in these matters. He has already given me a sworn deposition. I'm having it transcribed now."

McDonald listened carefully and nodded. "From what I'm told Warner is in Hawaii at the moment. Let's hold off seizing the church files until he returns. He might just bolt if he gets word from his people on the inside."

The two men talked another five minutes. "I'll have everything I need for the D.A.'s office here in Chicago by the end of the month. Warner will be back by then."

McDonald rubbed his hands to keep them warm. "Yeah, I'm sure the witness will hold, Chief. Okay. I'll stay in touch."

McDonald hung up with a smug sense of satisfaction. Through the years he had been involved in several fruitless investigations. It felt good to win one.

It was late in the afternoon on Monday when Ray Havens knocked on the door of an elderly couple from First Community. Despite the incredible events at church, he had decided to maintain his daily schedule of visiting the sick. With the help of a map drawn by Ron Simmons, he had found his way to this day's first appointment with little trouble.

The shades were drawn halfway in the living room window of this modest bungalow on the near north side of Chicago. A long wheelchair ramp angled its way up to the front door.

Dr. Ray rang the bell and patiently waited. An elderly woman in her eighties peered out the side window, then opened the door for him.

"Good afternoon, Mrs. Crosby, I'm Pastor Ray Havens from First Community Church. I called earlier," he said. He took off his hat in a show of respect.

"Why, of course. Dr. Havens, won't you please come in? Albert has been so excited to hear you were coming," she said. The home had the faint smell of medicine. The front room had an old wool carpet, a dark piano with faded pictures of children and grandchildren on top of it, and a 1950s-style sofa.

"He's not had a good day," whispered Mrs. Crosby. "Albert is in quite a bit of pain."

"I'm so sorry to hear that, Mrs. Crosby. I shall not stay long," said Dr. Ray.

Mrs. Crosby led him back to the family room which had become a makeshift hospital room. A large steel hospital bed was pushed up against the paneled wall. The head of the bed had been raised up to a thirty degree angle, and a frail, slightly jaundiced man shivered underneath a white thermal blanket.

When Dr. Ray entered the room, the man turned his large, hollow eyes toward him. "Is that you, Dr. Havens?" he said in a weak but cheerful voice.

"It is indeed, my good man," said Dr. Ray. "I stopped by to spend a few moments with you if I might."

"Praise the Lord. It is so good to meet you. We've heard so much about you." The man raised his gaunt arm and gestured for him to come closer. Dr. Havens walked over to the bed and took his hand.

"I hear something wonderful is going on at church," the man said in a raspy voice.

"Unlike anything I've ever seen in my life, Mr. Crosby," said Dr. Ray. "There were seven hundred people at this morning's prayer meeting. I do believe I've gotten a peek at heaven in the last few days, Mr. Crosby."

The man put his hands together in a victory clasp. "Then my prayers have been answered. I have been praying for a stirring to occur in our city every day for the last ten years." Dr. Ray could see tears in the old man's eyes. "I feel like Simeon in the New Testament," he said. "You remember him, Dr. Havens? The old man who met Joseph and Mary in the Temple when they brought Jesus to be dedicated."

"I do indeed, sir."

"When he saw our Savior's face he said, 'Lord, now You are letting Your servant depart in peace, according to Your word; for my eyes have seen Your salvation.'"

"You do know your Scriptures, Mr. Crosby," smiled Dr. Ray.

"I started memorizing the New Testament when I was five years old," said the old man. He started to cough, and it took several seconds for him to get his breathing back under control. He looked up at Dr. Ray with a pleading yet serene expression, "I don't have long, Dr. Havens," he said. "But I'm ready. Will you pray with me?"

Dr. Havens glanced over to Mrs. Crosby, who had large tears in her eyes. "Let's pray that God's will be done, Mr. Crosby," he said.

Dr. Ray took out his pocket Bible and read the Twenty-Third Psalm to Mr. Crosby and his wife. Then the three of them prayed, holding hands. When they were done, Mrs. Crosby and Dr. Ray walked back into the living room, out of earshot of her husband.

"Thank you so much for coming," she said. "I can't bear to watch Albert suffer like this much longer." She reached for a handkerchief in her sweater pocket and covered her eyes.

"You love him very much, don't you?" said Dr. Ray. She didn't look up but nodded her head. "He's a dear man of God, Mrs. Crosby. I can tell that by just the few things he said."

She wiped her eyes and looked again at Dr. Ray, "I'm so worried, Dr. Havens. The government won't pay for any more of his medicine. He's reached his quota for expenditures on this form of cancer. Our savings are just about gone. I don't know what I'm going to do," she said.

Dr. Ray understood her predicament. The national health insurance plan had gone badly into debt after just a few years of operation. To cut costs, the president and Congress had set limits on how much could be spent on terminal illnesses. Government policy was now quietly designed to encourage the elderly and terminally ill to sign living wills and refuse further treatment.

"I shall bring your need to the attention of the church leadership," said Dr. Ray. "We have a special fund for such situations. Let me assure you, Mrs. Crosby, we won't stand by and watch your husband denied of the medical care he needs."

"Thank you, thank you so much," said the woman. She grasped his hand and shook it hard. Then she turned and walked away so the preacher would not see her cry.

"It's good to welcome you back this evening," said Dr. Ray from the pulpit. It was seven o'clock and the crowd in front of him was estimated in excess of fifteen hundred people. Because the sanctuary only seated fourteen hundred, ushers had been forced to set up chairs in the gymnasium. Closed-circuit monitors carried a live video feed to the overflow crowd.

"Let's begin this evening with singing, shall we?" Dr. Ray said. The song leader stepped to the microphone and led the congregation in half an hour of communal music. Like the day before, the singing had a certain harmony, an effortless unity about it that was hard to describe.

Dr. Havens stayed seated. The pianist continued to play softly. Finally, he stepped up to the microphone and said gently, "I do believe some of you would like the opportunity to describe what God has done in your life during the past twenty-four hours. I just ask that you be brief, be sensitive to the issue of confidentiality, and let what you say be for the good of all."

Immediately, a housewife got up and moved to a microphone. Several mikes had been set up in the aisles and balcony to give members easy access.

"I have, for the last twelve years of my marriage, tried to change my husband, Timothy," she said. "Yesterday, God showed me why that was wrong. I've been trying to make him over in my image when the Bible clearly says he was made in the image of God. Yesterday at this altar, I gave Timothy back to God. And for the first time in our marriage, I now feel free to love him. That's all I wanted to say." Timothy stepped out of his pew and met his wife in the aisle. The couple hugged once, then twice, and then sat down together.

Next in line was a teenage boy with long hair on one side of his head who wore torn jeans and a large earring. He put one hand in a pocket and then the other. He leaned at an angle and looked down. Finally he spoke. "If anyone had told me a week ago I'd be standing here talking to you in church, you know, I would have assumed they were high or something."

The audience sat in supportive silence. "As some of you know, my mom left home when I was just five years old. For a long while it was just my dad and me. Things were pretty cool between us. But then he married my stepmom. Well, I kind of resented that and decided to get back at him. So my stepmom and me, we would get in fights. Bad ones. A couple of times I threatened to run away. Once I did.

"Yesterday something really weird happened to me. Actually, something good. My dad made me go to church with him and my stepmom. I didn't like that. I tried to block out Dr. Ray here. But I couldn't."

The boy smiled nervously. "When I was here praying, God showed me my hate. It wasn't my stepmom I hated, but . . ."

The teenager's voice broke. He struggled for control. "But it was my real mom that I hated." He covered his eyes with his hands. "So . . . so what God told me was . . . your mom may have left you . . . but I never will." He started to cry openly.

Dr. Havens walked over to the boy and put an arm around him. "Go ahead, son," he whispered, "we're all with you."

The boy, in a halting voice, finished his statement, "So last night, I went home and I told my stepmom, 'I know you tried to be a friend to me . . . but I never let you. Will you give me another chance?'" The pitch of the teenager's voice got higher. "She said, 'Ben, I forgive you, and I love you.' And I said, 'Mom, I love you too.' I just want to thank Jesus for taking away my hate. Even toward my real mom."

Dr. Havens leaned over to the microphone and said, "I think this boy has real courage, what do you all think?" The audience, as one person, rose to their feet in a deafening applause. The boy was instantly surrounded on stage by other teenagers from the church.

The evening went on in similar fashion for almost two hours. Dr. Havens was able to deliver a short message on the importance of balance in the Christian life, and then prepared to announce the benediction.

"I have been asked to announce that we have scheduled another six A.M. prayer meeting. And a noon service tomorrow. The deacons have also scheduled a worship service tomorrow evening. Again, the church will remain open tonight as long as any of you wish to stay."

With a look of serenity and a gleam of love in his eyes, Dr. Havens raised his right hand and prayed, "Now to Him who is able to keep you from stumbling, and to present you faultless before the presence of His glory with exceeding joy, to God our Savior, Who alone is wise, be glory and majesty, dominion and power, both now and forever. Amen."

With the service concluded, a group of people filed out of the sanctuary while an even larger group chose to stay on. Dr. Havens and Beulah had just put their coats on.

"Dr. Havens, I'm afraid we have a problem," a man said. It was Henry Styles, a custodian dressed in gray work clothes and black boots. His salt-and-pepper hair was combed straight back. His cheeks were red, and his quivering hands suggested his years of battling alcoholism had taken their toll.

Henry was dry now, but seldom, if ever, attended services.

"What is it, Mr. Styles?" Dr. Ray said.

"It's our trash can, sir," he replied. "Someone left something in there. In fact, a lot of something."

"Like what, Henry?" Dr. Ray said.

"I think you should come and see this for yourself."

Dr. Ray and Beulah looked at each other, then agreed to go with Henry. "Please, Henry, you lead the way." He led them out back to a large, metal trash can.

Outside, the church custodian took Dr. Ray aside, "No offense, Pastor Havens, but I don't think it would be proper for your wife to see what's in there."

"Beulah, would you wait here a moment for us, dear?" said Dr. Ray.

"Certainly, darling," said Beulah. She turned away and wrapped her arms around herself trying to keep warm in the frigid night air.

The janitor lifted the cover off and let it crash against the side with a loud bang. "This here can is plumb full of these," said the janitor. He reached in and grabbed a handful of magazines, which could best be characterized as both soft and hard-core pornography. A number of video cassettes were also thrown in there, most unmarked.

"A few of these magazines here still have mailing address labels on them."

He held one of the less objectionable ones up for Dr. Ray to see the address label. "I'm sorry to say so, Pastor, but this is the name of a man who goes to this church," said the janitor.

Dr. Ray glanced only momentarily at the magazine the janitor held, then turned away. "Thank you, Henry. You can close the lid now. I think I know what's happened here. Can you empty this can into the dumpster?"

"Yes, sir, I believe I can."

"Then please do so. Then, tomorrow morning, I want you to call the garbage company and arrange for a special pick-up. And Henry—"

"Yes, sir?"

"I can trust you that the name of the man will not be circulated in the church?"

"I understand, Reverend."

"I knew I could depend on you." He slapped the old custodian on the back. "Henry, this trash can here represents very good news."

The elderly janitor furrowed his eyebrows. "I'm not sure I'm following you, Reverend."

"Henry, I suspect that even as we speak, a family and marriage in this church have been given a second chance."

"This stuff ain't no good for a marriage, is it?"

"No, my good man, it isn't." Henry closed the lid and the two men walked back toward Beulah.

"Dr. Havens, I'm not a religious person," said the janitor. "Fact is, I'm not the church-goin' type. So maybe you can explain something to me. Just what in the world is going on inside this place? Why won't these folks go home?"

"Henry, why don't you join Beulah and me for a cup of coffee? It's my treat."

"I'm sorry, sir, but I've got to buff the floors tonight," he replied.

"That can wait. It's time Beulah and I got to know you better. I know a wonderful pie shop close to here. It will be on company time," said Dr. Ray.

"If you say so, sir."

"Indeed, I do."

As they walked back into the church, the outside floodlight cast a special brilliance across the parking lot. If an ordinary blacktop, covered with snow and parked cars, could somehow reflect the light of purity and forgiveness, this one did.

On the campus of Randolph University, the spiritual awakening began its third day. Because the number of students in the chapel had now surpassed half the student body, a decision had been made to cancel classes.

An angry Professor Porter confronted Dean Prestwick in the hallway just outside the faculty lounge. "So, it's just as I suspected," he said. "We have capitulated the cause of higher education in favor of sawdust trail revival meetings."

"Professor, really . . ."

"I must inform you, Dean, that I am now circulating a petition calling for a full faculty meeting to vote on your decision to cancel classes."

The dean remained calm. "If it's your intention to draw me into an argument with you, Dr. Porter, I'm afraid I'm going to disappoint you. My decision to cancel classes is based simply on the fact we now have neither enough students nor enough faculty to hold classes. I have not altered reality on campus, I have only recognized it for what it is."

"Then punish them!" said the professor. "Give the students zeros. Fire those faculty members who will not fulfill their academic duties. You have that authority."

"Dr. Porter, I would think it would be obvious to everyone that there is an Authority at work on this campus far greater than what I possess. Why don't you come with me to the chapel and see for yourself what's occurred?"

Porter turned away. "I wouldn't be caught dead in that assembly of religious hysterics."

"If I may ask, what is it you are afraid of, Dr. Porter?"

"Afraid? I'm not frightened of anything. Except for the academic reputation of this institution. It may already be damaged beyond repair. When other colleges learn we've canceled classes so students can weep at an altar rail, we may never again be seen as a credible institution of higher learning."

"Are you aware, Dr. Porter, as I'm certain you must be, that virtually all of the Ivy League schools experienced spiritual renewals at some time in their history? Harvard, Yale, Brown, and others were founded to educate young people in spiritual as well as academic matters. That has not hindered them from being taken seriously, has it?" She raised her brow in expectation of an answer.

The professor blinked at her.

"Dr. Porter—Hastings, if I may call you by your first name," said the dean, "please come to chapel with me. Just for an hour. You're an open-minded individual. Shouldn't you examine the evidence before reaching a conclusion?"

Porter knew he had been checkmated. "Out of deference to our professional relationship, I will acquiesce, Dean Prestwick. But one hour only, no more."

"Shall we be going, Hastings?"

The two walked off together in the direction of the chapel. The classrooms and offices they passed were empty.

As the dean and the reluctant professor entered the back door of the chapel, they found students seated on the hard tile floor. Several used their winter coats as cushions on the cold floor. They strained to hear what was being said over the speakers above the door.

"May we get through?" asked Dean Prestwick politely. The students quickly moved aside. The dean and Professor Porter were able to pick their way through the maze of legs and coats like soldiers delicately working their way across a minefield.

The dean opened the door to the main auditorium. A young female student usher met them, saying, "I'm sorry, there's no more room—" She took a second look at the two. "Oh. Dean Prestwick, Professor Porter. Excuse me. I'll ask someone to give up their seats."

She walked down the aisle and tapped two young women on the shoulder. The two students looked back and nodded, then picked up their books and left their seats.

"I've never seen the chapel this full outside of commencement," said Porter.

"Amazing, isn't it?" said the dean.

The young usher then signaled for them to come forward.

"Thank you so much," said the dean to the two young women who passed by them in the aisle.

"Our pleasure, Dean," one replied.

Once seated, they took off their coats and sat back to listen. The student body president stood at the podium.

"As some of you know," he said, "I have been accepted to Harvard Law School in the fall." The young man had good looks and a natural charisma about him. "I've always considered getting into a major law school the top priority of my life. But in the last few days I've had a chance to consider the goals, or should I say the gods, in my life. What I discovered is that most of them are . . . well, idols. Idols made of prestige, ego, and a desire for money." Professor Porter tapped his finger on the arm of his chair.

"Don't get me wrong—there's nothing wrong with law school. It's just that I'm supposedly a campus leader. Actually, I've been anything but that. I've followed exactly what our culture dictates success to be. I've dated women who feed my own ego. I've run with the right crowds to maintain my image. I've pursued a pre-law major, not out of any concern for justice or to help others, but because I wanted to make money, big time money, as soon as I got out of law school." Like a good attorney, he used his eyes to study the entire room.

"I've made all the right moves to be successful—except one. That's to stop and ask, *What does God call success?*" Professor Porter folded his hands and looked down.

"Would anyone consider a man that ended up with only twelve followers and who was executed as a criminal a success? No. Not in my value system. But He was. That's why if I do go on to law school, it will be for one purpose and one purpose only—to glorify Jesus Christ with all I say and do, for the rest of my life. If you want, I'm willing to give back the job of student body president. You deserve someone with a greater heart for God than what I've had."

With that said, he stepped away from the microphone and sat down.

Chaplain Vincent stood up. "I don't think we need to follow Robert's Rules of Order in this matter. Let's take a straw poll. Everyone in favor of Kevin remaining on as president, quietly stand." There was a rumble in the room as students stood to their feet. Dean Prestwick strained her head to look around the auditorium. Less than a dozen students had stayed seated.

"I think you have your answer, Kevin," said the chaplain. Kevin smiled and nodded his head.

The chaplain continued, "Dr. Simonson, chairman of our New Testament department, has asked if he could have a few moments to speak this morning." The chaplain invited the professor to the platform. A man in his late sixties, dressed in a somewhat rumpled brown suit, stood up and walked slowly toward the stage. With wire-rimmed glasses and a handkerchief in his pocket, he looked the part of an aging theologian.

"As many of you know," he said in a deep voice, "the last several years at Randolph have been marked by intense in-faculty debate over a number of issues. At times, this debate has become heated and even acrimonious.

"On one occasion, which still causes me great regret, I called another member of this faculty a coward and a failed scholar." The professor took off his glasses and folded them on the lectern. "This morning as I rose for my devotions, I tried to pray and found that I could not. It was as if the heavens were made of brass. I asked God what was wrong, and He directed me toward this portion of Scripture." The man opened a small New Testament retrieved from his suit pocket. "It is found in Matthew, chapter five, verses twenty-three and twenty-four: 'Therefore if you bring your gift to the altar, and there remember that your brother has something against you, leave your gift there before the altar, and go your way. First be reconciled to your brother, and then come and offer your gift.'"

He closed his Bible. "This is very difficult for me to say because I am a proud man by nature. But God has convicted me of a serious error in my life. Not a doctrinal heresy but a heresy of the heart. I used my theological convictions as an excuse to attack the character of another person. I failed to remember Jesus' ultimate command, 'You shall love your neighbor as yourself.'"

Professor Porter sat up in rapt attention.

"I'm quite afraid I loved my stature on this campus; I loved being right, more than I loved other people. That is a serious error. A sin."

The professor scanned the audience with his hand above his eyes. "Is Professor Melton here?" A man with a beard and flannel shirt stood as students turned their heads. "Professor, I apologize publicly for remarks I publicly made concerning you. They were petty, mean-spirited, and totally unbecoming a Christian scholar. I ask your forgiveness, as I ask the forgiveness of the students gathered here."

All of the audience turned toward Professor Melton to see his reaction. These two men had been at odds for decades.

The bearded professor moved to a microphone. "If I may, Dr. Simonson?" Dr. Simonson smiled and gestured for him to speak.

"Dr. Simonson, students, and fellow faculty, very few of you know what I am about to say. Some twenty-five years ago, when I was a student at Randolph, I took a theology course from Dr. Simonson. He gave me a *D* on a paper I turned in on why Christians should oppose military service. That day I made a vow to get back at him. After I finished my doctoral work, I was hired at Randolph. Part of my desire to return here was to purposely use my position to irritate, agitate, and undermine this professor at every turn.

"My generation taught me to distrust authority. I see now that distrust was part of a larger problem of not wanting to submit to God or anyone else. Dr. Simonson, my brother, you spoke before I did. But I fully intended to stand this morning and ask you to please forgive me for twenty-five years of living out a foolish vendetta."

"I don't believe what I'm seeing," whispered Dr. Porter to the dean. "Those two have been at each other's throats for years. They're on exact opposite ends of the political spectrum."

"It sounds to me as if they are rather the same in many respects," said Dean Prestwick.

Dr. Simonson walked over to the organist who was seated in the choir loft. He whispered something to the gentleman, and the two agreed. Dr. Simonson walked back to the microphone and said, "Friends and colleagues, you won't find this song in the hymn book, I can guarantee you. But I'd like to lead this entire audience in singing 'For He's a Jolly Good Fellow' in honor of my friend, Professor Melton. Will you join me?"

Laughter rocked the auditorium. One by one students and faculty members stood up. The organist, after an introduction filled with flourishes and runs, began the chorus. No one could remember louder singing in the chapel in years. It was almost deafening. The audience alternated between using Dr. Simonson's and Professor Melton's names in the song. The two men stood on the stage and directed the audience together. The celebration went on for over ten minutes.

Somewhere in the middle of the chorus, Hastings Porter rose to his feet and began singing with enthusiasm. Dean Prestwick looked over at Dr. Porter while he sang. When he realized he had been caught, a smile broke out on his face. *Why not?* he gestured to her. The two sang together as the joy of unity took hold of Randolph University.

"So you decided to take a little vacation of your own, is that right?" said José Martinez, the Roosevelt High School counselor. Seated in a chair in front of him was a depressed but defiant Eric Warner.

"You guessed it," said Eric.

"Why don't you tell me how you ended up getting arrested for truancy?" said Martinez.

"There's nothing to tell. I was hanging around a mall this afternoon. A security guard thought he saw me steal something from a record shop. So he called the police."

"Did you steal anything?"

"Nope." Eric played with a piece of paper he had made into a paper airplane. He refused to make eye contact with the guidance counselor.

"How can I reach your parents?"

"You can't."

"Where are they?" said Martinez. "It's not like your parents to leave you hanging out on the street."

"Well, that's what they did, Mr. Martinez. My great and famous father decided he needed a trip on the Love Boat, so he took off with my mom."

"And left you home alone?"

"Naw. There was a lady staying with me from church."

"Where's she?"

"In the hospital. She got hit by a car."

"You expect me to believe that?"

"It's the truth."

"Listen, Warner, I get all sorts of stories from students every day. Shoot me straight."

Eric remained silent. He tossed the plane, which looped once, then fell to the ground.

Martinez put his foot up on Eric's chair. "I'm serious, Eric. Time is running out for you."

Eric sat up, "I'm telling the truth. The woman who was supposed to watch me got hit by a car. That's why I'm staying with Dustin Jacobs. Call his parents if you don't believe me."

"Maybe I will," said Martinez. He picked up the phone, and looked at Eric to see his reaction. Eric didn't flinch. Martinez put the phone down. He thought for a moment, then pulled up a chair close to the boy. "Eric, this isn't making any sense.

You've never been in trouble before. This isn't like you. Tell me what's going on? Drugs? A girlfriend?"

Eric bit his lip and looked up at the counselor. He wanted to tell him the whole truth, but he couldn't. The risks were too high. "There's nothing to tell, okay?"

"Eric, please, I want to help."

The boy folded his arms and stared straight ahead.

"Okay, son, have it your way. I'll assume you're telling me the truth. But I'm going to have to call Dustin's dad and have him come in and sign for you. I'll meet with the principal today to decide what we do with you. My guess is in-school suspension."

"Big deal," mumbled Eric.

Martinez got Dustin's father's work number off his computer and called him. He agreed to pick up Eric, but he couldn't come until five. Martinez thanked him and hung up.

"I'm sending you to the detention room," said Martinez. "You can wait there for Mr. Jacobs." He walked over to Eric and pointed his finger in his face, "If you're not in school tomorrow morning by 7:50, I may have you suspended for the week. Understand?"

"Can I go to my locker now?" said Eric. Eric had left money in his locker and wanted to pick it up.

Martinez looked at his watch. "You have exactly three minutes to get back here. Got it? Three minutes."

"Got it," said Eric. He got up and walked out of the office. Out in the hallway he checked both directions before he ventured out. It was clear. He moved quickly up the stairs to his locker. He whirled the dial on it and jerked it opened.

He took a step back in horror.

A plastic doll hung inside with a rope around its neck. A note was taped to it. "You roughed up one of our men, Warner. The price is now doubled. Pay up tomorrow or die. Any questions?"

Eric slammed the locker shut and leaned against it. *I need to get back to the office,* he thought. He took off down the hallway. Several times he thought he heard someone following him. He didn't dare look. He raced down the stairs two at a time. He bolted around the corner and into the principal's office. *I made it,* he thought. *I'm safe in here. I'll just stay here until Dustin's father comes.*

"Back in school, Warner?" said a voice. Eric glanced over, and his heart nearly stopped. Seated on the sofa next to him was a member of the Squires.

"Thanks for the ride, Jane. Can you be back here about two o'clock to pick me up?" said Karin.

"Sure," said Jane Phelps, a freshman who lived on Karin's floor. "But are you sure you don't want me to stay with you?"

"No, they're just doing routine tests today. They may take a biopsy, but that's all," said Karin. Karin had lied to the freshman girl about the purpose of the visit to the Women's Health Clinic. She had convinced Jane that a Pap smear had come back with mixed results. She told the girl she had been referred to the clinic because of their OB/GYN specialists.

"If you need me any sooner, please call. I'll be glad to come right over," said Jane.

"Thanks, I appreciate it," said Karin. She slammed the door on the white BMW Jane's father had given her. Karin walked toward the clinic. Several protesters were gathered across the street. Karin quickly turned away from them.

"Please don't do it," a woman shouted. "Unborn women have rights too."

"God loves you and your baby," said another.

"It's murder," shouted another.

Karin pretended not to hear them. Two employees quickly walked out of the building and took her by either arm and escorted her into the clinic.

"I'm sorry you had to run that gauntlet," said one of the women. "Someday it will be illegal for those fanatics to be there. They're a menace."

Karin said very little. She was escorted to a desk where she had to sign a number of consent papers. Next she went to an examination room where mandatory tests and blood work were done. Finally, Karin was led to a procedure room where she lay down on a hospital bed. Her heart beat quickly, but her emotions were numb.

I have no choice, she told herself. *I tried, but no one would listen. This isn't my fault. It's Jeff's. I wouldn't be doing this if he would have married me.*

Next to her lay a woman who looked the same age as she. "Are you a little scared?" she asked Karin. "I've never done anything like this before."

"Not really," said Karin, who worked hard not to show her own fear. "I'm just trying not to think about it."

"My priest says this is a sin," said the girl. "Do you think it is? What happens if something goes wrong and I die?"

"Shh," said Karin. "Don't say that. You'll be just fine." Karin knew they both needed to get their minds off what was about to happen. So, she started to softly sing a song she had learned as a little girl, in Girl Scouts. Soon the other girl joined in. They both felt better.

"We're ready for you now."

The two women stopped singing and saw a nurse who had a mask over her face standing in front of them. Karin's fingers went numb. Her heart began to race.

The nurse started toward her. "I'm not sure," Karin said to her. "I'm not sure I'm ready yet."

"Just relax, sweetheart. I'm not here for you," said the nurse. "I'm here for Alyce."

The other woman managed a trembling smile at Karin. The nurse pushed up the gates on either side of the bed.

"Good-bye," she said. "Thanks."

"You'll be fine," said Karin.

The woman glanced at Karin one more time before she went through the double doors. She gave her the Girl Scout sign.

When she had gone, Karin let out an audible sigh of relief. She closed her eyes and tried to think about other things.

Her solitude was soon interrupted by a male voice, "Excuse me, Karin. I'm here to take your blood pressure."

She looked up to see a young male nurse smiling at her. He wrapped the black pressure band around her left arm and pumped it up. He held a stethoscope to her arm as he released the pressure on the cuff.

"Looking good, Karin," said the male nurse.

"You called me Karin. My name is Jill," said Karin. "Why did you call me Karin?"

The male nurse looked at her and smiled. "Did I call you Karin? I apologize."

"How do you know who I am?" demanded Karin. He ignored her question and continued to record her vital signs on a chart. "Excuse me," said Karin in a louder voice, "why did you call me Karin?"

"Her name will be Katherine," said the nurse without looking up.

"Whose name will be Katherine?" said Karin. This was starting to get weird and Karin didn't like it.

"The little girl that's going to bring much joy to a couple. They've prayed for a child for years." The nurse put down the chart and looked directly at Karin. "You're in good hands. I've got to go and check on others."

He patted her on the hand, then left the room.

Karin began to perspire. *How did he know who I was?* she thought. *And Katherine. What's this about Katherine?*

"Nurse!" Karin shouted. "Nurse! I want to see a nurse." Despite her call, no one responded. Finally, two minutes later, another nurse appeared through the doors dressed in green scrubs.

"Ready, sweetheart?" she said.

"I want the name of that male nurse who just took my blood pressure," said Karin.

"You just relax, Jill," said the female nurse.

"No, you don't understand. I want the name of the man who just took my blood pressure. I have the right to know that."

"Look, Jill, you're upset. You just close your eyes, and we'll take care of you."

"But there was a man here who knew my name," said Karin.

"Jill, we all know your name. Now just settle down, honey."

Back at the dormitory, Jane Phelps trudged up the steps to the women's dormitory. She happened to meet Sally Jensetter coming down the steps from the other direction.

"Hope everything turns out all right with Karin," said Jane.

"Me too," said Sally. Sally took another step or two, then stopped. "What did you just say, Jane?"

"I said I hope everything turns out all right with Karin, your roommate." Jane couldn't understand the confusion in Sally's eyes. "I gave her a ride to the Women's Health Clinic this morning," said Jane. "I'm going to pick her up at two."

"You what?" said Sally. "You drove her to an abortion clinic?"

"Come on, Sally, that's not why Karin is there. She's just getting a Pap smear and possibly a biopsy. I sure hope it all turns out fine."

Sally leaned back against the rail. "Oh, Jane! What time did you take her there?"

Now Jane began to looked concerned. "About seven-thirty this morning. She told me you would have taken her but that you had a test. Right?"

"Oh, no," Sally said again. Without saying good-bye, Sally bolted back up the stairs into the dormitory.

EIGHTEEN

I guess this is good-bye," said Steven Warner. He reached out and shook the hand of his friend, Ted. The two were dressed in loud Hawaiian shirts and khaki trousers. They stood on the dock at the island of Oahu.

"Hey, it was a terrific cruise," said Ted. "Thanks for running with me."

"Thanks for listening. I have no idea whether or not I have a job when I get home."

"It really doesn't matter, Steven," said Ted. "Remember what we decided over dinner last night? We work to live, we don't live to work."

"It's got me worried, Ted."

"About what?"

Steven looked down and scratched the dock with his toe. "I don't know, it's like . . . being rejected by people who really count in your life."

"Like your dad?"

"Yeah, like my dad," said Steven.

"Are you feeling bad about yourself again?" Ted asked.

"I guess so."

"Let me encourage you. When someone does something that leaves you feeling lousy about who you are, quietly say to yourself, 'Hey, fella, I give you back your shame. It's yours, not mine, and I don't believe in stealing.'"

Steven laughed, "I like that. I'm going to remember that."

"Remember that when you talk to your dad, Steven," said Ted. "He doesn't mean to hurt you, he just isn't in touch with his own feelings of shame."

"Hey, it's been fun," said Steven. "Call me if you come through Chicago. Brenda and I would love to have you two stay at our home."

"Likewise, if you come our direction," said Ted. Ted put his sunglasses back on, picked up his bags, smiled, and headed toward the taxi.

"Nice guy," Steven said to himself.

He turned and looked for Brenda. She stood in the welcome line where islanders dressed in traditional Hawaiian garb placed rings of flowers around the necks of tourists.

"Oh, Steven, isn't it just paradise?" she sighed.

"Too bad we have to leave today," he said.

Brenda looked away, "I know, Steven. I just can't believe how close we came to actually having a vacation. Then, for all this to happen." Her voice quivered.

Steven reached out and lifted her chin up so that she looked directly into his eyes, "I'll make it up to you, Belinda. I promise I will. You'll see."

She managed a smile.

"Come on, Brenda, we've got a plane to catch. If all goes well we could be back in Chicago by eleven A.M. their time." Steven picked up their bags and headed toward the curb to hail a taxi.

Brenda took one last glance at the beautiful ocean and the breaking surf.

Steven was four steps ahead of her when he turned around and noticed she wasn't following him.

A doctor stood at Karin's bedside wearing surgery blue scrubs and latex gloves. Karin looked around the room. Two nurses stood next to him. One was assigned to a surgical tray with a green napkin draped over it. It contained gleaming stainless steel sterilized surgical equipment.

"Doctor, can I ask you a question?" said Karin.

"Let's get this going," the doctor said.

"Doctor, I said I wanted to ask you a question," insisted Karin.

The doctor picked up a hypodermic needle.

"Wait . . . wait a minute," said Karin.

"What is it, Jill?" said the nurse. "Dr. Herman is in a hurry this morning. He has several other patients waiting."

"I just wanted to ask a simple question," said Karin in a weak voice.

"Ask it," said the doctor in a gruff voice.

"Is it too early to tell if it's a boy or a girl?"

"That's not important this morning, Jill. Getting you safely through this procedure is," said the doctor. He looked up at the nurse and nodded. She reached over with the needle.

"Just breathe deeply, Jill, and you'll feel very little pain," said the doctor. The local anesthetic was now injected.

Karin sat up, "I want an answer to my question! Could I find out if my baby is a boy or a girl?" she said.

"Quiet her down, nurse," said the doctor.

"I want an answer!" demanded Karin. "I won't allow you to continue unless you tell me."

Karin could see the dismayed pairs of eyes looking at one another. She decided to up the ante. "My dad is a lawyer, and if you don't tell me the answer, I'll have him sue every one of you."

The doctor looked over his mask at the others and shook his head in disgust. "Let's hold off a minute."

The doctor leaned over and stared down at Karin. "We'd have to perform some expensive tests to answer your question. There's no point. You're terminating this pregnancy. Now may we please get on with this? You've already put me fifteen minutes behind schedule." He nodded to the nurses again.

"This will take only a moment," said the doctor.

Her name is Katherine, thought Karin. *He said her name will be Katherine. Oh my word, I'm killing Katherine.*

"No!" she shouted. "I don't want this."

"Calm her down!" demanded the doctor. Two nurses held Karin down. "Stop!" cried Karin.

Several minutes later the doctor emerged from the procedure room and tore off his latex gloves. "Katherine," he grumbled. He cursed again and went to scrub.

Local newspapers in Covington Park were now aware of the events taking place at the church and at the college. They decided to send one of their free-lance reporters, Christie McNair, and her photographer, Shaqmar Phillips, to investigate. It was almost noon when their car approached the church.

"There it is now," said Christie. She pointed to the large steeple and colonial brick structure that rose above the tree line.

"Look at that, Christie," said Shaqmar. "The lot is full of cars. There isn't a parking space for blocks." As the two circled the church in a decade-old compact car, Shaqmar scrambled to get a lens on his camera. "I think I should get a picture of this."

The two finally pulled to a stop in the parking lot of an Italian restaurant three blocks from the church.

"You have everything you need?" asked Christie.

"Think so," said Shaqmar. He looked like an alpine mountain climber with all his packs and equipment dangling from his belt. He checked over each bag and was satisfied. "Let's go."

It was Wednesday. Because light faded early in the afternoon, Christie and Shaqmar had decided to take in the lunch service to get the best possible shots.

"I can't believe I get assignments like this," said Christie as she got out of the car. "What's next? Aliens appear at Founders' Day Parade?"

"I hear you," said Shaqmar. "I've got no time for religion either. All it is is folks talking one way and living another and the preacher making a good living off everybody."

"We never went to church growing up," said Christie. "Sunday was our day for sleeping in. But I tried it a few times in college. That's when I decided the world would be a better place if I did something about social justice. Who needs bad music and irrelevant sermons?"

"Ain't that the truth?" said Shaqmar. "My sociology prof used to say, 'Eleven A.M. is the most segregated hour in America.' As far as I can see, nothing's changed."

"Let's just get this over with and get out of here," said Christie. "I've got to take my cat to the vet."

The two walked around the corner and stopped. Not only was the parking lot full, but there were buses from other churches parked in the streets. She studied the names painted on the sides. "Shaqmar, look."

"What is it?" he answered. His eye was focused through the lens of his camera.

"The buses that are here. Look at that one. Second Baptist Church of Elroy. There's another—Rock of Gilead. Isn't that in the city somewhere?"

The photographer put down his camera. He looked at the address painted on the side of the blue vehicle. "Yeah, that's the south side of Chicago."

As the two got closer to the church, Christie stopped again. "Listen, do you hear that? It sounds like a band or something."

Shaqmar grinned. "It's gospel music, Christie. That's a black choir singing in there. I may need to get a picture of this." Shaqmar reached down to his nylon bag and unzipped a pocket. He took out a special film for indoor lighting and loaded a second camera. As they walked up to the front door, they could both hear the words of the old black spiritual, "Ride On, King Jesus."

Christie pulled the door open. The sound of a large choir hit them like a shock wave. An usher in a casual sweater stepped up to greet them. "Good afternoon. Phil Crawford's my name. Glad you could join us."

"Uh, I'm Christie McNair," said the reporter, extending her hand. "This is Shaqmar Phillips. We're from the *Daily Examiner*."

Phil shook their hands. "We've got overflow seating in the gymnasium," he said. "I'm sorry, but the fire marshal won't allow any more people in the sanctuary."

"When did this get started today?" asked Christie. She took out her pad and scribbled a few notes.

"Oh, this is our noon prayer service," said Phil.

"Is this your choir?" asked Christie.

"No, we called and asked several other churches to join us. You can see for yourself what the response was."

"Do you mind if we take some pictures?" asked Shaqmar. "We won't sit down and we'll leave quickly so we don't violate the fire marshal's orders."

"Fine, just as long as you don't disrupt the service," said Phil. "Could I ask that you not use the flash?"

Christie looked at Shaqmar; he nodded okay.

"Thanks," said Phil. "God bless both of you."

"Yeah, sure," mumbled Christie. She motioned for Shaqmar to follow her into the sanctuary.

They managed to work their way up to the sanctuary door, "Ready Shaqmar? Here we go," said Christie. She opened the door, squeezed through those standing at the back, and managed to break free into an open space.

Up on the stage stood a 100-voice black choir, swaying from side to side. The piano and the organ blended together in an energizing, exulting sound that had almost everyone on his or her feet.

"I don't believe what I'm seeing," said Shaqmar. "Black folks and white folks together like this."

"This doesn't happen often in churches, does it?" said Christie.

"Not in this city," said the photographer as he aimed and clicked his camera. He took several more shots, then put his bags down and took out his tripod. Christie furiously took notes. The choir reached a crescendo, then ended with a majestic final measure. The congregation roared their approval.

A black minister walked up to the microphone. "Thank you so much. Praise the Lord. This has been a very special day for God's people. Amen?"

"Amen," came the response in unison.

"We wish to thank Dr. Havens and the others here at First Community for their invitation to sing this afternoon. Our soloist, Danata Wilson, has one more song we'd like to leave you with. She's going to sing for us 'There is a Balm in Gilead.'"

"I always liked that song," whispered Shaqmar.

"It's a spiritual that dates back to the days of slavery," said the black pastor. "It speaks of the healing God offered our people when they were in bondage. It also speaks to the healing God can bring to our lives through Christ today. If you know it, join Danata on the second verse."

A young black woman stepped forward. Her eyes seemed to sparkle with the light of heaven. As the piano played the soft introduction, she bowed her head. Then quietly, almost inaudibly, with a pure soprano voice she began to sing, "There is a balm in Gilead, to heal the sin-sick soul. Oh, there is a balm in Gilead, to make the wounded whole."

The song, like a well-aimed arrow, pierced Christie's heart. It produced a feeling she had never experienced before. It was warmth, it was love, it was magnetism. *What's going on?* she thought. The sense of love continued to surround her. Tears began to form in her eyes. She found herself encountering a force she could not comprehend. It was conviction and attraction, flowing together at the same time.

What in the world is happening to me? She looked over at Shaqmar. He stood motionless as well.

When the soloist reached the second verse, Christie was coming undone on the inside. It was as if she could see herself as she really was for the first time in her life. The pride. The arrogance. The fear. The anger. It was all suddenly in front of her. The old Christie was at war with this new, powerful, loving Presence.

Without saying a word, she put her notebook back in her pocket and started up the side aisle.

"Christie!" said Shaqmar in a loud whisper. "Where in the world are you going?" He looked around, then decided to follow her. She walked up to the altar and stood. Tears flowed freely down each cheek.

The eyes of the entire congregation were now on Christie. The soloist looked down at her and smiled as she continued to sing. One of the women from the choir stepped out of the loft and made her way down to the reporter. She put her arm around Christie and hugged her as the journalist cried.

Shaqmar stood about ten feet away, bewildered by what had overcome Christie. The black pastor walked down and extended his hand to the photographer.

At that moment, the Presence reached out to Shaqmar too. It was as if a Person, unseen, a Father, was standing there, welcoming him into His arms. Shaqmar started to tremble. He wanted to run. But where could he go?

The pastor looked the photographer in the eye. "Brother, it's time you come home," he said.

His sense of his need for God became so intense he thought he would cry out. Shaqmar dropped to his knees right there. The pastor knelt beside him and prayed. In less than five minutes it was over. They stood up, hugged one another, and then turned toward the congregation.

"Please, everyone join us in the chorus," said the pastor. The entire auditorium reverberated with the beautiful, melodic chorus of the old spiritual.

Later that afternoon, Christie found a pay phone in the basement of the church. She called her newspaper and asked for the managing editor. "Adam, this is Christie. I've got the story. But seriously, I need to tell you in person."

■

That same morning, the door burst open at the CheckMate Detective Agency. Ingrid was wearing a red leather jacket, with pants and boots to match.

Fulton was seated at his desk. He looked at his watch and smiled. "You're right on time, Ingrid."

"What makes you think my name is Ingrid?"

"Oh, Mrs. Gustav, you're forgetting my trade," said Fulton. He stood up and stretched, revealing a shoulder holster under his coat. "Do you think I would risk my job and reputation for just any dame that comes charging in here, demanding I cooperate in forgery and blackmail?" He pointed to a chair, "Have a seat, Mrs. Gustav."

"Save the etiquette," snapped Ingrid. "Just give me the tapes and the letters. I've got the money. Do you have what you're supposed to?"

"Oh, we'll get around to them in a minute or two," he said. "Before we discuss that transaction, why don't you tell me why you're trying to destroy an innocent reverend?"

"It's none of your business."

"My sources tell me the man is clean. Married. Two children. Nice guy. What's he done to you?"

Ingrid glared at Fulton. "Shut up and give me the tapes!"

"You shut up, lady. I've just about had it with you."

Anger and hatred began to growl within Ingrid. In an unearthly voice she threatened, "You don't know who you are dealing with, Fulton! I could drop you dead right here on the spot. I could send you into an agony that would make death welcome. If you don't turn over those tapes and letters to me at this very moment—" She walked around and pointed her finger in his face. "Do you understand, you fool?"

Fulton suddenly felt pain in his stomach. His face became ashen and he felt nauseated. An overwhelming sense of fear gripped him. "Lady, what's going on here, what are you doing to me? What are you, some kind of witch or something?" His pain grew worse.

He scrambled around the table and picked up the satchel and threw it at her. "Get out!" he begged. "Get out of here right now! Keep your money. I don't want it. Do you hear me? Keep it and just get outta here."

Ingrid stood with her arms crossed and laughed. "So, Mr. Fulton, you've decided to quit asking questions. That's good. Because if you ask any more, I'll come back."

She threw an envelope with money on the table. "Here, take this. After all, I am an honest woman." She picked up the satchel and walked out the door.

Fulton leaned over a waste can and became violently sick.

NINETEEN

"Rachel, I'm calling to say I want my name taken off that petition," said Diane, an older woman who had been part of her small group.

"Diane, you can't be serious. How many times have we talked about this? Warner is a false shepherd. You aren't going to defend a false shepherd, are you?"

"I listened to you, Rachel. For a long time I believed you, especially when you said it was nothing personal. But I'm not buying that any longer. God showed me this week how wrong it is for me to be involved in this. I want you to take my signature off the petition, now."

"Diane, please. You're not getting caught up in all this hype at church, are you? Just wait. It will be over—"

"I wouldn't call what I've experienced 'hype,' Rachel. For the first time in years, Christ seems real to me again. But I had to come face-to-face with the fact that I was wrong to be involved with this plan of yours. It's wrong, Rachel. What you're doing is all wrong."

"Who are you to tell me that I'm wrong and you're right, Diane?"

"Rachel, why do you hate the pastor? Is it because your dad was a minister?"

"Leave my dad out of this. Besides, I don't hate him. He's just a . . . misguided individual. He's full of pride and arrogance. He puts himself before other people—"

"Rachel, you almost had me convinced. But last Sunday I went home and searched my Bible. I didn't go to sleep until five o'clock the next morning. You know what I found?"

"What?" said Rachel in a condescending voice.

"I found that the Bible teaches we are to honor those in authority over us. Those who teach and lead us are worthy of double honor. Double honor, Rachel. Yet, all our group did was tear down, criticize, and ridicule the pastor. It was sin, Rachel. S-i-n."

"You're telling me I'm in sin?"

"According to what God's Word says, yes, Rachel, you are." There was a long silence. Diane could feel Rachel's anger.

"Diane, I didn't want to say this to you, but you've forced the issue. Remember when you told the group your husband had no money sense? That he forced you into chapter eleven bankruptcy?"

"Yes," she replied with hesitation. "I'm sorry I said that too. I had no business saying things like that about my husband to the group."

"I'm afraid that incident clearly proves you two haven't been walking close to the Lord."

"What do you mean?"

"Wasn't your husband nominated to serve on the missions committee for next year?"

"Yes. So?"

"I wonder if the nominating committee is aware of that information?"

There was a long silence on the phone. "Rachel Brewster, you wouldn't—"

"I, of course, would prefer to keep such information confidential. If you leave your name on the petition to remove Warner . . ."

"That's blackmail, Rachel."

"Really, Diane? You're the one who told the entire group the most intimate details of your marriage. If you didn't want others to know, why did you tell us?"

"I can't believe you're doing this to me."

"I knew you'd come to your senses and see that this is for the good of everyone."

"I wish I had seen you for who you really are long ago," said Diane. "I should have walked out the first day you and the others started criticizing Pastor Warner. I'm sorry I didn't. I really am sorry. You're evil. You're actually evil."

"Oh, shut up, Diane," said Rachel. "You're no one to be judging me. You keep this up and I might also find a convenient time to remember your little confession to the group. Remember? That you once had feelings for another man at work."

"You wouldn't! That was ten years ago—before I was a Christian."

"Diane, does your husband know about that little incident?"

"Rachel, God has changed my life these last few days. I pity you. I pity you because you have taken the name of God and used it to try and destroy His church. I tremble for you, Rachel. The Lord isn't going to allow this to go on forever."

"If I were you I'd stop this very moment, Diane. If you try to stop me, I'll ruin your life and marriage so badly that you'll never recover from it."

"Lord Jesus, have mercy on this woman," Diane began to pray. "Show her the deception and hate in her life before—"

The sound of Diane praying pushed Rachel over the edge. "I said shut up! You're nothing but a cheap—" Rachel called her the most degrading name one woman can call another. She slammed the receiver down. Rachel sat by the phone and trembled with anger. Her plan was coming apart, one person at a time. She knew the spiritual events taking place at church were dismantling her power base hour by hour. She had to act fast. She picked up the phone and speed-dialed a familiar number.

"Hello," said an older woman's voice.

"I don't have time to explain. So listen carefully. I'm calling for Warner's resignation tomorrow at church. After the noon service. We'll go with the names we have. If we wait any longer, it may be too late."

"Rachel, do you think it will work?"

"It's got to. We're so close. We're so very close. Are you with me?"

"I'm with you."

"All right. We meet tomorrow at eleven A.M. at the church. Gather the others. Bring whatever men you can find. We'll finalize our strategy then."

"Rachel?"

"Yes?"

"God bless you, dear."

"God bless you too."

Rachel was about to hang up the receiver when a man's hand reached from behind and clicked it down. "I think that's enough of that." Rachel shrieked. She turned around and there stood Ed behind her with an angry look on his face.

"Ed! You almost scared me to death."

"I don't feel like apologizing in this case," he said.

"Why didn't you tell me you were coming home early? You frightened me out of my wits—" Rachel got up and pushed him out of the way.

"I'm home because the heating system failed at work. They closed the building early." Ed wouldn't let her get away, "I want to know once and for all, what's going on? What's this about Pastor Warner? And while you're at it, why don't you tell me who this Ingrid is, or should I say, Tiffany Evans? Why did she threaten you the other night?"

Rachel attempted to push past her husband, "It's my business, not yours."

Ed again stepped in front of her. "Not so fast, Rachel. I won't be put off this time. I'm not leaving until I get the full story." Ed grabbed her arm.

"Let go of me, Ed," said Rachel, her teeth clenched. "I'm warning you. I'll . . . I'll call the police and tell them you're abusing me."

Ed walked over to the phone, took the receiver off the wall, and handed it to her. "Go ahead, call, Rachel." Rachel glared at her husband. She reached out for the receiver, then changed her mind. She hung it up.

"If you are part of a scheme to get rid of our pastor, I think I have a right to know about it," said Ed.

Rachel turned around and pointed at her husband. "Oh, you do, do you? I'm the one who's had to make all the hard decisions. You're nothing but a spineless wimp."

Ed flinched ever so slightly. "Stop it, Rachel."

"Why? Because it's true?"

"I said stop it, Rachel."

"You've been a poor excuse for a lover since the day I met you."

"Rachel, no."

"I married you because I pitied you. So just go back to your miserable little job at your miserable little company and let me worry about what's right and wrong at church."

Ed tried to put his arms around her, "Rachel, I wasn't trying to be mean. I'm just worried. That woman threatened you the other night. You are getting phone calls at all hours of the day and night. It just has to stop."

Rachel pointed her finger at him, "Ed, I'll only say this once. You stay out of this. If you try and interfere, I'll leave you."

"Rachel, you don't mean that."

"I mean exactly that, Ed. You interfere with my plans and I'll divorce you. I'll take the house, our savings, the car—everything."

Rachel pushed him away. She walked out of the kitchen.

"Rachel, come back, please. Come back so we can talk about this."

Rachel was already gone and headed up the stairs. Ed heard a door slam. He knew what that meant. He was locked out. It would be hours, or even days, before she would speak to him again.

He sat for a long while by himself at the table. An hour later, he put on his coat and walked out the door. If he was going to eat supper, it would be alone.

Sally Jensetter stood in the cold morning air and frantically pushed the intercom button outside the door of the Women's Health Clinic.

"May I help you?" came the voice.

"I need to come in, right away," said Sally.

"Do you have an appointment?" replied the voice.

"I don't need an appointment. I want in. My best friend is inside. She needs me."

"Oh, so you're here to pick up a patient?" said the voice. "Which patient are you here with?"

"Karin Warner. Now will you please let me in?" Sally glanced back toward the street where Jane Phelps had the car idling. Exhaust from the engine formed a huge cloud behind the trunk in the cold, icy, afternoon air.

"I'm looking at the list," said the receptionist. "We don't have a Karin Warner registered here. Are you sure you have the right clinic?"

"Listen, Karin was dropped off here this morning. The woman who dropped her off is with me. Now can I please come in? I'm freezing out here."

"Our policy does not allow anyone in without an appointment."

"It's ten degrees out here," said Sally in a harsh voice. There was a pause.

"I really shouldn't do this . . ."

Sally heard a buzzer sound, and she pulled the door open. She was met by a stern-faced security guard who opened the inner door for her. She glanced around the waiting room for Karin, but she was nowhere to be found.

"Please sign in at the desk," the guard said.

"Why, thank you," smiled Sally. She was relieved to just have gotten in.

"May I help you?" said the receptionist at the end of the lobby. Sally pulled off her scarf and gloves and walked over to her.

"I'm here to pick up Karin Warner. W-a-r-n-e-r," said Sally. The woman glanced down her charts and then turned toward her computer. She entered the name, and the receptionist used a pencil to go down the list of names.

"I'm sorry, but you must be mistaken. There's no Karin Warner at this clinic. Perhaps you should try our Northside Clinic."

I know she's here, Sally thought. *I can feel it, and I'm not leaving without her.* Out of the corner of her eyes she spotted a door with a sign: "No Admittance. Authorized Personnel Only." *That's it*, thought Sally.

She turned back to the woman at the desk, "Maybe you're right. Maybe I do have the wrong address. Sorry to bother you." She noticed that the security guard never took his eyes off her.

"I hope you have better luck elsewhere," said the woman. She went back to entering data into her computer.

Sally walked away from the desk in the direction of the door. She stopped to put on her gloves and scarf and rebutton her coat. *I've got to find a way to get through that door*, she thought. The radio on the belt of the security guard crackled, and the man quickly grabbed it and answered the call. Someone in the parking lot couldn't get her car started. He put on his coat and went out through the front door.

Good. That takes care of Rambo, thought Sally. *Now if I can just get through that door*. Sally opened her purse and pretended to be concerned about her makeup. *Come on, come on. Someone open it.*

A minute later, the door opened and a technician in a white coat carrying a package for a courier emerged. *It's now or never*, thought Sally. She casually walked in the direction of the technician and right past him. Just before the door closed shut, Sally bolted for it. She managed to grab the edge of the door with her fingernails and keep it from closing. She pulled the door open and disappeared through it.

The receptionist happened to look up. "Hey!" she said. "You're not allowed in there!" But Sally had been too quick. She closed the metal door behind her and scanned the hallway for any sign of Karin. In front of her, a small sign with an arrow pointing down the hallway said, "Recovery Room."

Oh, Lord, she prayed, *I hope it's not too late.*

Sally checked for more clinic personnel, then headed down the corridor. She could hear the door open behind her from the lobby. "She went in there," said a woman's voice.

Sally ran down the short hallway and pushed through the double doors in front of her. All at once she found herself in a large room with at least four steel hospital beds positioned against different walls.

"What are you doing in here?" said a nurse who wore a paper hair net and blue scrubs.

Sally ignored her question and went from bed to bed.

"I must ask you to leave at once," said the nurse.

Sally's eyes were frantic with worry. In the third bed, she finally spotted her roommate's familiar blonde hair.

"Karin!" she cried.

Two security men burst through the door behind her. The receptionist was right behind them.

"That's her!" the woman shouted. The two private security guards rushed Sally and grabbed her by either arm.

Half asleep, Karin opened her eyes, "Sally? Sally, is that you?"

"It's me, Karin. Karin, please tell me you didn't."

"Come on, lady, you're outta here," said the beefy security guard.

"Wait," mumbled Karin. "Leave her alone."

"She's not allowed in here," said the guard.

"Let go of me!" said Sally. She jerked her arms to free herself.

"Do you know this woman?" said the nurse to Karin.

"Yes, she's my roommate from college. Please, let her go."

"I'm here to pick her up," said Sally, turning her defiant face toward the bigger guard. "Now let go of me."

The guards looked at one another, then at the head nurse.

"What's your name?" said the nurse.

"I'm Sally Jensetter."

"Sally, are you aware it's a crime to unlawfully enter a clinic and disrupt the personnel?"

"I'm just here to pick up my roommate."

The nursed turned toward Karin, "Jill, is this the person you designated to pick you up today?"

"Jill?" said Sally. "That's not Jill! That's Karin Warner. My roommate."

"Let her stay," pleaded Karin.

Sally leaned toward Karin, "Please, Karin, you didn't . . . tell me you didn't."

"She needs to go back to the lobby," said the head nurse. "And see that she stays there until Ms. Davis is ready to go home."

"Sure thing," said the guard. The two men walked Sally toward the door.

"I won't leave you, Karin," cried Sally. The guards escorted her back to the lobby.

"You stay right here," said Rambo, pointing to a chair.

"Yeah, yeah," said Sally.

"Bobby, you stay with her," said the other guard. "Just to make sure."

"My pleasure," said Rambo.

Ten minutes later, Sally sat up. "Jane," she said out loud. "I forgot about Jane." She looked at her watch. *Oh, no.* She turned to the security guard. "Our driver is still waiting for us outside."

"So?" said the guard. He popped another Dorito in his mouth and chewed it in a disinterested fashion.

"Could someone go out and tell her to go home until we call her?"

"Like who?" said the guard.

"Like you."

The heavy-set guard with a moustache and receding hairline just smiled at her. "Ma'am, what makes you think I'm going to leave you in here all by yourself so you can go barging back where you don't belong?" Another Dorito disappeared into his mouth.

"You have my word. I'll stay right here. Just go and tell my driver to go home."

"Why don't you tell her yourself?"

"Because, I don't trust you either. If I go outside, you might not let me back in."

"Wouldn't that be a shame?" he said. "Looks like we're both stuck here, doesn't it, ma'am?"

"Could you at least ask someone else to go outside and tell her?" asked Sally. He stopped his chewing for a moment.

"Reckon I can do that," he said. He pulled his radio off his belt and held it up to his mouth, "Phil, this is Danny. There's a lady parked out front . . ." He stopped and turned to Sally, "What kind of car is she driving?"

"A white BMW."

"Phil, find the lady out front in a white BMW. Tell her she's supposed to go home and wait for a call from . . ."

"From Sally."

"From Sally," the guard repeated.

"Roger, Danny," came the response.

"There you go," said the guard. He took a second look at Sally and changed expressions. "As long as we're stuck here for a while, my name is Danny. Danny McDawson. You wouldn't be interested in going out for a drink after work, would you?"

In a quiet, determined voice she said, "No, thank you."

"You don't need to get so edgy about it. Just trying to be friendly." He picked up a magazine.

Sally got up and moved two seats away from him.

"Hey, where you going?" Rambo said.

"Nowhere," she replied.

It was almost twelve-thirty when a nurse finally entered the waiting area, asking, "Is there a Sally Jensetter here?"

"That's me," said Sally. She sat up and put down her magazine.

"Ms. Davis is ready to be released now. Please come with me." Sally felt relieved to be going home. But then, a second thought hit her: *Karin has had an abortion. What am I going to say to her?*

In less than sixty seconds the large door opened, and Karin emerged in a wheelchair. She was dressed in a flannel shirt and jeans, a blanket draped across her lap. Sally had never seen Karin's face so pale and drained. Her hair was matted down and her eyes looked swollen.

She looks awful, Sally thought. *But I need to keep it together for Karin's sake.* She walked over and hugged Karin. "So how's my roomie?" she said in the most cheerful voice she could muster.

"Thanks for coming, Sally," said Karin weakly.

"Please read these instructions and call the clinic if any of these symptoms appear," said the nurse. "Will you please sign here, Jill?" She thrust a clipboard at Karin. Karin didn't even bother to read the form. She weakly scribbled her signature and handed it back.

"Is the car ready?" said the nurse.

The car. I forgot about a car. "Uh, our driver had to leave," said Sally. "Would you call a taxi for us?"

The nurse looked put out. "You can call, there's a phone by the receptionist's desk."

"Sorry for the bother," said Karin.

"Hey, no problem," said Sally. "I'll be back in just a moment." Despite Sally's brave exterior, her heart was broken in two. *I should have seen this coming,* she thought to herself. *Maybe I could have stopped this from happening.*

She looked through the Yellow Pages and found cabs. She called one and then went back to sit down next to Karin. She pulled a chair up next to Karin and cradled her roommate's head on her shoulder. She could feel Karin shiver, so Sally wrapped her own coat around her.

Ten minutes later, the front door of the clinic opened, and a short burly man in a leather jacket appeared in the lobby. The stub of a cigar was in his mouth and he wore a Chicago Bears cap. "Taxi for Jensetter," he announced.

"That's us," said Sally. "Come on, Karin, we're going home." She got up and took hold of the handlebars of the wheelchair.

"I'll do that," said the nurse. "Regulations." She pushed Karin out into the arctic wind and up to the door of the taxi. Despite the cold temperatures a small contingent of pro-life demonstrators remained huddled in prayer across the street. Sally stopped to glance over at the group. She could see several young women, some with small children bundled up in strollers.

When Sally helped Karin to her feet, one of the young mothers across the road yelled out, "God still loves you."

"Get her in the car!" said the nurse. "She doesn't need this." Sally helped Karin in, and the nurse slammed the door shut behind them.

As the taxi pulled out of the lot, Karin looked out the window. For a moment her eyes caught those of one of the women in the group. *I know her*, thought Karin.

The familiar woman was the wife of the youth pastor at First Community Church. She stared at Karin. *No, it couldn't be*, the woman said to herself. *It just couldn't be.*

"Where to, ma'am?" said the cab driver without looking back. Sally was just so relieved to get Karin out of the clinic, she hadn't thought of where to take her next.

I can't take her back to the dorm in this condition, thought Sally. "Just keep driving, I'll tell you where in a minute," said Sally.

"You got it, lady," said the cab driver. He shook his head and punched the meter setting.

A minute later Sally had an idea. "Driver, take us to Covington Park."

"What's the address, ma'am?" said the cabbie. Sally gave him a street number.

"But that's my address," said Karin. "You can't take me home. I can't go home today, Sally." She sounded ready to cry.

"Calm down, Karin. There's nobody home, remember? Maggie's in the hospital. Eric is at a friend's. Your parents won't be back for ten days. I can take care of you there. Do you still have your key?"

Karin pointed toward her purse, "In there. With my car keys." Sally dug through Karin's purse and found the key ring.

"Is this it?"

"Yeah, the silver one."

"Don't worry, Karin. I'll take care of you until you're feeling better."

"I'm so tired. And I hurt. Sally? The cramps really hurt."

"Yeah?"

"Promise me one thing," said Karin.

"What's that?"

"Whatever happens, you won't tell my parents."

Sally hesitated, "I don't know, Karin."

"Sally, you must promise me." Karin leaned forward and looked like she might faint.

"Okay, I promise."

Karin leaned back against the door and closed her eyes. It took nearly twenty minutes to reach the Covington Park exit. At last, the orange and yellow cab pulled up in front of the Warner house.

The cab driver got out and opened the door. He looked in at the two young women. He took his cigar out of his mouth and pointed at Sally. "You take care of your friend there," he said. "She don't look so hot."

"I will," said Sally. She paid the driver and then took Karin by the arm up the sidewalk. No one had shoveled snow for days and the walk was treacherous. Sally reached the front door and dug in her pocket to find the key. She held Karin, who seemed to be sweating, with one arm and tried to fit the key in the lock with the other. Finally, the door swung open.

"I've got to use the bathroom," said Karin.

"Do you need my help?" asked Sally.

"No, I think I can make it." Sally helped her down the hallway to the main bathroom. She let go of Karin, and Karin went inside. *I'd better stay here*, thought Sally. *Karin looks so bad.*

Sally started to shiver. Someone had left the thermostat turned down. *This cold can't be good for Karin*, thought Sally. She went down the hallway and searched for the thermostat. She found it in the den. She cranked it up from 62 degrees to 72 degrees. *That's more like it.*

She walked back to the main bathroom, but the door was still closed. "Karin?" she said through the door. "Are you all right?" There was still no answer. Sally spoke louder. "Karin, I said are you okay?" Still no reply. "Karin, answer me." Sally started to push on the handle of the door. The door opened, then went thud against something on the floor.

Sally squeezed her head through the door and looked around, then down. "Karin!" she cried. Karin lay sprawled on the floor, her eyes out of focus. Sally managed to push her way in, then bent down next to her unconscious roommate.

She tried to revive her, without success. With adrenaline pounding through her body, she got up and ran into the kitchen. She grabbed the phone and punched in 9-1-1.

"Emergency dispatch," came the voice. "May I help you?"

"I—I need an ambulance—immediately! My friend is unconscious. She's on the floor of the bathroom—her eyes are half open—" Sally started to hyperventilate.

"Just calm down, ma'am. The address I have on the screen is 715 Foxfire Lane. Is that correct?"

"Yes. I think so. I'm not sure."

"I'm dispatching paramedics right now. Please stay on the line."

"But she looks awful. She looks so bad . . ." Sally started to cry uncontrollably.

"We'll be there in just a minute. Stay calm. Was she still breathing?"

"I think so."

The dispatcher continued to ask questions and type the information into the computer.

It was five P.M. when Dustin's father pulled up at Roosevelt High to pick up Eric.

"Please sign here," said Martinez, the school counselor.

Mr. Jacobs scratched his signature, "I'll make sure he gets home okay." He glanced over at Eric. Eric had his back turned to both of them.

"He's all yours," said José Martinez. "Just make sure he's back here by 7:50 tomorrow morning."

"Will do. His parents called this morning from Hawaii and said they'll be back in Chicago tomorrow."

"What did you say?" said Eric. He suddenly came to life.

"Your mom called from Hawaii. They're cutting their trip short. They should arrive sometime tomorrow morning. About eleven our time."

"If you see Dr. Warner, ask him to give me a call, will you, Mr. Jacobs?" said Martinez. He glanced over at Eric. "I need to discuss some attitude problems."

"Sure thing, Mr. Martinez. Sorry about the trouble." He looked down at Eric again with a scowl. "We had no idea he was skipping school. I'll personally escort him to your office tomorrow morning."

"Thank you, sir," said Martinez. The two men shook hands, and Dustin's dad zipped up his all-weather designer jacket. He turned to Eric, "Let's go, big fella, supper's waiting at home."

Eric said little as the two trudged through the snow to the parking lot. Mr. Jacobs bent over to unlock Eric's door when he noticed something on the side of his new car. He stepped back. "What?" Someone had used a car key to scratch the letter S on the door while he had been inside the building.

"I don't believe it!" said Mr. Jacobs. He got down and ran his finger over it and cursed under his breath. Eric swallowed hard. The sky was getting dark. Mr. Jacobs stood up and kicked the car tire with his foot. "That's a brand new Lexus. It's probably going to cost a thousand dollars to have this repainted. I am angry, really angry!"

He walked back and forth, looking at the scratch, then kicking the snow so it flew four or five feet down the sidewalk.

"Get in the car, Eric," he snapped. "If you hadn't pulled this stunt at school, this might not have happened to my car."

Eric slumped into the seat and pulled the door shut. Mr. Jacobs gunned the accelerator and the car sped away from the school.

Later that night after a quiet supper, Eric and Dustin went up to Dustin's room. They sat on the edge of their beds while loud stereo music pulsated through the room.

"You really got busted, man," said Dustin.

"You think your dad knows who did his car?" said Eric.

"I don't think so. He'll get over it. But it's you I'm worried about. That S was for you, man."

"I suppose, but I'm not worried," said Eric.

"You're not worried? What planet are you on?"

"I've got what you might call . . . a group protection policy," said Eric.

"What are you talking about?"

"I'm going to join the Excaliburs."

"The Excaliburs? You? You must be joking."

"Shows you how much you know. Who do you think I was with at the mall today when I got busted?"

"You were with the Excaliburs?"

. "That's right, idiot. We agreed that if I join, the Squires will think twice about messing with me." Eric lay down on his bed and put his hands behind his head. He looked over at Dustin, "And that, my friend, is what you call security."

"Warner, do you have any idea what it takes to join the Excalibur?"

"Maybe."

"I've heard you've got to hurt someone—bad."

"Dustin, you worry about you. I'll worry about me. Later, man." Eric reached over and put on his own headphones.

It was Thursday morning and the halls of Roosevelt High were filled with the typical noise and confusion of an average day.

"So, Eric, my man, ready for a little initiation?" said a teenager dressed in an athletic jacket, the name of a professional NFL team emblazoned on the back.

"Yeah, I'm ready," said Eric. Several Excalibur gang members stood around him. Dustin's dad had kept his word and had personally escorted Eric into the school office. But Eric had talked Mr. Martinez into letting him go to his first class early. Just as soon as he had gotten out of the office, he had headed to the prearranged meeting place of the Excalibur—the boys' bathroom on the first floor.

"How do we know a preacher's kid won't wimp out on us?" asked one of the gang members who wore a short haircut. "What if church boy here gets scared?"

"You don't need to worry about me," said Eric.

"Do you got the guts to belong to this gang?"

"You'll see," said Eric.

"So who's it going to be, Warner?" said the leader. "Which of the Squires do you take out?"

"I haven't made up my mind yet. But when I do, you'll be the first to know."

The bell rang and the group started to disperse. The leader intentionally bumped into Eric as he left, "Remember, Warner, you fail us just once . . ."

"And what about you? Can I depend on you if I get jumped by the Squires?"

"We protect our own," said the leader. "You'll see."

Eric was left standing by himself in the hallway. The first bell rang, but Eric still had one stop to make at Dustin's locker. He slung his dufflebag over his shoulder and headed upstairs. When he reached Dustin's locker, he took out a piece of paper with a combination written on it.

Dustin doesn't need this as much as I do, thought Eric. Eric reached inside the locker and felt around for Dustin's gun. It wasn't in the coat. He dug through his shelf. Not there either. He stooped down and searched the bottom of the locker. *It's gone. That worm took his gun home.* Eric slammed the door of the locker shut and collapsed against it.

"Don't you know the rules, Warner? You're not supposed to make noise in the hallway during classes."

Eric whirled around. A member of the Squires stood leaning against a locker. He started toward Eric. "Do you think you can just walk back into this school without first paying your dues?"

Eric ran the other direction, but he was stopped short when another member of the Squires stepped in front of him. "Where do you think you're going?" he said. The two gang members began closing in on Eric.

"It's payback time, Warner," said the other in a menacing voice. "You hurt one of ours, didn't you?"

The two had Eric trapped between them. His heart started to pound so hard he was certain it would burst. Like a cornered animal, he glanced with fright for any escape route he could find. There was none.

"It's time you learned a little lesson in respect," said one. Eric felt a steel object jam against his back.

It's a knife, he thought. *They're going to stab me.*

"Just keep walking and keep your mouth shut," said the Squire. "We're going outside to help you learn the proper way to treat a Squire."

"That's right," said the other. "And if you're still alive when we're finished, you won't make the same mistake a second time."

If I go outside, I'm a dead man, Eric thought. He knew he had only seconds to make his move. They pushed him in the direction of the stairs. When they turned the corner to go down, they ran into an adult coming up the stairs from the other direction.

"Mr. Martinez!" shouted Eric.

"Hey, what are you doing out of class, Warner?" said the counselor. "What are you all doing here?"

"Help! They've got a knife and they're going to kill me!" Eric shouted.

The two Squires grabbed Eric and jerked him up the stairs away from the counselor. Martinez charged up the stairs after them. "Hey, you two, what do you think you're doing!"

One of the gang members reached inside his shirt and produced a gun, "Get back you—" He shouted an obscenity at the counselor. Martinez froze in his tracks. "You make one move toward us and Warner's dead meat, got it?" shouted the gang member.

Martinez held up his hands in a defensive gesture. "Now look, boys. If this is a fight or something, we can work it out. Okay? Let's just calm down and find a way to deal with this. Put down the gun."

"Get out of our way before I blow your head off!" shouted one of the boys. For the first time Martinez looked genuinely frightened. The taller gang member, Derek, had Eric's arms pinned behind his back. The shorter gang member, Tony, kept the gun pointed at Martinez.

"Just move aside and you won't get hurt," said Tony. Martinez hesitated. "Now!" The boy cocked the trigger on the gun.

"Please don't let them take me, Mr. Martinez. Please!" pleaded Eric.

The counselor looked anguished but slowly backed away. "I have no choice but to do what they say, Eric. But I'm warning the both of you!" He pointed at the two gang members, "If anything happens to Eric, you both will pay."

"Get out of our way," snarled Tony. The counselor began to back down the stairs one step at a time. *There's a fire alarm at the bottom of each stairwell*, thought Martinez. *If I can just get to it, it might give me the distraction I need.*

The gang members were getting nervous. "Get out of here now!" shouted Tony. He pointed the gun at Martinez's face.

"Okay, boys, have it your way," said Martinez in a calm voice. He walked backwards carefully. When he reached the bottom step, he knew the fire alarm was just to his left, within his grasp. *Now!* he thought. He reached over and jerked the lever down. A deafening buzz erupted just above their heads. The startled boys looked up, and Martinez lunged for Tony. But the counselor tripped on the stairs and fell short. The boy aimed at Martinez and fired. Martinez dropped to the ground, holding his thigh. The sound of the gunshot could barely be heard above the loud blare of the fire alarm.

The doors to classes burst open and students and teachers poured out into the hallways. They assumed it was another fire drill. Martinez lay face down on the floor, writhing in pain.

"You idiot!" shouted Derek. "You shot him!"

"We've got to get out of here!" said Tony. They turned to run down the hallway but were met by a sea of students swarming toward the exit. Tony flashed the gun at the first group to reach him.

"He's got a gun!" a girl screamed. Another wave of teenagers passed by her and started down the stairs. They found Martinez in a pool of blood.

"Someone's been shot!" a student shouted. Bedlam broke loose as students who turned and ran back up the stairs collided with those trying to come down.

"Now's our chance!" yelled Tony. The boys ran down the stairs past Martinez, dragging Eric with them. "This way, Derek, let's go!" But the first floor was already a mass of humanity with students, teachers, and administrators pushing toward the doors.

"Not that way, fool, this way!" shouted Derek. He grabbed Eric and pulled him back up the stairs. The two dragged Eric down the hall and into the first empty classroom they found. Derek slammed the door behind him.

"Let's kill him and get out of here!" said Tony.

"Why did you have to go and shoot that teacher, man!" demanded Derek. "Now we're wanted, man. This place is going to be crawling with the boys in blue."

"So let's get rid of Warner and go out the window," said Tony.

"Yeah, right. And lose our only ticket out of here?"

The wail of sirens could now be heard in the distance. Derek ran over to the window and looked out. Red emergency vehicles were followed by blue and red lights racing down the street.

"The police!" said Derek. Police as well as fire units responded to fire alarms at school in Covington Park.

"Just shut up and let me think," said Tony. He pointed the gun at Eric. "Get down and stay down, or you're a dead man! Got it?"

Eric nodded his head, and sat down on the floor. Tony kept the gun aimed at him.

"I say we grab Warner and walk outta here," said Tony. "If anyone tries to stop us, we plant one in Warner." The sound of more sirens filled the air.

"Then what happens after we shoot him, idiot?" said Derek. "They shoot us."

"Okay. Okay. I need to think, man. Give me time to think," said Tony. He scratched his head and paced back and forth. Within minutes the entire street was filled with squads from the Covington Park police force. More units responded when a hysterical teenage girl burst into the office to report that Mr. Martinez had been shot.

Uniformed officers with shotguns now jumped from their vehicles and ran toward the school.

"If we don't get out now, we won't get out," said Derek, breathing hard. "Let's go for it."

"Okay, man," said Tony. "On my count, we open the door and head for the stairway at the other end of the hall. We go downstairs and through the cafeteria. The police are still out front."

"Ready, man?"

"Yeah, I'm ready."

Tony pointed the gun at Eric, "Stand up, fool. You try one smart move and I'll put a bullet between your eyes." Eric nodded in fright. Tony took another deep breath. "Okay, one, two, three, and now!" They pulled the door open and the trio charged into the hallway.

They had gone less than six steps down the hall when a voice called out behind them, "Hold it right there! Police!" The boys whirled around to find an officer with his .357 Magnum pointed at them. "Get down on the floor! All three of you! Right now!"

Tony stuck the barrel of the gun into Eric's cheek. "Get back, pig, or you'll have a corpse on your hands!" he shouted back. The officer blanched. He had assumed all three of the boys were gang members.

"Please, officer! Help me!" cried Eric.

"Stay back!" shouted Tony. The two gang members pulled Eric back toward the room. The officer was helpless to stop them.

"Open the door, Derek!" shouted Tony. Derek opened the door while Tony continued to hold Eric out in front of them, as a shield. They disappeared through the door and it slammed shut.

The policeman grabbed his radio, "This is Higgins. I'm on the second floor. Officer needs assistance. I've got two white male suspects. They have a white, male hostage. I repeat, they have a hostage."

Inside, Derek grabbed three or four metal desks and slammed them against the door. He then went around and dumped over eight desks and formed a circular barricade. "They won't have a clear shot at us this way," said Derek.

Tony jerked Eric by the collar and threw him into the middle of the circle, "Get down and stay down!" he shouted. Eric climbed on his hands and knees into the circle of desks. Tony and Derek followed close after him. When all three were inside, Derek reached out and sealed the circle shut. All three boys lay sprawled out on the cold tile floor.

Patrol cars from neighboring suburbs and county sheriff's deputies continued to descend on the school. Meanwhile paramedics, wearing flak jackets, made their way through the school until they found Martinez. Helmeted policemen stood guard while the paramedics went to work on the unconscious man.

"Can you get a pulse?" asked one.

The paramedic leaned down with his stethoscope and listened. "Yeah, it's weak. Looks like he's lost a lot of blood. Let's get him out to the truck, stat," said the paramedic. They quickly moved Martinez onto a collapsible stretcher and pulled an oxygen mask over his face. They ripped open a package with a needle and started an IV.

Within sixty seconds the team burst out of the school and ran full speed toward the truck. Once he was loaded inside, the strobe lights on top of the ambulance came alive like a meteor shower. The vehicle screeched away from the curb and headed toward the nearest trauma center.

Eric looked up and could see the flash of the lights on the classroom wall from the ambulance as it headed down the street. He put his head down and fought back the tears. *You tried to save me, Mr. Martinez. Why?*

■

That hour, across town, the scene was considerably quieter and more orderly at the AIDS Homeless Shelter. A large plastic banner hung on the wall behind two volunteers that said, "Don't Leave AIDS Victims Out in the Cold."

"Thank you. I'll put you on the list, sir," said the volunteer at the phone desk. He hung up the receiver and wrote down another name. He turned toward the other volunteer and shook his head. "I don't know what to make of it."

"Make of what, Jim?" said the other man.

"This is the seventh phone call I've had this week from Covington Park."

"You're kidding?"

"No. I've actually had over a half dozen calls from people wanting to know if they could help the shelter."

"You mean give money?"

"No."

"Then what?"

"Are you ready for this?" Jim asked.

"Try me."

"They either want to come and cook or clean or—"

"Or what?"

The volunteer turned his chair so he looked directly at his colleague. "Or they offer to keep people in their homes if we run out of room."

The two men just stared at each other.

"In Covington Park? You can't be serious."

"I am."

Maggie Dunlop rolled over in her hospital bed at County General and moaned. She had been in constant pain since the accident. Her arm was still suspended in a tight sling. The concussion had at first left her vision blurred, but today it had begun to clear.

"How are we doing this beautiful morning, Mrs. Dunlop?" asked the male nurse who stood by her bed.

"Oh, I'm just glad to be alive, son, that's all," chuckled Maggie.

The young nurse stood by her bed and smiled.

"They said I was left lying on the street for nearly half an hour," sighed Maggie. "No one wanted to get involved. That type of thing."

"Well, thank God you're doing better," said the young man.

"If my Heavenly Father had wanted me home, I guess that's where I'd be right now, wouldn't I?"

"I guess it wasn't your time," said the nurse.

Maggie managed to sit up a little. "Ow, that hurts," she said. She looked over at the young man. "Young man, may I ask you a question?"

"Certainly."

"Are you a believer?"

"Yes, ma'am, I am."

"That's good news to me."

The nurse reached into his pocket, "This is for you. Came this morning. A volunteer left it on the desk because you were still asleep." He handed Maggie an envelope.

"Would you hand me my reading glasses, please?" she said.

"Surely." He walked over to a mobile eating tray and picked up Maggie's reading glasses. She adjusted the bows behind each ear and then looked down through the bottom of her bifocals. It was a get-well card.

"Just a note to say we love you. Get better soon. Signed, All Your Friends at First Community." There was a P.S. at the bottom of the page. "Don't forget to pray for Karin and Eric."

"Now I wonder who sent this?" she mused. She put the card down. "Karin and Eric, my goodness. I haven't prayed for them for days." She tried to fold her hands, but the pain quickly reminded her that one arm was still in a cast.

She lay back and closed her eyes, "Lord, thank You for putting me in a place where all I can do is pray. I couldn't get up and be busy if I wanted to. Thank You, Jesus, for allowing me to be exactly where I can serve You best. Now, about Karin and Eric—"

TWENTY

Early on Thursday morning, two nurses waited in the cafeteria line at County General.

"I'll take a coffee and bagel, please, no butter," said one nurse to an employee behind the counter.

"I'll have an omelet," said the other. "Use Egg Beaters, please."

"Coming right up," he said.

"I don't know how much longer I can take the graveyard shift," said the first nurse. "I'm thinking of asking for a transfer out of emergency. I might be able to get some daytime hours."

"I know what you mean," said the other nurse as she rubbed her forehead with the back of her hand. "I got an offer last week to work in a clinic. It's less pay, but decent hours."

"Say, did you hear the story on that girl that came in yesterday afternoon?"

"You mean the one they had in surgery last night?"

"Yeah. I talked to Dr. Frankl this morning. Nearly lost her. Low blood pressure when they brought her in."

"Trauma?"

"Hemorrhaging. A deep cervical tear. Her friend thought she had had an abortion."

"Well, did she?"

"No, she regained consciousness. Told the paramedics she made the doctor stop the abortion."

"Why, for heaven's name? What kind of back-alley doctor would start, then stop after dilation?"

"Who knows? I wouldn't be surprised if a lawsuit comes out of this."

"Did they save the baby?"

"So far."

"Here you are, ladies. A bagel with no butter, coffee, and a no-egg omelet. Anything else?" The employee put both plates up on the counter.

"No, thanks," said one.

The two nurses picked up their orders and walked down the line to pay the cashier.

"Flight attendants, please be seated." The wings of the Boeing 757 tilted slightly as the pilot adjusted his trajectory for touchdown. It was Thursday morning, and Flight 853 from San Diego to Chicago was right on schedule.

"Please put your tray table up, sir," said a flight attendant.

"Oh, thank you, I had forgotten," said Steven. He closed his book and pushed his small tray table into the locked position in the seat in front of him.

"It looks so cold down there," said Brenda. Beneath them sprawled the city and suburbs of Chicago. A white blanket of snow draped most of the cityscape. It formed a seamless quilt of white, except for the dark ribbons of asphalt that criss-crossed the neighborhoods.

Steven glanced at his watch, "Better set this for Central Standard Time again. Let's see, it must be 10:35."

"I'm calling Karin just as soon as we land," said Brenda. "Eric is in school right now. I hope Maggie, the poor dear, is going to be all right."

"Can I ask a favor?" said Steven. "Please make it quick. I need to get to church just as soon as I can."

"Steven, don't you think we should see Karin first? Maybe Maggie too?"

Steven turned toward his wife; he looked worried. "Brenda, this is probably the most critical day of my life. I need to get to the church. We can check on the kids just as soon as I find out what's happened."

Brenda started to object, then stopped. This was not the time to start the Same Old Fight. But soon her desire to see her children overrode her restraint. "Steven. You said things were going to be different when we got back. Remember?"

"Brenda," Steven tried to keep his voice down, "do you think I asked for a rebellion at church? Do you think I'm anxious to walk into this buzz saw? Maybe if you hadn't torn up Dr. Ray's telegram I could have handled this sooner. Okay?"

So we're back to business as usual, thought Brenda. The loud thump of the plane's wheels hitting the runway told them they were home. The pilot reversed the engines and the howl of screaming turbines shook the cabin. The plane trembled as it decelerated on the runway. The O'Hare terminal appeared out the window.

"Please remain in your seats until the captain has turned off the *fasten seat belt* sign," cautioned a male voice over the intercom.

The plane slowed down and turned toward a long, gray ramp that extended from the terminal. The plane jerked one last time as the pilot set the brakes. People jumped from their seats and pulled down winter coats, briefcases, and handbags from the overhead bins.

Steven jumped up and retrieved their coats, handing Brenda's to her. "I just want an hour at the church," he said. "Just an hour, I promise. Then we can go see Eric and Karin."

Brenda swallowed her hurt. "Okay, Steven."

"Thanks, Brenda." He leaned over and gave her a quick kiss. "Let's go see if I have a job or if I'm selling insurance now." His hair had that disheveled look that told her he was nervous. Steven could never keep his hair straight when he was worried.

That same morning, high atop an office complex in downtown Chicago, a group of executives met in closed session. The group enjoyed a spectacular view of the city. Ice green reflective windows and angular shaped buildings formed a panoramic backdrop to their discussions. They sipped coffee and joked with one another.

The weekly sales review had just started.

"If this downturn continues, we're going to have a hard time explaining it to New York," said a balding man in his late fifties. Seated at the end of the table, with employees to his right and left, he was obviously the boss.

"We've had over fifty cancellations in Covington Park alone this week," he said. "What's the story, Kay?"

"I have marketing working on it, Henry," she replied.

"What are they hearing?" said another young executive.

"I have a preliminary list of responses right here," said the female executive. She opened a file and took out three pages stapled together. "Why don't I read a sampling of answers?"

"Fine with me," said the boss. "Let's hear it, Kay."

"For example," she said as she scanned the page, "'I'm canceling the Adult Channel because my home has become a sacred place to me. I've paid too high a price for your brand of entertainment.'"

"Excuse me, Kay," said the young executive, "but when they say 'too high a price,' are they referring to our cost structure?"

"No, I don't think so," said the woman. "Listen to the rest and you'll get the idea. Second customer: 'Our bodies are intended to be a temple of God's Spirit. You treat them as if they're a landfill.' Or this one: 'Your depiction of normal behavior is anything but normal. Your explicit programming saddens the heart of our Creator.'"

"Oh, now I get it," said the young executive. He leaned back in his swivel chair and laughed out loud. "What we're facing, ladies and gentlemen, is another tactic on the part of the wacko religious right. I saw this at the last place I worked. It works this way. These kooks sign up for the cable service, particularly stations like ours, then cancel all at once to make a statement. It's bogus. These people aren't our real customers."

"I don't know, Mike," said Kay.

"Listen, I know the type. They hate sex and carry 12-pound Bibles. So what's new? Tell me something I don't know."

"I think you're wrong in this case," said the female executive. "I checked on the subscription history of several of these customers. All the people on the list have been subscribing to our service for at least three years or longer. Some have taken our channel for as long as eight years. At least, that's according to our records."

"So?" said the young executive.

"So, there goes your theory. They aren't new customers. They've been with us for years. Something else is going on."

"Like a boycott?" asked the boss.

"I asked marketing about that possibility. They've received no advance information about one. Usually these church groups don't keep it a secret. We'd know if one was coming. This is . . ." The woman stopped, wondering if she should finish her sentence.

"Yes, Kay?" said the boss.

"Well, sir, I think this is spontaneous."

"I don't buy it, Kay," said Mike. "You're trying to tell us that it's just a coincidence that fifty people, all in one week, all from one geographic area, call to cancel our channel based on moral objections?" He looked around the room and smirked, "What are the odds of that happening?"

"What do you make of it, Kay?" asked the boss. "Is someone working against us we don't know about?"

"I honestly don't know," said the woman.

"Then find out," snapped the boss. "I just hope this doesn't continue, or New York is going to start screaming. And if they make life difficult for me, I'll make it difficult for the rest of you."

The room got quiet.

The young executive leaned forward. "I've got a suggestion."

"Let's hear it," said the boss.

"I suggest we get down on our knees and pray this doesn't continue." The room was quiet for a moment, then the entire group broke out in laughter.

"All right, let's get on to other business," he said. An hour later everyone had left the room. Everyone, except Kay. She just sat there, reading and rereading the customers' comments.

The black airport limousine pulled up in front of First Community Church. The driver walked around and opened the door for Brenda and Steven.

He handed the driver a fifty-dollar bill for their fare. "Thanks, and keep the change," said Steven.

"Steven, look at this," said Brenda. "I haven't seen this many cars since last Easter." The lot was jammed with cars parked bumper to bumper. "I wonder what's going on."

"I don't know, dear. Let's find out." They picked up their suitcases and walked toward the church. Steven felt like a stranger entering someone else's house.

When they slipped in a side door of the lobby, a number of people turned around and stared at them in disbelief.

"Pastor, is that you?" said one of the ushers. "It is! Welcome home!" Immediately a group of people swarmed Steven and Brenda and welcomed them back. One man hugged Steven so tightly that he thought he would break in half.

"We're so glad to see you," said one person after another. The warm welcome left both Steven and Brenda just a little dazed. They hadn't been expecting this type of homecoming.

Everyone is so happy, thought Steven. *What's happened here?*

"You weren't due for another week," said one of the older members. "You must have heard about what happened." He smiled from ear to ear.

"I did hear you had decided to hold extra meetings, so I thought you might need someone to take the offerings," quipped Steven. The group laughed and then hugged them some more.

"Pastor, you won't believe everything that's happened here since last Sunday," said the man.

"I want to hear all about it," said Steven. "But first, where is Dr. Havens?"

"He's up front leading the service right now," said the usher. "Why don't you go up and join him? He'll be thrilled to see you."

"Who's here today?"

"We've got students from Randolph University. They're telling about what's happened on their campus. It's incredible, Pastor. Absolutely incredible."

"I wonder if Karin is here," said Brenda.

"Haven't seen her yet," said the usher. "Can I take you up front?"

Steven put his hands up. "No, thanks. At least not yet. I don't want to disrupt the service."

"Anything you say, Pastor. Oh, it's good to see you again," said the usher. He shook Steven's hand one more time. Steven glanced at Brenda with a look that asked, *Do you know what's going on?*

She shook her head no. The usher led Steven and his wife through a back corner door of the sanctuary. Their view of the platform was obscured. They decided to sit down on chairs against the wall.

It wasn't just the warm welcome that had thrown Steven off balance; there was also this vague feeling someone was following him. From the moment he had gotten out of the limousine, he was conscious of a Presence. Moment by moment, it seemed to be getting closer to him.

A young woman in a wheelchair was at the microphone. "I grew up in a home that on the outside looked like a good home," she said. "My parents were leaders in our church. We were there every Sunday. They gave regularly. But behind closed doors, at home, it was a different story. My parents almost never spoke to each other, or us.

"My dad was a research specialist. He went all over the world consulting with international companies. But he ignored me. He ignored my brother. And my sister. And my mom. To me, he was a stranger. Mom got lonely, so she started her own business.

"When my dad died a few years ago, I couldn't understand why I didn't cry at the funeral. Then it hit me. As far as I was concerned, he had been dead and buried in my life long before he ever got sick."

Steven glanced through the bulletin that had been printed for the service. He couldn't get away from the vague feeling that he wasn't alone. Someone was looking at him, and he didn't dare look back. Try as he did to block out what the woman was saying up front, her words seemed to cut through.

"I thought I could grow up without the love and affection each child needs and it wouldn't matter. But in these last few days God has dealt with me about my denial. My anorexia, which I hid so long at school, is no longer a secret. I've gone for help this week."

The girl maintained perfect composure. "The counselor helped me figure out why I had been trying to starve myself to death. It's because I didn't feel worthy to live. You can't feel worthy to live if you've never experienced love."

Steven stared at the floor and tapped his foot.

"But God has done something wonderful in my life this week. I've started to eat again. I've actually gained weight since Monday. But I won't tell you how much." The crowd laughed.

"Let me just say to all of you moms and dads sitting out there," the girl said, "the greatest gift you can give your children is the gift of your time and your love. It doesn't matter what else you accomplish in this life. If you end up losing your children, you've lost it all."

Steven didn't dare look at Brenda.

"How can your kids believe there's a God in heaven who loves them if you don't even talk to them? My dad's neglect and workaholism nearly cost me my life. Don't make the same mistake with your children. I've forgiven my dad this week. But you know what? Dad's not here for me to tell him that. I wish he were. But maybe you still have time to tell your kids you love them. Why don't you?"

Brenda tried to reach for Steven's hand, but he pulled it away.

The young woman opened a Bible on her lap. "Let me read something kind of neat. God showed it to me this week. I think it explains what God's doing on our campus." She flipped through several pages. "Here it is. It's in Malachi, chapter four: 'Behold, I will send you Elijah the prophet before the coming of the great and dreadful day of the LORD. And he will turn the hearts of the fathers to the children, and the hearts of the children to their fathers, lest I come and strike the earth with a curse.'"

She closed her Bible. "Dads, it's when you start putting your children first again in your lives that this land will be healed. Until that happens . . . well, maybe the problems we're experiencing in our society with drugs, and gangs, and STDs are just what we deserve."

She looked over at the audience, then sat down.

"I've got to go check my mail, Brenda," Steven said. He got up and walked away.

"But Steven—wait."

Steven ignored her plea. He pushed his way through the crowd toward the church offices. He was immediately spotted by more people. "Look, it's the pastor!" said someone. "It is!" Several people tried to shake his hand or catch his attention, but he hurried right past them.

"It must be an emergency," he heard someone say. Steven was determined to get away from the Presence. He walked right through the reception area of the main offices hardly saying a word to anyone.

"Pastor Warner?" said the receptionist.

"I can't talk right now," snapped Steven. He hurried down the hallway and closed the door behind him. His whole body was alive with tension, and he couldn't slow it down.

"Pastor Warner, welcome home," came a voice over the intercom. It was Elizabeth.

"Thank you, Elizabeth. Listen, I need a favor. I want to be left alone. Don't let anybody in here."

There was a slight pause. "Yes, yes Pastor. I understand. Glad to know you're back."

"Thanks." Steven reached over and turned off his intercom. He rubbed his chin and stared at the desk. He turned in his swivel chair and glanced at the credenza behind him. There on the ledge stood pictures of Brenda, Eric, and Karin.

The room seemed to close in on him. *This is crazy*, he thought. *I'm crazy. What's happening to me? Get a grip on it, Steven.* He beat his hand on his desk. But the pressure continued to build. It was starting to become intolerable. He glanced again at the pictures of his family on the credenza. He reached over and set each picture facedown. *There, now you can't stare at me*, he thought. But it didn't do any good. The tension in his spirit continued to escalate.

He was caught in the vise grip of conviction that seemed to turn a notch tighter by the minute. He had never known such spiritual agony in his life. "What do You want from me?" he said out loud. "What do you want?" He put his head down and began to cry. Not simply weeping, but guttural, deep sobs. He fell to his knees.

There was a knock on his office door.

"I'm busy now!" Steven said quite loudly. He didn't want anyone to see him like this. The door opened ever so slowly. He scrambled to get back to his feet. But it was too late. The person was already in the room. Up on one knee, Steven could only see a pair of man's legs as they approached him. He looked up. He thought he must be seeing things.

Less than six feet away stood a seventy-five-year-old man in a blue sport coat and gray pants.

"Dad? What—what in the world?" Steven was stunned.

The older man said nothing. His eyes glistened with tears. Ralph Warner moved toward his son with slow, deliberate steps. When the two men reached each other, they collapsed into each other's arms.

Each tried to say something, but it was impossible. The torrent of tears began.

"What do you suppose is going on in there?" whispered one secretary to another out in the next room. They pretended not to hear, but the noise inside was too loud to be ignored.

"I've come to ask your forgiveness, my son," said the father. "I'm . . . so sorry for the way I treated you." The men held on to each other, certain the other would drop to the floor if either of them let go.

"Dad, I need you so much," said Steven. The familiar look of anger and sternness was gone from Ralph Warner's face. In some respects, it now had the softness of a five-year-old boy.

Steven struggled to get his words out. "Oh, Dad, forgive me. Forgive me for what I've carried against you all these years," said Steven. "It was just . . . just that I wanted you . . . to want me."

"Oh, my son, my son," said the father. He reached and pulled Steven again to himself. It was some time before the two men sat down in chairs. But when they finally did let go of each other, it was done. Their souls had been emptied. And they had been filled again.

Steven wiped his eyes, "How, Dad? How did you get here?" His pain was now replaced by joy.

His father's face was red and swollen from tears, but a smile fought its way through. "God brought me here, Steven, that's all I can say."

"How?" asked Steven.

"I called the church on Monday to ask when you'd be returning from your trip. They let me talk to Dr. Havens. He told me what was happening here, about the trouble—and the revival. He asked me to pray with him."

Ralph Warner's voice became emotional. "When I hung up, your mother and I decided we needed to come out here. It was mainly for my sake. I knew I needed God to do something in my life. And when we drove into the parking lot here, it happened . . ." Steven's father could not finish his sentence.

Steven did something he had never done in his adult life. He got up and took his father's hand in his. "It's okay, Dad. I understand—I do. The same thing has happened to me."

The two men held hands. "Dad, can we pray?" It seemed an odd request for one minister to make to another, but in fact the two men had never prayed together, alone, in their entire lives.

"Please, please, let's do, Steven," said Ralph Warner.

Steven reached over and hugged his dad. "Lord," Steven began, "how can I thank You for this moment? You sent my father to look for me—while I was yet a long way off. Forgive me. For the years I spent running from You . . . and from Dad."

Now it was Steven's father's turn. He spoke in soft, sincere tones, not the managed and modulated preacher's voice Steven had remembered hearing as a boy. "Lord God Almighty, Your Word says, 'Fathers, do not provoke your children to wrath, but bring them up in the training and admonition of the Lord.' I must confess, for most of my life I didn't listen to Your warning. I see now how I provoked my children to anger. I held up standards they could never meet. And I knew I couldn't meet them either." Steven hugged his dad tighter. "I tried to hide my fears behind a stern and unrelenting heart. I need Your forgiveness, as I need Steven's. Thank You that it's not too late for Jesus Christ to turn my heart to my children again."

"It's already been done, Dad, it's already done," whispered Steven.

The door to the office opened and both men looked up. There was Brenda and Steven's mother. The women took one look at their husbands and burst into tears. All four of them hugged one another and cried until they had no more tears.

■

The SWAT team member peered through the scope of his high-powered rifle. He lay with his hat turned backward and his finger on the trigger, waiting for the word.

Next to him on the roof lay Lieutenant Plinski. He was in charge of field operations for the area SWAT team. He peered through his binoculars and tried to assess the situation. He reached over and picked up his walkie-talkie and put it next to his face. The black metal felt ice-cold in the outdoor wind. "This is Raven Two to Command," he said.

"Go ahead, Raven Two," crackled a voice through the receiver.

"We definitely have only three subjects in the room."

"That's three persons. Roger."

"They are barricaded behind metal desks. I have not been able to determine which one has the weapon."

"Roger, Raven Two."

The lieutenant tapped his team member on the shoulder, "Jed, do you have a clean shot at the taller boy?"

The man squinted through the scope. "Yup. Got him right in the cross hairs."

The lieutenant motioned to the other marksman who lay on the roof some fifteen feet away. They used specific hand motions to communicate in situations like this. The black-uniformed marksman made a cross-hair symbol using two fingers. The lieutenant nodded.

"This is Raven Two," said Lieutenant Plinski. "Patriots One and Two have a clean shot at both suspects. But the hostage is sandwiched closely between them on the floor. I advise against, repeat, against, active measures at this point."

"Understood, Raven Two. Negotiators are now active on the scene."

"Ten-four." The lieutenant looked down on the street. A black sedan arrived on the south side of the school. Three men and a woman got out of the car and were met by the Covington

Park police. A yellow tape had been used to cordon off the entire block. Confused students and frantic parents were assembled in the gymnasium trying to locate one another. No one knew yet who the gang members were or who their hostage was.

The lieutenant stared into the classroom through his binoculars. He could see that one of the boys was holding a gun against the ribs of the boy in the middle. He squinted and studied the clothes the boys wore. "The Squires," he said to himself. "I should have known."

"Right this way, please," said the school principal, Mr. Tufton. An administrator in his early sixties, with gray hair and a small moustache, he welcomed the hostage negotiators into the main office.

"Do we know who's upstairs yet?" said Jim O'Hara, the chief negotiator.

"I'm afraid not, sir," said Tufton. "We're going through our records right now. With the flu going through the school, it's made it more difficult. We have only a partial list of people accounted for. We're going to have to call through the entire roster."

"How long will that take?" he grunted.

"We have nine hundred students, officer," said the principal.

O'Hara grunted and walked away.

"How about the counselor that was shot?" asked the woman negotiator. "What's the word on him?"

"He's in serious condition," said Tufton.

"Does he have a family?" she asked.

"A wife and two daughters in college."

"Let's not say anything about the counselor's condition to the boys upstairs in the room," said O'Hara. "We need to try to calm them down right now. Where's the intercom system?"

"Right this way," said Tufton. He led the hostage negotiation team into a small office with a large control panel. "The different room numbers are listed under the switches," he said. "We believe this is the classroom they're in." He pointed to a small black switch with the number *209* painted in white beneath it.

"Have you made any contact with them yet?" O'Hara asked.

"No, we were advised against doing that by the Covington Park police," said Tufton.

"Good," grunted O'Hara. He turned to his colleagues. "Okay, let's get started." The team members took off their coats and began to unload their bags. They contained laptop computers with modem connections, portable telephones, and recording devices.

"I'm going to have to ask that everyone be kept out of this area," said the negotiator to Tufton. "No one comes in or out unless we authorize it, understood?"

"You will have our full cooperation," said the principal.

"Get me that list of students not accounted for just as soon as possible. It could make a difference."

"Understood," said Tufton. He turned and walked out of the small control room.

"Oh, one other thing," said O'Hara.

"Yes, officer?"

"Keep me posted on Martinez."

"You never believe something like this will happen, but I guess it does, doesn't it?" said Tufton.

"Nope."

Sally Jensetter lay stretched out on a couch in the hospital waiting room, fast asleep. She was exhausted from her all-night vigil and had drifted off only minutes earlier.

"Would you like some coffee, ma'am?" said a kindly voice.

Sally blinked at the person and then slowly sat up. It was a male nurse. He handed her a cup of steaming coffee.

"Why thank you," she said. She leaned over and took a sip. "That should help me wake up."

The man sat down beside her. "Did you try and reach Miss Warner's parents yet?"

Sally took a long sip of the coffee, then set it down. "No, I haven't. Karin made me promise that I'd tell no one. Particularly them. I wish I had never agreed to it." Sally reached up and ran her hand through her long, dark brown hair, then leaned back and closed her eyes. "They don't tell you about this on television do they?"

"About what?" asked the nurse.

"About things like this. I mean, they say abortion is safe now since it's legal. Tell that to Karin." She reached down and took another sip of coffee. "And the television sitcoms and soap operas. They treat sex like it's entertainment. A toy or something. Well, it's not."

"The truth is dangerous," said the male nurse. "Maybe that's why we don't hear much of it these days."

"I guess there's nothing I can do for Karin but pray," said Sally. She put her head down and rested her arms on her knees. Exhaustion left her thoroughly wrung out.

"Does Karin have friends who pray?" asked the nurse.

Sally looked up. "I suppose so."

"Have you called them?" said the nurse.

"No, uh . . . I didn't want anyone else to know about this. For Karin's sake."

"If Karin or the baby dies, will people know about it?" he asked.

Sally thought it over. "I see your point." She sat up again and straightened her hair. "Thanks. You've given me an idea. Would you excuse me?"

"Sure thing."

Sally took out her purse and opened a small mirror. She rubbed some makeup on her face and then snapped the compact shut. She stood up and headed out into the lobby straight to a phone. She put money in the phone and dialed the familiar number.

"Grandhurst Dormitory. Lisa Fredrickson speaking."

"Lisa. This is Sally. I'm at County General. I can't explain everything, but there's an emergency. It's about Karin. I need you to get five girls from the floor and get them together in your room."

"What's happened to her, Sally?"

"Lisa, she needs prayer. I'll tell you more later. Send Jane Phelps over here right away. Tell her to meet me in the lobby of the emergency room. Here's why . . ."

TWENTY-ONE

"**Y**our Honor, may I approach the bench?" asked the tired-looking attorney. The Family Court for Ashland County, which included Covington Park and several other upper-income suburbs, was now in session. It was midmorning on Thursday.

The walnut-paneled room was quite attractive, despite the sad business that was transacted there each day. The room was decorated with deep blue carpeting, recessed lighting, and black cushioned seats for the gallery. The judge's bench was made of solid oak with a hand-carved insignia of the county seal on the front of it. Yet because of escalating violence in family courts across the nation, two armed bailiffs now stood on duty at all times.

"Come forward, counsel," said the judge. The lawyer, a tall man in a dark suit, approached the bench.

"Your Honor, I have a somewhat unusual request to make of the court," he said.

"What is it?" the judge asked. "Another stay of proceedings? I'm not sure if I can tolerate any further delays. I have several more cases to hear this month."

The lawyer looked down and scratched his ear. "No, Your Honor, that isn't my request. You see, my client wishes to drop her suit against the defendant altogether."

"She wants to *what*?" said the judge. "We've spent the last five days of this court's time listening to the plaintiff's case. Now she wants the suit dismissed? Why, counselor?"

The lawyer could hear the anger in the judge's voice—anger which no doubt was justified. The attorney leaned forward and said in a low voice, "It seems that last night my client underwent some sort of 'spiritual' experience."

The judge raised his eyebrow.

"If I may continue, Your Honor. It seems she attended church somewhere in the area last evening. She called me at five o'clock this morning and said she intended to drop the suit. She said . . ." The lawyer took another deep breath, "she also wishes to retract her testimony. The claims her husband beat her and the children were false. She said she invented all of it in order to win a large settlement. She now admits to being involved in an ongoing affair, which she says she broke off last night."

The judge glared at the lawyer. "Are you telling me your client initiated a baseless action and then perjured herself in this court?"

The lawyer folded his hands on the front of the judge's bench. "I'm afraid that's about the size of it, Your Honor."

"Would the counsel for the defendant please approach the bench?" barked the judge. He leaned back in his swivel chair and tapped his desk with his gavel.

The opposing attorney, a short man weighing perhaps 250 pounds, and wearing an ill-fitting brown suit, got up and approached the bench. "Yes, Your Honor?"

The judge leaned forward. "Mr. Perkins, Mr. Savowitz here tells me his client wishes to drop her suit against your client. She admits to fabricating her testimony and has indicated she is guilty of a marital tryst that has led to the dissolution of the marriage."

The lawyer was momentarily speechless. "Your Honor, I—"

"Oh, if I may, Your Honor," said the other attorney, "my client wishes to convey something to her husband."

"What's that?" said the judge.

"It seems—" the attorney cleared his throat. "It seems she wishes to ask—to ask—"

"Yes, counsel, get on with it."

"Well, it seems that my client wishes to ask the defendant for his forgiveness."

The husband's attorney turned around and looked at the man seated at the table behind him. The ordeal of five grueling days of painful proceedings and cross-examination was etched in his face. The lawyer then looked at the neatly dressed woman seated at the other table. The acrimony in her eyes, which he had seen so frequently during the trial, had all disappeared. It was replaced by a serenity that seemed oddly out of place in divorce court.

"Your Honor," said the husband's attorney, "I have maintained my client's innocence in these matters all along. May I please confer with my client?"

"So granted, counsel," said the judge. The lawyer walked back to the table and sat down by the husband. He whispered to his client, pointed to the woman's attorney, then pointed to the man's wife. The man's facial expression went from pain, to confusion, to total bewilderment. He whispered something back to his lawyer. When the five-minute consultation was over, the husband put his head down on the table.

The attorney returned to the bench.

"Counselor, is your client ill?" asked the judge.

"Uh, he's fine, Your Honor," said the attorney.

"I see. I thought he might be ill. Have you reached a conclusion in this matter?" asked the judge.

"Yes, we have. My client wishes to ask the court's forbearance regarding his wife's testimony. He asks that she not be charged for her perjury. And—"

"And?" said the judge.

"And he wants her to know he still loves her. And—"

The judge again raised his eyebrow. "And?"

"She's welcome to come home. He made a reference to Hosea and Gomer as precedent."

"Hosea and Gomer?" said the woman's attorney. "Who in the world are they? A law firm?"

"No, counselor," chuckled the judge. "I'm no expert in matters pertaining to theology, but I believe he is making reference to two Old Testament characters. Gomer was a 'lady of the night,' if you will. She cheated on her husband, Hosea, numerous times. Yet, God told Hosea to take her back, and well—he did."

The woman's attorney was frustrated, "Your Honor, could I ask for a recess?"

"It looks as if you're too late for that," said the judge. He used his gavel to point behind them. The two lawyers turned around and there stood the husband and wife in each other's arms.

"Oh, my goodness," said the taller attorney.

"Counsel," said the judge, "I suggest you go and inform the couple's three children of these new developments."

"Certainly, Your Honor." He walked down the center aisle, through the small gate, and out into the lobby.

The judge picked up the gavel and whacked it on the bench, "The case of Fulmont versus Fulmont is dismissed. This court will be in recess until one o'clock this afternoon."

The husband and wife continued their reconciliation, oblivious to everything and everyone around them. Three frightened-looking elementary school-age children slowly walked through the double wooden doors into the courtroom. When the youngest child saw their parents hugging one another, he began to cry. The children ran to their parents, and the entire family became one large embrace.

The judge, not normally given to emotion, fought back tears as he watched the scene unfold. The father picked up the little girl in his arms. The little boy tugged on his mother's skirt. The family walked out as a unit, hand in hand.

"Counselor, I'd like to speak with you off the record."

"Of course, Your Honor," the woman's lawyer replied. He had packed his things and was preparing to leave.

"I don't know where your client went last evening, but please find out. I'd like to send more families there."

"So would I, Your Honor."

■

"We have it down to twenty students," said the secretary in the principal's office. She handed the principal and Captain O'Hara a list of the students unaccounted for at home or inside the gymnasium. They were now four hours into the standoff.

"Excellent work, Mrs. Watkins," said Tufton. He grabbed the computer printout and scanned the names.

"This has all the smell of a gang feud," said Captain O'Hara. "One of the SWAT members radioed that he recognized the gang garb through the window. Are any of the boys on this list known to be gang members?"

"Some are honor roll students," said Tufton. "I think we can safely cross them off."

"I wouldn't be so certain of that," said O'Hara. "We've arrested boys who lived in 800,000-dollar homes for gang and drug-related offenses. Just because they have bucks and brains doesn't mean they have a family."

A uniformed patrolman entered the office. He led with him a young student dressed in a gray T-shirt with an odd symbol on the front. "This boy says he has information that might help us," said the patrolman.

"Well, kid, what do you know about this?" said O'Hara.

"I heard about Mr. Martinez. Everyone has," said the boy. He looked down and wiped his nose. "I'll be straight with you. I'm a member of the Excaliburs."

"Yes?" said Tufton.

"I haven't done anything wrong. I'm in it just for self-defense."

"Against who?" said Tufton.

"Against the Squires."

"The Squires?" said O'Hara. "Are they involved in this?"

"Yeah, I think so. You see, we just had someone join us this week. He said the Squires were going to kill him. They were forcing him to pay for protection."

The principal got up from his desk and walked over to the boy. "Who was it, son? Who were they threatening?"

"Eric Warner is his name, sir."

"Eric Warner?" said the principal. "Why, that's impossible. He's the son of one of the leading ministers in the area. He couldn't be involved in this."

"Let me see the list," said O'Hara. He took his finger and scanned the paper. "Warner, Eric. Tenth grade."

"Excuse me for overhearing," said Mrs. Watkins, the secretary to the principal. "I believe Warner was also brought in as a truant this week. If I remember right, Mr. Martinez handled the matter."

"Wait," said Tufton. "Now that I think of it, Mr. Martinez mentioned Eric's name to me last night before I left. We were going to discuss it further today."

"That's it," said the hostage negotiator. He turned to another police officer. "Get over to his home right away. We need his parents here on the double."

"Yes, sir," said the officer.

"Excuse me, again," said Mrs. Watkins. "But when we called his home yesterday, no one answered. We tried his father's work number. The receptionist said Dr. Warner was out of the country with his wife. Eric's been staying at the home of a Dustin Jacobs."

"Well, try the church and his home one more time," said O'Hara. "We need to find someone related to the boy."

The negotiator turned back to the Excalibur gang member, "I want you to do one more thing for us."

The boy flipped his hair out of his eyes and looked up, "Yeah. What is it?"

The captain handed him the list of names on the paper. "Look at this. Which of these boys are members of the Squires?" The boy took the sheet and sat down to study it.

"Yeah. Here's one," he said. "Derek Thorton. He's their leader." He continued to study the list. "That's the only name I recognize. No, wait a minute. Barton. Tony Barton. Word is he's done the drive-by shootings for the gang."

O'Hara stuck out his hand. "Thanks, kid. You may have just saved three lives." The boy reluctantly shook hands and was then led out of the office by another officer.

Once he was gone, O'Hara's expression changed radically, "It's worse than I thought," he said to his team. "We have a kid upstairs who's not afraid to kill. One wrong move on our part, and Eric Warner is dead."

He pointed to an assistant. "Notify the SWAT team. We may have to take down the room. I want those two gang members in their sights at all times. Got it?"

"Yes, sir," said the team member.

"Now, let's pray we don't mess up."

"Good afternoon, boys, this is Jim O'Hara of the Ashland County Sheriff's department." The unexpected voice over the intercom in Room 209 made the two gang members tense up. Tony stuck his gun into Eric's ribs. "You shut up."

"I hear you," whispered Eric.

"We don't want to talk to no sheriff," shouted Tony. "You and the other pigs clear outta here, or we kill this guy. Cool?"

"I can assure you, boys, no one wants to hurt you. We just want to talk. That's all. You have some grievances you need to talk about, don't you?" said O'Hara.

"What should we do?" whispered Derek. "What if this is some kind of trick?"

"Let me do the talking," said Tony.

"How would you boys like something to eat?" said O'Hara. "Just name it. Pizza. Burgers. Fries. It's on me today."

"We're not hungry," shouted Tony. "We just want you and your men to get out of here. Got it?"

"Oh, we'll leave when it's time," said O'Hara. "But there's no need to rush anything. You men have had a hard day. Tell me about your girlfriend, Tony. Is she good-looking?"

Derek punched Tony, "They know our names, man. They know who we are."

"Hey, Derek. I hear you're quite the ladies' man yourself," said O'Hara. "You two have it all. Good-looking babes, hot cars—"

"Will you shut up!" shouted Tony. "Look, we're giving you ten minutes to clear out or we hurt somebody. Ten minutes!"

"Tony, my man, chill. Your mom is on her way over here. Why don't you just sit and relax until she gets here. Either of you guys ever owned a Trans Am?"

"He's trying to wear us down," said Tony. "Don't listen to him, Derek."

"Hey, guys, I had a car in high school. It was a '57 Chevy. Maybe the best car ever built. Bright red. Long fins. Four barrel carburetor. Ever been in one?"

"Shut up," said Tony. "I'm not talking about cars with any pig like you."

"Hey, Eric, I bet you're hungry too," said O'Hara. At the mention of his own name Eric sat up. Tony reached over and shoved his head back down. "Try that again and you're dead, Warner," he seethed.

"Okay, so you know we've got Warner," shouted Derek. "That doesn't change a thing. We want outta here in nine minutes, or we start target practice up here. I'm not jiving."

"Tony, you're a good man," said O'Hara. "You're a natural leader. How about it? Do you see a stint in the Marines after high school? Maybe the Air Force?"

"I said nine minutes!" Tony leaned above the desks and fired a round into the window by the door to the hallway. The glass shattered in the shape of a spider's web.

Across the street the lieutenant heard the gunshot over the radio patch he had into the intercom system. He grabbed his binoculars and squinted through them. He picked up his walkie-talkie. "This is Raven Two. I heard a gun report. A window has been shattered but no one is harmed that I can see. I repeat, gunfire in the room, no casualties."

The marksmen both leaned forward with their fingers on the triggers of their rifles. On top of the school building, just one floor above Room 209, three SWAT team members stood in full battle gear. Their mission was to rappel down and fire both tear gas and flash and bang grenades through the windows into the classroom. Other team members, located on the second floor out of sight of the room, would then storm the room. Their mission would be to suppress fire, and rescue the hostage.

"Just give me the word, Captain," shouted the lieutenant through his walkie-talkie. "We're in position and ready to go."

That same day, about noon, a group of five women and two men huddled inside a Sunday school room in the basement of First Community Church.

"Thank you all for coming," said Rachel Brewster. She glanced around the table. Her following was now down to fewer than half a dozen. They had managed to persuade two husbands to join their cause.

"Jim and Greg, thanks for coming," said Rachel. "It's men like you who belong on the deacon board. Not the group of Warner yes-men we currently have."

"This is the Lord's church," said one of the men. "That's worth fighting for, isn't it?"

"You bet it is," answered one of the women.

"Before we pray, let's review our strategy," said Rachel. "First, one of you gets the microphone. Then you turn it over to me. I present the petition. Then each of you takes a turn to speak in favor of it. Spread yourself around the sanctuary, so it doesn't look like we're together. I want this to look as spontaneous and widespread as possible. Got it?"

"Should we sit with our spouses?" asked one of the men.

."Of course. If you can recruit anyone else before we make our move, please do so. We're going to need as many people as possible to make this work."

"What about those who've asked to have their names removed from that list?" asked one woman.

"I've taken care of that," smiled Rachel. "Most have decided to leave them on."

"Well, praise the Lord."

"Are you nervous, Rachel?" asked one of the men. "I mean, it may be you against a whole room full of people caught up in this 'revival' or whatever you want to call it."

"I'm a little frightened," she answered. "But today I found encouragement again from the Word." She opened her large Bible. "Let me share the promise the Lord gave me." She paged through her Bible. "Yes, here it is. 'Though an army may encamp against me, My heart shall not fear; Though war may rise against me, In this I will be confident.' Psalm 27:3."

"Beautiful," said one person.

"Right on," said another.

"Let's join hands and pray before we go out to do battle," said Rachel. The group bowed their heads and prayed fervently for the next twenty minutes.

The meeting upstairs had gone well past one o'clock when Ray Havens stepped up to the pulpit. The crowd was divided into small prayer groups throughout the sanctuary.

"Please pardon me," said the Southern preacher over the noise, "but I do believe I have a delightful surprise for everyone." The room quieted down. "I'd like to introduce to you a special guest who just arrived an hour ago. Will you welcome back with me, your pastor, Dr. Steven Warner."

There was an audible gasp heard in the pews, followed by an outbreak of applause. As Steven made his way to the podium, the congregation responded with a standing ovation.

People sitting in the front row could see tears on his face. He smiled and acknowledged their applause. He motioned for them to sit down. But the applause went on.

He turned with a slight look of embarrassment to Dr. Ray. Dr. Ray smiled at him and continued to clap with the others. Again Steven motioned for the people to sit down.

Rachel and her group had just reached the auditorium level of the church when they heard the applause inside.

"What's the ruckus?" she asked one of the ushers in the lobby.

"Haven't you heard?" he said with a grin from ear to ear. "Pastor Warner is back!"

The color went completely out of Rachel's face. "He's *what*?"

"He and his wife came back just before lunch. Isn't it wonderful?"

"Oh, yeah, just wonderful," muttered Rachel. She glanced over at the others. It was too late. They had already entered the auditorium to find seats. She had no opportunity to retrieve them now. *I may be able to use this to my advantage*, thought Rachel. *This could be the break I've been waiting for.*

"Thank you so much, thank you so much, my friends," said Steven. At last the audience sat down. "I really wasn't expecting this kind of welcome. I—really don't deserve it.

"I am—I should say Brenda and I are—simply overwhelmed by what we have seen here today." His voice quivered. "I cannot believe what God has done in our church in the short time we have been gone."

An older couple in the front row nodded and smiled at him.

"I need to be honest with you," he said. His voice became more serious. "When I left First Community Church almost three weeks ago, I left a tired, empty man. I had been running on empty for months, no, years. I had tried so hard to be—" Steven faltered at this point. He turned away, then regained his composure. "I had tried so hard to be everything you wanted me to be."

Steven smiled through his tears. "I guess I had cared more about what you thought about me than what God thought."

Perfect, thought Rachel. *This is perfect.*

Steven continued, "Let me be clear. You never asked me to be a people-pleaser. I did it because I needed to do it." People leaned forward to be certain they didn't miss a word. "What

I'm trying to say," said Steven in a half-broken voice, "is that I failed you wonderful people. I failed you because I made an idol out of a good thing—my ministry. And God's Word says He will not share His glory with anyone else."

He's doing it for me, thought Rachel. *He's self-destructing. I won't even need the petitions.*

"I replaced God at the center of my life with something that didn't belong there—my career. That was wrong. Terribly wrong." Steven's face shone with a love Brenda had rarely seen, "I love all of you, and hope you will find it in your hearts to forgive me."

Steven bowed his head. Dr. Ray drew him close to himself. Handkerchiefs appeared all throughout the congregation. Silent tears streamed down Brenda's face. Steven's father and mother were visibly moved.

I've won, thought Rachel.

"Why don't you tell the people the rest of the truth?" came a voice.

All heads in the sanctuary immediately turned to see who had broken the silence of the moment. There in the middle aisle stood a rigid *Tiffany Evans*, dressed in a red blazer and dark black slacks.

"Excuse me, ma'am," said Dr. Ray from the pulpit. "But I don't believe we have recognized anyone for comment at this time." Steven stood at his side, perplexed.

"Pastor Warner, why don't you tell them the rest of the story?" she repeated.

Steven stepped to the microphone. "I don't think I understand, Mrs. Evans."

"Then let me refresh your memory," she said in a defiant voice. She turned toward the congregation. "Not many of you would know this. We kept it our secret. But Pastor Warner and I have been more than just pastor and parishioner for some time now."

"What?" someone said out loud. A collective gasp occurred throughout the congregation.

"That's right," she said. "Pastor Warner and I have been lovers for the last several months." The color drained out of Steven's face. He looked toward Brenda, who sat motionless.

"It can't be!" someone cried out.

"I don't believe it!" said another. Steven stood stunned, unable to react.

Ingrid, I should have guessed she'd try something like this, thought Rachel. *I should have made my move sooner. This day is mine.*

"That's a very serious charge you're making, ma'am," said Dr. Ray. "May I remind you that the Word of God clearly says in First Timothy, chapter five, 'Do not receive an accusation against an elder except from two or three witnesses'?"

"Are you asking me for other witnesses?" said Ingrid. "Then you shall have your witnesses." She reached in her purse and produced a cigarette case with a cassette player inside. She held it up to the microphone and punched the play button.

"We're almost never intimate anymore," said the female voice.

"I'm embarrassed to admit this," said the male voice. "But I have an appointment I had completely forgotten." The voice sounded distinctly like that of Steven Warner's.

"Wait a minute," said Steven from the platform, "that's not—"

"That's not what, Pastor?" said Tiffany. She switched off the tape player. "Are you denying that's your voice?"

"No—but—that isn't the way it happened."

The congregation started to rumble with conversation.

"What I mean is, my remarks are being taken out of context," said Steven. His face was beet red, and perspiration started to form on his brow.

"Ladies and gentleman of the congregation," said Tiffany. "I have more tapes like that one." She held up a handful of cassettes. "I'll gladly turn them over to the official board for their review. I think you'll discover the man you have trusted as pastor has violated your trust—and mine. I came seeking help and guidance, not an affair. He took advantage of me."

"Sit down!" someone shouted.

"This is completely out of order!" shouted Ralph Warner, Steven's father.

It was difficult for anyone to be heard. The room broke into a tumult. As Dr. Ray scanned the audience, he could see groups of two and three bowed in prayer in different portions of the auditorium.

Brenda got up and ran out of the sanctuary. Steven's mother followed her.

"This is neither the time nor the place for public accusations, Mrs. Evans," said Dr. Havens in a firm voice. "We have done our brother Warner a terrible disservice this day by entertaining such a heinous charge in this setting. According to Scripture, this matter should have been first brought to the board. I will not allow any further discussion of this issue."

"Not so fast, Dr. Havens," came a voice from the balcony. "I believe other members of this congregation should be allowed to speak." Rachel Brewster stood at the balcony microphone and held up a document for all to see. "I have in my hand today a petition signed by one hundred and fifty members of this congregation. It demands a congregational meeting to conduct a vote of no-confidence in Pastor Warner."

You fool, thought Ingrid. *You'll pay for this.*

The audience, already reeling from Tiffany's bombshell, had no idea how to react.

"I'm not surprised to learn of these 'developments' today," said Rachel. "There have been many of us who have suspected for some time that we had a false teacher among us."

"Sit down right now!" said an older man seated close to Rachel. "You can't talk about my pastor this way."

"Shut up and let her speak!" said one of the women in Rachel's small group who had stood up and walked to a microphone. "Let this woman speak. Or are we afraid of the truth?"

The older man was silenced.

"You've all heard Pastor Warner's confession today, haven't you?" said Rachel. "You've heard from his own mouth that he's guilty of sin. Idolatry, I believe he said. Now we hear he's guilty of adultery too. What more evidence do we need? I move that we dismiss Pastor Warner for violating our trust and disgracing the gospel."

"I second that motion!" said one of the men in Rachel's group.

"This is out of order!" shouted an usher.

"It's never out of order to deal with sin!" said Rachel.

A ruckus broke out as one group of people began to shout at the other. Dr. Ray interrupted, "I must ask for quiet in this sanctuary. The Scriptures tell us everything must be done in decency and order."

"You have no authority over us!" shouted one of Rachel's followers. "Give us our real church leaders. Where is our deacon chairman? I demand we hear from him." Unfortunately, Howard Svendsen hadn't been able to get the day off work, so he wasn't there. Phil Crawford stood in the back of the sanctuary and watched the church on the verge of coming apart.

"I can't allow this to happen," he whispered to his wife, who stood by him. "Pray for me."

He pushed his way to the front of the auditorium and walked up onto the stage. He whispered something in Dr. Ray's ear. He nodded his approval and pointed him toward Steven. Steven was seated in a stage chair with his head bowed. Phil walked over to him and whispered something. He reached down and hugged him, then walked up to the microphone.

"Excuse me," he said in a loud, determined voice. "Excuse me." The noise started to subside. "I am a member of the Board of Deacons, and I demand that order be restored." The congregation at last complied. "First Corinthians 14:40 clearly states, 'Let all things be done decently and in order.' What's going on here is a direct violation of that commandment."

As if the air had been let out of a tire all at once, the atmosphere in the room seemed spent of energy for the moment.

"Thank you," said Phil. "The Lord can only be honored today if we conduct ourselves as brothers and sisters."

Several *amen's* could be heard in the congregation.

"I have listened to the charges made against our brother, Pastor Warner, this afternoon. Frankly, I don't believe any of them," he began.

"So he's got you fooled too, Crawford!" shouted Rachel. "That's the problem with this deacon board. All you can say is yes."

Ingrid sighed angrily. *She doesn't know what she's doing,* she thought. *She's a fool.* Her hatred toward Rachel grew by the moment.

"Mrs. Brewster, another outburst such as that and I will instruct the ushers to escort you from this auditorium," said Phil.

Rachel seemed poised to hurl another insult, but then she thought better of it.

"Okay, Deacon Crawford, have your say, but you can't hide the truth," said Rachel. "The pastor has already admitted his guilt."

"Let me begin with you, Mrs. Evans," said Phil Crawford. Ingrid was startled. "I would like to ask you a simple question," Phil said.

The woman stood up and moved to the microphone, "Anything you wish, sir. My life's an open book."

"Just a yes or no will do," said Phil. "Do you believe that Jesus Christ is God's incarnate Son come in the flesh?"

Tiffany seemed to twitch. "Why would you ask that? That's what this church teaches, doesn't it?" she said.

"You haven't answered my question, Mrs. Evans," said Phil. "Do you believe Jesus Christ is God's Son come in the flesh? Yes or no?"

"That's what the Bible says," she answered. The woman seemed to have lost a degree or two of her defiance. "Besides, I don't see what this has to do with the fact your pastor and I had an affair. As I said, it all started when I came for help and the pastor ended up taking advantage of me."

Steven shot up from his seat, "That's a lie, Tiffany, and you know it is!" Phil turned toward Steven and discreetly motioned for him to sit down. Steven complied, but the look of incredulity and anger on his face still lingered.

"I'll ask one more time, Mrs. Evans," said Phil in a calm voice. "Simply confess that Jesus Christ is God's Son come in the flesh."

"I won't be put on trial here," she said in an angry voice. She pointed at Steven, "There's the man who belongs on the witness stand."

"Is Jesus Christ God's Son come in the flesh?" said Phil. "Is He or isn't He?"

Tiffany appeared to swallow hard. She started to say something, but the words seemed to stick in her throat. She tried to speak, but she couldn't.

"If you believe that Jesus is God's Son, why do you find it difficult to say so?" said Phil. He turned toward the music leader. "Mrs. James, now would be a good time to sing a favorite chorus of mine: 'Jesus, Name Above All Names.'"

The pianist began to play the melody softly. "Won't the congregation please join me?" said Phil. At first only a few people sang along. But little by little, the number of voices grew. The song grew louder and louder. The words and the soft, lovely harmony seemed to replace the acrid air of tension in the room with a fresh and clean scent.

As the music continued, Tiffany rubbed the temples of her head and shook it back and forth. With each stanza, she seemed more upset.

"Stop it!" she finally shouted. "Stop it right now. I can't stand this any longer!" She threw the tapes at the altar and stormed out of the sanctuary with her hands over both ears.

She pushed the back door open and stumbled out into the winter air. The group continued to sing, with an ever-increasing reverence.

"Sir," a voice said. "May I say something?" A man in a leather waist coat asked.

Phil motioned for the congregation to stop singing. "And who are you, sir?" he asked.

"My name is Jason Fulton. I'm a private investigator. I'd like an opportunity to refute the charges made against your reverend this afternoon."

All eyes turned toward the detective. Phil looked at Dr. Ray. Dr. Ray nodded his head.

"Okay, Mr. Fulton," said Phil. "If you can shed further light on this matter, we welcome you to the microphone." The detective got out of his seat and approached the altar.

It was obvious he was not comfortable in public. He chewed his gum nervously and ran his hand several times over his head before he said something. "Look folks, I ain't no preacher," he began. "I'm a former Chicago cop, vice squad, now a private detective. I came over here because I feel like Reverend Warner over here deserves an even break." He pointed toward Steven.

"I'll be honest. I don't mind bringing down a politician, an alderman here or there, even a mayor if he or she deserves it. Hey, if they've been cheating on their spouse, I don't mind blowing the whistle." He chewed his gum even more vigorously.

Who is this bozo? thought Rachel. *I wish he'd shut up so I can finish off Warner.*

"But, hey," said the detective, "I don't believe in messing with the Man upstairs—you know what I mean? So when this lady comes in and tells me she's been with the reverend but then gives me some tapes to redo, something don't seem right." The detective blew his nose in his handkerchief. "Sorry. As I was saying, I listened to those tapes. The Reverend here is clean

as a whistle. He never did anything with her. She was setting
him up, see?"

The noise began to grow in the crowd once more. Steven
put his head down. The detective looked over at him and
smirked. "Yeah, that's right, Rev. The lady, Ms. Evans, Gustav, whatever her alias is, she gave me some letters to forge too.
I took those letters and the tapes, and I walked them right over
to the state attorney's office. The police lab did the rest. We
set her up. Right now I would suspect that dame is in a squad
car somewhere on her way to County for booking."

"I knew it, Pastor!" someone shouted. "I knew it couldn't
be true!" The audience rose to their feet with cheering and
boisterous applause. Brenda had been brought back into the
auditorium by Beulah and her mother-in-law to hear the
detective's story. She ran up on stage and embraced her husband. Dr. Ray held his hands up and clasped them together in
joy.

Phil went over and put his arm around the detective, and
the applause went wild in the auditorium. Fulton seemed a
little embarrassed but nodded with gratitude. He shook hands
with Steven, Dr. Ray, and Phil and then left the stage.

Rachel, who had watched this entire scenario from the
balcony, collapsed on the floor. Then she began to quiver and
tremble.

A woman got up and went over to her. "Rachel, are you all
right? What's wrong?" Rachel couldn't reply, but instead
rocked back and forth on the carpet. Those around could hear
her moan. First it was a quiet, almost chantlike sound. Then
it grew louder and louder, like a wounded animal crying for
help. More people began to gather around her. Her body began
to convulse with agony. She let out one shriek, then another.

"She's having a seizure of some kind!" someone called from
the balcony. "Call the paramedics!"

Phil Crawford, aware of what might be happening, leaned
quietly over the microphone and said, "In the name of Jesus,
I order the powers that bind this woman to themselves be

bound." All at once Rachel seemed to go limp. The noise she had been making stopped at once. The people around her stood back in astonishment. Several men helped her into a pew, where she began to weep.

Steven got up from his seat and moved to the pulpit. "Rachel, this is your pastor. Rachel, I mean this. Jesus Christ loves you. Brenda and I love you. In fact, Christ has poured out His very life's blood on your behalf. Today, He's calling you to accept His offer of full, complete forgiveness."

Rachel sat with her head in her hands. "Rachel," Steven continued, "God can set you free. He can fill you with His love. Have you ever accepted Christ as your personal Savior?"

Rachel shook her head no. The women in her group couldn't believe what they were witnessing.

"Rachel, God loves you more than you will ever know. Would you like to receive His gift of eternal life and know true freedom and power?"

Rachel nodded yes. "Will all the congregation please join me in praying for Rachel?" said Steven. "I'm going to ask every woman in the congregation that loves Rachel to please stand and pray for her right now." Scores of women, including some from her study group, stood to pray. "Will one of you lead in prayer for her right now?" asked Steven.

"Father, Rachel is not an enemy, but a victim," said Melissa, the young mother who had left her group. "Let the love You have for her wash over her in this moment. Set her free from whatever deceptions she may have accepted as truth. Show her true power, the power of a new life in the person of Jesus Christ. Amen."

"Amen," said Steven. "Rachel, it's entirely up to you. But I believe Jesus is calling you to Himself today. If you're prepared to trust Christ as your Savior, come down so we can pray with you."

As a dumbfounded congregation watched, Rachel stood up. Two women helped her down the balcony stairs and up the aisle to the front of the church. As the Warners and Rachel embraced, she began to weep aloud—no longer a cry of agony or torment but one of release and cleansing. "I'm free," she said out loud. "Praise God, I'm really free." Her eyes, which, only moments ago, had been filled with anger and pain, were now soft and clear, almost translucent. They seemed filled with light.

"Look at what's happened to her," someone whispered. A holy awe and fear seemed to settle over the congregation.

"I can't believe it," Rachel said as the women embraced her. "I'm free. I'm really free. Christ is alive! He's alive!"

"I believe we are ready to dismiss this afternoon's service," said Dr. Ray from the pulpit. "Let's finish with a song we used to sing at camp meetings when I was a boy in Mississippi. We called it 'Old One Hundred.' I believe you know it as 'The Doxology.'"

The country preacher led out in a clear, melodic tenor voice: "Praise God from whom all blessings flow . . ."

In the back of the squad car Ingrid thrashed about as if bound by invisible ropes. She was wearing handcuffs.

"You have nothing on me!" she hissed at the detective in the front seat. "Nothing! I'll have your badge before the day is done."

In the front seat a plainclothes detective with a cigar in his mouth turned around. "Lady, I've already read you your rights. Conspiracy to commit forgery and conspiracy to commit blackmail are felonies. If I were you, I'd try and think of the number of a good attorney. But for now, why don't you just try and sit still?"

He turned and flipped on the car radio to a country music station. All of Ingrid's angry threats and insults were drowned out by the old Hank Williams tune, "Your Cheatin' Heart."

The celebration at church had just ended when an usher approached Steven with an ashen face.

Steven slapped him on the back, "Sam, what's wrong with you? You look ill."

"Pastor, we just got a call in the office. It's about your son, Eric."

Steven and Brenda glanced at each other. "What is it, Sam? Is he all right?" demanded Brenda. "Is Eric okay?"

The hesitation in the usher's face frightened them.

"Don't tell me," said Brenda.

"The school just called. Your son is in serious trouble. The police are on the phone." Steven pushed the usher aside and ran to his office. In less than five minutes he had borrowed Phil Crawford's car, and he and Brenda went screeching out of the church lot. People in the sanctuary could hear the sound of his tires squealing.

TWENTY-TWO

Steven, hurry, please," said Brenda. She pressed her hands against the dashboard as if to urge the vehicle to go faster. "I knew we should have called Eric the moment we landed," she sobbed. "If anything happens to him—"

"Brenda, we can't think like that," said Steven. He weaved back and forth between cars. Whenever a clear stretch of road opened up he stomped on the accelerator. He screeched to a halt behind a UPS truck that had stopped to make a delivery. He edged out into the oncoming lane, then gunned the engine again.

They were only a few blocks from the high school when Steven jerked the wheel and pulled the car to the side of the road.

"What in heaven's name are you doing!" said Brenda. "Our son may be dead. Get this car back on the road!"

Steven took a deep breath and looked over at his wife. "Darling, I know this seems irrational. But this situation is already out of our control. I've tried to control everyone, everything around me for the last twenty years. If anything is going to change in our home, it needs to start now. Let's pray."

Brenda saw something in her husband's face that she hadn't seen since seminary. It was peace. Though he looked concerned, even anguished, about Eric, Steven was different.

"All . . . right Steven, I trust you," she said.

"Come close to me," he said. Brenda slid over, and Steven wrapped his arms around her.

"Father God in heaven," he began, "I have never been more scared in my entire life. My boy, my own flesh and blood, may already be dead. I pray that's not the case. My busyness robbed him of my time and attention, and now, I'm asking for something I don't deserve. I'm asking You to spare him, to spare the both of us. Whatever it is I need to learn through this, let me learn it completely, that I might never have to go through something like this again."

Brenda could feel the hot tears drip off Steven's cheeks. He held her even tighter in his embrace.

"So, dear God," finished Steven, "if You see fit, let him emerge from this awful situation alive. In Christ's name, amen."

Brenda hugged Steven, "I love you so much, Steven."

"I love you too," he whispered. "More than I ever have."

Steven sat up, looked in his rearview mirror, and jerked the gearshift into drive. "Let's go."

Steven was one block from Roosevelt High when he came to a squad car parked horizontally across the road. All four sides of the intersection had been roped off. Several red flares burned hot on the pavement.

Steven stopped his car less than three feet from the door of the squad car. The police officer glanced at Steven and climbed out of his car. It was clear he was upset. "If I wasn't so busy, buddy, I'd write you up. What do you think you're doing barreling up this street and nearly hitting my car?"

Steven recognized the policeman as the same officer he had met the morning the church had been vandalized. "Officer, it's me, Reverend Warner. I'm Eric Warner's father. The boy who's being held hostage in the school."

The policeman's expression changed at once. "So it's you, Reverend. I thought I had a drunk driver on my hands."

"Do you know anything about our son?"

Brenda leaned toward the window. "Please, tell us what's happened."

"The word on the radio is that they're all still inside the building," he said.

"Oh, thank you, God," breathed Brenda.

"Can you get us into the school?" said Steven.

"Just follow me," he said. He turned and waved to his partner who walked over and untied the police ribbon.

The officer jumped in the car, hit his lights, and headed through the open intersection. Steven was right on his bumper.

"Oh, my word, Steven," said Brenda. "Look at this." The school was a sea of flashing red, yellow, and blue lights. Fire trucks, ambulances, squad cars, and other emergency vehicles filled the school's parking lot.

The police car in front of Steven pulled up to a black sedan. Steven parked the car and waited. A detective in a tan trench coat approached the squad car. The policeman pointed at Steven and Brenda. The detective motioned for the Warners to climb out. Steven and Brenda emerged from separate sides of the car and converged on the investigator.

"I'm Steven Warner, this is my wife, Brenda," he said. "We're Eric's parents."

"Detective Calhoun." He reached out and shook hands. "The suspects are two high school-aged kids. Gang members. Right now all we know is that they're upstairs and they have a gun. We're doing everything we can to talk them into giving up. If that doesn't happen, we have a special weapons and tactics team in place." The detective pointed at the roof of a building across the street. The Warners clearly saw snipers lying on the rooftop.

"Those men have rifles," said Brenda. "They mustn't start shooting. They might hit Eric."

"We won't do anything we don't have to do, Mrs. Warner," said the detective. "Right now we have the best hostage negotiators in the city inside trying to talk them out. But if anything goes wrong," he pointed again to the roof, "we may need help."

Brenda stood with her hands pressed against her face. Steven reached out and put his arm around his wife. "Officer, can you take us inside?"

"Let me check with our negotiators," he said. He went to his car and pulled out his radio mike. He turned away from the Warners and spoke into it for about two minutes. Steven and Brenda stood with their heads down, holding on to one another.

The detective dropped the mike onto the seat of his car and walked back. "Okay, here's the story. The captain wants to talk with you. But I must advise you that I cannot guarantee your safety in a situation like this. We think the building is secure, but there may be other gang members hidden inside. In the event we have to take down the second floor, there's the possibility of gunfire."

Brenda bit her lip and shook her head no.

"You'll have to sign a release form to go in," said the detective.

"We'll do it," said Steven.

"And you must promise me you won't interfere in any way with the negotiations underway. Agreed?"

The Warners looked at each other. "Agreed."

The detective looked inside his car and produced a clipboard with a release form on it. He looked at his watch, jotted down some information, and handed it to the couple to sign. They both scribbled their signatures. The detective turned and whistled to a uniformed officer, "Hey, Sergeant, I need you."

"Yes, sir?" said the older patrolman.

"These are the parents of the hostage. I want them taken to the central office. You and Mulhaney escort them."

"Will do, sir," said the patrolman. With shotguns pointed straight up, two heavily armed officers marched the Warners through the side door of the school building. They were met by two additional heavily armed officers inside.

Steven couldn't believe it was the same school he had been to only a month before. It had been transformed from an ordinary high school into an armed camp. Helmeted members of the SWAT squad walked past, dressed in dark clothing and with black camouflage paint smeared on their faces. The hallway crackled with the sound of radio transmissions. The school had taken on the atmosphere of a siege in progress.

"This way, folks," said their escort. They walked into the principal's office. A worried-looking man with a loosened tie and white shirt looked up from a table where maps were spread out in front of him. Several people stood around him.

"Excuse me, Captain O'Hara," said the escort. "These are the Warners, Eric's parents." O'Hara walked away from the schematic diagrams of the school he had been reviewing with a janitor.

"Pleased to meet you, Mr. and Mrs. Warner. Captain O'Hara, head of the Crisis Resolution Unit." He reached out his hand.

"Good afternoon, Captain," said Steven. "I'm Steven, this is my wife Brenda."

"Have you talked with Eric yet?" said Brenda. "How is he? Is he hurt?"

"I heard him over the intercom just a few minutes ago, Mrs. Warner. His captors won't allow us to talk directly to him. As far as we know, he's still unharmed."

"Thank you, Jesus," said Brenda.

"Are they going to let him go?" said Steven.

"I think so, but when, I can't say," replied O'Hara. "We've been talking with them for two hours now. They've been up there for almost seven. They gave us one deadline, but it passed, oh—" He looked at his watch. "About 45 minutes ago."

"How did you know they wouldn't shoot Eric?" said Brenda.

"Experience, ma'am," smiled O'Hara. "Hostage-takers often make serious threats right at the start. They're scared. They want out right away. But they also know if they plug their hostage, they've lost their last card."

The Captain turned away and lit a cigarette. "Besides," he used his cigarette to point out the window across the street, "I have four men with 30.06 rifles who have the two gang members in their sights at all times. I let those two punks know that, just to give them something to think about."

"What's next?" asked Steven. "How do we get them to surrender?"

"Wait." The captain blew smoke in the air.

"For how long?" Brenda said.

"For as long as we have to," he replied.

"When can I talk to my son?" said Steven.

"I'll have to think about that," said O'Hara. He pointed at Steven with the cigarette in his hand. "Right now, I'm trying to arrange for the mothers of the suspects to get here."

"Good," said Brenda. "Maybe they can talk their boys into surrendering."

"Huh," said O'Hara. "We can't locate either one."

"What about their dads?" asked Brenda.

"Dads? What dads?" said the detective. "Why don't you two just sit down until I call you." He turned and went back to the table where the diagrams were laid out.

"I say we make our move right now," said Derek. "They wouldn't dare shoot us. Not with preacher's little boy here."

"Just how stupid are you, man?" said Tony. "You heard the pig. They've got rifles on us. We stand up and try to walk out, and we're both dead."

Eric lay facedown and tried not to think about what might happen. For him, the day had seemed like an eternity. But as he lay there, he had a chance to think about his life. He remembered the time as a little boy he had gotten trapped in a neighbor's storage shed one summer day. He had cried and cried, yet no one came. He spent almost two hours in there before Karin came looking for him. She heard his voice and was finally able to pry open the door.

Karin, Karin where are you now? thought Eric. *Come get me, Karin. I want to go home.*

Eric's sister Karin lay in a hospital room in County General under mild sedation. Nurses came in and checked her vital signs from time to time, but there was little change. The fluids she had received had helped her vital signs, but they were watching her closely for signs of further internal hemorrhaging.

Meanwhile, a group of six young women prayed in Lisa Fredrickson's room back on campus. They sat on chairs and beds.

"Lord, touch Karin's life at this moment," one prayed. "Spare her life and the life of her child."

The siege at Roosevelt High was now in its eighth hour. O'Hara paced the room while the Warners sat nervously on a couch.

"Any word about the mothers yet?" said O'Hara to a subordinate.

"Sorry, Captain," came the reply from a team member who put the phone down. "We're still trying to reach Mrs. Thornton. Mrs. Barton is out of town."

"Out of town?" said O'Hara.

"Yeah. We got hold of a neighbor who told us she and her new boyfriend went to Vegas for five days. The neighbor was supposed to keep an eye on Tony."

"Terrific. Just terrific," muttered the Captain. "What about Mrs. Thornton. Where's she?"

"We've managed to get hold of her daughter at home. She says her mother works two jobs. Won't be home until midnight."

"Well, can she give us her mother's work number?" shouted O'Hara.

"I'm sorry, sir. She's six years old. All she knows is that her mom works in the city at a restaurant. We're working on it."

The captain mumbled something to himself, then turned and pointed at Steven. "Mr. Warner, it looks like you're all we've got."

"What?" said Steven.

"We're going to have to use you to try and talk to the boys," he said.

"Sure, if you think it would help."

"Now look, Mr. Warner," said O'Hara. "You've heard of the good cop/bad cop routine? This is it. I've played hardball with them. You come in now and play the part of their buddy. Their advocate. Someone they can trust. Get what I'm saying?"

"I think so."

"Good."

"They need a friend, Mr. Warner. You be that friend. If it goes bad, I'll take over."

"I'll do my best," said Steven. He got up and hugged his wife. Through her tears, she looked up at him with admiration. "If anyone can do it, Steven, you can."

Steven spent the next several minutes in a briefing with the negotiation team. When they were done, O'Hara and Steven walked into the control room to the intercom system. The team had played easy listening elevator music over the intercom for the last hour.

O'Hara looked over at Steven. "Ready?"

"Ready," said Steven. He drew a deep breath and prayed silently for wisdom.

The captain hit the switch and the music stopped. He picked up the microphone, "Hi fellas. Jim O'Hara again. Getting tired? I don't blame you. It's been almost four hours since lunch. Too bad you didn't take me up on my offer for some food. But the offer still stands. Hey, more good news. There's someone who wants to talk to you. He says he's here to help you boys get out of this mess."

He turned and pushed the microphone toward Steven. Steven swallowed hard. "Hi, fellas, this is Steve Warner. I'm a pastor here in town."

Eric sat up. "Dad? Dad, is that you?" A hand reached up and covered Eric's mouth and pulled him back down.

"I ought to kill you for that," growled Tony. But Eric didn't care, he pulled the hand off his mouth and shouted, "Dad! Come get me! Please—" Tony reached over and whacked Eric on the side of the head with the butt of the pistol. "Oh!" cried Eric as he slumped down.

Steven heard Eric's cry and started to get up. The Captain put his hand on his shoulder and gestured for him to keep his cool. Steven sat back down. *At least I know he's alive*, he thought.

"Hey, Tony, Derek," said Steven. "I know what it's like to not have many friends. To be misunderstood. That's why I came over. I want to make sure no one harms you."

"Sure you are," shouted Tony. "The moment we let your kid go, they kill both of us."

"That's not true," said Steven. "It took some doing, but I think we've got a deal with the captain. He's agreed that if you set Eric free, he'll give you safe conduct and a personal escort to the County Juvenile facility. Then we can sort this thing out."

"No deal, Warner," snarled Tony. "You tell the pigs to clear out. Now. They've got five minutes. If they don't, your boy buys the farm. Got it?" Tony once again stuck his head up over the barricade and fired his gun at an overhead projector on a stand. The force of the bullet knocked the machine over and sent shards of glass flying everywhere.

Steven pushed the microphone away. "Captain, that's gunfire!" The captain grabbed his walkie-talkie. "Raven Two, what have you got?"

"Suspect fired at an overhead projector. The hostage appears unharmed."

"Did you say *unharmed*?"

"Affirmative, sir. Gunfire was directed away from him."

Steven hit his fist on the table. "Captain, you've got to do something. Now! The next shot may be aimed at Eric."

"Calm down, Mr. Warner, your boy is still safe. They're just bluffing," said O'Hara.

"How do you know?" said Steven. "They're boys. They're scared. They might do anything. Order your men in."

"No, Mr. Warner, not yet. Please, I've seen this before. We're getting somewhere, trust me."

"You call gunshots *getting somewhere*?" Steven got up and walked over to the window.

"You falling apart on me, Reverend?"

"Okay, I'm sorry," said Steven. "This hasn't been an easy day."

"Let's go back on," said O'Hara.

"Wait, what if we offered the boys a better deal?"

"No deals."

"No, look. I've got an idea. I go up and offer myself as an exchange for Eric. Then the three of us leave the building together."

"Yeah, right. Then I've got two hostages instead of just one," said O'Hara. "Out of the question."

"Captain, those boys know you won't open fire with me standing between them. Right now they want out of there more than we want them out. It's worth a try. It might get Eric out alive."

The captain got up and rubbed his chin, "No, you're not trained for this type of thing. I can't let you—"

"Captain, I'm a shepherd."

"So?" grunted O'Hara.

"That's just it. Part of a shepherd's training is learning to lay down his life for others. I've spent a lifetime preparing for today."

The captain thought it over. "No, I don't think so. Too risky."

"Captain, I don't care if I come out of that room alive or not. I do care if Eric does. Please. Let's give it a try."

The captain stared at Steven. "All right, Warner. Let's see if the boys want to deal."

The two men sat down at the console again. Steven switched on the microphone, "Fellas, this is Steve Warner again. Hey, listen to this. I've just talked it over with Captain O'Hara, and we've decided to meet your terms."

Tony punched Derek and smiled, "What did I tell you? Leave it to me and we're out of here." Eric couldn't believe it. *Dad, how could you sell me out?* he thought.

Tony put his head over the barricade, "Okay, Warner. You clear out the pigs and nobody gets hurt. We want a car with a full tank of gas and a thousand dollars in a bag in the front seat. No cops anywhere, hear? One cop and we kill your kid. When we get out of this town, we'll let him go. Fair enough?"

"It's a good plan, Tony," said Steven. "But with one catch. I come up there and you exchange Eric for me. Then we walk out together."

Eric opened his eyes. *He'd do that for me?* thought Eric. He had a sudden impulse. He put his head up and yelled, "Dad, don't do it. They'll kill you, too."

Tony pointed the pistol at Eric, "Shut up!" Tony thought it over for a moment, "No deal, Warner. It's a setup."

"No it isn't, Tony," said Steven. "I'll come up alone. Unarmed. I walk into the room and you let Eric go. I stay. Then we all walk out together. It's that simple."

"We could get out of here, man," whispered Derek to Tony. "The preacher wouldn't be lying. Let's do it." Tony bit his nail on his left hand.

"Come on, Tony," said Derek. "No preacher is going to come in here and shoot us."

The sweat on Tony's upper lip was visible. "I don't know, I just don't know," he said. "I need time to think."

"Come on, man," said Derek. "Let's do it."

"All right!" Tony shouted up at the intercom. "You clear out the pigs. Then you come up here and your boy goes free. But no tricks, understand?"

"You have my word, Tony."

"I won't let you do it, Steven," said Brenda. "I can't lose both of you in one day."

Steven put his hands on her shoulders. "Brenda, that's our son up there."

"I know," she whispered. "I'm so scared."

"Here, Mr. Warner, put this on," said a hostage negotiator. He handed Steven a thin Kevlan bulletproof vest.

"I don't think so," said Steven. He handed the vest back to the officer.

"But Reverend Warner, if they start shooting—"

"If they see this under my shirt, they might just think it's a setup and start shooting. No, I go just as I am." The team member looked to O'Hara for support.

"It's up to him," said O'Hara.

"No vest," said Steven.

"Okay," said O'Hara. He put out his cigarette. "Let's go over this for the final time." The entire group huddled and reviewed the plan. Police cars would pull back from the front of the school. Steven would go up with escorts to the second floor, then go it alone from there. The SWAT team would be ready to move on O'Hara's command. A light blue unmarked car would be driven to the middle of the parking lot and the car door left open. Steven would walk out with the two gang members and get in the car. A transmitter hidden in the car would allow another unmarked car to track their movements.

Twenty minutes later, everything was in place.

"Good-bye, sweetheart," said Steven. He leaned over and kissed his wife. "I'll bring Eric back. I promise I will."

"I love you, Steven," she said.

He walked out, followed by two team members. O'Hara glanced at Brenda and smiled. "You've got a good man, lady," said the captain.

"I know," she replied.

"Okay, folks, this is it," said O'Hara.

O'Hara walked back into the intercom room. He sat down, took a deep breath, and flipped on the switch. "Boys, this is O'Hara. This is how it's going to happen. Reverend Warner is on his way up right now. He's coming alone. When he gets up there, he'll open the door. When he gets inside, you let Eric go, and the Reverend stays with you. Wait three minutes for Eric to get out of the area. Then you're free to go. Reverend Warner will walk out with you. You'll see a blue car parked in the street. It's yours."

"Okay, O'Hara," shouted Tony. "But one wrong move and I waste Dad and Sonny Boy here."

Steven walked slowly up the stairs to the second floor. Only members of the SWAT team were up there. Steven conferred with the officer in charge, they shook hands, and he continued on toward the room.

He turned the corner and started down the hallway. His mind went back to the day he had met Eric in school and canceled their plans. *I wish I had that day back*, he thought.

He looked at the room numbers above the doors—202, 205, 207, and at last, 209. *This is it*, he thought. *Please God, take care of Eric.*

He stepped up to the door and looked through the window of the classroom. The room was a mess—desks overturned, shattered glass, papers everywhere on the floor.

"Yea, though I walk through the valley of the shadow of death," whispered Steven to himself, "I will fear no evil." Steven reached out and knocked on the door.

Slowly a head rose above the desks. A figure clad in a black T-shirt and jeans got up. He looked much younger than Steven had imagined.

Tony motioned at Steven, and Steven approached the door. He turned the handle slowly and opened it. He walked inside the classroom.

"Are you Tony or Derek?" asked Steven.

"I'm Tony," said the boy. He pointed the .38-caliber gun at Steven's chest. "Now just walk in here nice and slow."

"Where's Eric?" said Steven. "I want to see him."

Tony turned around. "Get up, Warner. Your daddy's here to let you go home for supper."

Eric got up. Steven flinched when he saw his son's bruised and swollen face. His wanted to lash out at his son's tormentors, to hurt them for what they had done. But he couldn't allow himself the luxury of anger at this moment.

"Thanks, Dad, for coming," said Eric. His eyes were filled with tears.

"Sorry I took so long," said Steven.

"Cut this jive," said Tony. "Let's get it over with." He walked back and shoved a gun into Eric's ribs, "Get going."

"Boys, I want you to know something," said Steven.

"What?" snarled Tony.

"I don't hate you for what you've done."

"Well, isn't that special?" said Tony.

"No, I mean it. No matter what you've done today, there's a God in heaven who loves both of you."

Tony cursed at him.

Steven ignored the insult. "I only wish you'd give up and give others a chance to help you," he said.

"Help us into prison, you mean," said Derek. "Besides, it wasn't my idea to shoot Martinez. It was Tony's!"

Tony turned toward his partner. "Shut up! Can't you see what the preacher's trying to do?" He turned toward Steven with hate glowing in his eyes. "Listen, Preacher, no one on this earth cares whether I live or die? See? No one."

"I care, Tony. Christ has a better plan for your life than this."

At the mention of the name of Christ, Derek seemed to weaken. "I don't want to die, Reverend. Really. I don't."

"No one's going to die today," said Steven. "Someone already did."

"Who? Martinez?" snapped Tony.

"No, he's still alive. I'm talking Jesus. He was a ransom. Like I am. He traded His life for yours."

Tears began to roll down Derek's cheeks. He turned away and wiped his eyes with his sleeve.

"Shut up, Preacher!" shouted Tony.

"What are you afraid of?" said Steven. "That I might be right? That God may actually love you?"

Suddenly, Derek began to experience the Presence.

"What does it take, man?" said Derek.

"Simple, Derek. 'If you confess with your mouth the Lord Jesus and believe in your heart that God has raised Him from the dead, you will be saved.' It's that simple."

Derek shook. "I believe, Reverend Warner, I do."

"I said shut up!" snapped Tony. He walked back and took hold of Eric. "Get out of here!" He shoved Eric toward Steven, but as he did so, Tony's boot slipped on a shard of broken glass. He went down backward, and as he fell the gun went off. Derek grabbed his stomach and crumpled to the floor. Steven knew it was now or never. He threw himself onto Tony. The gun sounded a second time.

Across the street the SWAT commander saw the boys go down and heard the gun discharge twice over his radio. "Delta Ten! Delta Ten!" he shouted into his walkie-talkie. "Delta Ten" was the code phrase for attack. Immediately ropes dropped over the side of the building and three commandos rappelled down to the window level. Two fired flash and bang grenades through the window while the other shot tear gas into the room. The room exploded with white light and a deafening roar.

The SWAT team members on the second floor charged down the hallway from both ends. They were inside the room in less than seven seconds. The classroom became an inferno of smoke, noise, and shouting.

Downstairs in the office, Brenda heard the shudder of the grenades going off. She jumped up and ran toward the control room, "Steven! Eric!" she screamed.

It lasted less than thirty seconds.

"Raven Ten, this is Bravo Leader, room secured," crackled the voice over the radio. "We have casualties."

Paramedics rushed up the steps with stretchers and emergency kits. Police formed a corridor to clear the way for the wounded to be carried out.

Brenda and O'Hara ran out of the office. They headed for the door where the team would emerge.

Brenda stood by the stairwell with her hand up to her mouth and waited. First one stretcher, then another.

"Oh Lord, please don't let it be Steven and Eric," she prayed.

The boy on the first stretcher had an oxygen mask pulled over his nose. His face was covered with grime from the smoke. Before Brenda could get a good look at him, he was rushed down the sidewalk and loaded into the back of an ambulance.

The boy on the next stretcher sat up and coughed. Brenda recognized the familiar brown hair.

"Eric!" shouted Brenda. She broke free from the group and ran up to the stretcher. He looked up and smiled. "Hi, Mom," he whispered.

"My baby!" she cried out.

One of the paramedics looked up at her. "He took in a hefty dose of tear gas. But he'll be all right."

Next came a stretcher with Tony lying on it. He coughed and gasped for air.

Where's Steven? thought Brenda. Her legs began to feel weak. The principal steadied her with one arm. "Tell me— please tell me he's all right." She turned and buried her face in her hands.

"I've been through church board meetings that were worse," came a weak voice from behind her.

"Steven!" she cried. He stood on the stairs, his face black with soot and burn marks. He coughed and gasped for air, and he managed to walk only with the assistance of a paramedic.

"Steven!" She ran and threw herself into her husband's arms. Smoke inhalation and the shock of the experience had left him a little dazed.

"I said I'd bring him home," smiled Steven as he held his wife close to him.

Steven and Brenda stumbled over to Eric's stretcher in the street. "How about that game of one-on-one, Eric?" said Steven. He picked up his son's hand and kissed it, "I love you."

"You—you almost got yourself killed," said Eric. "For me. Why?"

"Because there is someone whose life is more precious to me than my own life," said Steven. "His name is Eric."

His son reached up and put his arms around his dad's neck.

"We're going to have to take him in to have his lungs checked," said the paramedic. "He also has leg lacerations. You should probably see a doctor too, Reverend Warner."

Steven coughed again. "Oh, I'll be fine. Do you mind if we ride with him to the hospital?"

"Hop in," said the paramedic.

"What about the other two boys?" asked Brenda.

"One is in critical condition with a stomach wound," said the paramedic. "The other boy just has smoke inhalation."

The Warners walked into the waiting area of the emergency room at County General. Steven looked like he had spent the day fighting a forest fire, and Brenda showed the effects of jet lag. It was just that morning they had flown in from Hawaii.

At the hospital, Derek's wounds received top priority. The hospital staff quickly rushed him into emergency surgery.

Eric had suffered a number of surface cuts on his legs from flying glass when the SWAT team fired tear gas into the room. "These will need stitches," a nurse said. "Otherwise, I think he's fine." She listened to Steven breathe and decided he didn't need further attention. Brenda and Steven decided to wait in the lobby until a doctor could tend to Eric.

"Why haven't we been able to reach Karin?" said Brenda. "No one on campus seems to know where she is. This morning I tried her room a dozen times. No answer."

"Let's try again in just a minute," said Steven.

As they sat trying to catch their breath, two young college girls walked through the electric doors that led to the receptionist's desk.

"Let's go see how Karin is doing," said Sally to Jane Phelps. They had just returned from supper at a restaurant near the hospital.

Steven saw them and sat up. *Don't I know that girl?* he thought. On an impulse, he got up and decided to follow them.

"Steven, where are you going?" said Brenda.

"I'll tell you in just a minute," he replied. He walked, then jogged to catch up with the two young women. They turned around, and when they saw his appearance, they turned around again and walked quickly away from him.

That's Sally, thought Steven. *Karin's roommate.* "Sally, wait! Please wait!" he yelled.

Without looking back, the two girls started to pick up speed. They were afraid.

"No, please. It's me, Reverend Warner," he said.

Sally was the first to stop. She turned slowly around.

"Dr. Warner?" she said. His clothes, his face, the smell of tear gas—it was hard to believe this was the pastor of one of the largest churches in town. "Is that you?" gasped Sally.

"Yes, it's me." He glanced down at himself. "Oh, you're probably wondering why I look like this," he said. "I—uh, I spent some time at my son's school today."

By now the other girl had joined Sally. "Hi, I'm Jane Phelps." Steven reached out with a grimy hand, then pulled it back.

"Sorry, Jane, I guess I need to wash up. Did I hear you mention Karin's name a minute ago?" said Steven.

The girls exchanged glances, but neither said a word.

"What is it? Where is she?" said Steven.

"Then you don't know?" said Jane.

"Know what?" said Steven. His heart rate started to climb.

"About Karin—and Jeff?" asked the freshman.

Sally nudged Jane to be quiet. After all, she had promised Karin she'd never tell her parents. But the freshman girl didn't get the message.

"Sure, I know about those two," said Steven. "I've never had much time for the boy. They've been dating on and off. Right?"

Again the two girls looked at each other.

"What's wrong?" said Steven. "What's going on with Karin and Jeff? Tell me. I want to know."

Sally drew a long breath. "Reverend Warner, we need to sit down somewhere where we can talk. I think you might want to get your wife, too—if she's here."

The confusion on Steven's face gave way to concern. "All right, Sally," he said slowly. "She's in the lobby. Why don't you two come back with me where we can talk?"

The trio walked back down the hallway into the emergency room waiting area.

"Brenda, look who I found," said Steven.

"Sally!" shrieked Brenda. She got up and hugged her daughter's roommate.

"This is Jane Phelps," Sally said. "She lives on Karin's floor."

"Wonderful," sighed Brenda. "Can you tell us where we can reach her? We've tried all day to get hold of her—it's been some kind of day."

"Uh, Mr. Warner, Mrs. Warner, there's something you both should know," said Sally. "I promised Karin I'd never tell you this, but I think it's time to break that promise."

Worry filled Brenda's eyes. "What is it girls? What's wrong?"

Sally sat down next to Brenda and took her hand. She explained everything that had happened to Karin.

"Oh, no—oh, no," said Brenda. Steven said nothing; he just bowed his head on his wife's shoulder. The two of them had very little left in emotional or physical reserves to absorb this latest news.

"I thought you two knew," said Jane.

"What room is she in?" said Steven.

"She's in room 347," said Sally.

"How could you keep such a thing from us?" said Brenda, fighting back tears. "She's our daughter!"

Sally lowered her head. "I'm so sorry, Mrs. Warner. She made me promise."

"This is no time to argue," said Steven. "We've got to see her. Come on, Brenda."

"What about Eric?" asked Brenda. "We just can't leave him in the emergency room."

"We'll call down from Karin's room," said Steven. "If there's a problem, they'll know where to reach us."

The two girls sat with tears in their eyes as the Warners got up to leave.

"Mr. and Mrs. Warner?" said Jane.

"Yes?" said Brenda as she turned around.

"I just want to say, well, what a wonderful person Karin really is. Despite what's happened. Please tell her we're down here. We're praying for her. Lots of people are praying for her."

"Thank you, Jane," said Brenda. The Warners turned and headed for the elevators. Steven and Brenda rushed into an open elevator and punched "3". It seemed to take forever for the doors to close. At last they were on their way upstairs. After what seemed aeons, the doors opened.

They glided past trays and medical equipment like professional skiers negotiating a slalom course. They counted down the room numbers until they found Karin's. Steven was the first to go in. A frail, blonde girl with an ashen face and closed eyes lay on the bed.

"Karin!" he cried. He rushed up to her bedside and took the girl's hand. "Oh, my little girl. It's me. It's Dad." Brenda was close behind. She rushed over and threw her arms around her daughter's neck. By now a nurse stood outside the door.

"Looks like Karin has visitors," she said.

"We're her parents," said Brenda, her voice choked with emotion. "What's wrong with our daughter?"

Karin opened her eyes halfway and struggled to focus.

"Mom? Is that you?" she moaned.

"Oh, darling," said Brenda.

"It's me, too, sweetheart, it's Dad," said Steven. "We're right here with you." He knelt next to her bed and held onto her hand.

"Karin has had some bleeding problems," said the nurse. "We're doing the best we can to save the baby."

Karin looked frightened. "Daddy, I'm so sorry . . ."

"Can I speak with you outside?" asked the nurse. She motioned them both toward the door.

"Come on, honey," said Brenda. "The nurse needs to speak with us."

But Steven wouldn't let go of his daughter.

"I imagine my appearance here today is quite a surprise to most of you," said Dr. Porter, a professor at Randolph University. It was Thursday evening and the Stirring on campus showed no signs of slowing down. Even though it was seven o'clock at night, the chapel remained packed.

Dean Prestwick stood against the back wall with a barely disguised smile on her face.

"I am here tonight to say God has done something in my life really quite extraordinary," he said. Both faculty and students listened in rapt attention.

"When I was the age of most of you here this evening, I experienced a distinct call to overseas mission work," he said. No one, particularly his colleagues, could believe what they were hearing. "I resisted that call. I ran from it. In fact, I've run from it for nearly thirty years."

"You see, I was raised in a small, fundamentalist church in Iowa. My dad was a missions agency executive. When I was only fifteen, he died of a heart attack. I became embittered toward God. I blamed Him for taking my father. I hardened my heart. I hardened it to the point that I've actually turned young men and women away from pursuing seminary training or missions work.

"I did it to get back at—" Porter paused for a moment, determined to maintain control. "I—did it—to pay God back—for—" He stopped again. "I have been so filled with anger all these years—" His voice reached almost a whine. "Because I so missed my father." Silently, he put his head down. No one knew what to do.

Dean Prestwick quietly made her way toward the front of the chapel. She walked up onto the stage and over to the professor, who stood bent over. She placed her hand on his back.

"Let's all stop for a moment and pray for our esteemed colleague and professor, Dr. Porter," she said. They all lowered their heads.

"Dear God," she said, "it is not those who wrestle with You that displease You, but those who ignore You. Our good friend, Dr. Porter, has wrestled with You as Jacob once did. Like Jacob, bless him now that the match has ended. In Christ's name, amen."

Dr. Porter, still struggling to regain his composure, chose to go and sit down. The dean surveyed the assembly of students and faculty and said, "I'm sure this will be news to all of you, but this morning Dr. Porter submitted his resignation to my office."

There was a commotion throughout the chapel.

"What?" said a faculty member. "It's been rejected, I trust."

"I called Dr. Porter as soon as I received it and asked him to please reconsider. Yet when he explained to me the reason behind his departure, I reluctantly chose to accept it."

"Please reconsider!" someone else said.

"I understand your sentiments entirely," she responded. "But Dr. Porter is resigning from Randolph to seek a position as an instructor in a school in Asia. This is no ordinary school.

Dr. Porter will be teaching within the confines of a leprosarium."

There was a moment of silence, then a female student, one of Dr. Porter's advisees, stood up. In a clear, lovely soprano voice, she began to sing: "Amazing grace, how sweet the sound—" In a moment the entire assembly joined her. Soon the entire room reverberated with the familiar song. Dr. Porter, buoyed by the sound of the hymn, rose slowly from the chair.

"How are you, sis?" Eric stood in the door of Karin's room with his mother close behind him.

"Eric? Is that you?" said Karin, turning her head toward the door.

"Yeah. It's me."

"Thanks for coming."

"Sure, no problem." Eric looked back at his mom.

"Go in," she whispered.

Eric approached the bed cautiously. "I came up here to tell you something," he said.

"Where have you been?" she said.

"Oh, I had to stay after school for something," he joked. "I just stopped by to say something."

"What's that?"

"Thanks for coming to get me when I was locked in the shed," he said.

Karin laughed quietly. "Eric, that was years ago."

"I love you, Karin," he said. "Please get better."

TWENTY-THREE

The prayer vigil on Karin's floor was in its ninth hour. Despite the ordeal, none of the girls gathered in prayer were prepared to leave. Not before they received the assurance that Karin and her baby would live.

The hours dragged on. Doctors and nurses routinely updated the Warners on Karin's condition. Dr. Ray had heard of the incident at Roosevelt High and had spent the afternoon with Beulah in an emergency prayer meeting. Once he received news it was over, he tracked Steven and Brenda down at County General.

Now, everyone in the waiting room was asleep, including Dr. Ray. It was four o'clock in the morning when a male nurse touched Steven on the shoulder. He had been asleep in a Lazy Boy recliner.

"Reverend Warner," said the young male nurse. "Please wake up. The hour has come."

Steven rubbed his eyes, "What? What did you say?" He leaned forward and looked at the other sleeping figures in the room.

"Let's let them sleep," said the nurse. "All I need is you."

"What is it?" said Steven. "Is something wrong? Is it Karin?"

"Shh," said the nurse. "Just come with me." Still somewhat groggy, Steven stumbled to his feet. He followed the nurse down the hallway toward his daughter's room.

"In there," said the nurse. He pointed into Karin's room. Still confused, Steven walked through the door. A soft table lamp next to Karin's bed washed the room in a peaceful, amber color. Karin was sitting up.

"Daddy, come in," she said. "Did you meet them?"

"Meet who, sweetheart?" said Steven.

"The nurses who just left," she smiled. "There were six of them." There was a strength in her voice that surprised Steven. As Steven walked closer he noticed that a tinge of color had returned to her cheeks. "They prayed for me for nearly two hours," Karin said.

Steven leaned over to take a closer look at his daughter. "Karin, you look different."

"The doctor was just in here, Daddy," she said. There was a glimmer of light in her eyes. "He let me hear the heartbeat."

"Karin, what about the hemorrhaging?" asked Steven.

"She's out of danger," said a voice behind them. It was a woman doctor. "Too early to tell, but a slow heartbeat like that often means it's a female. Of course, that's just folklore. I'll check in on her again later this morning. See you then." The doctor smiled and walked back to the desk.

Steven stood there, not knowing whether to laugh or cry with joy. He wrapped his arms around his daughter and rocked her like a little child. "Oh, thank you, God," he said over and over and over.

Around eight o'clock in the morning Steven took Brenda and Eric home. For the first time in a long time, they all ate breakfast together. Karin was due to be released in three or four days. The answering machine flashed "28," indicating the number of calls they had received while they were gone.

"These can wait," said Steven. "Hey, Eric, how about a little game of one-on-one?"

"You've got to be kidding, Dad," said Eric. "I need some sleep."

"Sleep? You can sleep anytime. Or are you afraid of my monster slam dunk?"

"In your dreams, Dad."

"Let's go." Eric and his dad put on their warm clothes and headed out into the winter morning. The sun sparkled off the snow with a brilliance that could shame the color of rare gems.

Steven had just made his first three-point shot when a car pulled in the driveway. Eric picked up the ball, "Who's that, Dad?"

"I don't know, son. But I'll find out." Steven walked toward the car.

A middle-aged man in a trench coat got out and produced a badge. "Mr. Warner? Joe McDonald. Treasury Department. I'd like to ask you a few questions."

"Certainly," said Steven. "May I ask what this is all about?"

"I'm conducting a criminal investigation, sir," said McDonald. "I have a search warrant and court order that allow me to seize all financial documents pertaining to First Community Church."

"What?" said Steven.

"Shall we go inside?" said McDonald.

Steven turned toward Eric. "It will be just a few minutes, big guy." Eric turned away and started taking shots on his own.

"There had better be a good reason for this, Mr. McDonald," said Steven. "I'm in the middle of a basketball game with my son. Between him and you, he's my first priority."

McDonald didn't like Warner's attitude. "You may find this a more serious matter than you think, Reverend Warner."

Steven reached for the back door when Brenda opened it and surprised them both. "Oh, Steven, I didn't realize we had company," she said. "There's a phone call for you. You need to take it right away."

"Is it about Karin?"

"No, sweetheart," she said. "It's the police." Brenda looked again at the stranger.

"Brenda, I'd like you to meet Mr. McDonald. He's with the Treasury Department."

"Hello, Mr. McDonald," she smiled. "Steven, there's been another break-in at church. They caught someone this time."

"You're kidding," he said. "Not another burglary?" He turned toward the agent, "Look, Mr. McDonald, whatever is on your mind it's going to have to wait. This is the second break-in this year. This time they've finally caught someone. If you'll please excuse me."

"You won't mind if I follow you?" said the agent.

"Be my guest," said Steven. "You said you wanted the files didn't you?" He turned to his wife. "Honey, can you call the church for me? Tell them I'm on my way over."

Steven started for his car, then remembered Eric. *Not this time*, he thought to himself. He walked over to his son who stood with a ball under his arm.

"Eric, there's been another burglary at church. They've got a suspect. I've got to go down there. I want you to come along. Will you, please?"

The boy looked down, then raised his head. He had a huge smile. "Sure thing, Dad. Besides, you might need someone who knows Tae Kwon Do." He made a few martial arts moves, then punched his dad.

"All right, big guy, let's go."

During the drive to the church the agent kept a close tail on Steven and Eric. Steven couldn't have cared less. The scene at the church was like an instant replay of the first break-in episode. The squad cars. An officer filling out forms. Even the same police officer stood in the hallway.

"Good morning, Reverend Warner," said the policeman.

"Good morning, officer," he replied. "This is becoming a habit, isn't it?"

"Maybe this is the last time we'll be needed here," said the policeman. "We've got a suspect in the office. A neighbor saw him trying to open the back door around four o'clock this morning and decided to call us. We came and searched the lot and found the back door open. We didn't find anyone inside the first time. So we left an officer hidden in the building. He caught the suspect coming out at six o'clock. The suspect had been hiding in the safe."

"Who is it?" said Steven.

"You may know him," said the officer. "He claims to be a member of your congregation."

"He's what?" Steven followed the officer down the corridor into the main office. Seated in the reception area was a young man slumped down in a chair.

"Todd!" said Steven. "What in the world are you doing here?" It was Todd Branstrom, the young lawyer Steven had eaten lunch with the day the waitress spilled water and coffee on him. "What in the world are you doing here?" said Steven.

"It's you?" said Joe McDonald.

The lawyer looked away and scowled.

"How do you know Todd?" said Steven.

"I spent an entire evening taking a deposition from him at his home. He's the one who sent information to our IRS office implicating you and others in a money-laundering scheme. The U.S. attorney's office is prepared to call him as a grand jury witness against you and others at this church." Steven was dumbstruck.

"We searched him and found this card in his wallet," said the officer. He handed Steven a business card. "Does this name make any sense to you?"

Steven studied the card, "Ingrid Gustav, Director, The New Consciousness Center," he read. Steven looked at the young man in disbelief. "You were involved with Tiffany?"

"We booked a woman by this name yesterday on felony charges," said the police officer. "It looks like we might have someone else to add to the list."

"I know my rights," said the lawyer. "I don't have to say a word. I wish to call my attorney."

"But Todd, why?" said Steven.

"Ingrid knows what true power is. You don't. It's not over, Warner," said the young man with spite. "Believe me, it's not over."

"All right, wise guy, let's get going," said the officer. "Oh, by the way, we found these inside his coat pocket." The policeman held up several computer tapes. Steven carefully examined one.

"They're used by our treasurer," said Steven.

The treasury agent shook his head. "I need to use your phone, Reverend Warner. I'm afraid my investigation has been seriously compromised."

Steven pointed toward the desk, "Be my guest."

"Dad, are you in some kind of trouble?" said Eric.

"Only if we don't get back to our game," he replied. Steven pretended to do one or two basketball moves, then grabbed his son and hugged him. The two of them walked out of the office, then raced down the hallway to see who would be first out the back door.

EPILOGUE

In the weeks and months that followed, the Stirring spread to the communities surrounding Covington Park. In each place, a similar pattern occurred. Churches that had once been dead or divided were revitalized and mended. Pastors who had been driven from churches by factions and in-fighting were invited back for public services of confession and reconciliation. As a result, several pastors who had left the local church returned to active ministry.

There was also a change in relationships between pastors. Where petty jealousies and arguments had once divided them, a new spirit of love and cooperation replaced distrust and competition.

In the local business community, a dramatic drop in employee theft and absenteeism occurred. The number of sexual harassment suits and employee grievances filed also plunged. Employers and corporate leaders were forced to create flexible schedules to allow for executives to participate in their children's lives again. It became commonplace in Covington Park to see high-level executives attend their sons' or daughters' school play or awards assembly in the middle of the day.

Crime showed significant drops in those communities most affected by the Stirring. The decreased demand for drugs on the street resulted in the financial breakup of several of the county's drug cartels. With fewer dollars from illegal drug sales available, the trade in illegal weapons also suffered.

In the inner city, where gang violence and single parenthood had been epidemic, men returned to raise the children they had fathered. The result was the dissolution of many of the area's most powerful and dangerous gangs. In several communities, it became safe to walk the streets again at night.

Racial tensions also subsided in many parts of the city as the church led the way in reconciliation. Suburban and urban churches began holding joint worship services, and several congregations exchanged pulpits on special Sundays. Affluent churches chose to commit funds and resources to networking with urban churches. Reconciliation marches, led by pastors and lay leaders from several racial groups, became an annual event.

In local government, the change in values and the revitalization of the family began having an impact. Local and state referendum initiatives that promoted euthanasia and physician-assisted suicide were soundly defeated.

Abortion clinics in the county were forced to consolidate as demand dropped off significantly. Eventually, many went out of business altogether in and around Covington Park.

As the number of two-parent families increased, education improved and test scores soared for the first time in three decades in the area. School-based clinics that distribute birth control devices became less and less popular. Eventually, the idea was shelved altogether in area schools.

As for Dr. Ray and Beulah, he was offered a position as the first professor of prayer and spiritual life at Randolph University. He declined, preferring instead to follow the Stirring as it spread to other cities.

Randolph University underwent a profound change. Students went out at their own expense to share their story at other campuses. As a result, revival began to spread to other colleges and universities. Thousands of students made decisions to commit their lives to Christ. A great number chose to pursue full-time ministry and mission careers. On those campuses where the Stirring occurred, date rapes and other violent incidents almost disappeared.

Maggie Dunlop recovered. She helped organize an extensive ministry to local and county jails, leading literally hundreds of inmates to faith in Christ.

Rachel and Ed Brewster became active in anti-cult ministries. Rachel was also invited from time to time to discuss the deception of the New Age movement on local talk shows. Ingrid, indicted for her role in the break-ins at the church and for conspiracy to commit forgery and blackmail, fled the country while on bail. She was rumored to be living among a Druid sect in England. Todd Branstrom was convicted of numerous felonies, including burglary and destruction of data and property, and was sentenced to four years in prison.

Karin Warner chose to put her baby girl, whom she named Katherine, up for adoption. Karin later married a seminary student and the two of them began an orphanage in Brazil for street children. They eventually had three children of their own.

Eric went on to graduate with honors from high school, and was awarded a full basketball scholarship to a state university. He later entered seminary and chose youth ministry as a career. Derek recovered from his gunshot wound and was sent to serve out his sentence at a church-operated ranch in Montana for troubled teenagers.

Tony, who failed to express any remorse for his part in the attempted murder of Martinez, was tried as an adult and sentenced to ten years in the state's maximum security prison. Martinez recovered and returned to his duties at Roosevelt High.

Steven and Brenda were given a surprise vacation to the Caribbean by the congregation six months later. They also became active in marriage enrichment weekends. He set up an office in his house where he worked two days a week. For the remainder of his days in the ministry, Steven rarely, if ever, missed supper at home.

ABOUT THE AUTHOR

Robert Moeller is an author and writer, frequent guest speaker, and contributing editor to *Leadership Journal*. His first book, *For Better, For Worse, For Keeps*, a non-fiction marriage book, was released this year by Multnomah. He has previously served as a pastor, radio ethics correspondent, and director of communications at Trinity Evangelical Divinity School. Bob and his wife, Cheryl, have been married fifteen years, and are the parents of four children.